"There he stood stock still, staring"

[Page 398.]

MARY-'GUSTA

BY

JOSEPH C. LINCOLN

AUTHOR OF "THANKFUL'S INHERITANCE," "KENT KNOWLES: 'QUAHAUG,'" ETC.

Lincoln. Mary-'Gusta.
Mary-'Gusta is a little orphan girl who is
taken in charge by her step-father's two
old partners, Captain Shadrach Gould and
Zoeth Hamilton. She makes one of a unique
household of which these two, together with
an old sea-cook, Isaiah Chase, are the members. The old men think they are taking
care of the little girl, but as a matter
of fact she mothers all three of them.
The two partners keep a general store and
all but ruin themselves and their business
trying to give Mary-'Gusta advantages beyond their means. Fortunately she dis-
covers their straits and comes home to
manage affairs for them and prevent dis-
aster.

37961

D. APPLETON AND COMPANY

NEW YORK   LONDON

1916

N. D. S. U. LIBRARY
FARGO, N. D.

LIST OF ILLUSTRATIONS

37961

MARY-'GUSTA

CHAPTER I

ON the twentieth day of April in the year 19—, the people—that is, a majority of the grown people of Ostable—were talking of Marcellus Hall and Mary-'Gusta.

A part of this statement is not surprising. The average person, no matter how humble or obscure, is pretty certain to be talked about on the day of his funeral, and Marcellus was to be buried that afternoon. Moreover, Marcellus had been neither humble nor obscure; also, he had been talked about a good deal during the fifty-nine years of his sojourn on this planet. So it is not at all surprising that he should be talked about now, when that sojourn was ended. But for all Ostable—yes, and a large part of South Harniss—to be engaged in speculation concerning the future of Mary-'Gusta *was* surprising, for, prior to Marcellus's death, very few outside of the Hall household had given her or her future a thought.

On this day, however, whenever or wherever the name of Marcellus Hall was mentioned, after the disposition of Marcellus's own bones had been discussed and those of his family skeleton disinterred and articulated, the conversation, in at least eight cases out of ten, resolved itself into a guessing contest, having as its problem this query:

"What's goin' to become of that child?"

For example:

Mr. Bethuel Sparrow, local newsgatherer for the *Ostable Enterprise,* seated before his desk in the editorial sanctum, was writing an obituary for next week's paper, under the following head:

"A Prominent Citizen Passes Away."

An ordinary man would probably have written "Dies"; but Mr. Sparrow, being a young and very new reporter for a rural weekly, wrote "Passes Away" as more elegant and less shocking to the reader.

It is much more soothing and refined to pass away than to die—unless one happens to be the person most concerned, in which case, perhaps, it may make little difference.

"The Angel of Death," wrote Mr. Sparrow, "passed through our midst on Tuesday last and called to his reward Captain Marcellus Hall, one of Ostable's most well-known and influential residents."

A slight exaggeration here. Marcellus had lived in Ostable but five years altogether and, during the last three, had taken absolutely no part in town affairs—political, religious or social. However, "influential" is a good word and usual in obituaries, so Bethuel let it stand. He continued:

"Captain Hall's sudden death——"

Erasure of "death" and substitution of "demise." Then:

"—Was a shock to the community at large. It happened on account of——" More erasures and substitutions. "—It was the result of his taking cold owing to exposure during the heavy southeast rains of week before last which developed into pneumonia. He grew rapidly worse and passed away at 3.06 P.M. on Tuesday, leaving a vacancy in our midst which will be hard to fill, if at all. Although Captain Hall had resided in Ostable but a comparatively short period, he was well-known and respected, both as a man and——"

Here, invention failing, Mr. Sparrow called for assistance.

"Hey, Perce," he hailed, addressing his companion, Mr. Percy Clark, who was busy setting type: "What's a good word to use here? I say Marcellus was respected both as a man—and somethin' else."

"Hey?" queried Percy, absently, scanning the eight point case. "What d'ye say?"

"I asked you what would be a good thing to go with 'man'?"

"Hey? I don't know. Woman, I guess."

"Aw, cut it out. Never mind, I got it:

"—As a man and a citizen. Captain Hall was fifty-nine years of age at the time of his demise. He was born in South Harniss and followed the sea until 1871, when he founded the firm of Hall and Company, which was for some years the leading dealer in fresh and salt fish in this section of the state. When the firm——

"I say, Perce! 'Twouldn't do to say Marcellus failed in business, would it? Might seem like hintin' at that stuff about his sister and the rest of it. Might get us into trouble, eh?"

"Humph! I don't know who with. Everybody's talkin' about it, anyway. Up to the boardin' house they've been talking about mighty little else ever since he died."

"I know, but talk's one thing and print's another. I'm goin' to leave it out.

"When the firm went out of business in 1879, Captain Hall followed the sea again, commanding the ships

Faraway, Fair Wind, and *Treasure Seeker,* and the bark *Apollo.* Later he retired from the sea and has not been active in the same or otherwise since. In 1894 he married Augusta Bangs Lathrop, widow of the late Reverend Charles Lathrop, formerly pastor of the Congregational Church in this town. Captain Hall had been residing in his native town, South Harniss, but after his marriage he took up his residence in Ostable, purchasing the residence formerly owned by Elnathan Phinney on Phinney's Hill, where he lived until his lamented demise. Mrs. Hall passed away in 1896. The sudden removal of Captain Hall from our midst leaves a stepdaughter, Mary Augusta Lathrop, aged seven. The——"

Here Mr. Sparrow's train of thought collided with the obstruction which was derailing many similar trains in Ostable and South Harniss.

"I say, Perce," he observed, "what's goin' to become of that kid of Marcellus's—his wife's, I mean? Marcellus didn't have any relations, as far as anybody knows, and neither did his wife. Who's goin' to take care of Mary-'Gusta?"

Percy shook his head. "Don't know," he answered. "That's what all hands are askin'. I presume likely she'll be looked after. Marcellus left plenty of money, didn't he? And kids with money can generally find guardians."

"Yup, I guess that's so. Still, whoever gets her will have their hands full. She's the most old-fashioned, queerest young-one ever I saw."

So much for Mr. Sparrow and his fellow laborer for the *Enterprise.* Now to listen for a moment to Judge Baxter, who led the legal profession of Ostable; and to Mrs. Baxter who, so common report affirmed, led the Judge. The pair were upstairs in the Baxter house, dressing for the funeral.

"Daniel," declared Mrs. Baxter, "it's the queerest thing I ever heard of. You say they don't know—either of them—and the child herself doesn't know, either."

"That's it, Ophelia. No one knows except myself. Captain Hall read the letter to me and put it in my charge a year ago."

"Well, I must say!"

"Yes, I know, I said it at the time, and I've been saying it to myself ever since. It doesn't mean anything; that is, it is not binding legally, of course. It's absolutely unbusinesslike and unpractical. Simply a letter, asking them, as old friends, to do this thing. Whether they will or not the Almighty only knows."

"Well, Daniel, I must say I shouldn't have thought you, as his lawyer, would have let him do such a thing. Of course, I don't know either of them very well, but, from what little I've heard, I should say they know as much about what they would be supposed to do as—as you do about tying a necktie. For mercy sakes let me fix it! The knot is supposed to be under your chin, not under your ear as if you were going to be hung."

The Judge meekly elevated the chin and his wife pulled the tie into place.

"And so," she said, "they can say yes or no just as they like."

"Yes, it rests entirely with them."

"And suppose they say no, what will become of the child then?"

"I can't tell you. Captain Hall seemed pretty certain they wouldn't say no."

"Humph! There! Now you look a little more presentable. Have you got a clean handkerchief? Well, that's an unexpected miracle; I don't know how you happened to think of it. When are you going to speak with them about it?"

"Today, if they come to the funeral, as I suppose they will."

"I shall be in a fidget until I know whether they say yes or no. And whichever they say I shall keep on fidgeting until I see what happens after that. Poor little Mary-'Gusta! I wonder what *will* become of her."

The Judge shook his head.

Over the road between South Harniss and Ostable a buggy drawn by an aged white horse was moving slowly. On the buggy's seat were two men, Captain Shadrach Gould and Zoeth Hamilton. Captain Gould, big, stout, and bearded, was driving. Mr. Hamilton, small, thin, smooth-faced and white-haired, was beside him. Both were obviously dressed in their Sunday clothes, Captain Shadrach's blue, Mr. Hamilton's black. Each wore an uncomfortably high collar and the shoes of each had been laboriously polished. Their faces, utterly unlike in most respects, were very solemn.

"Ah hum!" sighed Mr. Hamilton.

Captain Shadrach snorted impatiently.

"For the land sakes don't do that again, Zoeth," he protested. "That's the tenth 'Ah hum' you've cast loose in a mile. I know we're bound to a funeral but there ain't no need of tollin' the bell all the way. I don't like it and I don't think Marcellus would neither, if he could hear you."

"Perhaps he can hear us, Shadrach," suggested his companion, mildly. "Perhaps he's here with us now; who can tell?"

"Humph! Well, if he is then I *know* he don't like it.

Marcellus never made any fuss whatever happened, and he wouldn't make any at his own funeral no more than at anybody else's. That wasn't his way. Say nothin' and keep her on the course, that was Marcellus. I swan I can hardly make it seem possible that he's gone!"

"Neither can I, Shadrach. And to think that you and me, his old partners and lifelong chums as you might say, hadn't seen nor spoken to him for over two years. It makes me feel bad. Bad and sort of conscience-struck."

"I know; so it does me, in a way. And yet it wasn't our fault, Zoeth. You know as well as I do that Marcellus didn't want to see us. We was over to see him last and he scarcely said a word while we was there. You and me did all the talkin' and he just set and looked at us—when he wasn't lookin' at the floor. I never saw such a change in a man. We asked—yes, by fire, we fairly begged him to come and stay with us for a spell, but he never did. Now it ain't no further from Ostable to South Harniss than it is from South Harniss to Ostable. If he'd wanted to come he could; if he'd wanted to see us he could. We went to see him, didn't we; and *we* had a store and a business to leave. He ain't had any business since he give up goin' to sea. He——"

"Sshh! Shh!" interrupted Mr. Hamilton, mildly, "don't talk that way, Shadrach. Don't find fault with the dead."

"Find fault! I ain't findin' fault. I thought as much of Marcellus Hall as any man on earth, and nobody feels worse about his bein' took than I do. But I'm just sayin' what we both know's a fact. He didn't want to see us; he didn't want to see nobody. Since his wife died he lived alone in that house, except for a housekeeper and that stepchild, and never went anywhere or

7

had anybody come to see him if he could help it. A reg'lar hermit—that's what he was, a hermit, like Peleg Myrick down to Setuckit P'int. And when I think what he used to be, smart, lively, able, one of the best skippers and smartest business men afloat or ashore, it don't seem possible a body could change so. 'Twas that woman that done it, that woman that trapped him into gettin' married."

"Sshh! Shh! Shadrach; she's dead, too. And, besides, I guess she was a real good woman; everybody said she was."

"I ain't sayin' she wasn't, am I? What I say is she hadn't no business marryin' a man twenty years older'n she was."

"But," mildly, "you said she trapped him. Now we don't know——"

"Zoeth Hamilton, you know she must have trapped him. You and I agreed that was just what she done. If she hadn't trapped him—set a reg'lar seine for him and hauled him aboard like a school of mackerel—'tain't likely he'd have married her or anybody else, is it? I ain't married nobody, have I? And Marcellus was years older'n I be."

"Well, well, Shadrach!"

"No, 'tain't well; it's bad. He's gone, and—and you and me that was with him for years and years, his very best friends on earth as you might say, wasn't with him when he died. If it hadn't been for her he'd have stayed in South Harniss where he belonged. Consarn women! They're responsible for more cussedness than the smallpox. 'When a man marries his trouble begins'; that's gospel, too."

Zoeth did not answer.

Captain Gould, after a sidelong glance at his companion, took a hand from the reins and laid it on the Hamilton knee.

"I'm sorry, Zoeth," he said, contritely; "I didn't mean to—to rake up bygones; I was blowin' off steam, that's all. I'm sorry."

"I know, Shadrach. It's all right."

"No, 'tain't all right; it's all wrong. Somebody ought to keep a watch on me, and when they see me beginnin' to get hot, set me on the back of the stove or somewheres; I'm always liable to bile over and scald the wrong critter. I've done that all my life. I'm sorry, Zoeth, you know I didn't mean——"

"I know, I know. Ah hum! Poor Marcellus! Here's the first break in the old firm, Shadrach."

"Yup. You and me are all that's left of Hall and Company. That is——"

He stopped short just in time and roared a "Git dap" at the horse. He had been on the point of saying something which would have been far more disastrous than his reference to the troubles following marriage. Zoeth was apparently not curious. To his friend's great relief he did not wait for the sentence to be finished, nor did he ask embarrassing questions. Instead he said:

"I wonder what's goin' to become of that child, Mary Lathrop's girl. Who do you suppose likely will take charge of her?"

"I don't know. I've been wonderin' that myself, Zoeth."

"Kind of a cute little thing she was, too, as I recollect her. I presume likely she's grown up consid'ble since. You remember how she set and looked at us that last time we was over to see Marcellus, Shadrach?"

"Remember? How she looked at *me*, you mean! Shall I ever forget it? I'd just had my hair cut by that

9

new barber, Sim Ellis, that lived here 'long about then, and I told him to cut off the ends. He thought I meant the other ends, I cal'late, for I went to sleep in the chair, same as I generally do, and when I woke up my head looked like the main truck of the old *Faraway*. All it needed was to have the bald place gilded. I give you my word that if I hadn't been born with my ears set wing and wing like a schooner runnin' afore the wind I'd have been smothered when I put my hat on—nothin' but them ears kept it propped up off my nose. *You* remember that haircut, Zoeth. Well, all the time you and me was in Marcellus's settin'-room that stepchild of his just set and looked at my head. Never took her eyes off it. If she'd said anything 'twouldn't have been so bad; but she didn't—just looked. I could feel my bald spot reddenin' up till I swan to man I thought it must be breakin' out in blisters. 'Never see anybody that looked just like me, did you, Sis?' I says to her, when I couldn't stand it any longer. 'No, sir,' she says, solemn as an owl. She was right out and honest, I'll say that for her. That's the only time Marcellus laughed while we was inside that house. I didn't blame him much. Ho, ho! Well, he ain't laughin' now and neither are we— or we hadn't ought to be. Neither is the child, I cal'late, poor thing. I wonder what will become of her."

And meanwhile the child herself was vaguely, and in childish fashion, wondering that very thing. She was in the carriage room of the barn belonging to the Hall estate—if the few acres of land and the buildings owned by the late Marcellus may be called an estate—curled up on the back seat of the old surrey which had been used so little since the death of her mother, Augusta Hall, four years before. The surrey was shrouded from top to floor with a dust cover of unbleached muslin through which the sunshine from the carriage room windows filtered in a mysterious, softened twilight. The covered surrey was a favorite retreat of Mary-'Gusta's. She had discovered it herself—which made it doubly alluring, of course—and she seldom invited her juvenile friends to share its curtained privacy with her. It was her playhouse, her tent, and her enchanted castle, much too sacred to be made common property. Here she came on rainy Saturdays and on many days not rainy when other children, those possessing brothers or sisters, played out of doors. She liked to play by herself, to invent plays all her own, and these other children—"normal children," their parents called them—were much too likely to laugh instead of solemnly making believe as she did. Mary-'Gusta was not a normal child; she was "that queer Lathrop young-one"—had heard herself so described more than once. She did not like the phrase; "queer" was not so bad—perhaps she was queer —but she had an instinctive repugnance to being called a young-one. Birds and rabbits had young-ones and she was neither feathered nor furred.

So very few of the neighborhood children were invited to the shaded interior of the old surrey. Her dolls—all five of them—spent a good deal of time there and David, the tortoise-shell cat, came often, usually under compulsion. When David had kittens, which interesting domestic event took place pretty frequently, he —or she—positively refused to be an occupant of that surrey, growling and scratching in a decidedly ungentlemanly—or unladylike—manner. Twice Mary-'Gusta had attempted to make David more complacent by bringing the kittens also to the surrey, but their parent had promptly and consecutively seized them by the scruff of their necks and laboriously lugged them up to the hay-mow again.

Just now, however, there being no kittens, David was slumbering in a furry heap beside Mary-'Gusta at one end of the carriage seat, and Rosette, the smallest of the five dolls, and Rose, the largest, were sitting bolt up-right in the corner at the other end. The christening of the smallest and newest doll was the result of a piece of characteristic reasoning on its owner's part. She was very fond of the name Rose, the same being the name of the heroine in "Eight Cousins," which story Mrs. Bailey, housekeeper before last for Marcellus Hall, had read aloud to the child. When the new doll came, at Christmas time, Mary-'Gusta wished that she might christen it Rose also. But there was another and much beloved Rose already in the family. So Mary-'Gusta re-flected and observed, and she observed that a big roll of tobacco such as her stepfather smoked was a cigar; while a little one, as smoked by Eben Keeler, the grocer's delivery clerk, was a cigarette. Therefore, the big doll being already Rose, the little one became Rosette.

Mary-'Gusta was not playing with Rose and Rosette at the present time. Neither was she interested in the peaceful slumbers of David. She was not playing at all, but sitting, with feet crossed beneath her on the seat and hands clasped about one knee, thinking. And, although she was thinking of her stepfather who she knew had gone away to a vague place called Heaven—a place variously described by Mrs. Bailey, the former house-keeper, and by Mrs. Susan Hobbs, the present one, and by Mr. Howes, the Sunday school superintendent—she was thinking most of herself, Mary Augusta Lathrop, who was going to a funeral that very afternoon and, after that, no one seemed to know exactly where.

It was a beautiful April day and the doors of the carriage house and the big door of the barn were wide open. Mary-'Gusta could hear the hens clucking and the voices of people talking. The voices were two: one was that of Mrs. Hobbs, the housekeeper, and the other belonged to Mr. Abner Hallett, the undertaker. Mary-'Gusta did not like Mr. Hallett's voice; she liked neither it nor its owner's manner; she described both voice and manner to herself as "too soothy." They gave her the shivers.

Mr. Hallett's tone was subdued at the present time, but a trifle of the professional "soothiness" was lacking. He and Mrs. Hobbs were conversing briskly enough and, although Mary-'Gusta could catch only a word or two at intervals, she was perfectly sure they were talking about her. She was certain that if she were to appear at that moment in the door of the barn they would stop talking immediately and look at her. Everybody whom she had met during the past two days looked at her in that queer way. It made her feel as if she had something catching, like the measles, and as if, somehow or other, she was to blame.

She realized dimly that she should feel very, very badly because her stepfather was dead. Mrs. Hobbs had told her that she should and seemed to regard her as queerer than ever because she had not cried. But, according to the housekeeper, Captain Hall was out of his troubles and had gone where he would be happy for ever and ever. So it seemed to her strange to be expected to cry on his account. He had not been happy here in Ostable, or, at least, he had not shown his happiness in the way other people showed theirs. To her he had been a big, bearded giant of a man, whom she saw at infrequent intervals during the day and always at night just before she went to bed. His room, with the old-fashioned secretary

against the wall, and the stuffed gull on the shelf, and
the books in the cupboard, and the polished narwhal horn
in the corner, was to her a sort of holy of holies, a place
where she was led each evening at nine o'clock, at first
by Mrs. Bailey and, later, by Mrs. Hobbs, to shake the
hand of the big man who looked at her absently over
his spectacles and said good night in a voice not unkindly
but expressing no particular interest. At other times she
was strictly forbidden to enter that room.

Occasionally, but very rarely, she had eaten Sunday
dinner with Marcellus. She and the housekeeper usually
ate together and Mr. Hall's meals were served in what
the child called "the smoke room," meaning the apartment just described, which was at all times strongly
scented with tobacco. The Sunday dinners were stately
and formal affairs and were prefaced by lectures by the
housekeeper concerning sitting up straight and not disturbing Cap'n Hall by talking too much. On the whole
Mary-'Gusta was rather glad when the meals were over.
She did not dislike her stepfather; he had never been
rough or unkind, but she had always stood in awe of
him and had felt that he regarded her as a "pesky
nuisance," something to be fed and then shooed out of
the way, as Mrs. Hobbs regarded David, the cat. As
for loving him, as other children seemed to love their
fathers, that the girl never did. She was sure he did
not love her in that way, and that he would not have
welcomed demonstrations of affection on her part. She
had learned the reason, or she thought she had: she was
a *stepchild;* that was why, and a stepchild was almost as
bad as a "changeling" in a fairy story.

Her mother she remembered dimly and with that recol-
lection were memories of days when she was loved and
made much of, not only by Mother, but by Captain Hall

also. She asked Mrs. Bailey, whom she had loved and whose leaving was the greatest grief of her life, some questions about these memories. Mrs. Bailey had hugged her and had talked a good deal about Captain Hall's being a changed man since his wife's death. "He used to be so different, jolly and good-natured and sociable; you wouldn't know him now if you seen him then. When your mamma was took it just seemed to wilt him right down. He was awful sick himself for a spell, and when he got better he was like he is today. Seems as if *he* died too, as you might say, and ain't really lived since. I'm awful sorry for Cap'n Marcellus. You must be real good to him when you grow up, Mary-'Gusta."

And now he had gone before she had had a chance to grow up, and Mary-'Gusta felt an unreasonable sense of blame. But real grief, the dreadful paralyzing realization of loss which an adult feels when a dear one dies, she did not feel.

She was awed and a little frightened, but she did not feel like crying. Why should she?

"Mary-'Gusta! Mary-'Gusta! Where be you?"

It was Mrs. Hobbs calling. Mary-'Gusta hurriedly untwisted her legs and scrambled from beneath the dust cover of the surrey. David, whose slumbers were disturbed, rose also, yawned and stretched.

"Here I be, Mrs. Hobbs," answered the girl. "I'm a-comin'."

Mrs. Hobbs was standing in the doorway of the barn. Mary-'Gusta noticed that she was not, as usual, garbed in gingham, but was arrayed in her best go-to-meeting gown.

"I'm a-comin'," said the child.

"Comin', yes. But where on earth have you been? I've been hunting all over creation for you. I didn't suppose you'd be out here, on this day of all others, with—with that critter," indicating David, who appeared, blinking sleepily.

"I must say I shouldn't think you'd be fussin' along with a cat today," declared Mrs. Hobbs.

"Yes'm," said Mary-'Gusta. David yawned, apparently expressing a bored contempt for housekeepers in general.

"Come right along into the house," continued Mrs. Hobbs. "It's high time you was gettin' ready for the funeral."

"Ready? How?" queried Mary-'Gusta.

"Why, changin' your clothes, of course."

"Do folks dress up for funerals?"

"Course they do. What a question!"

"I didn't know. I—I've never had one."

"Had one?"

"I mean I've never been to any. What do they dress up for?"

"Why—why, because they do, of course. Now don't ask any more questions, but hurry up. Where are you goin' now, for mercy sakes?"

"I was goin' back after Rose and Rosette. They ought to be dressed up, too, hadn't they?"

"The idea! Playin' dolls today! I declare I never see such a child! You're a reg'lar little—little heathen. Would you want anybody playin' dolls at your own funeral, I'd like to know?"

Mary-'Gusta thought this over. "I don't know," she answered, after reflection. "I guess I'd just as soon. Do they have dolls up in Heaven, Mrs. Hobbs?"

"Mercy on us! I should say not. Dolls in Heaven! The idea!"

"Nor cats either?"

"No. Don't ask such wicked questions."

Mary-'Gusta asked no more questions of that kind, but her conviction that Heaven—Mrs. Hobbs' Heaven—was a good place for housekeepers and grown-ups but a poor one for children was strengthened.

They entered the house by the kitchen door and ascended the back stairs to Mary-'Gusta's room. The shades in all the rooms were drawn and the house was dark and gloomy. The child would have asked the reason for this, but at the first hint of a question Mrs. Hobbs bade her hush.

"You mustn't talk," she said.

"Why mustn't I?"

"Because 'tain't the right thing to do, that's why. Now hurry up and get dressed."

Mary-'Gusta silently wriggled out of her everyday frock, was led to the washstand and vigorously scrubbed. Then Mrs. Hobbs combed and braided what she called her "pigtails" and tied a bow of black ribbon at the end of each.

"There!" exclaimed the lady. "You're clean for once in your life, anyhow. Now hurry up and put on them things on the bed."

The things were Mary-'Gusta's very best shoes and dress; also a pair of new black stockings.

When the dressing was finished the housekeeper stood her in the middle of the floor and walked about her on a final round of inspection.

"There!" she said again, with a sigh of satisfaction. "Nobody can say I ain't took all the pains with you that anybody could. Now you come downstairs and set right where I tell you till I come. And don't you say one single word. Not a word, no matter what happens."

She took the girl's hand and led her down the front stairs. As they descended Mary-'Gusta could scarcely restrain a gasp of surprise. The front door was open—the *front* door—and the child had never seen it open before, had long ago decided that it was not a truly door at all, but merely a make-believe like the painted windows on the sides of her doll house. But now it was wide open and Mr. Hallett, arrayed in a suit of black, the coat of which puckered under the arms, was standing on the threshold, looking more soothy than ever. The parlor door was open also, and the parlor itself—the best first parlor, more sacred and forbidden even than the "smoke room"—was, as much of it as she could see, filled with chairs.

Mrs. Hobbs led her into the little room off the parlor, the "back settin'-room," and, indicating the haircloth and black walnut sofa against the wall, whispered to her to sit right there and not move.

"Mind now," she whispered, "don't talk and don't stir. I'll be back by and by."

Mary-'Gusta, left alone, looked wide-eyed about the little back sitting-room. It, too, was changed; not changed as much as the front parlor, but changed, nevertheless. Most of the furniture had been removed. The most comfortable chairs, including the rocker with the parrot "tidy" on the back, had been taken away. One or two of the bolt-upright variety remained and the "music chair" was still there, but pushed back into a corner.

Mary-'Gusta saw the music chair and a quiver of guilty fear tinged along her spine; that particular chair had always been, to her, the bright, particular glory of the house. Not because it was beautiful, for that it distinctly was not; but because of the marvellous secret hidden beneath its upholstered seat. Captain Marcellus had brought it home years and years before, when he was a sea-going bachelor and made voyages to Hamburg.

In its normal condition it was a perfectly quiet and ugly chair, but there was a catch under one arm and a music box under the seat. And if that catch were released, then when anyone sat in it, the music box played "The Campbell's Are Coming" with spirit and jingle. And, moreover, kept on playing it to the finish unless the catch was pushed back again.

To Mary-'Gusta that chair was a perpetual fascination. She had been expressly forbidden to touch it, had been shut in the dark closet more than once for touching it; but, nevertheless, the temptation was always there and she had yielded to that temptation at intervals when Mrs. Hobbs and her stepfather were out. And the last time she had touched it she had broken the catch. She had wound up the music box, after hearing it play, but the catch which made it a perfectly safe seat and not a trap for the unwary had refused to push back into place. And now there it was, loaded and primed, so to speak, and she was responsible. Suppose—Oh, horrible thought!—suppose anyone should sit in it that afternoon!

She gasped and jumped off the sofa. Then she remembered Mrs. Hobbs' parting command and stopped, hesitating. Mr. Hallett, standing at the end of the hall, by the front door, heard her move and tiptoed to the sitting-room.

"What's the matter, little girl?" he whispered, soothingly.

"No-nothin'," gasped Mary-'Gusta.

"You're sure?"

"Ye-yes, sir."

"All right. Then you set down on the sofa and keep still. You mustn't make any noise. The folks are comin' now. Set right down on the sofy, that's a good girl!"

So back to the sofa went Mary-'Gusta, trembling with apprehension. From her seat she could see along the hall and also through the other door into the "big settin'-room," where, also, there were rows of chairs. And, to her horror, these chairs began to fill. People, most of them dressed in church-going garments which rattled and rustled, were tiptoeing in and sitting down where she could see them and they could see her. She did not dare to move now; did not dare go near the music chair even if going near it would have done any good. She remained upon the sofa, and shivered.

A few moments later Mrs. Hobbs appeared, looking very solemn and Sundayfied, and sat beside her. Then Judge and Mrs. Baxter were shown into the little room and took two of the remaining chairs. The Judge bowed and smiled and Mrs. Baxter leaned over and patted her hand. Mary-'Gusta tried to smile, too, but succeeded only in looking more miserable. Mrs. Hobbs whispered to her to sit up straight.

There was a steady stream of people through the front door now. They all entered the parlor and many stayed there, but others passed on into the "big settin'-room." The chairs there were almost all taken; soon all were taken and Mr. Hallett was obliged to remove one of those in the small room. There were but two left empty, one a tall, straight antique with a rush seat, a family heirloom, and the other the music chair. Mary-'Gusta stared at the music chair and hoped and hoped.

Mr. Sharon, the minister, entered and shook hands with the Judge and Mrs. Baxter and with Mrs. Hobbs and Mary-'Gusta. He also patted the child's hand. Mrs. Hobbs whispered to him, with evident pride, that it was "goin' to be one of the biggest funerals ever given in Ostable." Mr. Sharon nodded. Then, after waiting a moment or two, he tiptoed along the front hall and took up his stand by the parlor door. There was a final rustle of gowns, a final crackle of Sunday shirtfronts, and then a hushed silence.

The silence was broken by the rattle of wheels in the yard. Mr. Hallett at the door held up a warning hand. A moment later he ushered two people in at the front door and led them through the parlor into the "big settin'-room." Mary-'Gusta could see the late comers plainly. They were both men, one big and red-faced and bearded, the other small, and thin, and white-haired. A rustle passed through the crowd and everyone turned to look. Some looked as if they recognized the pair, but they did not bow; evidently it was not proper to bow at funerals.

Mr. Hallett, on tiptoe, of course, glided into the little room from the big one and looked about him. Then, to the absolute stupefaction of Mary-'Gusta, he took the rush-seated chair in one hand and the music chair in the other and tiptoed out. He placed the two chairs in the back row close to the door of the smaller room and motioned to the two men to sit.

Mary-'Gusta could stand it no longer. She was afraid of Mrs. Hobbs, afraid of Mr. Hallett, afraid of the Baxters and all the staring crowd; but she was more afraid of what was going to happen. She tugged at the housekeeper's sleeve.

"Mrs. Hobbs!" she whispered, quiveringly. "Oh, Mrs. Hobbs!"

Mrs. Hobbs shook off the clutch at her sleeve.

"Sshh!" she whispered. "Sshh!"

"But—but please, Mrs. Hobbs——"

"Sshh! You mustn't talk. Be still. Be still, I tell you."

The small, white-haired man sat down in the rush-seated chair. The big man hesitated, separated his coat tails, and then he, too, sat down.

And the music box under the seat of the chair he sat in informed everyone with cheerful vigor that the Campbells were coming, Hurrah! Hurrah!

Captain Shadrach Gould arose from that chair, arose promptly and without hesitation. Mr. Zoeth Hamilton also rose; so did many others in the vicinity. There was a stir and a rustle and whispered exclamations. And still the news of the imminent arrival of the Campbells was tinkled abroad and continued to tinkle. Someone giggled, so did someone else. Others said, "Hush!"

Mrs. Judge Baxter said, "Heavens and earth!"

Mrs. Hobbs looked as if she wished to say something very much indeed.

Captain Shadrach's bald spot blazed a fiery red and he glared about him helplessly.

Mr. Hallett, who was used to unexpected happenings at funerals—though, to do him justice, he had never before had to deal with anything quite like this—rushed to the center of the disturbance. Mrs. Hobbs hastened to help. Together and with whisperings, they fidgeted with the refractory catch. And still the music box played—and played—and played.

At last Mr. Hallett gave it up. He seized the chair and with it in his arms rushed out into the dining-room. Captain Shadrach Gould mopped his face with a handkerchief and stood, because there was nowhere for him to sit. Mrs. Hobbs, almost as red in the face as Captain Shad himself, hastened back and collapsed upon the sofa. Mr. Sharon cleared his throat.

And still, from behind the closed door of the dining-room the music chair tinkled on:

"The Campbells are coming! Hurrah! Hurrah!"

Poor little guilty, frightened Mary-'Gusta covered her face with her hands.

CHAPTER II

"AND now, gentlemen," said Judge Baxter, "here we are. Sit down and make yourselves comfortable. I shall have a good deal to say and I expect to surprise you. Sit down."

Captain Gould and Mr. Hamilton were in the Judge's library at his home. The funeral was over, all that was mortal of Marcellus Hall had been laid to rest in the Ostable cemetery, and his two friends and former partners had, on their return from that cemetery, stopped at the Judge's, at the latter's request. He wished, so he said, to speak with them on an important matter.

"Why don't you sit down, Captain?" asked the Judge, noticing that, although Zoeth had seated himself in the rocker which his host had indicated, Shadrach was still standing.

Captain Shadrach laid a hand on the back of the arm-chair and regarded the lawyer with a very grave face, but with a twinkle in his eye.

"To tell you the truth, Judge," he said, slowly, "I don't cal'late I ever shall set down again quite so whole-hearted as I used to. You spoke of a surprise, didn't you? I've had one surprise this afternoon that's liable to stay with me for a spell. I'm an unsuspectin' critter, generally speakin', but after that—Say, you ain't got a brass band nor fireworks hitched to *this* chair, have you?"

Judge Baxter laughed heartily. "No," he said, as soon as he could speak. "No, Captain, my furniture isn't loaded."

24

The Captain shook his head. "Whew!" he whistled, sitting down gingerly in the armchair. "Well, that's a mercy. I ain't so young as I used to be and I couldn't stand many such shocks. Whew! Don't talk to *me!* When that devilish jig tune started up underneath me I'll bet I hopped up three foot straight. I may be kind of slow sittin' down, but you'll bear me out that I can *get up* sudden when it's necessary. And I thought the dum thing never would *stop!*"

Mr. Hamilton stirred uneasily. "Hush, hush, Shadrach!" he pleaded. "Don't be so profane. Remember you've just come from the graveyard."

"Come from it! By fire! There was a time there when I'd have been willin' to go to it—yes, and stay. All I wanted was to get out of that room and hide somewheres where folks couldn't look at me. I give you my word I could feel myself heatin' up like an airtight stove. Good thing I didn't have on a celluloid collar or 'twould have bust into a blaze. Of all the dummed outrages to spring on a man, that——"

"Shadrach!"

"There, there, Zoeth! I'll calm down. But as for swearin'—well, if you knew how full of cusswords I was there one spell you wouldn't find fault; you'd thank me for holdin' 'em in. I had to batten down my hatches to do it, though; I tell you that."

Mr. Hamilton turned to their host. "You'll excuse Shadrach, won't you, Judge," he said, apologetically. "He don't mean nothin' wicked, really. And he feels as bad as I do about Marcellus's bein' took."

"Course I do!" put in the Captain. "Zoeth's always scared to death for fear I'm bound to the everlastin' brimstone. He forgets I've been to sea a good part of my life and that a feller has to talk strong aboard ship.

Common language may do for keepin' store, but it don't get a vessel nowheres; the salt sort of takes the tang out of it, seems so. I'm through for the present, Zoeth. I'll keep the rest till I meet the swab that loaded up that chair for me."

The Judge laughed again. Then he opened his desk and took from a drawer two folded papers.

"Gentlemen," he said, gravely, "I asked you to come here with me because there is an important matter, a very important matter, which I, as Captain Hall's legal adviser, must discuss with you."

Captain Shadrach and Zoeth looked at each other. The former tugged at his beard.

"Hum!" he mused. "Somethin' to do with Marcellus's affairs, is it?"

"Yes."

"Want to know! And somethin' to do with me and Zoeth?"

"Yes, with both of you. This," holding up one of the folded papers, "is Captain Hall's will. I drew it for him a year ago and he has appointed me his executor."

Zoeth nodded. "We supposed likely he would," he observed.

"Couldn't get a better man," added Shadrach, with emphasis.

"Thank you. Captain Hall leaves all he possessed— practically all; there is a matter of two hundred dollars for his housekeeper, Mrs. Hobbs, and a few other personal gifts—but he leaves practically all he possessed to his stepdaughter, Mary Lathrop."

Both his hearers nodded again. "We expected that, naturally," said the Captain. "It's what he'd ought to have done, of course. Well, she'll be pretty well fixed, won't she?"

Judge Baxter shook his head. "Why, no—she won't," he said, soberly. "That is a part of the surprise which I mentioned at first. Captain Hall was, practically, a poor man when he died."

That the prophesied surprise was now a reality was manifest. Both men looked aghast.

"You—you don't mean that, Judge?" gasped Zoeth.

"Poor? Marcellus poor?" cried Shadrach. "Why— why, what kind of talk's that? He didn't have no more than the rest of us when——" he hesitated, glanced at Zoeth, and continued, "when the firm give up business back in '79; but he went to sea again and made considerable, and then he made a whole lot in stocks. I know he did. You know it, too, Zoeth. How could he be poor?"

"Because, like so many other fortunate speculators, he continued to speculate and became unfortunate. He lost the bulk of his winnings in the stock market and—well, to be quite frank, Captain Hall has been a broken man, mentally as well as physically, since his wife's death and his own serious illness. You, yourselves, must have noticed the change in his habits. From being an active man, a man of affairs, he became almost a hermit. He saw but few people, dropped the society of all his old friends, and lived alone—alone except for his various housekeepers and Mary-'Gusta—the little girl, I mean. You must have noticed the change in his relations with you."

Mr. Hamilton sighed. "Yes," he said, "we noticed he never came to see us and—and——"

"And wasn't over'n above sociable when we come to see him," finished Captain Shadrach. "Yes, we noticed that. But I say, Judge, he must have had *some* money left. What became of it?"

"Goodness knows! He was a child, so far as money matters went, in his later years. Very likely he frittered it away in more stock ventures; I know he bought a lot of good for nothing mining shares. At any rate it has gone, all except a few thousands. The house and land where he lived is mortgaged up to the handle, and I imagine there are debts, a good many of them. But whatever there is is left to Mary-'Gusta—everyone calls her that and I seem to have caught the habit. It is left to her—in trust."

Captain Shadrach thought this over. "In trust with you, I presume likely," he observed. "Well, as I said afore, he couldn't have found a better man."

"He thought he could, two better men. I rather think he was right. You are the two, gentlemen."

This statement did not have the effect which the Judge expected. He expected exclamations and protests. Instead his visitors looked at each other and at him in a puzzled fashion.

"Er—er—what was that?" queried Mr. Hamilton. "I didn't exactly seem to catch that, somehow or 'nother."

Judge Baxter turned to the Captain.

"You understood me, didn't you, Captain Gould?" he asked.

Shadrach shook his head.

"Why—why, no," he stammered; "it didn't seem to soak in, somehow. Cal'late my head must have stopped goin'; maybe the shock I had a spell ago broke the mainspring. All I seem to be real sartin of just now is that the Campbells are comin'. What was it you said?"

"I said that Captain Marcellus Hall has left whatever property he owned, after his creditors are satisfied, to his stepdaughter. He has left it in trust until she becomes of age. And he asks you two to accept that trust and the care of the child. Is that plain?"

It was plain and they understood. But with understanding came, apparently, a species of paralysis of the vocal organs. Zoeth turned pale and leaned back in his chair. Shadrach's mouth opened and closed several times, but he said nothing.

"Of course," went on Baxter, "before I say any more I think you should be told this: It was Captain Hall's wish that you jointly accept the guardianship of Mary-'Gusta—of the girl—that she live with you and that you use whatever money comes to her from her stepfather's estate in educating and clothing her. Also, of course, that a certain sum each week be paid you from that estate as her board. That was Marcellus's wish; but it *is* a wish, nothing more. It is not binding upon you in any way. You have a perfect right to decline and——"

Captain Shadrach interrupted.

"Heave to!" he ordered, breathlessly. "Come up into the wind a minute, for mercy sakes! Do you mean to say that me and Zoeth are asked to take that young-one home with us, and take care of her, and dress her, and—and eat her, and bring her up and—and——"

He paused, incoherent in his excitement. The Judge nodded.

"Yes," he replied, "that is what he asks you to do. But, as I say, you are not obliged to do it; there is no legal obligation. You can say no, if you think it best."

"If we think—for thunder sakes, Baxter, what was the matter with Marcellus? Was he out of his head? Was he loony?"

"No, he was perfectly sane."

"Then—then, what——Zoeth," turning wildly to Mr. Hamilton, who still sat, pale and speechless, in his chair;

"Zoeth," he demanded, "did you ever hear such craziness in your life? Did you ever *hear* such stuff?"

Zoeth merely shook his head. His silence appeared to add to his friend's excitement.

"Did you?" he roared.

Zoeth muttered something to the effect that he didn't know as he ever did.

"You don't know! Yes, you do know, too. Speak up, why don't you? Don't sit there like a ship's figgerhead, starin' at nothin'. You know it's craziness as well's I do. For God sakes, say somethin'! *Talk!*"

Mr. Hamilton talked—to this extent:

"Hush, Shadrach," he faltered. "Don't be profane."

"Profane! Pup-pup-profane! You set there and—and— Oh, jumpin', creepin' Judas! I—I——" Language—even his language—failed to express his feelings and he waved his fists and sputtered. Baxter seized the opportunity.

"Before you make your decision, gentlemen," he said, "I hope you will consider the situation carefully. The girl is only seven years old; she has no relations anywhere, so far as we know. If you decline the trust a guardian will have to be appointed by the courts, I suppose. Who that guardian will be, or what will become of the poor child I'm sure I don't know. And Captain Marcellus was perfectly sane; he knew what he was doing."

Shadrach interrupted.

"He did!" he shouted. "Well, then, I must say——"

"Just a minute, please, I have a letter here which he wrote at the time he made his will. It is addressed to both of you. Here it is. Shall I read it to you, or had you rather read it yourselves?"

Zoeth answered. "I guess maybe you'd better read it,

Judge," he said. "I don't cal'late Shadrach nor me are capable of readin' much of anything just this minute. You read it. Shadrach, you be still now and listen."

The Captain opened his mouth and raised a hand. "Be still, Shadrach," repeated Zoeth. The hand fell. Captain Gould sighed.

"All right, Zoeth," he said. "I'll keep my hatch closed long's I can. Heave ahead, Judge."

The letter was a long one, covering several sheets of foolscap. It began:

To Shadrach Gould and Zoeth Hamilton, my old partners and friends.

DEAR SHAD AND ZOETH:

I am writing this to you because I have known you pretty much all my life and you are the only real friends I have got in this world.

"I was his friend, or I tried to be," commented Baxter, interrupting his reading; "but he considered you two, and always spoke of you, as his oldest and nearest friends. He has often told me that he knew he could depend on you. Now listen."

The letter went on to state that the writer realized his health was no longer good, that he was likely to die at any time and was quite reconciled.

I should be glad to go [Captain Hall had written], if it was not for one thing. Since my wife was took from me I care precious little for life and the sooner it ends the better. That is the way I look at it. But I have a stepdaughter, Mary Augusta Lathrop, and for her sake I must stick to the ship as long as I can. I have not been the right kind of father to her. I have tried, but I don't seem to know how and I guess likely I was too old to learn. When I go she won't have a relation to look out for her. That has troubled me a lot and I have thought about it more than a little, I can tell you. And so I have decided to leave her in your care. I am hoping you will take charge of her and bring her up to be a good girl and a good woman, same as her mother was before her. I know you two will be just the ones for the job.

"Jumpin' fire!" broke in Shadrach, the irrepressible.

"Hush, Shadrach," continued Mr. Hamilton. "Go on, Judge."

Baxter continued his reading. The letter told of the will, of the property, whatever it might be, left in trust for the child, and of the writer's desire that it might be used, when turned into money, for her education. There were two pages of rambling references to stocks and investments, the very vagueness of these references proving the weakening shrewdness and lack of business acumen of Captain Hall in his later years. Then came this:

When this first comes to you I know you will both feel you are not fitted to take charge of my girl. You will say that neither of you has had any children of his own and you have not got experience in that line. But I have thought it over and I know I am right. I couldn't find better pilots afloat or ashore. Shadrach has been to sea and commanded vessels and is used to giving orders and having them carried out. He sailed mate with me for a good many voyages and was my partner ashore. I know him from truck to keelson. He is honest and able and can handle any craft. He will keep the girl on the course she ought to sail in her schooling and such and see she does not get on the rocks or take to cruising in bad company. Zoeth has had the land training. He is a pious man and as good outside the church as he is in, which is not always the case according to my experience. He has the name all up and down the Cape of being a square, honest storekeeper. He will look out for Mary's religious bringing up and learn her how to keep straight and think square. You are both of you different from each other in most ways but you are each of you honest and straight in his own way. I don't leave Mary in the care of one but in the charge of both. I know I am right.

"He said that very thing to me a good many times," put in the Judge. "He seemed to feel that the very fact of your being men of different training and habits of thought made the combination ideal. Between you, so he seemed to think, the girl could not help but grow up as she should. I am almost through; there is a little more."

I want you fellows to do this for my sake. I know you will, after you have thought it over. You and I have been through good times and bad together. We have made money and we have seen it go faster than it came. Shad has seen his savings taken away from him, partly because I trusted where he did not, and he never spoke a word of complaint nor found a mite of fault. Zoeth has borne my greatest trouble with me and though his share was far away bigger than mine, he kept me from breaking under it. I have not seen as much of you lately as I used to see, but that was my fault. Not my fault exactly, maybe, but my misfortune. I have not been the man I was and seeing you made me realize it. That is why I have not been to South Harniss and why I acted so queer when you came here. I was sort of ashamed, I guess. You remember when the old Hall and Company firm started business there were four of us who agreed to stick by each other through foul weather and fair till we died. One of that four broke his promise and pretty nigh wrecked us all, as he did wreck the firm. Now I am asking you two to stick by me and mine. I am trusting and believing that you are going to do it as I write this. When you read it I shan't be on hand. But, if I am where I can see and hear I shall still be believing you will do this last favor for your old messmate.

MARCELLUS.

Judge Baxter folded the sheets of foolscap and laid them on the table. Then he took off his spectacles and wiped them with his handkerchief.

"Well, gentlemen?" he said, after a moment.

Captain Gould drew a long breath.

"I don't think it's well," he observed. "I think it's about as sick as it can be, and I cal'late Zoeth feels the same; eh, Zoeth?"

Mr. Hamilton did not answer. He neither spoke nor moved.

"Of course," said the lawyer, "it is not necessary that you make up your minds this instant. You will probably wish a few days to think the matter over in and then you can let me know what you decide. You have heard the letter and I have explained the situation. Are there any questions you would like to ask?"

Shadrach shook his head.

"No, not far's I'm concerned," he said. "My mind is made up now. I did think there wasn't anything I wouldn't do for Marcellus. And I would have done anything in reason. But this ain't reason—it's what I called it in the beginnin', craziness. Me and Zoeth can't go crazy for anybody."

"Then you decline?"

"Yes, sir; I'm mighty sorry but of course we can't do such a thing. Me and Zoeth, one of us a bach all his life, and t'other one a—a widower for twenty years, for us to take a child to bring up! My soul and body! Havin' hung on to the heft of our senses so far, course we decline! We can't do nothin' else."

"And you, Mr. Hamilton?"

Zoeth appeared to hesitate. Then he asked:

"What sort of a girl is she?"

"Mary-'Gusta? She's a bright child, and a well-behaved one, generally speaking. Rather old for her years, and a little—well, peculiar. That isn't strange, considering the life she has led since her mother's death. But she is a good girl and a pretty little thing. I like her; so does my wife."

"That was her at the cemetery, wasn't it? She was with that Hobbs woman?"

"Yes."

"I thought so. Shadrach and I met her when we was over here two years ago. I thought the one at the graveyard was her. Poor little critter! Where is she now; at the house—at Marcellus's?"

"Yes; that is, I suppose she is."

"Do you—do you cal'late we could see her if we went there now?"

"Yes, I am sure you could."

Zoeth rose.

"Come on, Shadrach," he said, "let's go."

The Captain stared at him.

"Go?" he repeated. "Where? Home, do you mean?"

"No, not yet. I mean over to Marcellus's to see that little girl."

"Zoeth Hamilton! Do you mean to tell me—— What do you want to see her for? Do you want to make it harder for her and for us and for all hands? What good is seein' her goin' to do? Ain't it twice as easy to say no now and be done with it?"

"I suppose likely 'twould be, but it wouldn't be right. Marcellus asked us to do this thing for him and——"

"Jumpin' Judas! *Asked* us! Do you mean to say you're thinkin' of doin' what he asked? Are you loony, too? Are you——"

"Shh, Shadrach! He asked us, as a last favor, to take charge of his girl. I feel as you do that we can't do it, 'tain't sensible nor possible for us to do it, but——"

"There ain't any buts."

"But the very least we can do is go and see her and talk to her."

"What for? So we'll feel meaner and more sneaky when we *have* to say no? *I* shan't go to see her."

"All right. Then I shall. You can wait here for me till I come back."

"Hold on, Zoeth! Hold on! Don't——"

But Mr. Hamilton was at the door and did not turn back. Judge Baxter, who was following him, spoke.

"Sit right here, Captain," he said. "Make yourself as comfortable as you can. We shan't be long."

For an instant Shadrach remained where he was. Then he, too, sprang to his feet. He overtook the lawyer just as the latter reached the side door.

"Hello, Captain," exclaimed Baxter, "changed your mind?"

"Changed nothin'. Zoeth's makin' a fool of himself and I know it, but he ain't goin' to be a fool *all* by himself. I've seen him try it afore and 'tain't safe."

"What do you mean?"

The Captain grunted scornfully.

"I mean there's safety in numbers, whether it's the number of fools or anything else," he said. "One idiot's a risky proposition, but two or three in a bunch can watch each other. Come on, Judge, and be the third."

CHAPTER III

THE white house on Phinney's Hill looked desolate and mournful when the buggy containing Judge Baxter and his two companions drove into the yard. The wagon belonging to Mr. Hallett, the undertaker, was at the front door, and Hallett and his assistant were loading in the folding chairs. Mr. Hallett was whistling a popular melody, but, somehow or other, the music only emphasized the lonesomeness. There is little cheer in an undertaker's whistle.

Captain Gould, acting under the Judge's orders, piloted his horse up the driveway and into the back yard. The animal was made fast to the back fence and the three men alighted from the buggy and walked up to the side door of the house.

"Say, Judge," whispered the Captain, as they halted by the step, "you don't cal'late I can find out who loaded up that music-box chair on me, do you? If I could meet that feller for two or three minutes I might feel more reconciled at bein' fool enough to come over here."

Mrs. Hobbs answered the knock at the door—she invited them in. When told that they had come to see Mary-'Gusta she sniffed.

"She's in her room," she said, rather sharply. "She hadn't ought to be let out, but of course if you want to see her, Judge Baxter, I presume likely she'll have to be. I'll go fetch her."

"Wait a minute, Mrs. Hobbs," said Baxter. "What's the matter? Has the child been behaving badly?"

Mrs. Hobbs' lean fingers clinched. "Behavin' badly!" she repeated. "I should say she had! I never was so mortified in my life. And at her own father's funeral, too!"

"What has she done?"

"Done? She——" Mrs. Hobbs hesitated, glanced at Captain Shadrach, and left her sentence unfinished. "Never mind what she done," she went on. "I can't tell you now; I declare I'd be ashamed to. I'll go get her."

She marched from the room. Zoeth rubbed his forehead.

"She seems sort of put out, don't she," he observed, mildly.

Baxter nodded. "Susan Hobbs has the reputation of getting 'put out' pretty often," he said. "She has a temper and it isn't a long one."

"Has she been takin' care of Marcellus's girl?" asked Zoeth.

"Yes. As much care as the child has had."

Captain Shad snorted. It was evident that the housekeeper's manner had not impressed him favorably.

"Humph!" he said. "I'd hate to have her take care of me, judgin' by the way she looked just now. Say," hopefully, "do you suppose *she* was the one fixed that chair?"

They heard Mrs. Hobbs on the floor above, shouting:

"Mary-'Gusta! Mary-'Gusta! Where are you? Answer me this minute!"

"Don't seem to be in that room she was talkin' about," grumbled Shadrach. "Tut! Tut! What a voice that is! Got a rasp to it like a rusty saw."

Mrs. Hobbs was heard descending the stairs. Her face, when she reëntered the sitting-room, was red and she looked more "put out" than ever.

"She ain't there," she answered, angrily. "She's gone."

"Gone?" repeated Zoeth and Shadrach in chorus.

"Gone?" repeated the Judge. "Do you mean she's run away?"

"No, no! She ain't run away—not for good; she knows better than that. She's sneaked off and hid, I suppose. But I know where she is. I'll have her here in a minute."

She was hurrying out again, but the Captain detained her.

"Wait!" he commanded. "What's that you say? You know where she is?"

"Yes, or I can guess. Nine chances to one she's out in that barn."

"In the barn? What's she doin' there—playin' horse?"

"No, no. She's hidin' in the carriage room. Seems as if the child was possessed to get out in that dusty place and perch herself in the old carryall. She calls it her playhouse and you'd think 'twas Heaven the way she loves to stay there. But today of all days! And with her best clothes on! And after I expressly told her——"

"Yes, yes; all right. Humph! Well, Zoeth, what do you say? Shall we go to Heaven and hunt for her? Maybe 'twill be the only chance some of us'll get, you can't tell," with a wink at Baxter.

"Hush, Shadrach! How you do talk!" protested the shocked Mr. Hamilton.

"Let's go out to the barn and find the young-one ourselves," said the Captain. "Seems the simplest thing to do, don't it?"

Mrs. Hobbs interrupted.

"You don't need to go at all," she declared. "I'll get her and bring her here. Perhaps she ain't there, anyway."

"Well, if she ain't there we can come back again. Come on, boys."

He led the way to the door. The housekeeper would have accompanied them, but he prevented her doing so.

"Don't you trouble yourself, ma'am," he said. "We'll find her. I'm older'n I used to be, but I ain't so blind but what I can locate a barn without a spyglass."

"It won't be any trouble," protested the lady.

"I know, but it might be. We'll go alone."

When the three were in the back yard, and the discomfited housekeeper was watching them from the door, he added:

"I don't know why that woman rubs my fur the wrong way, but she does. Isaiah Chase says he don't like mosquitoes 'cause they get on his nerves. I never thought I wore my nerves on the back of my neck, which is where Isaiah gets skeeter-bit mostly, but anyhow, wherever they be, that Hobbs woman bothers 'em. There's the barn, ain't it? Don't look very heavenly, but it may seem that way after a spell in t'other place. Now where's the carriage room?"

The door of the carriage room was open, and they entered. A buggy and the muslin draped surrey were there, but no living creature was in sight. They listened, but heard nothing.

"Mary! Mary-'Gusta!" called Baxter. "Are you here?"

No answer. And then, from beneath the cover of the surrey, appeared a fat tortoise-shell cat, who jumped lightly to the floor, yawned, stretched, and blinked suspiciously at the visitors.

"Humph!" grunted Captain Shadrach. "There's one stowaway, anyhow. Maybe there's another; I've had 'em come aboard in pairs."

The Judge walked over to the surrey, and raised the

cover. From behind it came a frightened little squeal.

"Oh, there you are!" said Baxter. "Mary-'Gusta, is that you?"

There was a rustle, a sob, and then a timid voice said, chokingly, "Yes, sir."

"Come out," said the Judge, kindly. "Come out; here are some friends who want to meet you."

Another sob and then: "I—I don't want to."

"Oh, yes, you do. We won't hurt you. We only want to see you and talk with you, that's all. Come, that's a good girl."

"I—I ain't a good girl."

"Never mind. We want to see you, anyway. I guess you're not very bad."

"Yes, I—I am. Is—is Mrs. Hobbs there?"

"No. Come now, please."

A moment's wait, then, from beneath the cover, appeared a small foot and leg, the latter covered by a black stocking. The foot wiggled about, feeling for the step. It found it, the cover was thrown aside and Mary-'Gusta appeared, a pathetic little figure, with rumpled hair and tear-stained cheeks. Rose and Rosette, the two dolls, were hugged in her arms.

Judge Baxter patted her on the head. Zoeth and Shadrach looked solemn and ill at ease. Mary-'Gusta looked at the floor and sniffed dolefully.

"Mary-'Gusta," said the Judge, "these two gentlemen are old friends of your father's and," with a pardonable stretching of the truth, "they have come all the way from South Harniss to meet you. Now you must shake hands with them. They like little girls."

Mary-'Gusta obediently moved forward, shifted Rosette to the arm clasping Rose, and extended a hand. Slowly she raised her eyes, saw Mr. Hamilton's mild, gentle face and then, beside it, the face of Captain Shadrach Gould. With a cry she dropped both dolls, ran back to the surrey and fumbled frantically with the dust cover.

Baxter, surprised and puzzled, ran after her and prevented her climbing into the carriage.

"Why, Mary-'Gusta," he demanded, "what *is* the matter?"

The child struggled and then, bursting into a storm of sobs, hid her face in the dust cover.

"I—I didn't mean to," she sobbed, wildly. "I didn't mean to. Honest I didn't. I—I didn't know. I didn't mean to. Please don't let him. *Please!*"

The Judge held her close and did his best to calm her.

"There, there, child," he said. "No one's going to hurt you."

"Yes—yes, they are. Mrs. Hobbs said she shouldn't wonder if he knocked my—my head right off."

"Knocked your head off! Who?"

"Him."

She raised her hand and pointed a shaking finger straight at Captain Shadrach.

All three of her hearers were surprised, of course, but in the case of the Captain himself amazement was coupled with righteous indignation.

"Wha-what?" he stammered. "Who said so? What kind of talk's that? Said *I* was goin' to knock your head off? *I* was?"

Baxter laughed. "No, no, Mary-'Gusta," he said; "you're mistaken. Mrs. Hobbs couldn't have said any such thing. You're mistaken, dear."

"No, I ain't," with another sob; "she did say so. She said he would knock my head—ah—ah—off and—

and put me in jail, too. And I didn't mean to do it; honest, truly I didn't."

The Judge looked at his companions and shook his head as if the conundrum was beyond his guessing. Captain Shad groaned.

"By fire!" he ejaculated. "All hands have gone loony, young-ones and all. And," with conviction, "I'm on the road myself."

Zoeth Hamilton stepped forward and held out his hands.

"Come here, dearie," he said, gently; "come here and tell me all about it. Neither me nor the Cap'n's goin' to hurt you a mite. We like little girls, both of us do. Now you come and tell me about it."

Mary-'Gusta's sobs ceased. She looked at the speaker doubtfully.

"Come, don't be scared," begged Zoeth. "We're goin' to be good friends to you. We knew your father and he thought everything of us. You ain't goin' to be afraid of folks that was your Pa's chums. You come here and let's talk it over."

Slowly Mary-'Gusta crossed the room. Zoeth sat down upon an empty box near the door and lifted the girl to his knee.

"Now you ain't afraid of me, be you?" he asked quietly.

Mary-'Gusta shook her head, but her big eyes were fixed upon Captain Shadrach's face.

"No-o," she faltered. "I—I guess I ain't. But you wasn't the one I did it to. It was him."

Judging by the Captain's expression his conviction that all hands, himself included, had lost their reason was momentarily growing firmer.

"*Me?*" he gasped. "You done somethin' to me and I—well, by Judas, this is——"

"Hush, Shadrach! What was it you done, Mary, that made you afraid of Cap'n Gould? Tell me. I won't hurt you and I won't let anybody else."

"*You* won't let—Zoeth Hamilton, I swan, I——"

"Be still, Shadrach, for mercy sakes! Now, what was it, dearie?"

Mary-'Gusta hesitated. Then she buried her face in Mr. Hamilton's jacket and sobbed a confession.

"I—I made it go," she cried. "I—I broke the—the catch—and it was wound up and—and it went off. But I didn't know. I didn't mean——"

"There, there, course you didn't. We know you didn't. What was it that went off?"

"The—the music chair. It was in the corner and Mr. Hallett took it and—and I couldn't say anything 'cause Mrs. Hobbs said I mustn't speak a word at the funeral. And—and he set in it and it played and—Oh, don't let him put me in jail! Please don't."

Another burst of tears. Mary-'Gusta clung tightly to the Hamilton jacket. Judge Baxter looked as if a light had suddenly broken upon the darkness of his mind.

"I see," he said. "You were responsible for the 'Campbells.' I see."

Shadrach drew a long breath.

"Whew!" he whistled. "So she was the one. Well, I swan!"

Zoeth stroked the child's hair.

"That's all right, dearie," he said. "Now don't you worry about that. We didn't know who did it, but now we do and it's all right. We know you didn't mean to."

"Won't—won't he knock my head off?"

"No, no, course he won't. Tell her so, Shadrach."

Captain Shadrach pulled at his beard. Then he burst into a laugh.

"I won't hurt you for nothin', sis," he said, heartily. "It's all right and don't you fret about it. Accidents will happen even in the best regulated—er—funerals; though," with a broad grin, "I hope another one like that'll never happen to *me*. Now don't you cry any more."

Mary-'Gusta raised her head and regarded him steadily.

"Won't I be put in jail?" she asked, more hopefully.

"Indeed you won't. I never put anybody in jail in my life; though," with an emphatic nod, "there's some folks ought to go there for frightenin' children out of their senses. Did that Mrs. Hobbs tell you I was goin' to— what was it?—knock your head off and all the rest?"

"Yes, sir, she did."

"Well, she's a—she's what she is. What else did she say to you?"

"She—she said I was a bad, wicked child and she hoped I'd be sent to the—the orphans' home. If she was to have the care of me, she said, she'd make me walk a chalk or know why. And she sent me to my room and said I couldn't have any supper."

Zoeth and the Captain looked at each other. Baxter frowned.

"On the very day of her father's funeral," he muttered.

"Can't I have any supper?" begged Mary-'Gusta. "I'm awful hungry; I didn't want much dinner."

Zoeth nodded. His tone, when he spoke, was not so mild as was usual with him.

"You shall have your supper," he said.

"And—and must I go to the orphans' home?"

No one answered at once. Zoeth and Captain Shad again looked at each other and the Judge looked at them both.

"Must I?" repeated Mary-'Gusta. "I—I don't want to. I'd rather die, I guess, and go to Heaven, same as Mother and Father. But Mrs. Hobbs says they don't have any dolls nor cats in Heaven, so I don't know's I'd want to go there."

Baxter walked to the window and looked out. Captain Shadrach reached into his pocket, produced a crumpled handkerchief, and blew his nose violently. Zoeth stroked the child's hair.

"Mary-'Gusta," he said, after a moment, "how would you like to go over to South Harniss and—and see me and Cap'n Gould a little while? Just make us a visit, you know. Think you'd like that?"

The Captain started. "Good land, Zoeth!" he exclaimed. "Be careful what you're sayin'."

"I ain't sayin' anything definite, Shadrach. I know how you feel about it. I just wanted to see how she felt herself, that's all. Think you'd like that, Mary-'Gusta?"

Mary-'Gusta thought it over. "I guess maybe I would," she said, "if I could take my dolls and David. I wouldn't want to leave David. Mrs. Hobbs don't like cats."

And at that moment Mrs. Hobbs herself appeared in the doorway of the carriage room. She saw the child and her eyes snapped.

"So she was here," she said. "I thought as much. Mary-'Gusta, what did you run away from that room for? Didn't I forbid you leavin' it? She's been a bad girl, Judge Baxter," she added, "and I can't make her behave. I try my best, but I'm sure I don't know what to do."

Captain Shadrach thrust both hands into his pockets.

"I tell you what to do," he said, sharply. "You go into the house and put some of her things into a valise or

46

satchel or somethin'. And hurry up as fast as you can."

Mrs. Hobbs was astonished.

"Put 'em in a satchel?" she repeated. "What for? Where's she goin'?"

"She's goin' home along with me and Zoeth. And she's got to start inside of half an hour. You hurry."

"But—but——"

"There ain't any 'buts'; haven't got time for 'em."

Mr. Hamilton regarded his friend with an odd expression.

"Shadrach," he asked, "do you realize what you're sayin'?"

"Who's sayin'? You said it, I didn't. Besides takin' her home with us today don't mean nothin', does it? A visit won't hurt us. Visits don't bind anybody to anything. Jumpin' Judas! I guess we've got room enough in the house to have one young-one come visitin' for— for a couple of days, if we want to. What are you makin' such a fuss about? Here you," turning to the housekeeper, "ain't you gone yet? You've got just thirteen minutes to get that satchel ready."

Mrs. Hobbs departed, outraged dignity in her walk and manner.

"Am—am I goin'?" faltered Mary-'Gusta.

Zoeth nodded.

"Yes," he said, "you're goin'. Unless, of course, you'd rather stay here."

"No, I'd rather go, if—if I can take David and the dolls. Can I?"

"Can she, Shadrach?"

Captain Shad, who was pacing the floor, turned savagely.

"What do you ask me that for?" he demanded. "This is your doin's, 'tain't mine. You said it first, didn't you? Yes, yes, let her take the dolls and cats—and cows and pigs, too, if she wants to. Jumpin' fire! What do I care? If a feller's bound to be a fool, a little live stock more or less don't make him any bigger one. . . . Land sakes! I believe she's goin' to cry again. Don't do that! What's the matter now?"

The tears were starting once more in the girl's eyes.

"I—I don't think you want me," she stammered. "If you did you—you wouldn't talk so."

The Captain was greatly taken aback. He hesitated, tugged at his beard, and then, walking over to the child, took her by the hand.

"Don't you mind the way I talk, Mary-'Gusta," he said. "I'm liable to talk 'most any way, but I don't mean nothin' by it. I like little girls, same as Zoeth said. And I ain't mad about the jig-tune chair, neither. Say," with a sudden inspiration, "here we are settin' here and one of our passengers has left the dock. We got to find that cat, ain't we? What did you say his name was— Solomon?"

"No, sir; David."

"David, sure enough. If I'd been up in Scripture the way Zoeth—Mr. Hamilton, here—is, I wouldn't have made that mistake, would I? Come on, let's you and me go find David and break the news to him. Say, he'll be some surprised to find he's booked for a foreign v'yage, won't he? Come on, we'll go find him."

Mary-'Gusta slowly rose from Mr. Hamilton's knee. She regarded the Captain steadily for a moment; then, hand in hand, they left the barn together.

Judge Baxter whistled. "Well!" he exclaimed. "I must say I didn't expect this."

Zoeth smiled. "There ain't many better men than Shadrach Gould," he observed, quietly.

CHAPTER IV

MARY-'GUSTA, even though she lives to be a very old woman, will never forget that ride to South Harniss. It was the longest ride she had ever taken, and that of itself would have made it unforgetable. Then, too, she was going visiting, and she had never been visiting before. Also, she was leaving Mrs. Hobbs and, for a time at least, that lady could not remind her of her queerness and badness. More than all, she was going on a journey, a real journey, like a grown-up or a person in a story, and her family—David and the dolls— were journeying with her. What the journey might mean to her, or to what sort of place she was going—these questions did not trouble her in the least. Childlike, she was quite satisfied with the wonderful present, and to the future, even the dreaded orphans' home, she gave not a thought.

Perched on the buggy seat, squeezed in between Captain Shad and Mr. Hamilton, she gazed wide-eyed at the houses and fields and woods along the roadside. She did not speak, unless spoken to, and the two men spoke but seldom, each apparently thinking hard. Occasionally the Captain would sigh, or whistle, or groan, as if his thoughts were disturbing and most unusual. Once he asked her if she was comfortable.

"Yes, sir," she said.

"Havin' a good time? Like to go to ride, do you?"

Mary-'Gusta assumed her most grown-up air.

"Yes, sir," she said. "I just love to travel. It's been the dream of my life."

49

"Gosh! I want to know!" exclaimed the astonished Shadrach; then he shook his head, chuckled, and ordered the horse to hurry up.

The dolls were arranged in a row against the back of the dashboard. In front of them, and between the Captain's feet and Zoeth's, the battered satchel containing the child's everyday dress and visiting essentials was squeezed. Mary-'Gusta's feet stuck straight out and rested on the top of the satchel. David, in a basket with the lid tied fast, was planted between the last mentioned feet. David did not appear to share his—or her—owner's love of travel. The cat wailed lugubriously at intervals.

Zoeth made the next attempt at conversation.

"Never been to South Harniss, have you, Mary-'Gusta?" he inquired.

"No, sir," gravely. "But," remembering the housekeeper's final charge not to forget her manners, if she had any, "I'm sure I'll like it very much."

"Oh, you are, eh? Well, that's nice. What makes you so sure?"

Mary-'Gusta reflected. She remembered what Mrs. Bailey had said after a week's visit in Bayport, which is fourteen miles from Ostable. "I think everybody enjoys a change of air," she observed.

"My soul and body!" exclaimed Mr. Hamilton.

Captain Shad looked down at his small passenger.

"How old are you, sis?" he demanded.

"I'm seven. But I ain't a sis; I haven't got any brothers or sisters."

"Oh! Well, that's a fact, too, now I come to think of it. How old did you say; seventy, was it?"

"No, sir. Seven. Did you think I said seventy?"

"Eh? No, I guess not."

"I couldn't be seventy. If I was I'd be lots bigger, you know."

"That's so; I presume likely you would."

More reflection. Then: "If I was seventy I guess you wouldn't have asked me."

"Sho! Wouldn't I? Why not?"

" 'Cause grown-up folks don't like to be asked how old they are. I asked Mrs. Hobbs how old she was once and she didn't like it."

"Didn't she?"

"No, sir. She told me to mind my own business."

The Captain laughed aloud. Then, turning to Mr. Hamilton, he said: "Say, Zoeth, Isaiah'll be a little mite surprised when he sees this craft make port, eh?"

Zoeth smiled. "I shouldn't wonder," he replied.

"Um-hm. I'd like to have a tintype of Isaiah's face. Well, sis—er, Mary-'Gusta, I mean—there's South Harniss dead ahead. How do you like the looks of it?"

They had emerged from a long stretch of woods and were at the summit of a little hill. From the crest of this hill the road wound down past an old cemetery with gray, moss-covered slate tombstones, over a bridge between a creek and a good-sized pond, on through a clump of pines, where it joined the main highway along the south shore of the Cape. This highway, in turn, wound and twisted—there are few straight roads on Cape Cod— between other and lower hills until it became a village street, the main street of South Harniss. The sun was low in the west and its light bathed the clustered roofs in a warm glow, touched windows and vanes with fire, and twinkled and glittered on the waters of Nantucket Sound, which filled the whole southern horizon. There was little breeze and the smoke from the chimneys rose almost straight. So, too, did the smoke from the distant tugs and steamers. There were two or three schooners far out, and nearer shore, a sailboat. A pretty picture, one which artists have painted and summer visitors enthused over many times.

To Mary-'Gusta it was new and wonderful. The child was in a mood to like almost anything just then. Mrs. Hobbs was miles away and the memory of the music chair and her own disgrace and shame were but memories. She drew a long breath and looked and looked.

"Like it, do you?" asked Zoeth, echoing his friend's question.

Mary-'Gusta nodded. "Yes, sir," she said. "It—it's lovely."

Captain Shadrach nodded. "Best town on earth, if I do say it," he said, emphatically. "So you think it's lovely, eh?"

"Yes, sir." Then, pointing, she asked: "Is that your house?"

The Captain grinned. "Well, no, not exactly," he said. "That's the town hall. Nobody lives there but the selectmen and they ain't permanent boarders—that is, I have hopes some of 'em 'll move after town-meetin' day. Our house is over yonder, down nigh the shore."

The old horse pricked up his ears at sight of home and the buggy moved faster. It rolled through the main street, where the Captain and Mr. Hamilton were kept busy answering hails and returning bows from citizens, male and female. Through the more thickly settled portion of the village it moved, until at a point where there were fewer shops and the houses were older and less up-to-date, it reached the corner of a narrow cross road. There it stopped before a frame building bearing the sign, "Hamilton and Company, Dry Goods, Groceries, Boots and Shoes and Notions." There was a narrow platform

"Squeezed in between Captain Shad and Mr. Hamilton, she gazed wide-eyed at the houses and fields"

at the front of the building and upon this platform were several men, mostly of middle age or older. Mary-'Gusta noticed that most of these men were smoking. If she had been older she might have noticed that each man either sat upon the platform steps or leaned against the posts supporting its roof. Not one was depending solely upon his own muscles for support; he sat upon or leaned against something wooden and substantial.

As the buggy drew alongside the platform the men evinced considerable interest. Not enough to make them rise or relinquish support, but interest, nevertheless.

"Hello, Shad!" hailed one. "Home again, be you?"

"Pretty big funeral, was it?" drawled another.

"Who's that you got aboard?" queried a third.

Captain Shadrach did not answer. Mr. Hamilton leaned forward. "Where's Annabel?" he asked.

"She's inside," replied the first questioner. "Want to see her? Hi, Jabe," turning his head and addressing one of the group nearest the door, "tell Annabel, Zoeth and Shad's come."

"Jabe," who was propped against a post, languidly pushed himself away from it, opened the door behind him and shouted: "Annabel, come out here!" Then he slouched back and leaned against the post again.

The door opened and a stout, red-faced young woman appeared. She looked much more like an Eliza than an Annabel. She had a newspaper in her hand.

"Hey?" she drawled. "Who was that hollerin'? Was it you, Jabez Hedges?"

Jabez did not take the trouble to answer. Instead he took a hand from his trousers pocket and waved it toward the buggy. Annabel looked; then she came down the steps.

"Hello!" she said. "I see you got back all right."

Zoeth nodded. "How'd you get along in the store?" he asked, anxiously. "How's business?"

"Wasn't none to speak of," replied Annabel carelessly. "Sold a couple of spools of cotton and—and some salt pork and sugar. Ezra Howland bought the pork. He wasn't satisfied; said there wasn't enough lean in it to suit him, but I let him have it a cent cheaper, so he took it."

Mr. Hamilton seemed a trifle disappointed. "Was that all?" he asked, with a sigh.

"Yup. No, 'twa'n't neither, come to think of it. Rastus Young's wife come in with her two young-ones and bought some shoes and hats for 'em."

"Did she pay cash?" demanded Captain Shadrach sharply.

"No; she said charge 'em up, so I done it. Say, ain't you comin' in pretty soon? It's 'most my supper time."

Zoeth opened his mouth to answer, but the Captain got ahead of him.

"It's our supper time, too," he said, crisply. "When we've had it you can have yours. Get dap, January."

The horse, whose name was Major but who was accustomed to being addressed by almost any name, jogged on. Mr. Hamilton sighed once more.

"I'm 'fraid one of us had ought to stayed in the store, Shadrach," he said. "Annabel means well, she's real obligin'; but she ain't a good hand at business."

Shadrach snorted. "Obligin' nothin'!" he retorted. "We're the ones that was obligin' when we agreed to pay her seventy-five cents for settin' astern of the counter and readin' the *Advocate*. I told you when you hired her that she wasn't good for nothin' but ballast."

"I know, Shadrach. I'd ought to have stayed to home

and kept store myself. But I did feel as if I must go to Marcellus's funeral."

"Sellin' them Youngs a whole passel of stuff and lettin' 'em charge it up!" went on Shadrach. "They owe us enough now to keep a decent family all winter. Reg'lar town dead-beats, that's what they are. You couldn't get a cent out of Rastus Young if you were to run a dredge through him."

Mr. Hamilton groaned remorsefully. "If I'd only stayed at home!" he said.

"If you'd stayed to home you'd have charged up the stuff just the same as she did. You're the softest thing, outside of a sponge, in this town. Anybody can impose on you, and you know it, Zoeth."

Zoeth's habitual mildness gave way to resentment, mild resentment.

"Why, Shadrach," he retorted, "how you talk! You was the one that charged up the last things Rastus's folks bought. You know you was."

The Captain looked as if he had been caught napping.

"Well, what's that got to do with it?" he sputtered. "'Twasn't nothin' but some corn meal and a few yards of calico. How could I help chargin' it up, with that woman cryin' and goin' on about their havin' nothin' to eat nor wear in the house? I couldn't let 'em starve, could I? Nor freeze neither?"

"'Twas only last week she did it," protested his partner. "Folks don't freeze in April, seems to me."

"Aw, be still! Don't talk no more about it. By fire!" with a sudden change of subject and a burst of enthusiasm, "look at that horse, will you! Turned right in at the gate without my pullin' the helm once or sayin' a word—knows as much as a Christian, that horse does."

The buggy had rocked and plowed its way over the

hummocks and through the sand of the narrow lane and was at the top of a grass-covered knoll, a little hill. At the foot of the hill was the beach, strewn with seaweed, and beyond, the Sound, its waters now a rosy purple in the sunset light. On the slope of the hill toward the beach stood a low, rambling, white house, a barn, and several sheds and outbuildings. There were lilac bushes by the front door of the house, a clam-shell walk from the lane to that door, and, surrounding the whole, a whitewashed picket fence. A sandy rutted driveway led from the rear of the house and the entrance of the barn down to a big gate, now wide open. It was through this gateway and along this drive that the sagacious Major was pulling the buggy.

Mary-'Gusta stared at the house. As she stared the back door was thrown open and a tall, thin man came out. He was in his shirtsleeves, his arms were bare to the elbow, and to Mary-'Gusta's astonishment he wore an apron, a gingham apron similar to those worn by Mrs. Hobbs when at work in the kitchen.

"Ahoy, there, Isaiah!" hailed the Captain. "Here we are."

The man with the apron took a big nickel watch from the upper pocket of his vest, looked at it, and shook his head. Upon his face, which was long and thin like the rest of him, there was a grieved expression.

"A little mite late, ain't we, Isaiah?" said Zoeth, hastily. "Hope we ain't kept supper waitin' too long?"

The tall man returned the watch to the pocket.

"Only twenty-three minutes, that's all," he drawled, with the resignation of a martyr. "Twenty-three minutes ain't much in a lifetime, maybe—but it don't help fried potatoes none. Them potatoes was ready at half-past five."

"Well, 'tain't six yet," protested Captain Shad.

"Maybe 'tain't, but it's twenty-three minutes later'n half-past five. Last thing you said to me was, 'Have supper ready at half-past five!' I had it ready. Them potatoes went on the fire at——"

"There! there!" interrupted the Captain. "Never mind the potatoes. We'll 'tend to them in a minute. Give us a hand with this dunnage. There's a satchel here and some more stuff. Sooner this craft's unloaded the sooner we can eat. All ashore that's goin' ashore."

Zoeth climbed out of the buggy. He lifted their passenger to the ground.

"Mary-'Gusta," he said, "here's where Cap'n Gould and I live. This is Mr. Isaiah Chase. Isaiah, this is Mary Lathrop, Cap'n Marcellus's little girl. She's come to—t——"

"To make us a little visit," put in the Captain, promptly. "You want to get acquainted with Isaiah, Mary-'Gusta; he's cook and steward for me and Mr. Zoeth. That's right; shake hands and be sociable."

Mary-'Gusta extended her hand and Mr. Chase, after wiping his own hand on the apron, pumped hers up and down.

"Pleased to meet you," he said, solemnly.

"Now for the dunnage," said Captain Shad. "There's the satchel and—and the other things. Look out for that basket! *Look out!*"

Mr. Chase had seized the basket and swung it out of the buggy. David, frightened at the sudden aërial ascension, uttered a howl. Isaiah dropped the basket as if it was red hot.

"What in tunket!" he exclaimed.

"Nothin' but a cat," explained the Captain. " 'Twon't hurt you."

"A cat! What—whose cat?"

"Mine," said Mary-'Gusta, running to the rescue. "He's a real good cat. He ain't cross; he's scared, that's all. Honest, he ain't cross. Are you, David?"

David howled and clawed at the cover of the basket. Mr. Chase backed away.

"A cat!" he repeated. "You fetched a cat—here?"

"Sartin we fetched it." Captain Shadrach was evidently losing patience. "Did you think we'd fetch an elephant? Now get out them—them doll babies and things."

Isaiah stared at the dolls. Mary-'Gusta stopped patting the basket and hastened to the side of the buggy. "I'll take the dollies," she said. "They're mine, too."

A moment later they entered the house. Mary-'Gusta bore three of the dolls. Mr. Hamilton carried the other two, and Isaiah, with the valise in one hand and the basket containing the shrieking David at arm's length in the other, led the way. Captain Shad, after informing them that he would be aboard in a jiffy, drove on to the barn.

The room they first entered was the kitchen. It was small, rather untidy, and smelt strongly of fish and the fried potatoes.

"Come right along with me, Mary-'Gusta," said Zoeth. "Fetch the satchel, Isaiah."

"Hold on," shouted the perturbed "cook and steward." "What—what in the nation will I do with this critter?"

The "critter" was David, who was apparently turning somersaults in the basket.

Zoeth hesitated. Mary-'Gusta settled the question.

"Put him right down, please," she said. "He'll be better soon as he's put down. He's never traveled before and it's kind of strange to him. He'll be all right and

I'll come back and let him out pretty soon. Mayn't I,
Mr.—Mr. Chase?"

"Huh? Yes, yes, you can if you want to, I cal'late.
I don't want to, that's sure."

He deposited the basket on the floor at his feet. Mary-
'Gusta looked at it rather dubiously and for an instant
seemed about to speak, but she did not, and followed
Mr. Hamilton from the kitchen, through the adjoining
room, evidently the dining-room, and up a narrow flight
of stairs.

"I cal'late we'll put her in the spare room, won't we,
Isaiah?" queried Zoeth, with some hesitation.

Isaiah grunted. "Guess so," he said, ungraciously.
"Ain't no other place that I know of. Bed ain't made,
though."

The spare room was of good size, and smelled shut up
and musty, as spare rooms in the country usually do. It
was furnished with a bureau, washstand, and two chairs,
each painted in a robin's egg blue with sprays of yellow
roses. There were several pictures on the walls, their
subjects religious and mournful. The bed was, as Mr.
Chase had said, not made; in fact it looked as if it had
not been made for some time.

"I've been cal'latin' to make up that bed for more'n
a month," explained Isaiah. "Last time 'twas unmade
was when Zoeth had that minister from Trumet here of
a Saturday and Sunday. Every day I've cal'lated to
make up that bed, but I don't seem to get no time. I'm
so everlastin' busy I don't get time for nothin', somehow."

"I can make the bed," declared Mary-'Gusta, eagerly.
"I can make beds real well. Mrs. Hobbs told me so—
once."

The two men looked at each other. Before either

could speak a tremendous racket broke out on the floor below, a sound of something—or somebody—tumbling about, a roar in a human voice and a feline screech. Mary-'Gusta rushed for the stairs.

"I knew he would," she said, frantically. "I was afraid somebody would. It was *right* in front of the door. Oh! David, dear! I'm a-comin'! I'm a-comin'!"

From the kitchen came Captain Shadrach's voice. It sounded excited and angry.

"Who in blazes left that dum critter right under my feet?" he hollered. "I—I swan, I believe I've broke my neck—or his—one or t'other."

When Zoeth and Isaiah reached the kitchen they found the Captain sitting in a chair, rubbing his knees, and Mary-'Gusta seated on the floor beside the open basket, hugging the frightened and struggling David.

"I—I guess he's all right," panted the child. "I was so afraid he'd be killed. You ain't killed, are you, David?"

David appeared to be remarkably sound and active. He wriggled from his owner's arms and bolted under the stove.

"No; he's all right," said Mary-'Gusta. "Isn't it nice he ain't hurt, Mr.—I mean Cap'n Gould?"

Captain Shad rubbed his knee. "Um—yes," he said, with elaborate sarcasm; "it's lovely. Course I don't mind breakin' both *my* legs, but if that cat had been—er—bruised or anything I should have felt bad. Well, Isaiah," he added, tartly, turning to the grinning "steward," "are them fried potatoes of yours real or just in your mind?"

"Eh? Why—why they're right there on the stove, Cap'n Shad."

"Want to know! Then suppose you put 'em on the table. I'm hungry and I'd like to eat one more square meal afore somethin' else happens to finish me altogether. By fire! if this ain't been a day! First that chair, and then that will and letter of Marcellus's, and then this. Humph! Come on, all hands, let's eat supper. I need somethin' solid to brace me up for tomorrow's program; if it's up to this, I'll need strength to last it through. Come on!"

That first supper in the white house by the shore was an experience for Mary-'Gusta. Mrs. Hobbs, in spite of her faultfinding and temper, had been a competent and careful housekeeper. Meals which she prepared were well cooked and neatly served. This meal was distinctly different. There was enough to eat—in fact, an abundance—fried cod and the fried potatoes and hot biscuits and dried-apple pie; but everything was put upon the table at the same time, and Mr. Chase sat down with the others and did not even trouble to take off his apron. The tablecloth was not very clean and the knives and forks and spoons did not glitter like those the child had been accustomed to see.

Even Mr. Hamilton, to whom most of the things of this world—his beloved store excepted—seemed to be unessential trivialities, spoke of the table linen.

"Seems to me," he observed, in his gentle and hesitating way, "this tablecloth's sort of spotted up. Don't you think so, Shadrach?"

Captain Shad's reply was emphatic and to the point.

"Looks as if 'twas breakin' out with chicken-pox," he replied. "Ain't we got a clean one in the locker, Isaiah?"

Mr. Chase's face assumed an aggrieved expression.

"Course we have," he answered, "but I didn't know you was goin' to have company."

"Neither did we. But we could stand a clean tablecloth, even at that."

"I've got somethin' to do besides changin' tablecloths every day."

"Every day! Every Thanksgivin' Day, you mean. This one——"

"Now, look-a-here, Cap'n Shad; you know well as I do that Sarah J. never come to do the washin' last week. She was down with the grip and couldn't move. If you expect me to do washin' as well as cook and sweep and keep house and—and shovel snow, and——"

"Shovel snow! What kind of talk's that? There ain't been any snow since February."

"Don't make no difference. When there was I shoveled it, didn't I? It ain't no use; I try and try, but I can't give satisfaction and I might's well quit. I don't have to stay here and slave myself to death. I can get another job. There's folks in this town that's just dyin' to have me work for 'em."

Captain Shadrach muttered something to the effect that if Isaiah did work for them they might die sooner. Mr. Chase rose from his seat.

"All right," he said, with dignity. "All right, this settles it. I'm through. After all the years I sailed cook along with you, Shad Gould, and after you beggin' me— yes, sir, beggin' on your knees, as you might say, for me to run this house for you long as you lived—after that, to—to—— Good-by. I'll try not to lay it up against you."

He was moving—not hastily, but actually moving— toward the kitchen door. Zoeth, who was evidently much disturbed, rose and laid a hand on his arm.

"There, there, Isaiah," he pleaded. "Don't act so. We ain't findin' any fault. Shadrach wasn't findin' fault, was you, Shadrach?"

"No, no, course I wasn't. Don't talk so foolish, Isaiah.

Nobody wants you to quit. All I said was—— Come back here and set down. Your tea's gettin' all cold."

To Mary-'Gusta it seemed as if the tea had been at least cool to begin with. However, Mr. Chase suffered himself to be led back to the table and attacked his supper in injured silence. Mary-'Gusta offered a suggestion.

"I guess I could wash a tablecloth," she said. "I always wash my dolls' things."

Her three companions were plainly surprised. The Captain was the first to speak.

"You don't say!" he exclaimed.

"Yes, sir, I do. And," with a glance at the silver, "I can scour knives and forks and spoons, too. I used to help Mrs. Hobbs scour 'em sometimes."

Even Shadrach had no remark to make. He gazed at the child, then at Zoeth, and drew a long breath.

As soon as supper was over the Captain and Mr. Hamilton hastened up to the village and the store.

"You better go to bed pretty soon, Mary-'Gusta," said Zoeth. "You're tired, I know. Isaiah'll make your bed for you. We'll be on hand and see you first thing in the morning. Isaiah'll go up with you and blow out your light and all. Good night."

The Captain said good night also and the pair hurried out.

When at ten o'clock they returned they found Mr. Chase up and awaiting them. Isaiah had a story to tell.

"I never see a young-one like that in this world," declared Isaiah. "You know what she done after you left? Helped me do the dishes. Yes, sir, by time, that's what she done. And she wiped 'em first-rate, too; good enough to satisfy *me,* and you know that means somethin' 'cause I ain't easy to satisfy. And talk! Say, I never had a child talk same as she does. How old is she, for the land sakes?"

Zoeth told them the visitor's age.

"Well, maybe so," went on Isaiah, "but she don't talk seven; nigher seventeen, if you ask me. Pumpin' me about funerals, she was, and about folks dyin' and so on. Said she cal'lated she'd have a doll's funeral some time. 'For mercy sakes, what for?' I says. 'Can't you think up anything pleasanter'n that to play? That kind of game would give me the blue creeps!' She thought that over —she generally thinks about a thing for five minutes afore she talks about it—and says she, 'I know,' she says, 'but a person must go to funerals and so it's better to get used to 'em and know how to behave. I shouldn't want my dolls,' she says, 'to do things at funerals that make people feel bad and laugh.' I couldn't get that through my head. 'If they felt bad they wouldn't laugh, would they?' says I. *'They* wouldn't—the ones that felt bad wouldn't,' says she, 'but others' might laugh at them. And that would make the person who was to blame feel *terribly.*' Now what was all that about? Can you make any sense of it?"

Captain Shadrach smiled sheepishly. "I cal'late me and Zoeth have an idea what she was drivin' at," he said. "Go on, Isaiah; what else did she say?"

"What didn't she say? Wanted to know if I thought God would knock anybody's head off that had done wrong, even if they didn't mean to. Yes, sir, that's what she said—if God would knock anybody's head off. Mine pretty nigh come off when she said that. I told her that, fur's I knew, He wasn't in the habit of doin' it. She said that Mrs. Hobbs told her that if she wasn't punished for her wickedness in this world she would be in the next. She was real kind of scared about it, seemed to me. Now what's she done that's wicked, a little critter like her?"

Zoeth said nothing, but he looked vexed and disturbed.

"I'd knock *somebody's* head off if I had my way," observed Shadrach. "Or if I didn't, I'd like to. Where is she now, Isaiah?"

"She's up in the spare room, asleep I cal'late. And she's got her dolls along with her, three on one side and two on t'other. Wanted me to be sure and wake all hands of 'em up on time in the mornin'. He, he! She undressed them dolls, every one of 'em, afore they turned in. Oh, yes, and she helped me make the bed, too. She *can* make a bed, blessed if she can't. And all the time a-talkin', one minute like a child and the next like a forty-year-old woman. She's the queerest young-one!"

"I guess she's had a kind of queer bringin' up," said Zoeth.

"Where's that—where's Saul—er—Elijah—what's his name—David?" asked the Captain. "Where's the cat?"

"He's out in the barn, locked in. She had to go out along with me when I toted him there, and kiss him good night and tell him not to be frightened, and goodness knows what all—you'd think she was that cat's mother, to hear her. How long's she goin' to stay?"

"Don't know," replied Shadrach, hastily. "That ain't settled yet."

"How'd you come to fetch her over here? You're the last ones I ever thought would be fetchin' a child to visit you. Say, you ain't cal'latin' to keep her for good, are you?"

Zoeth hesitated. Shadrach's answer was emphatic.

"Course not," he snapped. "What do Zoeth and me know about managin' a child? Keep her for good, the idea!"

Isaiah chuckled. " 'Cordin' to my notion," he said, "you

wouldn't have to know much. You wouldn't have to manage her. If she wasn't managin' you—yes, and me, too—inside of a month, I'd miss my guess. She's a born manager. You ought to see her handle them dolls and that cat."

When the two partners of Hamilton and Company went upstairs to their own bedrooms they opened the door of the spare room and peeped in. Mary-'Gusta's head and those of the dolls were in a row upon the pillow. It was a strange sight in that room and that house.

"I declare!" whispered Zoeth. "And this mornin' we never dreamed of such a thing. How long this day has been!"

"Judgin' by the state of my nerves and knees it's been two year," replied Shadrach. "I've aged that much, I swan to man. Humph! I wonder if Marcellus knows what's happened."

His tone was not loud, but it or the lamplight in her face awakened Mary-'Gusta. She stirred, opened her eyes and regarded them sleepily.

"Is it mornin'?" she asked.

"No, no," replied Zoeth. "It's only ten o'clock. Captain Shadrach and I was goin' to bed and we looked in to see if you was all right, that's all. You must go right to sleep again, dearie."

"Yes, sir," said Mary-'Gusta, obediently. Then she added, "I said my prayers to myself but I'll say 'em to you if you want me to."

The embarrassed Captain would have protested, but the girl's mind seemed to be made up.

"I guess I will say 'em again," she said. "There's somethin' in 'em maybe you'd ought to hear." She closed her eyes. "Please God bless Father—Oh, I forgot—bless Mrs. Hobbs and Cap'n Gould and Mr. Hamilton. I thought I'd ask him to bless you, you know, because I'm visitin' here. And bless David and Rose and Rosette and Emma and Christobel and Minnehaha. They're my dolls. And please, God, forgive me for breakin' the music chair and makin' it go off, because you know I am very sorry and won't do it again. And—and, Oh, yes!—bless Mr. Chase, Amen. You don't mind my puttin' you and Mr. Chase in, do you?"

"No, dearie, not a mite," said Zoeth.

Captain Shad, looking more embarrassed than ever, shook his head. "Good night," said Mary-'Gusta. Zoeth hesitated, then he walked over and kissed her.

"Good night, little girl," he said.

"Good night, Mr. Hamilton," said Mary-'Gusta. Then she turned expectantly toward the Captain. Shadrach fidgeted, turned to go, and then, turning back, strode to the bed, brushed the soft cheek with his rough one and hastened out into the hall. Zoeth followed him, bearing the lamp. At the door of the Captain's room, they paused.

"Well, good night, Zoeth," said Shadrach, brusquely.

"Good night, Shadrach. This—this is queer business for you and me, ain't it?"

"I should think 'twas. Humph! You said this morning that maybe Marcellus was alongside of us today. If he is he knows what's happened, don't he?"

"Perhaps he knows that and more, Shadrach. Perhaps he can see what'll happen in the future. Perhaps he knows that, too."

"Humph! Well, if he does, he knows a heap more'n I do. Good night."

CHAPTER V

MARY-'GUSTA awoke next morning to find the sun shining in at the window of her bedroom. She had no means of knowing the time, but she was certain it must be very late and, in consequence, was almost dressed when Isaiah knocked at the door to tell her breakfast would be ready pretty soon. A few minutes later she appeared in the kitchen bearing the pitcher from the washstand in her room.

"What you doin' with that?" demanded Mr. Chase, who was leaning against the door-post looking out into the yard.

"I was goin' to fill it," said the child. "There wasn't any water to wash with."

Isaiah sniffed. "I ain't had no time to fill wash pitchers," he declared. "That one's been on my mind for more'n a fortni't but I've had other things to do. You can wash yourself in that basin in the sink. That's what the rest of us do."

Mary-'Gusta obediently washed in the tin basin and rubbed her face and hands dry upon the roller towel behind the closet door.

"Am I late for breakfast?" she asked, anxiously.

"No, I guess not. Ain't had breakfast yet. Cap'n Shad's out to the barn 'tendin' to the horse and Zoeth's feedin' the hens. They'll be in pretty soon, if we have luck. Course it's *time* for breakfast, but that's nothing. I'm the only one that has to think about time in this house."

The girl regarded him thoughtfully.

"You have to work awful hard, don't you, Mr. Chase?" she said.

Isaiah looked at her suspiciously.

"Huh?" he grunted. "Who told you that?"

"Nobody. I just guessed it from what you said."

"Humph! Well, you guessed right. I don't have many spare minutes."

"Yes, sir. Are you a perfect slave?"

"Eh? What?"

"Mrs. Hobbs says she is a perfect slave when she has to work hard."

"Who's Mrs. Hobbs?"

"She's—she keeps house—that is, she used to keep house for my father over in Ostable. I don't suppose she will any more now he's dead. She'll be glad, I guess. Perhaps she won't have to be a perfect slave now. She used to wear aprons same as you do. I never saw a man wear an apron before. Do you have to wear one?"

"Hey? Have to? No, course I don't have to unless I want to."

Mary-'Gusta reflected.

"I suppose," she went on, after a moment, "it saves your pants. You'd get 'em all spotted up if you didn't wear the apron. Pneumonia is a good thing to take out spots."

Isaiah was surprised.

"What is?" he asked.

"Pneumonia. . . . No, I don't think that's right. It's pneumonia that makes you sick. Somethin' else takes out the spots. I know now; it's am-monia. It's very good for spots but you mustn't smell the bottle. I smelled the bottle once and it went right up into my head."

"What on earth are you talkin' about? The bottle went up into your head!"

"No, the ammonia smell did. It was awful; like—like——" she paused, evidently in search of a simile; "like sneezin' backwards," she added. "It was terrible."

Isaiah laughed. "I should think 'twould be," he declared. "Sneezin' backwards! Ho, ho! That's a good one!"

Mary-'Gusta's eyes were still fixed upon the apron.

"Mr.—I mean Cap'n Gould said you was the cook and steward," she observed. "I don't know as I know what a steward is, exactly. Is it the one that stews things?"

"Ha, ha!" roared Isaiah. Mary-'Gusta's dignity was hurt. The color rose in her cheeks.

"Was it funny?" she asked. "I didn't know. I know that a cook cooked things, and a baker baked things, so I thought maybe a steward stewed 'em."

Mr. Chase continued to chuckle. The girl considered.

"I see," she said, with a solemn nod. "It was funny, I guess. I remember now that a friar doesn't fry things. He is a—a kind of minister. *Friar Tuck* was one in 'Robin Hood,' you know. Mrs. Bailey read about him to me. Do you like 'Robin Hood,' Mr. Chase?"

Isaiah said he didn't cal'late that he knew anybody of that name. The dialogue was interrupted here by the arrival of Zoeth and, a moment later, Captain Shadrach. Breakfast was put upon the table in the dining-room and the quartette sat down to eat.

Mary-'Gusta was quiet during the meal; she answered when spoken to but the only questions she asked were concerning David.

"He's all right," said Captain Shad. "Lively as can be. He'll have a good time out in that barn; there's considerable many mice out there. Likes mice, don't he?"

"Yes, sir. He's a good mouser. Did he look as if he missed me?"

"Eh? Well, I didn't notice. He never mentioned it if he did. You can go see him after breakfast. What do you think she can find to do today, Zoeth?"

Mr. Hamilton had evidently considered the problem.

"I thought maybe she'd like to go up to the store 'long of you and me," he suggested. "Would you, Mary-'Gusta?"

Mary-'Gusta hesitated. "I'd like to very much," she said, "only——"

"Only what?"

"Only I've got to see to David and the dolls first. Couldn't I come up to the store afterwards?"

The Captain answered. "Why, I guess likely you could," he said. "It's straight up the road to the corner. You can see the store from the top of the hill back here. Isaiah'll show you the way. But you can 'tend to—what's that cat's name?—Oh, yes, David—you can 'tend to David right off. Isaiah'll give the critter his breakfast, and the dolls can wait 'til noontime, can't they?"

Mary-'Gusta's mind was evidently divided between inclination and duty. Duty won.

"They ain't dressed yet," she said, gravely. "And besides they might think I'd gone off and left 'em and be frightened. This is a strange place to them, same as it is to me and David, you know. None of us have ever been visitin' before."

So it was decided that she should wait until her family had been given parental attention, and come to the store by herself. The partners left for their place of business and she and Mr. Chase remained at the house. Her first act, after leaving the table, was to go to the barn and return bearing the cat in her arms. David ate a hearty breakfast and then, after enduring a motherly lecture concerning prudence and the danger of getting lost, was permitted to go out of doors.

Mary-'Gusta, standing in the doorway, gazed after her pet.

"I hope there's no dogs around here," she said. "It would be dreadful if there was a dog."

Isaiah tried to reassure her. "Oh, I cal'late there ain't no dog nigh enough to do any harm," he said; "besides, most cats can run fast enough to get out of the way."

The child shook her head. "I didn't mean that," she said. "I meant it would be dreadful for the dog. David doesn't have a mite of patience with dogs. He doesn't wait to see if they're nice ones or not, he just goes for 'em and then—Oh! He most always goes for 'em. When he has kittens he *always* does."

Mr. Chase's reply to this illuminating disclosure was that he wanted to know.

"Yes," said Mary-'Gusta, "David doesn't take to dogs, some way. Why don't cats like dogs, Mr. Chase?"

Isaiah said that he cal'lated 'twas the nature of the critters not to. Mary-'Gusta agreed with him.

"Natures are queer things, ain't they?" she said, solemnly. "I guess everybody has a nature, cats and all. Mrs. Hobbs says my nature is a contrary one. What's your kind, Mr. Chase?

"Do you suppose," she said, a few moments later, when the cook and steward had shown symptoms of doing something beside lean against the sink and whistle, "do you suppose you could get along for a few minutes while I went up and dressed my dolls?"

Isaiah turned to stare at her.

"Well," he stammered, "I—I cal'late maybe I could if

I tried hard. If you don't beat anything ever I see! What are you doin' with that pitcher?"

The girl was holding the wash pitcher under the pump.

"I'm fillin' it," she answered. "Then you won't have to have it on your mind any more. I'll hurry back just as fast as I can."

She hastened out, bearing the brimming pitcher with both hands. Isaiah gazed after her, muttering a word or two, and then set about clearing the breakfast table.

She was down again shortly, the two favorites, Rose and Rosette, in her arms. She placed them carefully in the kitchen chair and bade them be nice girls and watch mother do the dishes.

"I left the others in the bedroom," she explained. "Minnehaha ain't very well this mornin'. I guess the excitement was too much for her. She is a very nervous child."

Isaiah's evident amusement caused her to make one of her odd changes from childish make-believe to grown-up practicability.

"Of course," she added, with gravity, "I know she ain't really nervous. She's just full of sawdust, same as all dolls are, and she couldn't have any nerves. But I like to play she's nervous and delicate. It's real handy to say that when I don't want to take her with me. I'm a nervous, excitable child myself; Mrs. Hobbs says so. That's why I've hardly ever been anywhere before, I guess."

She insisted upon wiping the dishes while Isaiah washed them. Also, she reminded him that the table-cloth which had been so severely criticized the previous evening had not as yet been changed. The steward was inclined to treat the matter lightly.

"Never mind if 'tain't," he said. "It's good enough for a spell longer. Let it stay. Besides," he added, "the washin' ain't been done this week and there ain't another clean one aboard."

Mary-'Gusta smiled cheerfully.

"Oh, yes, there is," she said. "There's a real nice one in the bottom drawer of the closet. I've been huntin' and I found it. Come and see."

She led him into the dining-room and showed him the cloth she had found.

"It's a real pretty one, I think," she said. "Shall we put it on, Mr. Chase?"

"No, no, course not. That's the best tablecloth. Don't use that only when there's company—or Sundays."

Mary-'Gusta considered. She counted on her fingers.

"How long have we used this dirty one?" she asked.

"Eh? Oh, I don't know. Four or five days, maybe." Then, evidently feeling that the repetition of the "we" implied a sense of unwarranted partnership in the household management, he added with dignity, "That is, *I've* seen fit to use it that long."

The sarcasm was wasted. The girl smiled and nodded.

"That makes it all right," she declared. "If we put this one on now it'll be Sunday long before it's time to change. And we can wash the other one today or to-morrow."

"Oh, *we* can, eh?"

"Yes, sir."

Isaiah looked as if he wished to say something but was at a loss for words. The Sunday cloth was spread upon the table while he was still hunting for them.

"And now," said Mary-'Gusta, "if you're sure you don't need me any more just now I guess I'd like to go up and see the store. May I?"

She found the store of Hamilton and Company an exceedingly interesting place. Zoeth and his partner greeted her cordially and she sat down upon a box at the end of the counter and inspected the establishment. It was not very large, but there was an amazing variety in its stock. Muslin, tape, calico, tacks, groceries, cases of shoes, a rack with spools of thread, another containing a few pocket knives, barrels, half a dozen salt codfish swinging from nails overhead, some suits of oilskins hanging beside them, a tumbled heap of children's caps and hats, even a glass-covered case containing boxes of candy with placards "1 c. each" or "3 for 1 c." displayed above them.

"Like candy, do you?" asked Mr. Hamilton, noticing her scrutiny of the case and its contents.

"Yes, sir," said Mary-'Gusta.

"How about sassafras lozengers? Like them?"

"Yes, sir."

She was supplied with a roll of the lozenges and munched them gravely. Captain Shad, who had been waiting on a customer, regarded her with an amused twinkle.

"Sassafras lozengers are good enough for anybody, eh?" he observed.

"Yes, sir," replied Mary-'Gusta. Then she added, politely: "Only I guess these are wintergreen."

She stayed at the store until noon. Then she walked home with the Captain whose turn it was to dine first that day. The hiring of Annabel had been an unusual break in the business routine. Ordinarily but one of the partners left that store at a time.

"Well," inquired the Captain, as they walked down the lane, "what do you think of it? Pretty good store for a place like South Harniss, ain't it?"

"Yes, sir."

"I bet you! Different from the Ostable stores, eh?"

"Yes, sir; I—I guess it is."

"Um-hm. Well, how different?"

Mary-'Gusta took her usual interval for consideration.

"I guess there's more—more things in it with separate smells to 'em," she said.

Captain Shad had no remark to make for a moment. Mary-'Gusta, however, was anxious to please.

"They're nice smells," she hastened to add. "I like 'em; only I never smelled 'em all at the same time before. And I like the lozengers *very* much."

The two or three days which Captain Shad had set as the limit of the child's visit passed; as did the next two or three. She was busy and, apparently, enjoying herself. She helped Isaiah with the housework, and although he found the help not altogether unwelcome, he was inclined to grumble a little at what he called her "pesterin' around."

"I never see such a young-one," he told his employers. "*I* don't ask her to do dishes nor fill pitchers nor nothin'; she just does it on her own hook."

"Humph!" grunted Captain Shadrach. "So I judged from what I see. Does it pretty well, too, don't she?"

"Um-hm. Well enough, I guess. Yes," with a burst of candor, "for her age, she does it mighty well."

"Then what are you kickin' about?"

"I ain't kickin'. Who said I was kickin'? Only— well, all I say is let her do dishes and such, if she wants to, only—only——"

"Only what?"

"Only I ain't goin' to have her heavin' out hints about what *I* ought to do. There's two skippers aboard this craft now and that's enough. By time!" with another

76

burst, "that kid's a reg'lar born mother. She mothers that cat and them dolls and the hens already, and I swan to man I believe she'd like to adopt me. I ain't goin' to be mothered and hinted at to do this and that and put to bed and tucked in by no kid. I'll heave up my job first."

He had been on the point of heaving up his job ever since the days when he sailed as cook aboard Captain Shadrach's schooner. When the Captain retired from the sea for the last time, and became partner and fellow shopkeeper with Zoeth, Isaiah had retired with him and was engaged to keep house for the two men. The Captain had balked at the idea of a female housekeeper.

"Women aboard ship are a dum nuisance," he declared. "I've carried 'em cabin passage and I know. Isaiah Chase is a good cook, and, besides, if the biscuits are more fit for cod sinkers than they are for grub, I can tell him so in the right kind of language. We don't want no woman steward, Zoeth; you hear *me!*"

Zoeth, although the Captain's seafaring language was a trial to his gentle, churchly soul, agreed with his partner on the main point. His experience with the other sex had not been such as to warrant further experiment. So Isaiah was hired and had been cook and steward at the South Harniss home for many years. But he made it a practice to assert his independence at frequent intervals, although, as a matter of fact, he would no more have dreamed of really leaving than his friends and employers would of discharging him. Mr. Chase was as permanent a fixture in that house as the ship's chronometer in the dining-room; and that was screwed to the wall.

And, in spite of his grumbling, he and Mary-'Gusta were rapidly becoming fast friends. Shadrach and Zoeth also were beginning to enjoy her company, her unexpected questions, her interest in the house and the store, and shrewd, old-fashioned comments on persons and things. She was a "queer young-one"; they, like the people of Ostable, agreed on that point, but Mr. Hamilton was inclined to think her ways "sort of takin'" and the Captain admitted that maybe they were. What he would not admit was that the girl's visit, although already prolonged for a fortnight, was anything but a visit.

"I presume likely," hinted Zoeth, "you and me'll have to give the Judge some sort of an answer pretty soon, won't we? He'll be wantin' to know afore long."

"Know? Know what?"

"Why—why whether we're goin' to say yes or no to what Marcellus asked us in that letter."

"He does know. Fur's I'm consarned, he knows. I spoke my mind plain enough to pound through anybody's skull, I should think."

"Yes—yes, I know you did. But, Shadrach, if she don't stay here for good where will she stay? She ain't got anybody else to go to."

"She is stayin', ain't she? She—she's makin' us a visit, same as I said she could. What more do you want? Jumpin' fire! This fix is your doin' anyway. 'Tain't mine. If you had paid attention to what I said, the child wouldn't have been here at all."

"Now, Shadrach! You know you was the one that would fetch her over that very day."

"Oh, blame it onto me, of course!"

"I ain't blamin' anybody. But she's here and we've got to decide whether to send her away or not. Shall we?"

They were interrupted by Mary-'Gusta herself, who entered the barn, where the discussion took place, a doll under one arm and a very serious expression on her face.

"Hello!" hailed Zoeth. "What's the matter?"

Mary-'Gusta seated herself upon an empty cranberry

crate. The partners had a joint interest in a small cranberry bog and the crate was one of several unused the previous fall.

"There's nothin' the matter," she said, solemnly. "I've been thinkin', that's all."

"Want to know!" observed the Captain. "Well, what made you do anything as risky as that?"

Mary-'Gusta's forehead puckered.

"I was playin' with Jimmie Bacheldor yesterday," she said, "and he made me think."

Abner Bacheldor was the nearest neighbor. His ramshackle dwelling was an eighth of a mile from the Gould-Hamilton place. Abner had the reputation of being the meanest man in town; also he had a large family, of which Jimmie, eight years old, was the youngest.

"Humph!" sniffed Captain Shad. "So Jimmie Bacheldor made you think, eh? I never should have expected it from one of that tribe. How'd he do it?"

"He asked me about my relations," said Mary-'Gusta, "and when I said I hadn't got any he was awful surprised. He has ever so many, sisters and brothers and aunts and cousins and—Oh, everything. He thought 'twas dreadful funny my not havin' any. I think I'd ought to have some, don't you?"

The partners, looking rather foolish, said nothing for a moment. Then Zoeth muttered that he didn't know but she had.

"Yes," said Mary-'Gusta, "I—I think so. You see I'm —I mean I was a stepchild 'long as father was here. Now he's dead and I ain't even that. And I ain't anybody's cousin nor nephew nor niece. I just ain't anything. I'm different from everybody I know. And—and—" very solemnly— "I don't like to be so different."

Her lip quivered as she said it. Sitting there on the cranberry crate, hugging her dolls, she was a pathetic little figure. Again the partners found it hard to answer. Mr. Hamilton looked at the Captain and the latter, his fingers fidgeting with his watchchain, avoided the look. The girl went on.

"I was thinking," she said, "how nice 'twould have been if I'd had a—a brother or somebody of my very own. I've got children, of course, but they're only dolls and a cat. They're nice, but they ain't real folks. I wish I had some real folks. Do you suppose if—if I have to go to the —the orphans' home, there'd be anybody there that would be my relation? I didn't know but there might be another orphan there who didn't have anybody, same as me, and then we could make believe we was—was cousins or somethin'. That would be better than nothin', wouldn't it?"

Zoeth stepped forward and, bending over, kissed her cheek. "Never you mind, Mary-'Gusta," he said. "You ain't gone there yet and afore you do maybe Cap'n Shad and I can think up some relations for you."

"Real relations?" asked Mary-'Gusta, eagerly.

"Well, no, not real ones; I'm afraid we couldn't do that. But when it comes to make-believe, that might be different." He hesitated an instant, glanced at the Captain, and then added: "I tell you what you do: you just pretend I'm your relation, a—well, an uncle, that's better'n nothin'. You just call me 'Uncle Zoeth.' That'll be a start, anyhow. Think you'd like to call me 'Uncle Zoeth'?"

Mary-'Gusta's eyes shone. "Oh, yes!" she cried. "Then I could tell that Jimmie Bacheldor I had one relation, anyhow. And shall I call Cap'n Gould 'Uncle Shadrach'?"

Zoeth turned to his companion. "Shall she, Shadrach?" he asked, with a mischievous smile.

If it had not been for that smile the Captain's reply might have been different. But the smile irritated him. He strode to the door.

"Zoeth Hamilton," he snapped, "how long are you goin' to set here? If you ain't got anything else to attend to, I have. I'm goin' up to the store. It's pretty nigh eight o'clock in the mornin' and that store ain't open yet."

"Want to come along, Mary-'Gusta?" asked Zoeth. "She can come, can't she, Shad?"

"Yes, yes, course she can," more genially. "Cal'late there's some of those sassafras—checkerberry lozengers left yet. Come on, Mary-'Gusta, if you want to."

But the child shook her head. She looked wistful and a trifle disappointed.

"I—I guess maybe I'd better stay here," she said. "I ought to see to Minnehaha's sore throat. I'm goin' to put some red flannel 'round it; Mr. Chase says he cal'lates he knows where there is some. Good-by, Uncle Zoeth. Good-by—er—Cap'n Gould."

The partners did not converse on the way to the store. Zoeth made an attempt, but Shadrach refused to answer. He was silent and, for him, grumpy all the forenoon. Another fortnight passed before the subject of the decision which must, sooner or later, be given Judge Baxter was mentioned by either of the pair.

CHAPTER VI

MARY-'GUSTA was growing accustomed to the life in the South Harniss home. She found it a great improvement over that which she had known on Phinney's Hill at Ostable. There was no Mrs. Hobbs to nag and find fault, there were no lonely meals, no scoldings when stockings were torn or face and hands soiled. And as a playground the beach was a wonderland.

She and Jimmie Bacheldor picked up shells, built sand forts, skipped flat stones along the surface of the water at high tide, and picked up scallops and an occasional quahaug at low water. Jimmie was, generally speaking, a satisfactory playmate, although he usually insisted upon having his own way and, when they got into trouble because of this insistence, did not permit adherence to the truth to obstruct the path to a complete alibi. Mary-'Gusta, who had been taught by the beloved Mrs. Bailey to consider lying a deadly sin, regarded her companion's lapses with alarmed disapproval, but she was too loyal to contradict and more than once endured reproof when the fault was not hers. She had had few playmates in her short life and this one, though far from perfect, was a joy.

They explored the house together and found in the big attic and the stuffy, shut-up best parlor the most fascinating of treasure hordes. The former, with its rows of old trunks and sea chests under the low eaves, the queer garments and discarded hats hanging on the nails, the dusky corners where the light from the little windows scarcely penetrated even on a sunny May afternoon, was the girl's especial Paradise. Here she came to play by herself on rainy days or when she did not care for company. Her love of make-believe and romance had free scope here and with no Jimmie to laugh and make fun of her imaginings she pretended to her heart's content. Different parts of that garret gradually, in her mind, came to have names of their own. In the bright spot, under the north window, was Home, where she and the dolls and David—when the cat could be coaxed from prowlings and mouse hunts to quiet and slumber—lived and dined and entertained and were ill or well or happy or frightened, according to the day's imaginative happenings. Sometimes Home was a castle, sometimes a Swiss Family Robinson cave, sometimes a store which transacted business after the fashion of Hamilton and Company. And in other more or less fixed spots and corners were Europe, to which the family voyaged occasionally; Niagara Falls—Mrs. Bailey's honeymoon had been spent at the real Niagara; the King's palace; the den of the wicked witch; Sherwood Forest; and Jordan, Marsh and Company's store in Boston.

Jimmie Bacheldor liked the garret well enough, but imagination was not his strongest quality and the best parlor had more charms for him. In that parlor were the trophies of Captain Shadrach's seafaring days— whales' teeth, polished and with pictures of ships upon them; the model of a Chinese junk; a sea-turtle shell, flippers, head and all, exactly like a real turtle except, as Mary-'Gusta said, 'it didn't have any works'; a glass bottle with a model of the bark *Treasure Seeker* inside; an Eskimo lance with a bone handle and an ivory point; a cocoanut carved to look like the head and face of a funny old man; a Cuban *machete;* and a set of ivory

83

chessmen with Chinese knights and kings and queens, all complete and set out under a glass cover.

The junk and the lance and the *machete* and the rest had a fascination for Jimmie, as they would have had for most boys, but for him the parlor's strongest temptation lay in the fact that the children were forbidden to play there. Zoeth and the Captain, having been brought up in New England families of the old-fashioned kind, revered their parlor as a place too precious for use. They, themselves, entered it not oftener than three times a year, and Isaiah went there only when he felt inclined to dust, which was not often. Shadrach had exhibited its treasures to the children one Sunday morning when Zoeth was at church, but he cautioned them against going there by themselves. "You'd be liable to break somethin'," he told them, "and some of them things in there you couldn't buy with money. They've been brought from pretty much everywheres in creation, those things have."

But, in spite of the warning, or because of it, Jimmie was, as Isaiah would have said, "possessed" to visit that parlor. He coaxed and teased and dared Mary-'Gusta to take advantage of the steward's stepping out of the house or being busy in the kitchen to open that parlor door and go in with him and peep at and handle the treasures. Mary-'Gusta protested, but young Bacheldor called her a coward and declared he wouldn't play with cowards and 'fraid-cats, so rather than be one of those detestable creatures she usually swallowed her scruples and followed the tempter. It was a risk, of course, but a real adventure; and, like many adventurers, the pair came to grief. They took David into the parlor and the cat wriggled from its owner's arms, jumped upon the table, knocked the case containing the chessmen to the

84

floor, and not only broke the glass but decapitated one of the white knights.

Even the mild Mr. Hamilton was incensed when Isaiah told the news at supper time. And Captain Shad, who had bought those chessmen at Singapore from the savings of a second mate's wages, lost patience entirely.

"Didn't I tell you young-ones not to go into that parlor?" he demanded.

"Yes, sir," admitted Mary-'Gusta, contritely.

"Yes, by fire, I did! And you went just the same."

"Yes, sir."

"And you fetched that everlastin'—er—Goliath in there, too. Don't you know you've been a bad girl?"

"Ye—yes, sir."

Zoeth protested. "She ain't a bad girl, Shadrach," he said. "You know she ain't."

"Well—er—maybe she ain't, generally speakin'. I cal'late 'twas that Bacheldor brat that was responsible; but just the same I ain't goin' to have it happen any more. Mary-'Gusta, if you and that consarned—what's-his-name—Jimmie—go into that parlor again, unless Isaiah or one of us are with you, I—I—by the jumpin' Judas, me and Zoeth won't let you go to the Sunday school picnic. There! I mean that and so does Zoeth. Shut up, Zoeth! You do mean it, too. You know mighty well either your dad or mine would have skinned us alive if we'd done such a thing when we was young-ones. And," turning to the culprit, "if you fetch that cat in there, I'll—I'll—I don't know what I'll do."

The Sunday school picnic was to be held on the second Saturday in June and Mary-'Gusta wished to attend it. She had never been to a real picnic, though the other children in Ostable had described such outings in glowing colors. Now, although she, a visitor, was not a regular member of the South Harniss Methodist Sunday school, the superintendent personally had invited her to go and Zoeth and the Captain had given their consent. Not to go would be a heart-breaking calamity. She finally resolved to be very, very good and obedient from that time on.

But good resolutions are broken occasionally, even by grown-ups, and in childhood much can be forgotten in nine days. So, on the afternoon of the tenth day, which was the day before the picnic, Mary-'Gusta walking alone in the field which separated the Gould-Hamilton property from that of Abner Bacheldor, Jimmie's father—Mary-'Gusta, walking in that field, was depressed and melancholy. Her state of mind was indicated by the fact that she had left all her dolls, even Rose and Rosette, at home. She felt guilty and wicked and conscience-stricken. She had been a bad girl; only one other knew how bad she had been and he, being guilty likewise, would not betray her. But at home Isaiah Chase was, as he said, "heatin' himself to a bile" baking apple turnovers for her to take to the picnic. And Captain Shadrach had announced his intention of bringing her, from the store, candy and bananas to go into the lunch basket with the turnovers and sandwiches and cake. And the Captain had that very day called her a good girl. If he only knew!

There had been a flurry of excitement in the kitchen just after dinner. Mr. Bacheldor had appeared at the door with the request that he might "borrer the loan of Cap'n Gould's shotgun." The day before, at a quarter after four—Mr. Bacheldor was certain as to the time because he had been "layin' down two or three minutes on the sofy afore goin' out to look at some wood there was to cut in the shed, and I'd just got up and looked at the clock afore I looked out of the settin'-room winder"—looking out of that window he had seen a cat running from his henyard with one of his recently hatched Plymouth Rock chickens in its mouth.

"If I'd had a gun then," declared Abner, "I could have blowed the critter to thunder-and-gone. But I'll get him next time. Let me have the gun, will you, Isaiah? I know Shad'll say it's all right when you tell him."

That shotgun was a precious arm. It had been given to the Captain years before by the officers of a sinking schooner, whom Shadrach's boat's crew, led by Shadrach himself, had rescued at a big risk off the Great South School. It had the Captain's name, with an inscription and date, on a silver plate fastened to the stock. Isaiah was not too willing to lend it, but chicken stealing is a capital offense in South Harniss, as it is in most rural communities, and the cat caught in the act is summarily executed.

So Mr. Chase went to the Captain's room and returned with the gun.

"There you be, Ab," he said. "Hope you get the critter."

"Oh, I'll get him all right, don't you fret. Say, Isaiah —er—er——" Mr. Bacheldor hesitated. "Say," he went on, "you couldn't let me have two or three cartridges, could you? I ain't got none in the house."

Isaiah looked more doubtful than ever, but he brought the cartridges. After making sure, by inquiry and inspection, that they were loaded, the borrower started to go.

"Oh, I say, Ab," Mr. Chase called after him; "know whose cat 'twas?"

Mr. Bacheldor did not appear to hear, so the question was repeated. Abner answered without turning.

"I know," he declared. "I know all right," and hurried on. Isaiah looked after him and sniffed disdainfully.

"Anybody on earth but that feller," he said, "would have been ashamed to beg cartridges after beggin' the gun, but not Ab Bacheldor, no sir! Wonder he didn't want to borrer my Sunday hat to practice shootin' at."

Mary-'Gusta considered shooting a cat the height of cruelty and dreadfulness but she was aware of the universal condemnation of chicken stealing and kept her thought to herself. Besides, she had her own wickedness to consider.

She walked slowly on across the field, bound nowhere in particular, thinking hard and feeling very wretched and miserable. The pleasure of the next day, the day she had been anticipating, was spoiled already for her. If she went to that picnic without making a full and free confession she knew she would feel as mean and miserable as she was feeling now. And if she did confess, why then——

Her meditations were interrupted in a startling manner. She was midway of the field, upon the other side of which was a tumbledown stone wall, and a cluster of wild cherry trees and bayberry bushes marking the boundary of the Bacheldor land. From behind the wall and bushes sounded the loud report of a gun; then the tramp of running feet and an excited shouting:

"You missed him," screamed a voice. "You never hit him at all. There he goes! There he goes! Give him t'other barrel quick!"

Mary-'Gusta, who had been startled nearly out of her senses by the shot and the shouting, stood perfectly still, too surprised and frightened even to run. And then out of the bushes before her darted a scared tortoise-shell cat, frantically rushing in her direction. The cat was David.

"He's hidin' in them bushes," shouted the voice again. "Stay where you be, Pop. I'll scare him out and then you give it to him."

Mary-'Gusta stood still no longer. The sight of her idolized pet running for his life was enough to make her forget fright and everything else. She too ran, but not toward home.

"David!" she screamed. "Oh, David! Come here! David!"

David may have recognized the voice, but if so the recognition made no difference. The cat kept straight on. The girl ran across its path. It dodged and darted into a beachplum thicket, a *cul-de-sac* of tangled branches and thick grass. Before the animal could extricate itself Mary-'Gusta had seized it in her arms. It struggled and fought for freedom but the child held it tight.

"David!" she panted. "Oh, don't, David! Please be still! They shan't hurt you; I won't let 'em. Please!"

Through the bushes above the wall appeared the freckled face of Con—christened Cornelius—Bacheldor. Con was Jimmie's elder brother.

"He must have got through," he shouted. "He—no, there he is. She's got him, Pop. Make her put him down."

Mr. Abner Bacheldor crashed through to his son's side. He was carrying a gun.

"You put that cat down," screamed Con, threateningly.

Mary-'Gusta said nothing. Her heart was beating wildly but she held the struggling David fast.

"It's that kid over to Shad Gould's," declared Con. "Make her give you a shot, Pop."

Mr. Abner Bacheldor took command of the situation.

"Here, you!" he ordered. "Fetch that critter here. I want him."

Still Mary-'Gusta did not answer. She was pale and her small knees shook, but she neither spoke nor moved from where she stood. And her grip upon the cat tightened.

"Fetch that cat here," repeated Abner. "We're goin' to shoot him; he's been stealin' our chickens."

At this accusation and the awful threat accompanying it, Mary-'Gusta forgot her terror of the Bacheldors, of the gun, forgot everything except her pet and its danger.

"I shan't!" she cried frantically. "I shan't! He ain't! He's my cat and he don't steal chickens."

"Yes, he does, too," roared Con. "Pop and I see him doin' it."

"You didn't! I don't believe it! When did you see him?"

"Yesterday afternoon. We see him, didn't we, Pop?"

"You bet your life we did," growled Abner. "And he was on my land again just now; comin' to steal more, I cal'late. Fetch him here."

"I—I shan't! He shan't be shot, even if he did steal 'em. And I know he didn't. If you shoot him I'll—I'll tell Uncle Zoeth and—and Cap'n Gould. And I won't let you have him anyhow. I won't," with savage defiance. "If you shoot him you'll have to shoot me, too."

Con climbed over the wall. "You just wait, Pop," he said. "I'll take him away from her."

But his father hesitated. There were certain reasons why he thought it best not to be too arbitrary.

"Hold on, Con," he said. "Look here, sis, I'm sorry to have to kill your cat, but I've got to. He steals chickens and them kind of cats has to be shot. I see him myself yesterday afternoon. I told Isaiah Chase myself that . . . why, you was there and heard me! You heard me tell how I was lookin' out of the winder at quarter past four and see that cat——"

Mary-'Gusta interrupted. Her expression changed. She was still dreadfully frightened but in her tone was a note of relief, of confident triumph.

"You didn't see him," she cried. "It wasn't David; it wasn't this cat you saw. I *know* it wasn't."

"Well, I know it was. Now don't argue no more. You fetch that cat here or I'll have Con take him away from you. Hurry up!"

"I know it wasn't David," began Mary-'Gusta. Then, as Con started in her direction, she turned and ran, ran as hard as she could, bearing David in her arms. Con ran after her.

It was the cat that saved the situation and its life at the same time. Mary-'Gusta was near the edge of the pine grove and Con was close at her heels. David gave one more convulsive, desperate wriggle, slid from the girl's arms and disappeared through the pines like a gray projectile.

Mary-'Gusta collapsed on the grass and burst into frightened, hysterical sobs. Con took one or two steps after the flying cat and gave up the chase. Mr. Bacheldor, from behind the wall, swore emphatically and at length.

"Come here, Con, you fool," he yelled, when the expression of his true feelings had reached a temporary end. "Come here! let the kid alone. We'll get into trouble if we don't. As for that dummed cat, we'll get him next time. He'll see his finish. Come on, I tell you."

Con reluctantly rejoined his parent and the pair departed, muttering threats. Mary-'Gusta, the tears running down her cheeks, ran home to find David and plead with Mr. Chase for her pet's safety and protection from its persecutors. But Isaiah had gone up to the store on an errand. David, however, was crouching, a trembling heap, under the kitchen stove. The girl pulled him out, fled with him to the garret, and there, with the door locked, sat shivering and sobbing until Captain Shad came home for supper that night.

The Captain's first question when he arrived was concerning Mary-'Gusta's whereabouts. Isaiah said he had not seen her for two hours or more. And just then the child herself appeared, entering the kitchen from the door leading to the back stairs.

"Hello, Mary-'Gusta!" hailed Shadrach. "Thought you was lost. Supper's about ready to put on the table. Why, what's the matter? Been cryin', ain't you?"

Mary-'Gusta went straight to him and clutched his hand. "Please, Cap'n Gould," she begged, "will you come into the sittin'-room a minute? I—I want to ask you somethin'. I want you to do somethin' for me, will you?"

"Sartin sure I will. What is it?"

Mary-'Gusta glanced at Isaiah's face. "I'd—I'd rather tell you, just you alone," she said. "Please come into the sittin'-room."

She tugged at his hand. Much puzzled, he followed her through the dining-room and into the sitting-room.

"Well, Mary-'Gusta," he said, kindly, "now what is it? What's the big secret?"

Mary-'Gusta closed the door. She was very solemn and her lip quivered but she did not hesitate.

"It's about David," she said. "Somethin's happened to David. I—I'm goin' to tell you about it, Cap'n Gould."

She told of her adventure and of David's peril. Shadrach listened. When he heard of the accusation which was the cause of the affair he shook his head.

"My, my!" he exclaimed. "That's pretty bad, that is.

I'd hate to have your cat killed, Mary-'Gusta, land knows I would. But if the critter's a chicken thief——"

"But he ain't! I *know* he ain't!"

"Humph! You can't always tell, you know cats are cats and——"

"But I know David wasn't the cat that did it. I *know* he wasn't."

"Oh, you know, do you. Hm! you do seem pretty sartin, that's a fact. How do you know?"

The girl looked at him. "Please, Cap'n Gould," she said, "I—I'd rather tell you over to Mr. Bacheldor's. That's what I wanted to ask you; won't you please go right over to Mr. Bacheldor's with me? I—I'll tell you how I know when we're there."

Captain Shadrach was more puzzled than ever. "You want me to go to Ab Bacheldor's with you?" he repeated. "You want to tell me somethin' over there? Why not tell me here?"

"'Cause—'cause Mr. Bacheldor thinks David did it and he'll kill him. He said he would. I want *him* to know David wasn't the one. And if, if you're there when he knows, he'll know *you* know he knows and he won't dast shoot at David any more. Please come, Cap'n Gould. Please, right away."

Shadrach tugged at his beard. "Humph!" he muttered. "There's more 'knows' in that than there is knots in a snarled fish line. You want me as a witness, nigh's I can make out. Is that it?"

"Yes, sir. Will you go with me right off?"

"Right off, eh? Can't it wait till after supper?"

"I—I don't want any supper. *Please!*"

So supper was postponed, in spite of Isaiah's grumblings, and the Captain and Mary-'Gusta started forthwith for the home of their nearest neighbor. Mr.

Chase, his curiosity aroused, would have asked a dozen questions, but Mary-'Gusta would neither answer nor permit Shadrach to do so.

The Bacheldor family were at supper when the callers arrived. Abner himself opened the door and he looked rather embarrassed when he saw the pair on the steps. Captain Shad did not wait for an invitation to enter; he walked in and Mary-'Gusta followed him.

"Now then, Ab," said the Captain, briskly, "what's this about our cat stealin' your chickens?"

Mr. Bacheldor and Con, separately and together, burst into a tirade of invective against the offending David.

"That's all right, that's all right," broke in the Captain, crisply. "If that cat stole your chicken it ought to be shot. But are you sure of the cat? Do you know ours did it? This girl here says 'twasn't ours at all."

"I know a dum sight better," began Abner, savagely. But this time it was Mary-'Gusta who interrupted.

"Cap'n Gould," she said, "please ask him what time it was yesterday afternoon when he saw the cat run off with the chicken."

Bacheldor did not wait to be asked.

"'Twas quarter-past four yesterday afternoon," he declared. "I know the time."

"I don't see what the time's got to do with it," put in Shadrach.

"But it's got everything to do with it," urged Mary-'Gusta. "Honest truly it has."

"Oh, it has, eh? Why?"

"'Cause—'cause—Ask him if he's sure?"

Again Abner did not wait. "Course I'm sure," he replied. "I told Isaiah Chase—yes, and I told that young-one, too—that I looked at the clock just afore I looked

94

out of the window and see the critter in the very act. Yes, and Con see him too."

Mary-'Gusta stamped her foot in triumph. "Then it wasn't David," she said. "It wasn't David at all. 'Twas somebody else's cat, Mr. Bacheldor."

"Somebody else's nothin'! Don't you suppose I know——"

"Hold on! Heave to, Ab. Mary-'Gusta, how do you know 'twasn't our cat?"

"'Cause—'cause David was with me from four o'clock till most five; that's how. He was in the—in our house with me. So," triumphantly, "he couldn't have been anywhere else, could he?"

Con and his father both began a protest, but Shadrach cut it short.

"Keep still, for mercy sakes," he ordered. "This ain't Shoutin' Methodist camp meetin'. Let's get soundin's here. Now, Mary-'Gusta, you say the cat was with you from four till five; you're sure of that?"

"Yes, sir. I know because Mr. Chase had gone out and we knew he wouldn't be back until five 'cause he said he wouldn't. So we looked at the clock before we went in."

"Went in? Went in where?"

The girl hung her head. It was evident that the answer to this question was one she dreaded to make. But she made it, nevertheless.

"Before we went into—into the parlor," she said, faintly.

Captain Shad was the only one of her hearers who grasped the full significance of this confession. No, there was one other, and he turned red and then white.

"The parlor?" repeated the Captain, slowly. "The best parlor?"

"Ye-yes, sir."

"Do you mean you went into the best parlor over to our house and—*and took that cat in with you?*"

"Yes, sir."

"Well, I swan to man! Did you forget what I told you would happen if you went into that parlor again? And especially if you lugged that cat in? Did you forget that?

"N-no, sir. I didn't forget it. You—you said I couldn't go to the picnic."

Shadrach shook his head. "Well," he groaned, "if this don't beat the nation! What under the sun did you do it for?"

" 'Cause—'cause we wanted to play pirates with—with the swords and things," faltered Mary-'Gusta. "And we took David 'cause he was goin' to be one of the passengers on the ship we took. But," with a sudden return to the main point at issue, "that proves David wasn't the cat he saw, the one that stole his chicken."

The Captain looked at her. "By fire, it does, that's right," he muttered. Abner Bacheldor roared in indignation.

"It don't prove nothin'," he cried. "All it proves is that the kid's a liar. She's lyin' so's to save that dummed thief of a cat. All kids'll lie when they think they can make somethin' out of it."

Shadrach grunted. "Maybe so," he said, "but I ain't caught this one in a lie so far. And I doubt if she's lyin' now. Now, Mary-'Gusta, is there any way you can prove you was in that parlor, and—what's his name—David was there at the time you say? Is there?"

Again Mary-'Gusta hesitated. Her eyes wandered about the faces in the room, until their gaze rested upon the face of Jimmie Bacheldor. And Jimmie looked white and scared.

"N-no, sir, I—I guess not," she faltered.

"I guess not, too," declared Con, with a sarcastic laugh.

But the Captain was suspicious. He had seen the child's look.

"Hold on," he commanded. "There's more to this than a blind man could see through a board fence. Mary-'Gusta, was there anybody else except David in that parlor along with you? Was there?"

Mary-'Gusta looked at the floor.

"Yes, sir," she faltered.

"So? I kind of had an idea there might be. Who was it?"

Again the look and then: "I—I ain't goin' to tell."

Con laughed once more. "You bet she ain't," he exclaimed. "She can't. The whole yarn's a lie. Don't pay no attention to it, Pop."

Shadrach turned sharply in his direction. "*I'm* payin' attention to it," he snapped, "and that's enough. So you ain't goin' to tell, Mary-'Gusta, eh? Remember now, if you do tell it'll prove your story's true and David'll come out on top. Think it over."

Evidently Mary-'Gusta was thinking it over. Her eyes filled with tears, but she shook her head.

The Captain looked down at her. "Keepin' mum, eh?" he said. "Well, that's all right. I cal'late we're pretty good guessers, some of us, anyway. Jim," with a sudden look straight at the youngest member of his neighbor's family, who was fidgeting with his spoon and acting remarkably nervous, "what have you got to say? Have a good time in that parlor playin' pirates, did you?"

Jimmie gasped. The suddenness of the attack knocked his defenses flat. He gurgled, stammered, and then broke into a wail of distress.

"I—I didn't mean to," he sobbed, wildly. "'Twas her. She said do it; I never. I—I——"

"Why, Jimmie Bacheldor!" exclaimed Mary-'Gusta, shocked into protest by her fellow culprit's distortion of the truth. "How can you say so! What a story! You know——"

"I guess he knows," broke in Shadrach. "And I cal'late I know, too. Now then, Jim, what time was it when you looked at the clock? Shut up, Abner, let the boy answer. Tell us, Jim; nobody'll hurt you."

"It—it was four o'clock," hollered Jimmie, in agony. "I—I never done it a purpose. I won't do so no more."

"No, I don't cal'late you will. Cal'late you won't have a chance. Well, Ab, I guess we've proved our client's case. Next time you go out cat shootin' you better be sure you're gunnin' for the right one. Come on, Mary-'Gusta."

Con Bacheldor sprang to his feet.

"Pop," he shouted, "be you goin' to let 'em go this way? And that cat stealin' our chickens right along. Ain't you goin' to tell 'em you'll kill the critter next time he comes on our land?"

Abner was silent. He seemed oddly anxious to see the last of his visitors. It was the Captain who spoke.

"No, Con," he said, crisply, "he ain't goin' to tell me that. And you listen while I tell *you* somethin'. If that cat of ours gets hurt or don't show up some time I'll know who's responsible. And then—well, then maybe *I'll* go gunnin'. Good night, all hands."

All the way back across the fields and through the grove the Captain was silent. Mary-'Gusta clinging to his hand was silent too, dreading what she knew was sure to follow. When they entered the kitchen Shadrach turned to her:

"Well, Mary-'Gusta," he said, "I'm glad your cat's turned out to be no chicken thief, but—but that don't alter what you did, does it?"

"No, sir," stammered the girl.

"No, I'm afraid it don't. I told you what would happen if you went into that parlor, and you went just the same. I cal'late you know what to expect, don't you?"

"Ye-yes, sir," in a low tone. "You mean I can't go to the Sunday school picnic."

Shadrach cleared his throat. He was not enjoying this episode, as a matter of fact his unhappiness was almost as keen as the child's. But as a boy he had been reared in the old-fashioned way, and he felt that he had a duty to perform.

"I'm afraid that's what I mean," he said, gravely. "Now set down and have your supper."

Mary-'Gusta tried hard to be brave, but the disappointment was too great. The tears streamed down her cheeks and she ran from the room. Shadrach strode after her.

"Here!" he called. "Mary-'Gusta, where are you goin'? Come back and have your supper."

But Mary-'Gusta did not come back. She was already on the stairs.

"I—I don't want any supper," she sobbed. "Please, oh, *please* don't make me eat it."

The Captain hesitated, turned back, and jerked his own chair to the table.

"Well," he demanded brusquely, "the supper's here and somebody's got to eat it, I cal'late. Fetch it on,

Isaiah! What are you starin' at me like that for, you dumbhead?"

Isaiah brought in the supper. Then he demanded to know what the fuss was all about. Shadrach told him. Isaiah's chief interest seemed to center on the attempted shooting.

"Why the son of a swab!" he cried, excitedly. "Of all the cheek I ever heard of in my life that Abner Bacheldor's got the heft! To borrer a man's own gun— yes, and cartridges, too—to kill that man's own cat with! Of all the solid brass! He never told me 'twas our cat. All he wanted to know was could he borrer your gun and somethin' to load it with. If I'd known——"

His employer interrupted him. *"What?"* he roared. "Do you mean to say that Ab Bacheldor came here and borrowed *my* gun to—to do what he done with?"

"Sartin sure he did. And only this very afternoon, too."

"And did he know whose cat 'twas?"

"He said he did. Mary-'Gusta was here 'long with me when he come. I says: 'Know whose cat 'tis?' and says he, 'I know all right!' I thought he acted kind of sheepish and funny. I—Here! where you goin'?"

The Captain was on his feet and his cap was in his hand.

"Goin'!" he snarled. "I'm going to make another call on Abner. And," with his hand on the latch, "if you hear somebody bein' murdered over in that direction you needn't call the constable, neither."

"But—but, hold on, Cap'n Shad! You ain't finished your own supper yet and Zoeth's waiting up to the store for you to come back so's he can come down and get his."

The reply was emphatic and, in its way, conclusive.

"To the blue brimstone with the supper!" roared Shadrach. "It can wait and so can Zoeth. If he can't he can do the next best."

He was absent for half an hour. When he returned Mr. Hamilton was in the dining-room. Shadrach entered, bearing the precious shotgun. He stood it carefully in the corner. There was a satisfied look in his eye.

"For goodness' sake, Shadrach!" exclaimed Zoeth, "what have you been thinkin' of? There I was waitin' and waitin' and hankerin' and hankerin' and no you nor no supper. I had to lock up the store finally. 'Twas either that or starve. I ain't a fault-finder, generally speakin', but I have to eat, same as other folks."

His partner paid not the least attention. His first remark was in the form of a question addressed to Mr. Chase.

"Look here, Isaiah," he demanded, "did I understand you to say that Mary-'Gusta was with you when that sculpin come to borrow my gun?"

"Yup. She was here."

"And she knew that he was goin' to shoot a cat with it?"

"Sartin, she heard him say so."

Shadrach strode to the mantel, took from it a hand lamp, lighted the lamp and with it in his hand walked from the room and ascended the stairs. Zoeth called after him, but he did not answer.

He entered Mary-'Gusta's room. The child was in bed, the dolls beside her. She was not asleep, however. The tear stains on her cheeks and the dampness of the pillow showed how she had spent the time since leaving the dining-room.

Shadrach put the lamp upon the washstand, pulled a chair beside the bed and sat down. He took her hand in his.

"Mary-'Gusta," he said, gently, "you knew 'twas my gun that Ab Bachelor was tryin' to shoot David with?"

Mary-'Gusta moved her head up and down on the pillow.

"Yes, sir," she said.

"You was here when he borrowed it?"

"Yes, sir. And then I knew it was yours when he had it there in the field. I saw the silver name thing on the handle. It kind of shined in the sun."

"Um-hm. Yes, yes. I see. You knew it, of course. But you didn't tell me. Why on earth didn't you? Didn't you know that if I'd realized that swab had borrered my gun to kill my cat that would have been enough? If the critter had stole a million chickens 'twouldn't have made any difference if I'd known *that*. The cheeky lubber! Well, he won't shoot at anything of ours for one spell, I'll bet. But why didn't you tell me?"

Mary-'Gusta's answer was promptly given.

"Why, 'cause," she said, "that was just it. I knew if you knew that you wouldn't care whether David stole the chicken or not. And I wanted you to know he didn't."

"Um, I see. But if you had told me you wouldn't have had to tell about the parlor. *I'd* never asked a single question."

"Ye-yes, sir; but I wanted you to know David doesn't steal chickens."

Shadrach swallowed hard. "I see," he said. "Yes, yes, I see. So just to clear that cat you was willin' to give up the picnic and everything."

Mary-'Gusta sobbed: "I—I did want to go so," she moaned.

The Captain lifted her from the pillow and put his arm about her.

"You *are* goin'," he declared, emphatically, "you just bet you're goin'."

"Oh! Oh, am I? Am I really? I—I know I hadn't ought to. I was a bad girl."

"You! You're a dummed good girl! The best and squarest—yes, and the spunkiest little girl I ever saw. You're a brick."

"I'm awful sorry I went into the parlor, Cap'n Gould."

"Blast the parlor! I don't care if you stay in there a week and smash everything in it. And—and, see here, Mary-'Gusta, don't you call me 'Cap'n Gould' any more. Call me 'Uncle Shad,' will you?"

Just before bedtime that night Mr. Hamilton broached a subject which had troubled him all day.

"Shadrach," he said, timidly. "I—I guess I ought to tell you somethin'. I know you won't want to talk about it, but seems 's if I must tell you. I had a letter this morning from Judge Baxter. He says he can't wait much longer for an answer from us about Marcellus's girl. He's got to know what we've decided to do with her."

Shadrach, who was smoking, took his pipe from his mouth.

"Well, give him the answer then," he said, shortly. "You know what 'tis, well as I do."

Zoeth looked troubled.

"I know you don't want to keep her," he said, "but——"

"Who said I didn't?"

"Who? Why, Shadrach Gould! You said——"

"I said a good many things maybe; but that's nothin'. You knew what I meant as well as I did."

"Why, Shadrach! You—you don't mean you *are* willin' to keep her—here, with us, for good? You don't mean *that?*"

The Captain snorted impatiently. "Don't be so foolish, Zoeth," he protested. "You knew plaguey well I never meant anything else."

CHAPTER VII

THE next day Captain Shadrach drove to Ostable and spent several hours in consultation with Judge Baxter. Adjusting matters by correspondence is a slow process at best, and the Captain, having surrendered unconditionally, was not the man to delay.

"I can settle more in ten minutes' talk," he told his partner, "than the three of us could in a month's letter-writin', especially if I had to write any of the letters. I never was any hand to write letters; you know that, Zoeth. And when I do write one the feller I send it to is liable to come around and ask me to read it 'cause he can't. Like as not I can't either, if it's had time to get cold, and there we are, right where we started. No, I'll go and see the Judge and when I fetch port tonight there'll have been somethin' done."

This prophecy was fulfilled. Before the Captain left Ostable for the homeward drive a good deal had been done. Judge Baxter, in his capacity as administrator, had already been looking into the affairs of his late client and, as he had expected, those affairs were badly tangled. When the outstanding debts were paid there would be little left, a thousand or two, perhaps, but certainly no more.

"So there you are, Shadrach," he said. "I'm mighty glad you and Zoeth have decided to keep the girl, but I'm afraid she'll come to you with very little property of her own. If she is to have the good education and all the rest that Marcellus wanted her to have I guess it'll be your money that pays for it. That's the honest truth, and I think you ought to know it."

The Captain nodded. "That's all right," he said. "I expected just about that, account of what you said the day of the funeral. Me and Zoeth are about as fur from bein' rich as the ship's cat is from bein' skipper, but we've put by a little and the store fetches us in a decent livin'. We'll take the young-one and do our best by her. Land knows what that best'll be," he added, with a dubious shake of the head. "Speakin' for myself, I feel that I'm about as competent to bring up a child as a clam is to fly."

Baxter laughed. "Marcellus seemed confident that you and Hamilton were perfectly suited to the job," he said.

"Um; yes, I know; Marcellus had confidence in a good many things, the stock market included. However, what is to be will be and we all have to take chances, as the feller that was just married said when he tackled his wife's first mince pie. You get those guardian papers, whatever they are, made out, and Zoeth and me'll sign 'em. As for the competent part— well," with a chuckle, "that child's pretty competent herself. I have a notion that, take it five or six years from now, it'll be her that'll be bringin' us up in the way we should go. I feel a good deal as if I was signin' on for a long voyage with the chances that I'd finish mate instead of skipper.

"Say, Judge," he added, just before leaving for home, "there's one thing more I'd like to say. 'Most everybody thinks Marcellus left his stepdaughter a consider'ble sight of money, don't they?"

"Why, yes; I suppose they do."

"All right, let 'em think so. 'Twill give 'em somethin' to talk about. They'll be guessin' how rich the child is instead of markin' off in the almanac the days afore Zoeth and me head for the poorhouse."

"Humph! I see. You don't care to have it known that you and your partner are adopting and supporting her purely from motives of kindness and generosity."

"Pooh! pooh! No generosity about it. Besides, Marcellus was kind and generous enough to us in the old days. Pity if we couldn't take our trick at the wheel now."

The Judge smiled. "You're a good deal more willing to take that trick than you were when I saw you last, Captain Shad," he observed. "You seem to have changed your mind completely."

The Captain grinned. "Well, yes, I have," he admitted. "Maybe 'tain't so big a change as you think; I have a habit of blowin' up a squall when I'm gettin' ready to calm down. But, anyway, that young-one would change anybody's mind. She's different from any girl of her age ever I saw. She's pretty as a little picture and sweet and wholesome as a—as a summer sweet apple. She don't pester, and she don't tease, and she don't lie—no, sir, not even when I'd consider layin' the course a p'int or two from the truth a justifiable proceedin'. She's got inside my vest, somehow or 'nother, and I did think I was consider'ble of a hardshell. She's all right, Mary-'Gusta is. I'm about ready to say 'Thank you' to Marcellus."

And so it was settled, and Mary-'Gusta Lathrop was no longer a visitor, but a permanent member of the odd household at South Harniss. She was delighted when she heard the news, although, characteristically, she said very little beyond confiding to her two "uncles" that she was going to be a good girl and not take David into the parlor again. The remainder of her "things" and belongings were sent over by the Judge and, in due time, the guardianship papers were signed.

"There!" exclaimed Zoeth, laying down the pen. "That settles it, I cal'late. Now, Mary-'Gusta, you're our little girl, mine and your Uncle Shad's, for good and all."

"Not quite so long as that, Zoeth," put in the smiling Shadrach. "We'll hang on to her for a spell, I shouldn't wonder; but one of these days, a hundred years from now or such matter, there's liable to be a good-lookin' young feller sparkin' 'round here and he'll want to marry her and take her somewheres else. What'll you say when it comes to that, Mary-'Gusta?"

Mary-'Gusta thought it over. "If 'twas a hundred years from now," she said, "I guess he wouldn't want me."

The Captain laughed uproariously. "Well, maybe we can discount that hundred some for cash," he admitted. "Make it twelve or fifteen years. Then suppose somebody—er—er——" with a wink at Zoeth—"suppose Jimmie Bacheldor, we'll say, comes and wants us to put you in his hands, what'll you say then?"

The answer was prompt enough this time.

"I'll say no," asserted Mary-'Gusta, with decision. "Jimmie Bacheldor hates to wash his hands; he told me so."

All that summer she played about the house or at the store or on the beach and, when the fall term began, the partners sent her to school. They were happy and proud men when Miss Dobson, the primary teacher, said the girl was too far advanced for the first class and entered her in the second. "Just natural smartness," Captain Shadrach declared. "Natural smartness and nothin' else. She ain't had a mite of advantages, but up she goes just the same. Why, Teacher told me she considered her a reg'lar parachute."

"A parachute's somethin' that comes down, ain't it," suggested Zoeth, remembering the balloon ascension he had seen at the county fair.

"Humph! So 'tis. Seems as if 'twasn't parachute she said. 'Twas—'twas——"

"Parasol?" suggested Isaiah, who was an interested listener.

"No, no; nor paralysis neither. Paragon, that's what 'twas. Teacher said that child was a paragon."

"What's a paragon?" asked Mr. Chase.

"I don't know. But it's what she is, anyway."

The paragon continued to progress in her studies. Also she continued, more and more, to take an interest in the housework and the affairs of her adopted uncles and Isaiah Chase. Little by little changes came in the life of the family. On one memorable Sunday Captain Shadrach attended church. It was the first time in a good many years and whether the congregation or Zoeth or the Captain himself was the more astonished at the latter's being there is a question. Mary-'Gusta was not greatly astonished. It was the result of careful planning on her part, planning which had as its object the relieving of Mr. Hamilton's mind. Zoeth never missed a Sunday service or a Friday night prayer meeting. And, being sincerely religious, he was greatly troubled because his friend and partner took little interest in such things.

Shadrach's aversion to churches dated back to a sermon preached by a former minister. The subject of that sermon was Jonah and the whale. The Captain, having been on several whaling voyages in his younger days, had his own opinion concerning the prophet's famous adventure.

If the minister had been a younger and more tactful man the argument which followed might have ended pleasantly and the break have been avoided. But the clergyman was elderly, as set in his ways as the Captain was in his, and the disagreement was absolute and final.

"The feller is a regular wooden-head," declared Shadrach, hotly. "I was willin' to be reasonable; I was willin' to give in that this Jonah man might have been out of his head and, after he was hove overboard and cast ashore, thought he'd been swallowed by a whale or somethin' or 'nother. I picked up a sailor once who'd drifted around in a boat for a week and he couldn't remember nothin' of what happened after the first day or so. If you'd told him he'd been swallowed by a mackerel he wouldn't have said no. But I've helped kill a good many whales—yes, and I've helped cut 'em up, too—and I know what they look like inside. No man, whether his name was Jonah or Jehoshaphat, could have lived three days in a whale's stomach. How'd he breathe in there, eh? Cal'late the whale had ventilators and a skylight in his main deck? How'd the whale live all that time with a man hoppin' 'round inside him? Think I'd live if I—if I swallowed a live mouse or somethin'? No, sir-ee! Either that mouse would die or I would, I bet you! I've seen a whole parcel of things took out of a whale's insides and some of the things had been alive once, too; but they wasn't alive then; they was in chunks and part digested. Jonah wasn't digested, was he? And the whale wasn't dead of dyspepsy neither. That's what I told that minister. 'You try it yourself,' I says to him. 'There's whales enough back of the Crab

Ledge, twenty mile off Orham,' said I. 'You're liable to run in sight of 'em most any fair day in summer. You go off there and jump overboard some time and see what happens. First place, no whale would swallow you; next place, if it did 'twould chew you or sift you fine first; and, third place, if you was whole and alive that whale would be dead inside of ten minutes. You try it and see.' Good fair offer, wasn't it? But did he take it up? Not much. Said I was a scoffer and an infidel and didn't know anything about Scripture! 'I know about whales, anyhow,' I told him. And he slammed off and wouldn't speak to me again. Don't talk to *me!* I'll never go inside that meetin'-house again."

And he never had until Mary-'Gusta coaxed him into it. She was a regular attendant at Sunday school, but on Sunday mornings in pleasant weather she had been accustomed to take a walk with Shadrach. These walks they both enjoyed hugely, but one bright morning she announced that she was not going for a walk, but was going to church with Uncle Zoeth. Shadrach was disappointed and astonished.

"Land sakes! What's this mean?" he demanded. "Thought you liked to walk with me."

"I do. I like it very much. But I don't think it's fair for me to do it every Sunday. Uncle Zoeth *always* goes to church and he feels real bad 'cause you don't go. He told me so. He says the church folks think you won't go to Heaven when you die and that makes him feel dreadful. He's goin' to Heaven, you know."

"Oh, he is, eh?"

"Of course. He couldn't help it, he's so good. Don't you think he'll go to Heaven, Uncle Shad?"

"Who? Zoeth? Sartin I do. If he don't, nobody will."

"Wouldn't it make you feel bad if you was afraid he wouldn't go there?"

"Humph! Maybe so, but I ain't afraid."

"I know, but he is afraid *you* won't. He thinks an awful lot of you; as much as you do of him, you know. Uncle Shad, I'm goin' to meetin' with Uncle Zoeth this mornin', and I want you to go with us; will you?"

The Captain pulled his beard.

"Look here, Mary-'Gusta," he said. "What's all this about, anyway? You don't cal'late I'd take you walkin' Sundays if I thought 'twas wicked, do you?"

"No, sir; but Uncle Zoeth thinks not goin' to church is wicked. If you and I went to church with him 'twould please him ever so much."

"Maybe so, but 'twould please you and me if he went walkin' with us. I've asked him times enough. Why can't he do what I want as well as my doin' what he wants?"

"'Cause he thinks it's wrong. You don't think goin' to church is wrong, do you, Uncle Shad?"

Shadrach shook his head. "By fire!" he exclaimed. "You're a regular young lawyer, you are, Mary-'Gusta. Judge Baxter hasn't got you beat when it comes to makin' out a case. Look here, now; be honest; hadn't you rather go to walk with me than go to that meetin'-house?"

"Yes, sir," frankly; "I'd rather."

"Oh, you had, eh? But all the same you want us to give up our walk and go to church every Sunday just to please Zoeth. Is that it?"

Mary-'Gusta took his hand. "No, sir," she said shyly, "but I thought perhaps we could divide up. You and I could go with him one Sunday and to walk the next

Sunday. That would be fair. I'm his little girl same as I am yours, Uncle Shad, ain't I?"

Shadrach was stumped, and he went to church that Sunday morning. The sermon had nothing to do with Jonah or the whale, so his feelings were not ruffled. Zoeth was mightily pleased and Mary-'Gusta was happy because he was. The plan of alternate Sundays was adopted. It was but one instance of the "managing" quality which the girl possessed. Isaiah declared that she wound all hands around her little finger, but even he seemed to enjoy the winding.

As she grew older Mary-'Gusta learned more and more concerning her uncles, their habits, their contrasting temperaments and their past history. She learned a little of Hall and Company, the prosperous firm of which they had been partners, with Marcellus Hall, her stepfather, as the head. Isaiah told her a little concerning the firm: "No bigger on Cape Cod," he declared. She asked why it had not continued in business. Mr. Chase brusquely answered that it hadn't, that's all, and would not give any particulars. She questioned the steward concerning Shadrach and Zoeth. The former had never married; that was funny; why hadn't he? Isaiah said he did not know. Hadn't Uncle Zoeth ever married, either? Yes, Zoeth had married.

"Who did——" began Mary-'Gusta, but Isaiah cut short the catechizing.

"You mustn't ask such questions," he declared.

"Why mustn't I?"

" 'Cause you mustn't. Your uncles wouldn't like it a mite if they knew you was pryin' into their affairs. You mustn't ever say a word about your Uncle Zoeth's gettin' married."

"Wouldn't he like me any more if I did?"

"No, you bet he wouldn't; he'd—I don't know's he wouldn't come to hate you. And you mustn't say it to Cap'n Shad neither."

The idea of being hated by Uncle Zoeth was a dreadful one and Mary-'Gusta avoided the tabooed subject. But she thought about it a good deal. She noticed that in neither of the two lots in the cemetery, one where the Goulds were buried and the other the Hamiltons, was a stone erected to the memory of the "beloved wife of Zoeth Hamilton," although other beloved wives of the former generations were commemorated. This seemed odd. As her education progressed she read more and more and from her reading she built up several imaginative romances with Zoeth as the hero, and as the heroines beautiful creatures who had died young, in shipwreck, probably, and whose names were not to be mentioned because. . . . She could not find a satisfactory solution of the because. Shipwreck or burial at sea she deduced from the fact of there being no grave in the cemetery. Mothers and fathers of several of her schoolmates had been buried at sea. Perhaps the late Mrs. Hamilton had been so buried. But Zoeth had never been a seafaring man.

One Saturday afternoon—she was about ten years old at the time—she was in the garret. The garret had taken the place of the old surrey at Ostable, and thither she retired when she wished to be alone to read, or play, or study. This afternoon she was rummaging through the old trunks and sea chests in search of a costume for Rose. It was to be a masculine costume, of course, for there was no feminine apparel in that garret, but in the games which the girl played when alone with her dolls, Rose, the largest of the family, was frequently obliged to change her sex with her raiment.

Mary-'Gusta had ransacked these trunks and chests pretty thoroughly on previous occasions, but this time she made a discovery. In an old trunk which had obviously belonged to Captain Shadrach she found a sort of pocket on the under side of the lid, a pocket closing with a flap and a catch. In this pocket were some papers, old receipts and the like, and a photograph. The photograph interested her exceedingly. It was yellow and faded but still perfectly distinct.

There was a large building standing on posts fixed in the sand, and beyond it were wharves and a glimpse of schooners and the sea. Barrels, a good many barrels, were piled upon the wharves and at the end of the building. Over the door was the sign, "Hall and Company, Wholesale Fish Dealers."

This sign of itself was interesting enough. Evidently here was the place where her stepfather and Captain Gould and Mr. Hamilton had done business years before. But more interesting still was the group of men standing on the platform under the sign. There were four of these men, dressed in clothes and hats which —especially the hats—looked queer and old-fashioned now. Two of the men Mary-'Gusta recognized, or thought she did. They were Captain Shadrach and Mr. Hamilton. Much younger they looked, of course; their hair was not gray and Zoeth wore a beard, while Shadrach had only a mustache. But, in spite of these things and the odd clothes they wore, she was sure she recognized them. And, having recognized them, she also recognized the man in the center of the group as her stepfather, Captain Marcellus Hall. The fourth man, evidently younger than the others, a handsome, square-shouldered chap in his shirtsleeves, she did not know.

She turned the photograph over. On its back was written:

Firm of Hall and Company. Taken August 19th, 1877.
      Marcellus Hall
      Zoeth J. Hamilton
      Edgar S. Farmer
      Shadrach B. Gould.

The names were in differing handwritings. Evidently each man had signed the photograph.

Mary-'Gusta scrutinized the photograph again. Then, with it in her hand, she descended to the kitchen. Isaiah was sitting in a chair by the stove reading a newspaper.

"Mr. Chase," said Mary-'Gusta, "who was Edgar S. Farmer?"

If that kitchen chair had been the never-to-be-forgotten piece of furniture with the music box beneath it and that box had started to play, Isaiah could not have risen more promptly. He literally jumped to his feet and the paper flew from his hands. He whirled upon the questioner.

"What?" he demanded. "What's that you said?"

He was pale, actually pale. Mary-'Gusta was frightened.

"Why—why, I just asked——" she faltered, "I just asked who—who—— What *can* be the matter, Mr. Chase?"

Isaiah waved his hand. "*What* did you ask?" he demanded.

"I asked—I asked who Edgar S. Farmer was, that's all. I didn't mean—I didn't know——"

"Be still! Be still, for mercy sakes! What do you know about Ed Farmer? Who told you about him?"

The girl was more frightened than ever. Isaiah's

next move did not tend to reassure her. He strode to the door, looked up the lane, and closed and locked the door before she could find words to answer.

"Now, then," he said, coming close to her and looking her straight in the face, "who told you about Ed Farmer?"

"Nobody told me. Honest, they didn't."

"Somebody must have told you; else how did you know?"

Mary-'Gusta hesitatingly held up the photograph. "It's written on this," she said.

Mr. Chase snatched it from her hand. He looked at the picture and then at her.

"It's written on the back," went on the girl.

Isaiah turned the photograph over.

"Humph!" he said suspiciously. "I see. Who gave this to you?"

"Nobody gave it to me. I found it in an old trunk up in the attic."

"Humph! You did, eh? Well, I swan to man! Have you showed it to anybody else but me?"

"No, sir. Honest, I haven't. I just found it this minute."

"Well, I swan, that's lucky. 'Twas in a trunk, eh? Whose trunk?"

"One of Uncle Shad's, I guess."

"Humph! I presume likely. Well, what made you ask about—about the one you did ask about?"

"I knew who the others were. I knew my father and Uncle Zoeth and Uncle Shad. But I didn't know who the Farmer one was. It says 'Firm of Hall and Company,' and all those names are signed. So I thought maybe Mr. Farmer was——"

"Never you mind who he was. He was a darned

blackguard and his name ain't mentioned in this house. That's all I can tell you and you mustn't ask any more questions. Why, if your Uncle Zoeth—yes, or your Uncle Shad either—was to hear you askin' about him— they'd—I don't know what they'd do. I'm goin' to tear this thing up."

He would have torn the photograph across, but the girl seized his hands.

"Oh, no, you mustn't," she cried. "Please don't. It isn't mine. It belongs to Uncle Shad. You mustn't tear it—give it to me."

Isaiah hesitated. "Give it to you?" he repeated. "What'll you do with it?"

"I'll put it right back where I found it. Truly, I will. I will, honest, Mr. Chase."

Isaiah reflected. Then, and with considerable reluctance, he handed her the photograph.

"All right," he said, "only be sure you do it. And look here, Mary-'Gusta, don't you ever touch it again and don't you ever tell either of your uncles or anybody else that you found it. You hear?"

Mary-'Gusta said that she heard. She ran to the garret and replaced the photograph in the pocket of the trunk. She did not mention it again nor did Isaiah, but thereafter when her active imagination constructed a life romance with Mr. Zoeth Hamilton as its hero, that romance contained a villain also, and the villain's name was Edgar S. Farmer. And the firm of Hall and Company, her father's firm, had a fourth and most mysterious partner who was a blackguard.

CHAPTER VIII

THE summers and winters came and went and Mary-'Gusta's birthdays came and went with them. She grew taller and more mature. Her place as assistant housekeeper was recognized now and even Isaiah consulted her on matters of household management. As for her uncles, she managed them whether consulted or not. They took the place of the discarded dolls; she was too old for dolls now, although David was still mothered and petted as much as ever. But when Uncle Zoeth had a cold it was she who insisted upon his wrapping up and saw that the wraps were ready, and if Uncle Shad was caught wearing socks with holes in them he was scolded and supplied with fresh ones. She selected the clothes they should wear and insisted that they black their boots on Sunday. She helped them in the store and it became occasionally possible for them to leave that place of business at the same time without engaging the services of Annabel. At first the partners, Captain Shadrach especially, protested against the supervision and the innovations, but Mary-'Gusta tactfully and diplomatically carried each point, and, after a time, the Captain ceased to protest and accepted the inevitable almost with meekness.

"No use, Zoeth," he said on one occasion; "I've talked and talked but I'm wearin' the necktie just the same. I told her 'twas too good to wear weekdays and it ought to be saved for Sunday, but it ain't Sunday and I've got it on. She said 'twas becomin' and the one I've been wearin' wasn't and that she crocheted it for me and I don't know what all. So here I am. Got so I ain't even boss of my own neck."

"Well, 'tis becomin'," observed Zoeth. "And she did crochet it for you. I noticed you didn't stop her tyin' it on you even while you was vowin' you wouldn't wear it."

Shadrach sighed. "To think," he groaned, "that I, Cap'n Shad Gould, a man that's handled as many fo'mast hands as I have, should come to be led around by the nose by a slip of a girl! By fire, I—I can't hardly believe it. It's disgraceful."

Zoeth smiled. "Oh, be still, Shadrach," he said. "You bear up under the disgrace as well as anybody ever I saw. You know perfectly well you was tickled to death to have her tie that necktie on you. You was grinnin' like a Chessy cat all the time."

"I wasn't, neither. I was chokin', not grinnin'. You don't know a grin from a choke."

Zoeth changed the subject. "It's a mighty pretty necktie," he declared. "There ain't anybody in this town, unless it's Philander Bearse's wife, that can crochet any better'n that girl of ours."

Shadrach snorted. "What are you talkin' about?" he demanded. "Etta Bearse never saw the day she could crochet like that. No, nor do anything else so well, either. Look at the way our candy trade has picked up since Mary-'Gusta fixed up the showcase. You cal'lated 'twas all right the way 'twas afore and thought 'twas foolish to change, but she changed it and —well, we've sold a third again as much candy."

Zoeth's smile broadened. "Seems as if I remember your sayin' a few things about that showcase," he remarked. "You gave me fits for lettin' her fuss with it.

Annabel was in t'other day and she said folks thought 'twas queer enough our lettin' a thirteen-year-old child run our store for us."

"She did, eh? She's jealous, that's what ails her. And to think of *her* sayin' it. That Annabel's all brass, like a ship's spyglass. By the jumpin' Judas! I'm proud of that showcase and I'm proud of Mary-'Gusta. She don't make many mistakes: *I* can't remember of her makin' any."

"Neither can I, not even in neckties. There, there, Shadrach! I know you. You talk about disgrace and such, but you're as crazy about Mary-'Gusta as—as——"

"As you are, eh? Well, maybe I am, Zoeth. When she was first willed to us, as you might say, I used to wonder how we'd ever get along with her; now I wonder how we got along without her. If she should be—er—took away from us, I don't know——"

"Sshh, shh, Shadrach! Don't talk about anything like that."

Mary-'Gusta was making good progress at school. At fourteen she graduated from the grammar school and in the fall was to enter the high school. She was popular among her mates, although she never sought popularity.

At picnics and church sociables she had always a small circle about her and the South Harniss boys were prominent in that circle. But Mary-'Gusta, although she liked boys and girls well enough, never showed a liking for one more than the other and she was too busy at the house and in the store to have her young friends hanging about. They bothered her, she said. As for having a particular friend of the other sex, which some of the girls in her class no older than she seemed to think a necessary proof of being in their teens, she laughed at the idea. She had her adopted uncles and Isaiah to take care of and boy beaux were silly. Talking about them as these girls did was sillier still.

That summer—the summer preceding Mary-'Gusta's fifteenth birthday—was the liveliest South Harniss had known. The village was beginning to feel the first symptoms of its later boom as a summer resort. A number of cottages had been built for people from Boston and New York and Chicago, and there was talk of a new hotel. Also there was talk of several new stores, but Hamilton and Company were inclined to believe this merely talk and did not worry about it. Their trade was unusually brisk and the demand for Mary-'Gusta's services as salesgirl interfered considerably with her duties as assistant housekeeper.

One fine, clear July morning she came up to the store early in order that the partners might go down to the house for breakfast. They had gone and she had just finished placing on the counters and in other likely spots about the store sheets of sticky fly paper. Flies are a nuisance in South Harniss in midsummer and Captain Shad detested them. Just as the last sheet was laid in place, a young fellow and a girl came in. Mary-'Gusta recognized them both. The girl was the seventeen-year-old daughter of a wealthy summer resident, a Mr. Keith from Chicago. The Keiths had a fine cottage on the bluff at the other end of the village. The young chap with her was, so gossip reported, a college friend of her brother. His surname was prosaic enough, being Smith, but his first name was Crawford and his home was somewhere in the Far West. He was big and good-looking, and the Boston papers mentioned him as one of the most promising backs on the Harvard Freshman eleven. Next year, so the sporting writers opined, he would almost certainly make the Varsity team. Most of Mary-'Gusta's feminine friends and acquaintances rated him "perfectly splendid" and regarded Edna Keith with envious eyes.

This morning both he and the Keith girl were arrayed in the gayest of summer regalia. Young Smith's white flannel trousers were carefully creased, his blue serge coat was without a wrinkle, his tie and socks were a perfect match, and his cap was of a style which the youth of South Harniss might be wearing the following summer, but not this one. Take him "by and large," as Captain Shadrach would have said, Crawford Smith was an immaculate and beautiful exhibit; of which fact he, being eighteen years of age, was doubtless quite aware.

He and the Keith girl were, so Mary-'Gusta learned, a committee of two selected to purchase certain supplies for a beach picnic, a combination clambake and marshmallow toast, which was to take place over at Setuckit Point that day. Sam Keith, Edna's brother, and the other members of the party had gone on to Jabez Hedges' residence, where Jabez had promised to meet them with the clams and other things for the bake. Edna and her escort, having made their purchases at Hamilton and Company's, were to join them at the "clam-man's." Then the whole party was to go down to the wharf and the sailboat.

Miss Edna, who was a talkative damsel, informed Mary-'Gusta of these facts at once. Also she announced that they must hurry like everything.

"You see," she said, "we told Sam and the rest we'd be at the clam-man's in ten minutes, and, if we're not there, Sam will be awfully cross. He hates to wait for people. And we've been too long already. It's all your fault, Crawford; you would stop to hear that fruit man talk. I told you you mustn't."

The "fruit man" was Mr. Gaius Small, and, although he stammered, he loved the sound of his own voice. The demand for a dozen oranges furnished Gaius with subject sufficient for a lengthy monologue—"forty drawls and ten stutters to every orange," quoting Captain Shad again.

"I told you you mustn't get him started," went on Miss Keith, gushingly. "He'll talk forever if he has a chance. But you would do it. Asking him if he kept pomegranates and bread-fruit! The idea! I'm sure he doesn't know what a pomegranate is. You were *so* solemn and he was *so* ridiculous! I thought I should *die*. You really are the drollest person, Crawford Smith! I don't know what I shall do with you."

It was evident that her opinion of young Smith was not different from that of other young ladies of her age. Also that Crawford himself was not entirely unconscious of that opinion. At eighteen, to be set upon a pedestal and worshiped, to have one's feeblest joke hailed as a masterpiece of wit, is dangerous for the idol; the effort of sustaining the elevated position entails the risk of a fall. Crawford was but eighteen and a good fellow, but he had been worshiped a good deal. He was quite as sensible as other young chaps of his age, which statement means exactly that and no more.

"Well," he said, with a complacent grin, "we learned how to pronounce 'pomegranate' at any rate. You begin with a pup-pup-pup, as if you were calling a dog, and you finish with a grunt like a pig. I wish I had asked him for a persimmon; then he'd have made a noise like a cat."

Miss Keith, when she recovered from her spasm of

merriment, declared her companion "perfectly killing."

"But we must hurry," she said. "We really must. Crawford, you buy the things. I should think of that fruit man and laugh all the time, I know I should."

She remained by the door and the young gentleman strolled to the counter. He cast an amused glance about the store; its display of stock was, thanks to Mary-'Gusta's recent efforts at tidiness, not quite the conglomerate mass it had been when the partners were solely responsible, but the variety was still strikingly obvious.

"Humph!" observed Crawford; "I've forgotten what we came to buy, but I'm sure it is here, whatever it is. Some emporium, this! Introduce me to the proprietor, will you, Edna?"

Edna giggled.

"She isn't the proprietor," she said. "She is just the clerk, that's all. Her name is—I've forgotten your name, dear. What is it?"

"Mary Lathrop," replied Mary-'Gusta, shortly. She objected to being addressed as "dear" and she strongly objected to the patronizing tone in which it was uttered. Edna Keith was older than she, but not old enough to patronize.

"Oh, yes, so it is," said the young lady. "But that isn't what everyone calls you. They call you something else—something funny—Oh, I know! Mary-'Gusta, that's it. I knew it was funny. Mary-'Gusta, this is Mr. Smith. He wants to buy some things. And he's in a *great* hurry."

"Charmed, Mary-'Gusta," said Mr. Smith. Mary-'Gusta did not appear charmed. She asked him what he wanted.

"Search *me*," said the young gentleman, cheerfully.

"There was a list, wasn't there, Edna? You have it, I think."

Edna produced the list, scrawled in pencil on the back of an envelope. Crawford looked it over.

"Sam's writing isn't exactly print," he observed, "but I can guess at it. Let's see—a pound of butter. Where's the butter department of this *Bon Marché*, Edna?"

Edna, after another convulsion, declared she didn't know.

"No doubt Miss—er—Mary Jane knows," went on her companion. "Why, yes, of course she does. Right there, behind the oilskin jacket. Remove jacket, open door—behold, the icebox and the butter. Neat, compact, and convenient. One pound only, Elizabeth Eliza. Thank you."

"Her name isn't Elizabeth Eliza," giggled Miss Keith. "Isn't he awful, Mary-'Gusta! You mustn't mind him."

"I don't," said Mary-'Gusta, promptly. "What else do you want?"

Crawford consulted the list. "The next item," he said, "appears to be a—er—certain kind of ham. I blush to mention it, but I must. It is deviled ham. Have you that kind of ham, Mary-'Gusta?"

Mary-'Gusta took the can of deviled ham from the shelf. Crawford shook his head.

"To think that one so young should be so familiar with ham of that kind!" he said. "She didn't speak its name, though. Suppose I had asked you what kind of ham you had, Miss—er—'Gusta, how would you have got around it?"

Mary-'Gusta did not answer. She was very angry, but she was determined that her tormentor should not know it.

"A young lady of few words," commented Mr. Smith.

"Next item appears to be six boxes of marshmallows. Where is the marshmallow department, Mary Jane?"

Mary-'Gusta hesitated. The tin boxes of marshmallows were on the shelf behind the counter under the candy case. But there was a fresh assortment in an unopened packing box in the back room, a box which had just come from the wholesale confectioner's in Boston. Her Uncle Zoeth had expressed a fear that those beneath the counter were rather stale.

Miss Keith fidgeted. "Oh, dear!" she exclaimed. "This is *so* slow. I know Sam and the rest won't wait for us at the clam-man's much longer."

Her companion whistled. "Is the word 'hurry' in the South Harniss dictionary, Edna?" he inquired. "How about it, Mary Jane?"

Mary-'Gusta was determined not to hurry. This superior young man wished her to do so and that was reason sufficient for delay.

Young Smith sighed resignedly. "Edna," he said, "suppose we sit down. The word is *not* in the dictionary."

There was but one chair, except those behind the counters, in the store. Miss Keith took that with an exclamation of impatience. Crawford Smith, whistling a mournful dirge, sauntered to the end of the counter and sat down upon a nail keg.

Mary-'Gusta also uttered an exclamation. It is well to look before one leaps, also, occasionally, before one sits. That keg had, spread across its top, a sheet of the fresh and very sticky fly paper. Before she could have protested, even if she had wished to do so, the young gentleman's spotless white flannels and the fly paper came in contact, close and clinging contact.

Mary-'Gusta put a hand to her mouth. Crawford

looked at her, caught the direction of her look, and looked in that direction himself. His whistle stopped in the middle of a note and his face immediately became a match for his socks and tie, a beautiful rich crimson, the chosen color of his University.

Miss Keith, from her seat by the door, could not see beyond the end of the counter. Consequently she was unaware of the mishap to the white flannels. But Mary-'Gusta saw and knew; also she could see that Mr. Smith knew.

"Oh, dear!" exclaimed Edna, impatiently. "We are dreadfully late now. We'll never get there on time. Sam won't wait for us; I know he won't. Where are those marshmallows? Can't you please hurry, Mary-'Gusta?"

Mary-'Gusta's eyes were sparkling. Her manner was provokingly deliberate. She took a box of marshmallows from beneath the counter.

"There are some here," she said, "but I'm afraid they aren't very fresh. The fresh ones, those that have just come, are in a box in the back room. That box hasn't been opened yet. If you can wait I'll open it for you."

Young Smith said nothing. Miss Keith, however, spoke her mind.

"Of course we can't wait," she declared. "I'm sure these will do. They will do, won't they, Crawford?"

And still Crawford remained silent. Mary-'Gusta, who was enjoying this portion of the interview as much as she had disliked its beginning, offered a suggestion.

"If you will just come here and look at these," she said, with mischievous gravity, addressing the young gentleman on the nail keg, "perhaps you can tell whether they're fresh enough."

The young gentleman did not rise. His face retained its brilliant color and his lips moved, but his answer was not audible. At his age the dread of appearing ridiculous, especially in the presence of a youthful and charming female, is above all others hateful. And Edna Keith was not the only girl in the picnic party; there were others. She would be certain to tell them. Crawford Smith foresaw a horrible day, a day of disgrace and humiliation, one in which he was destined to furnish amusement without sharing the fun. And Sam Keith, who had remarked upon the splendor of his friend's attire, would gloat—not only here in South Harniss, but elsewhere—in Cambridge, for instance. An older man would have risen, laughed whether he felt like laughing or not—and have expressed his opinion of fly paper. Crawford was not yet a man; he was in the transition stage, a boy fondly hoping that other people might think him a man. So he sat still until it was too late to rise, and then wished he had risen in the first place.

"My goodness!" exclaimed the fidgety Miss Keith, "why don't you look at them, Crawford? What are you waiting for?"

Mary-'Gusta, the box of marshmallows in her hand, regarded the boy on the nail keg. His eyes met hers and in them was a look of such utter misery that the girl relented. Her feeling of satisfied resentment changed to one almost of pity. She had been made to feel ridiculous herself at various times in her short life and she remembered the sensation. Mary-'Gusta, as has been mentioned before in this history, was old for her years.

She considered a moment. Then she thrust the box beneath the counter.

"I guess I'd better not sell you those, anyway," she

said with decision. "Uncle Zoeth said they weren't fresh. I'll open the case in the back room."

Edna stamped her foot.

"We can't wait for that," she declared. "We must go without them, I suppose. Oh, dear! And they depended on us to get them. It's so provoking. Now we can't have any toast at all and it would have been such fun."

Mary-'Gusta glanced once more at the occupant of the keg.

"I was thinking," she said, slowly, "that you needn't both wait unless you wanted to. Perhaps Miss Keith might go on and tell the others and—er—Mr. Smith could stay here until I opened the box. Then he could meet you at the boat."

Edna hesitated. "Shall I, Crawford?" she asked.

Her companion did not hesitate. "I think perhaps you'd better, Edna," he said. "I—I guess I won't be long."

Miss Keith hurried out. Mary-'Gusta turned her attention to the remaining visitor.

"You can get up now," she said. "Some of it will tear off, anyway, and if you hurry you will have time to run home and change your—your clothes."

Crawford was evidently much surprised, also his embarrassment was not lessened; but he rose.

"Then—then you knew?" he stammered.

"Of course I knew. I saw you sit down on it, didn't I? If I'd known what you were going to do I'd have told you to look out. But you did it so quick I couldn't. Now tear off as much as you can."

The young gentleman obeyed orders. "Does it show much?" he queried. "I can't see. Is there much left?"

Mary-'Gusta smiled. His contortions were as violent as they were vain. "There's enough," she said simply. "Here are the things you bought. Now go out of the back door and cut across the fields. It's the shortest way home."

Mr. Smith took his various parcels, including the six boxes of marshmallows which Mary-'Gusta produced from beneath the counter. "I thought you said these were stale," he observed, wonderingly.

"I said they weren't real fresh, but they're fresh enough for a toast. I said that so that the Keith girl wouldn't wait. I didn't think you wanted her to."

"You bet your life I didn't! So that's why you said you would have to open the other box? Just—just to help me out?"

"Yes. Now don't stop any longer. You'll have to run, you know. Go out the back way."

Crawford started for the door of the back room, but at that door he paused.

"Say," he said, feelingly, "this is mighty white of you, do you know it? And after the way I guyed you when I first came in! I guess I was rather fresh, wasn't I?"

"Yes, you were."

"Yes, yes, I guess I was. I thought you were just a country kid, you know, and I—say, by George, you *were* white. If I'd been you I'd have got square. You had the chance; 'twould have served me right for playing the smart Aleck. I beg your pardon. You're all *right!* And I'm awfully sorry I was such a chump."

It was a straightforward, honest apology and confession of fault. Mary-'Gusta was pleased, but she did not show it. He had referred to her as a kid and she did not like that.

"If you don't hurry—yes, and run like everything," she said, "you won't have time to get home and change and meet the others at the boat. And somebody else will see you, too. You'd better go."

The young man went without further delay. Mary-'Gusta watching from the back door saw him racing across the fields in the direction of the Keith cottage. When her uncles returned she said nothing of the occurrence. She considered it funny, but she knew Crawford Smith did not, and she was sure he would prefer to have the secret kept.

The following afternoon the partners of Hamilton and Company entertained a caller at the store. That evening Shadrach spoke of the call to Mary-'Gusta.

"That young Smith feller that's been visitin' the Keiths was in today," said the Captain. "Didn't want to buy nothin'; said he just happened in, that's all. Asked where you was, he did. I didn't know he knew you, Mary-'Gusta."

Mary-'Gusta, who was busy clearing the supper table, answered without looking round. "He and Edna Keith bought some things at the store yesterday," she said.

"Yes, so he said. He said tell you everything was all right and he had a fine time at the picnic. Seemed to cal'late you was a pretty bright girl. We knew that afore, of course, but it was nice of him to say so. He's leavin' on tomorrow mornin's train. Goin' way out West, he is, to Nevada; that's where he and his dad live. His ma's dead, so he told us. Must be tough to live so fur off from salt water: I couldn't stand it, I know that. Funny thing about that young feller, too; his face looked sort of familiar to me and Zoeth. Seemed as if he looked like somebody we knew, but of course we didn't know any of his folks; we don't know any Smiths from way off there."

The subject was dropped for the time, but two days later the expressman brought a package to the house. The package was addressed to Miss Mary Augusta Lathrop and contained a five-pound basket of expensive chocolates and bonbons. There was a note with it which read as follows:

Hope you'll like these. They are fresh, at least Huyler's people swear they are, but I don't believe they are as good as those marshmallows. And I *know* they are not as fresh as a certain person was at a certain time. Please eat them and forget the other freshness.

C. S.

You were a perfect little brick not to tell.

Mary-'Gusta was obliged to tell then, but she made her uncles and Isaiah promise not to do so. She, with the able assistance of the other members of the household, ate the contents of the basket in due time. The basket itself was taken to the parlor, where it was given a place beside the other curiosities. As for the note, that disappeared. And yet, if one had investigated the contents of the small drawer of Mary-'Gusta's bureau, where she kept her most intimate treasures, the mystery of its disappearance might have been solved.

It was the only epistle of its kind the girl had yet received; and, after all, good-looking young college men are what they are. And Mary-'Gusta, in spite of her queerness, was feminine—and human.

CHAPTER IX

WHEN Maru-'Guato was seventeen a great event took place. The happening which led to it was trivial enough, but the results were important and far-reaching. They led to the second great change in her life, a change as important as that brought about by her memorable "visit" to South Harniss.

She was a girl in years still, but tall for her age, and in thought and manner almost a young woman. Her management of her uncles and Isaiah was now complete. They no longer protested, even to each other, against the management and, in fact, gloried in it. The cook and steward accepted her orders concerning the daily marketing and he and she audited the monthly bills. The white house by the shore was a different place altogether now and "chicken-pox tablecloths" and tarnished silver were things of the forgotten past. At the store she had become almost a silent partner, and Hamilton and Company's "emporium" was, thanks to her judgment and tact, if not yet an up-to-date establishment, at least a shop where commodities to be sold were in places where they might be seen by prospective purchasers and readily located by the proprietors.

She spent a good deal of her time, except in school hours, at the store and much of the buying as well as the selling was done by her. The drummers representing New York and Boston wholesale houses knew her and cherished keen respect for her abilities as a selector and purchaser of goods.

'Say," said one of these gentlemen, after a lengthy session during which his attempts to work off several "stickers" had been frustrated by Mary-'Gusta's common sense and discernment—"Say, that girl of yours is a wonder, do you know it? She's the sharpest buyer I ever run across on my trips down here. I don't take a back seat for anybody when it comes to selling goods, and there's mighty little I can't sell; but I can't bluff her. She knows what's what, you hear me!"

Shadrach, to whom this remark was made, chuckled. "You bet you!" he declared, with enthusiasm. "Anybody that gets ahead of our Mary-'Gusta has got to turn out afore the mornin' watch. She's smart. Zoeth and me ain't aboard the same craft with her."

"I should say not. And you can't get gay with her, either. Most girls of her age and as good a looker as she is don't object to a little ragging: they're used to it and they like it—but not her. She isn't fishing for boxes of candy or invitations to dances. That line of talk means good-by and no sale where she is. Business and just business, that's all there is to her. How long are you goin' to keep her here?"

"How long? Why, forever, I hope. What are you talkin' about?"

The drummer winked. "That's all right," he observed. "You want to keep her, I don't doubt: but one of these days somebody else'll be wanting her more than you do. Mr. Right'll be coming along here some time and then—good night! She's young yet, but in a couple of years she'll be a queen and then—well, then maybe I'll stand a better chance of unloading those last summer caps the house has got in stock. Girls like her don't stay single and keep store; there's too much demand and not enough competition. Gad! If I wasn't an antique and married already I don't know but I'd be getting into line. That's what!"

Captain Shadrach was inclined to be angry, but, although he would not have admitted it, he realized the truth of this frank statement. Mary-'Gusta was pretty, she was more than that, and the line was already forming. Jimmie Bacheldor had long ago ceased to be a competitor; that friendship had ended abruptly at the time of David's narrow escape; but there were others, plenty of them. Daniel Higgins, son of Mr. Solomon Higgins, the local lumber dealer and undertaker, was severely smitten. Dan was at work in Boston, where he was engaged in the cheerful and remunerative business of selling coffins for the American Casket Company. He was diligent and active and his future promised to be bright, at least so his proud father boasted. He came home for holidays and vacations and his raiment was anything but funereal, but Mary-'Gusta was not impressed either by the raiment or the personality beneath it. She treated the persistent Daniel as a boy and a former schoolmate. When he assumed manly airs she laughed at him and when he invited her to accompany him to the Cattle Show at Ostable she refused and said she was going with Uncle Zoeth.

Dan Higgins was not the only young fellow who found the store of Hamilton and Company an attractive lounging place. Some of the young gentlemen not permanent residents of South Harniss also appeared to consider it a pleasant place to visit on Summer afternoons. They came to buy, of course, but they remained to chat. Mary-'Gusta might have sailed or picknicked a good deal and in the best of company, socially speaking, if she had cared to do so. She did not so care.

"They don't want me, Uncle Shad," she said. "And I don't want to go."

"Course they want you," declared Shadrach, stoutly. "If they didn't want you they wouldn't ask you, 'tain't likely. And I heard that young Keith feller askin' you to go out sailin' with him this very afternoon."

"You didn't hear his sister ask me, did you? There, there, Uncle Shad, don't worry about me. I'm having a good time; a very much better time than if I went sailing with the Keiths."

"What's the matter with the Keiths? They're as nice folks as come to South Harniss."

"Of course they are."

"Well, then! And you're as good as they are, ain't you?"

"I hope so. Uncle Shad, why don't you wear a white flannel suit in hot weather? Mr. Keith, Sam's father, wore one at the church garden party the other day."

The Captain stared at her. "Why don't I wear—what?" he stammered.

"A white flannel suit. You're as good as Mr. Keith, aren't you?"

"I guess I am. I don't know why I ain't. But what kind of a question's that? I'd look like a plain fool togged out in one of them things: anyway, I'd feel like one. I don't belong in a white flannel suit. I ain't no imitation dude."

"And I don't belong in Sam Keith's yacht. At least Mr. Keith and Edna would feel that I didn't. I don't want to be considered an imitation, either."

Shadrach shook his head. "You ain't like anybody else," he said. "You're a funny girl, Mary-'Gusta."

"I suppose I am; but I'm not as funny as I should be if I tried to *be* somebody else. No, Uncle Shad, you'll just have to bear with me as I am, funniness and all."

A few days after this Keith, senior, came into the store. He was not arrayed in the white flannels but was wearing a rather shabby but very comfortable tweed jacket and trousers and a white canvas hat of the kind which Hamilton and Company sold for fifty cents. His shirt was of the soft-collared variety and his shoes were what South Harniss called "sneakers."

John Keith's visits to Cape Cod were neither very frequent nor lengthy. His wife and family came in June and remained until late September, but his sojourns were seldom longer than a week at a time and there were intervals of a month or more between them. In Chicago he was the head of a large business and that business demanded close attention. When he left it he left his cares with it and enjoyed himself in his own way. That way included old clothes, golf, a boat, and just as few tea and garden parties as his wife would permit.

He was planning a fishing trip and had stopped at the store to buy some tobacco. The partners had gone home for dinner and Mary-'Gusta was tending shop. At that moment she was busy with the traveling representative of Messrs. Bernstein, Goldberg and Baun, of Providence, wholesale dealers in stationery, cards and novelties. The time was August, but Mr. Kron, the drummer, was already booking orders for the Christmas season. His samples were displayed upon the counter and he and Mary-'Gusta were deep in conversation.

"That's what you ought to have," declared Mr. Kron, with enthusiasm. "Believe me, there's goin' to be some call for that line of stuff this year. The house can't turn 'em out fast enough."

"But what is it?" asked Mary-'Gusta. "What's it for?"

"It's a combination calendar and beauty-box," explained Mr. Kron. "Hang it on the wall by your bureau —see? In the mornin' you can't remember what day it is. All right, there's the calendar. Then you want to doll yourself up for—well, for the party you're goin' to——"

"The same morning?" interrupted Mary-'Gusta.

Mr. Kron grinned. He was a young man and this was his first trip in that section. His clothes were neither modest nor retiring and he, himself, did not suffer from these failings. Also he prided himself on having a way with the ladies, especially the younger ladies. And Mary-'Gusta was distinctly the most attractive young person he had met on this trip.

He laughed in appreciation of the joke.

"Say," he observed, admiringly, "you're up to the minute, ain't you! You're some kidder, all right. Are there many more in this burg like you? If there are I'm goin' to move in and settle down. What?"

Mary-'Gusta did not laugh, nor did she answer. Instead, she turned to the gentleman who had entered the store.

"Good morning, Mr. Keith," she said. "Was there anything you wanted?"

Keith smiled. "No hurry," he said. "I've got a little time to kill and if you don't mind I'll kill it here. I'll sit down and wait, if I may. That boatman of mine will be along pretty soon."

He took the chair by the door. Mr. Kron continued his exploitation of the combination calendar and beauty-box.

"You are goin' to a party," he went on, "either that

night or that afternoon or sometime. Sure you are! Girls like you ain't handed the go-by on many parties in this neck of the woods—am I right? Well, then, when the time comes, you pull down the flap. There's your beauty-box, lookin'-glass, powder puff and powder, all complete. Now a novelty like that will sell——"

"We couldn't use it," interrupted Mary-'Gusta. "Show me something else."

Mr. Kron, disappointed but far from discouraged, showed her something else—many somethings. Concerning each he was enthusiastic, slangy, and familiar. Mary-'Gusta paid little attention to slang or enthusiasm; the familiarity she ignored utterly. She selected several of the novelties, a rather extensive line of Christmas cards, and in the matters of price and cash discounts was keen and businesslike. Keith watched and listened, at first with amusement, then with growing admiration for the girl's simplicity and good sense.

Mr. Kron's admiration was outspoken.

"Say," he said, as he repacked his samples, "you're a mighty clever buyer, do you know it? That line of stuff you've ordered is the cream, that's what it is. You made a mistake in not layin' in a dozen or two of those combination beauty-boxes, but that's all right. Here, have one for yourself. Take it with my compliments."

Mary-'Gusta declined. "No, thank you," she said.

"Why not? It don't come out of my pocket. The firm expects me to hand out little keepsakes like that. I've been plantin' 'em with the girls all the way down."

"No, thank you," she replied.

Mr. Kron, having finished his business as representative of Messrs. Bernstein, Goldberg and Baun, attempted a stroke of his own.

"Say," he said, "I've got a little spare time on my hands this evenin'; I shan't make the next town until tomorrow. There's a new movie theater just opened over to Orham. They tell me it's all to the mustard. I can hire a rig here and you and me might drive over tonight and take it in. What do you say, Kid?"

"No, thank you," said Mary-'Gusta again.

"But——"

"No, thank you. Good day."

She turned away to enter the order she had just given in a book on the desk. Mr. Kron tried again, but she did not appear to hear him. He grinned, observed "Oh, very well!" and, with a wink at Mr. Keith, went out, a suitcase in each hand.

Keith rose from the chair and, walking over to the counter, requested to be supplied with the tobacco he had come to buy. Mary-'Gusta gave it to him. Her cheeks were red and Keith was surprised to notice that she looked almost as if she would like to cry. He guessed the reason.

"That young man will get himself thoroughly kicked some day," he observed; "I'm not sure that I oughtn't to have done it myself just now. He annoyed you, I'm afraid."

Mary-'Gusta answered without looking at him.

"That's all right," she said. "I'm foolish, I guess. He meant to be nice, perhaps. Some girls may like that sort of niceness; I don't."

"Why didn't you tell him to get out?"

"I wanted to see his samples. It is time for us to buy our Christmas things and I had rather choose them myself, that's all."

"Oh! But Mr. Hamilton or the Captain—I should think——"

141

"Oh, they might have bought some that we couldn't sell."

"The beauty-boxes, for instance?"

Mary-'Gusta smiled. "Why, yes," she admitted; "perhaps."

"I see. But it was rather an ordeal for you. Do you have to endure much of that sort of thing?"

"No more than any girl who keeps store, I guess."

At the dinner table that evening Keith referred to his experience as listener in Hamilton and Company's shop.

"That girl with the queer name," he said, "a niece of those two old chaps who run the place, I believe she is. Do you know anything about her, Gertrude?"

Before Mrs. Keith could reply, Edna spoke:

"Ask Sam, Dad," she said, mischievously. "Sam knows about her. He just adores that store; he spends half his time there."

"Nonsense, Edna!" protested Sam, turning red. "I don't do any such thing."

"Oh, yes, you do. And you know about Mary-'Gusta too. He says she's a peach, Daddy."

"Humph!" grunted her brother, indignantly. "Well, she is one. She's got every girl in your set skinned a mile for looks. But I don't know anything about her, of course."

Mrs. Keith broke in. "Skinned a mile!" she repeated, with a shudder. "Sam, what language you do use! Yes, John," she added, addressing her husband. "I know the girl well. She's pretty and she is sensible. For a girl who has had no opportunities and has lived all her life here in South Harniss she is really quite remarkable. Why do you speak of her, John?"

Mr. Keith related a part of the conversation between Mary-'Gusta and Mr. Kron.

"She handled the fellow splendidly," he said. "She talked business with him and she wouldn't let him talk anything else. But it was plain enough to see that she felt insulted and angry. It seems a pity that a girl like that should have to put up with that sort of thing. I wonder if her uncles, old Mr. Hamilton and Captain Shadrach, realize what happens when they're not about? How would they take it, do you think, if I dropped a hint?"

Edna laughed. "You would have to be very careful, Daddy," she said. "Mr. Hamilton and the Captain idolize Mary-'Gusta and she just worships them. Besides, she isn't really their niece, you know. She is a young lady of independent means—at least, so everybody says."

Her father was surprised. He asked what she meant by "independent means." Mrs. Keith answered.

"The means are not very extensive, I imagine," she said. "The story is that this Mary-'Gusta—why they persist in calling her by that dreadful name I can't understand—is the daughter of a former friend and partner. Mr. Hamilton and Captain Gould adopted her and she has lived with them ever since. She has money of her own, though no two of the townspeople agree as to how much. I've heard it estimated all the way from five to fifty thousand. She never speaks of it and those queer old uncles of hers keep their affairs very much to themselves. But I agree with you, John; it is a shame that she should have to spend her life here in South Harniss. I think we ought to do something for her, if we can. I shall think it over."

Mrs. Keith was always doing something for somebody. At home in Chicago she was president of her women's club and identified with goodness knows how many charitable societies. In South Harniss she was

active in church and sewing circles. Her enthusiasm
was always great, but her tact was sometimes lacking.
South Harniss people, some of them, were inclined to
consider her as a self-appointed boss interfering where
she had no business.

Her husband looked a trifle dubious.

"Be careful, Gertrude," he cautioned. "Look out you
don't offend. These Cape Codders are self-respecting
and touchy, you know. Anyone interfering with their
private affairs is likely to get into trouble."

His wife resented the warning. "Don't throw cold
water on everything, John," she said. "I know more
about Cape Codders than you do. You only meet them
for a few weeks each summer. I flatter myself that *I*
know them and that they know and trust me. Of *course*
I shall be careful. And I shall think the Mary-'Gusta
matter over."

She did think it over and a week later she came to
her husband overflowing with the excitement of a brilliant idea. A cousin of hers, a maiden lady of sixty or
thereabouts, wealthy and a semi-invalid who cherished
her ill-health, was in need of a female companion. Mrs.
Keith was certain that Mary-'Gusta would be just the
person to fill that need.

Mr. Keith was by no means so certain. He raised
some objections.

"Humph," he said. "Well, Gertrude, to be frank, I
don't think much of the scheme. Cousin Clara has had
one companion after the other for thirty years. None
of them has stayed with her very long. She requires
a sort of combination friend and lady's maid and secretary and waitress, and I don't think our Mary-'Gusta
would enjoy that sort of job. I certainly shouldn't—
with Clara."

His wife was indignant. "I might have known you would be ready with the cold water," she declared. "Clara is—well, cranky, and particular and all that, but the opportunity is wonderful. The girl would travel and meet the best people——"

"She might remove their wraps, I admit."

"Nonsense! And if Clara took a fancy to her she might leave her a good sum of money when she died."

"Perhaps, providing the girl didn't die first. No, Gertrude, I'm sorry to disappoint you, but I don't think much of your idea. Anyway, according to my belief, you're approaching this thing from the wrong end. It isn't the girl herself you should try to influence, but her uncles, or guardians, or whatever they are. If I know her, and I've been making some inquiries, she won't leave them. She will consider that they need her at the house and store and she'll stay. They are the ones to influence. If the matter of her welfare and future was put to them in the right light they might—well, they might sacrifice themselves to benefit her."

"Rubbish! I know I'm right. She'll jump at the opportunity. I shall tell her about it this very afternoon."

"She won't accept; I'll bet on it."

His principal reason for non-belief in Mary-'Gusta's acceptance was his knowledge of his wife's lack of tact. The girl did not consider herself, nor was she, a subject of charity. And the position of combination friend and servant would not appeal to her. John Keith had an idea of his own concerning Mary-'Gusta, but it could wait until his wife's had failed.

It failed, of course, and Mrs. Keith, that evening, was indignant and angry.

"I never was so treated in my life," she declared.

145

"That girl didn't know her place at all. I'm through. I wash my hands of the whole matter."

"Wasn't she polite?" inquired Keith.

"Oh, she was polite enough, as far as that goes, but she wouldn't even consider my proposal. Wouldn't even hear me through. She said she had no thought of leaving South Harniss. She was quite satisfied and contented where she was. One would think I had come to ask a favor instead of conferring one. Why, she seemed to think my plan almost ridiculous."

"Did she say so?"

"No, of course she didn't. She thanked me and all that; but she snubbed me just the same. I'm disgusted. I'm through—absolutely and completely through trying to help that girl!"

Keith did not say, "I told you so"; in fact, he said little or nothing more at the time. But a day or two afterwards he called at the store. Zoeth and Captain Shadrach were alone there, their niece having gone down to the house, a fact of which the caller was aware.

The partners liked John Keith. They considered him, as Captain Shad said, "a first-rate, everyday sort of feller," who did not patronize nor put on airs, even though he was a "summer man" and rich. When he talked with them it was of things they understood, local affairs, the cranberry crop, fishing, and the doings of the Board of Selectmen. He was willing to listen as well as talk and he did not refer to permanent residents as "natives," a habit of his wife's which irritated the Captain extremely.

"Jumpin' fire!" said the latter on one occasion, "every time that woman calls us town folks 'natives' I feel as if she cal'lated I lived up a tree and chucked coconuts at folks. I don't wonder some of the South Sea Islands heathen eat missionaries. If I *ate* that woman she might agree with me; she don't as 'tis. Every time I say yes she says no, and that makes me think yes harder'n ever."

So Mrs. Keith was not popular with the South Harniss natives, perhaps because she tried so hard to be; her husband, who apparently did not try to be, was. He and his opinions were liked and respected. When he came into the store, therefore, on this occasion, Zoeth and Shad welcomed him, asked him to sit down, and the conversation began with the astonishing rise in the price of sea-front property and drifted from that to other timely and general topics.

Just how it drifted to Mary-'Gusta and her future neither of the partners could have told—however, drift there it did, and they found themselves chanting her praises to their caller, who seemed much interested.

"She is a remarkably capable girl," observed Mr. Keith. "And before we realize it she will be a young woman. Are you planning that she shall keep store and keep house for you the rest of her life, or the rest of yours?"

Zoeth shook his head. "Why," he said, mildly, "I don't know's we've planned much about it so fur. Those things sort of take care of themselves, always seemed to me. Or the Almighty takes care of 'em for us."

Their visitor smiled. "Someone else will be willing and anxious to take care of her before many years, or I miss my guess," he said. "She is likely to marry, you know. There must be some promising young fellows down here."

Shadrach sniffed. It was a subject he never discussed with his partner and did not like even to think about. The remark of the hat and cap drummer concerning the coming of a "Mr. Right" had troubled him not a little.

"Ugh!" he grunted; "there's promisin' ones enough. Most of those that are contented to stay here in South Harniss are nothin' *but* promise; they ain't so strong on makin' good. 'Tain't like 'twas when Zoeth and me were young ourselves. Now all the smart, ambitious boys go up to the city to work."

"Some of the girls go up there, too, don't they? To school, or college? Didn't I hear that Christopher Mullet's daughter was at school in Bridgewater?"

"Ugh!" grunted Shadrach again. "I cal'late you did hear. If you didn't you're the only one in town that ain't. Becky Mullet—yes, and Chris, too—ain't done anything but brag about their Irene's goin' off to what they call 'finishin' school.' Judas! I see *her* finish. She ain't got—I swan that girl ain't got anything in her head but gas, and every time she opens her mouth she loses enough of that to keep a lighthouse lit up all night."

"Shadrach," murmured Zoeth, "don't say such unlikely things about folks. Be charitable as you can."

"Judas! I am—as much as I can. If I wasn't charitable to that Mullet girl I'd be talkin' yet. I hove to afore I'd got scarcely under way."

Keith put in a word. "Finishing schools are not all bad, by any means," he said. "There are various kinds and grades, of course, but a good private school for girls is a fine thing. It teaches them to meet and judge people of all kinds, and that fine feathers don't always make fine birds. Then, too, a girl at a good school of that sort is under strict discipline and her acquaintances, male acquaintances especially, are chosen with care. Sixteen to eighteen is a dangerous age for the average girl.

"By the way," he added, "did your niece tell you of her experience with that traveling salesman the other day, the fellow selling Christmas novelties? No? Well, I happened to be here at the time. It was rather interesting."

He told of Mary-'Gusta's session with Mr. Kron. The partners listened with growing indignation.

"Well, by the jumpin'!" exclaimed Captain Shad. "Did you ever hear such brassy talk in your life! I wish to thunder I'd been here. There'd have been one mighty sick patient ready for the doctor and he wouldn't have been a South Harniss native either. But Mary-'Gusta didn't take none of his sauce, I tell you; that girl of ours is all right!"

"Yes, she is all right. But she didn't enjoy the experience, that was plain enough, and, so far as I can see, she is likely to have a good many others of the same kind. Now it isn't my business, I know that; you can tell me to shut up and clear out any time you like, of course; but do you think it is just fair to a girl like your niece to condemn her to a life of storekeeping or the alternative of marrying one of the promising young men you've been talking about? Don't you think such a girl as she is deserves a chance; every chance you can give her?"

The two partners stared at him open-mouthed. Shadrach, as usual, spoke first.

"Condemn her?" he repeated. "Condemn Mary-'Gusta? A chance? Why——"

"Hush, Shadrach," interrupted Zoeth. "Mr. Keith ain't done yet. He's goin' to tell us what he means. Go on, Mr. Keith, what do you mean?"

Keith, having broken the ice, and found the water not so chilly as he had feared it might be, plunged in.

"Well, I mean this," he said. "I confess frankly that I have been very favorably impressed by your niece. She is an unusual girl—unusually pretty, of course, but much more than that. She is simple and brave and sensible and frank. If she were my daughter I should be very proud of her. I know you are. She should have, it seems to me, the opportunity to make the most of her qualities and personality. I've been thinking about her a great deal ever since my call at the store here the other day. Now I've got a suggestion to make. You can take it or leave it, but I assure you it is made with the best of intentions and solely in her interest as I see it; and I hope you'll take it after you've thought it over. Here it is."

He went on to impart the suggestion. His hearers listened, Zoeth silently and Shadrach with occasional mutterings and exclamations.

"So there you are," said Keith in conclusion. "The school is a good one, one of the best in Boston. Two years there will do worlds for your niece. It has done worlds for other girls I have known. It is rather expensive, of course, but, as I understand it, Mary has money of her own of which you, as her guardians, have charge. She couldn't spend a portion of that money to better advantage."

Zoeth said nothing, but he looked at the Captain and the Captain looked at him.

"She *has* money of her own, hasn't she?" inquired Mr. Keith. "I have been told she was left an independent fortune by her father."

There was another interval of silence. The partners were quite aware of the general belief in Mary-'Gusta's independent fortune. They had not discouraged that belief. It was no one's business but theirs and their respect and affection for Marcellus Hall had prevented the disclosure of the latter's poverty. That secret not even Mary-'Gusta knew; she, too, believed that the money which paid for her clothes and board and all the rest was her own. Her uncles had helped her to think so.

So when their visitor asked the pointed question Zoeth looked at Shadrach and the latter shook his head.

"Yup," he answered, brusquely, "it's true enough, I cal'late. Marcellus left her all he had. But—but look here, Mr. Keith. Do I understand you to advise us to send Mary-'Gusta away—to school—for two years? Jumpin' fire! How—how could we? She—why, what would we do without her?"

"It would be harder for you here in the store, of course."

"The store! 'Tain't the store I'm thinkin' about; it's me and Zoeth. What'll *we* do without her? Why, she —why, no daughter could mean more to us than that girl does, and if Zoeth and me was her own—er—mother and father we couldn't think more of her. We'd be adrift and out of sight of land if Mary-'Gusta went away. No, no, we couldn't think of such a thing."

"Not even for her sake? She's worth a pretty big sacrifice, a girl like that."

A long discussion followed, a discussion interrupted by the arrival of occasional customers but resumed as soon as each of these individuals departed. Zoeth asked a question.

"This—this Miss—er—What's-her-name's school you're talkin' about," he asked, "a reg'lar boardin' school, is it?"

"Yes, but there are day pupils. It was my idea, provided you two were willing to listen to my suggestion at all, to suggest that Mary attend as a day pupil. She might live near the school instead of at it. That would be much less expensive."

"Um-hm," mused Shadrach, "but—but she'd have to live somewheres, and I for one would want to be mighty particular what sort of a place she lived at."

"Naturally. Well, I have thought of that, too, and here is suggestion number three: I have a cousin—a cousin of my first wife's—who lives on Pinckney Street, which is not far from the Misses Cabot's school. This cousin—Mrs. Wyeth is her name—is a widow and she hasn't too much money. She doesn't keep a boarding house exactly, but she has been known to take a few of what she calls 'paying guests.' She's very Bostonian and very particular concerning the references and family connections of those guests, but I think I could manage that. If your niece were placed in her care she would have a real home and meet only the sort of people you would wish her to meet."

He might have added that Mrs. Wyeth, being under many obligations, pecuniary and otherwise, to her wealthy Chicago relative, would need only a hint from him to give Mary-'Gusta the care and attention of a parent, a very particular, Boston first-family parent. But, unlike his present wife, he was not in the habit of referring to his charities, so he kept this information to himself.

Zoeth sighed. "I declare," he said, "you're mighty kind in all this, Mr. Keith. I know that you're sartin this goin' away to school would do Mary-'Gusta a sight of good. But—but I swan I—I can't hardly bear to think of our lettin' her go away from us."

"I don't wonder at that. Just think it over and we'll have another talk later."

CHAPTER X

MR. KEITH and the Captain had that later talk—several talks, in fact—and a week after their first one Captain Shadrach suddenly announced that he was cal'latin' to run up to Boston just for a day on business and that Mary-'Gusta had better go along with him for company. Zoeth could tend store and get along all right until they returned. The girl was not so certain of the getting along all right, but Mr. Hamilton as well as the Captain insisted, so she consented at last. The Boston trip was not exactly a novelty to her—she had visited the city a number of times during the past few years—but a holiday with Uncle Shad was always good fun.

They took the early morning train and reached Boston about ten o'clock. Shadrach's business in the city seemed to be of a rather vague nature this time. They called at the offices of two or three of his old friends—ship-chandlers and marine outfitters on Commercial Street and Atlantic Avenue—and then the Captain, looking at his watch, announced that it was pretty nigh noontime and he cal'lated they had better be cruisin' up towards Pinckney Street. "Got an errand up in that latitude," he added.

Pinckney Street was on the hill in the rear of the Common and the State House and was narrow and crooked and old-fashioned.

"What in the world are we doing up here?" queried Mary-'Gusta. "There aren't any wholesale houses here,

I'm sure. Haven't you made a mistake, Uncle Shad?"

Shadrach, who had been consulting a page of his pocket memorandum book, replied that he cal'lated he'd got his bearin's, and, to the girl's astonishment, stopped before a brick dwelling with a colonial doorway and a white stone step which actually shone from scrubbing, and rang the bell.

The maid who answered the bell wore a white apron which crackled with starch. She looked as if she too had, like the step, been scrubbed a few minutes before.

"This is No. ——, ain't it?" inquired the Captain. "Humph! I thought so. I ain't so much of a wreck yet but that I can navigate Boston without a pilot. Is Mr. Keith in?"

The maid, who had received the pilot statement with uncomprehending astonishment, looked relieved.

"Yes, sir," she said. "Mr. Keith's here. Are you the ones he's expectin'? Walk in, please."

They entered the house. It was as spotlessly tidy within as without. The maid ushered them into a parlor where old mahogany and old family portraits in oil were very much in evidence.

"Sit down, please," she said. "I'll tell Mr. Keith you're here."

She left the room. Mary-'Gusta turned to the Captain in amazed agitation.

"Uncle Shad," she demanded, "why on earth did you come *here* to see Mr. Keith? Couldn't you have seen him at South Harniss?"

Shadrach shook his head. "Not today I couldn't," he said. "He's up here today."

"But what do you want to see him for?"

"Business, business, Mary-'Gusta. Mr. Keith and me

are tryin' to do a little stroke of business together. We've got a hen on, as the feller said. Say, this is kind of a swell house, ain't it? And clean—my soul! Judas! did I move this chair out of place? I didn't mean to. Looks as if it had set right in that one spot for a hundred years."

Keith entered at that moment, followed by an elderly lady whose gown was almost as old-fashioned as the furniture. She was a rather thin person but her face, although sharp, was not unkind in expression and her plainly arranged hair was white. Mary-'Gusta liked her looks; she guessed that she might be very nice indeed to people she knew and fancied; also that she would make certain of knowing them first.

"Hello, Captain Gould," hailed Keith. "Glad to see you. Found the place all right, I see."

"Yes—yes, I found it, Mr. Keith."

"I thought you wouldn't have any difficulty. Mary, how do you do?"

Mary-'Gusta and Mr. Keith shook hands.

"Captain," said Keith, "I want to introduce you to my cousin, Mrs. Wyeth."

Mrs. Wyeth bowed with dignity.

"How do you do, Captain Gould," she said.

"Why—why, I'm pretty smart, thank you, ma'am," stammered Shadrach, rather embarrassed at all this ceremony. "Pleased to meet you, ma'am."

"And this young lady," went on Keith, "is Miss Mary Lathrop. Miss Lathrop, this lady is Mrs. Wyeth, my cousin."

Mary-'Gusta, with the uneasy feeling that Mrs. Wyeth's gaze had been fixed upon her since she entered the room, bowed but said nothing.

"And now," said Mr. Keith, heartily, "we'll have

luncheon. You're just in time and Mrs. Wyeth has been expecting you."

The Captain's embarrassment reached its height at this invitation.

"No, no," he stammered, "we—we can't do that. Couldn't think of it, you know. We—we ain't a mite hungry. Had breakfast afore we left home, didn't we, Mary-'Gusta?"

Keith laughed. "Yes, I know," he said; "and you left home about half-past five. I've taken that early train myself. If you're not hungry you ought to be and luncheon is ready. Emily—Mrs. Wyeth—has been expecting you. She will be disappointed if you refuse."

Mrs. Wyeth herself put in a word here. "Of course they won't refuse, John," she said with decision. "They must be famished. Refuse! The idea! Captain Gould, Mr. Keith will look out for you; your niece will come with me. Luncheon will be ready in five minutes. Come, Mary. That's your name—Mary—isn't it? I'm glad to hear it. It's plain and it's sensible and I like it. The employment bureau sent me a maid a week ago and when she told me her name I sent her back again. It was Florina. That was enough. Mercy! All I could think of was a breakfast food. Come, Mary. Now, John, do be prompt."

That luncheon took its place in Mary-'Gusta's memory beside that of her first supper in the house at South Harniss. They were both memorable meals, although alike in no other respects. Mrs. Wyeth presided, of course, and she asked the blessing and poured the tea with dignity and businesslike dispatch. The cups and saucers were of thin, transparent China, with pictures of mandarins and pagodas upon them. They looked old-fashioned and they were; Mrs. Wyeth's grandfather had bought them himself in Hongkong in the days when he commanded a clipper ship and made voyages to the Far East. The teaspoons were queer little fiddle-patterned affairs; they were made by an ancestor who was a silversmith with a shop on Cornhill before General Gage's army was quartered in Boston. And cups and spoons and napkins were so clean that it seemed almost sacrilegious to soil them by use.

Captain Shadrach did not soil his to any great extent at first. The Captain was plainly overawed by the genteel elegance of his surrounding and the manner of his hostess. But Mr. Keith was very much at ease and full of fun and, after a time, a little of Shadrach's self-consciousness disappeared. When he learned that grandfather Wyeth had been a seafaring man he came out of his shell sufficiently to narrate, at Keith's request, one of his own experiences in Hongkong, but even in the midst of his yarn he never forgot to address his hostess as "ma'am" and he did not say "Jumpin' Judas" once.

After luncheon Mr. Keith and the Captain left the house together. "Goin' to attend to that little mite of business I spoke to you about, Mary-'Gusta," explained Shadrach, confidentially. "We'll be back pretty soon. I cal'late maybe you'd better wait here, that is," with a glance at Mrs. Wyeth, "if it'll be all right for you to."

"Of course it will be all right," declared Mrs. Wyeth promptly. "I shall be glad to have her."

"Thank you, ma'am. If she won't be in the way I——"

"If she were likely to be in the way I should say so. She won't be."

"Yes—er—yes, ma'am," stammered Shadrach. "Thank you, ma'am."

When he and Mr. Keith were out of the house he drew a long breath.

"Judas!" he observed, feelingly. "Say, that cousin of yours don't waste any words, does she? When it comes to speakin' what's in her mind she don't fool around none. She's as right up and down as a schooner's fo'mast."

Keith laughed heartily. "Emily is blunt and outspoken," he said. "She prides herself on that. But she is as square as a brick. She never says one thing to your face and another behind your back."

"No, I—I judge that's so. Well, that's all right; I ain't got any objections to that way of talkin' myself. But say, if every woman was like her there wouldn't be many sewin' circles, would there? The average sewin' circle meetin' is one part sew and three parts what So-and-so said."

When the little mite of business had been transacted and the pair returned to the Wyeth house they found Mrs. Wyeth and Mary-'Gusta awaiting them in the parlor. The girl had the feeling that she had been undergoing a rather vigorous cross-examination. Mrs. Wyeth had not talked a great deal herself and her manner, though brusque and matter of fact, was kind; but she had asked questions about Mary-'Gusta's home life, about Captain Gould and Mr. Hamilton, about school and friends and acquaintances. And her comments, when she made any, were direct and to the point.

She and Mr. Keith exchanged looks when the latter entered the room. Keith raised his eyebrows inquiringly. She nodded as if giving emphatic assent to his unspoken question.

Shadrach and Mary-'Gusta left the house soon afterward. While the Captain and Mr. Keith were whispering together in the hall, Mrs. Wyeth bade the girl good-by.

"I like you, my dear," said the lady. "You seem to be a sweet, sensible girl, and I don't meet as many of that kind nowadays as I could wish. I am sure we shall be good friends."

"And *what* did she mean by that?" demanded Mary-'Gusta, as she and the Captain walked along Pinckney Street together. "Why should we be good friends? Probably I'll never meet her again."

Shadrach smiled. "Oh, you can't always tell," he said. "Sometimes you meet folks oftener'n you think in this world."

Mary-'Gusta looked at him. "Uncle Shad," she said, "what does all this mean, anyway? Why did you go to her house? And what was the mysterious business of yours with Mr. Keith?"

The Captain shook his head. "We've got a hen on, same as I told you," he declared. "When it's time for the critter to come off the nest you'll see what's been hatched same as the rest of us. How'd you like that Mrs. Wyeth? Had a pretty sharp edge on her tongue, didn't she?"

Mary-'Gusta considered. "Yes," she answered; "she was outspoken and blunt, of course. But she is a lady— a real lady, I think—and I'm sure I should like her very much when I knew her better. I think, though, that she would expect a person to behave—behave in her way, I mean."

"Judas! I should say so. Don't talk! I ain't felt so much as if I was keepin' my toes on a chalk mark since I went to school. I don't know what her husband died of, but I'll bet 'twasn't curvature of the spine. If he didn't stand up straight 'twasn't his wife's fault."

Mary-'Gusta's curiosity concerning the mysterious business which had brought them to the city became greater than ever before it was time to take the train for home. Apparently all of that business, whatever it might be, had been transacted when her uncle and Mr. Keith took their short walk together after luncheon. Captain Shadrach seemed to consider his Boston errand done and the pair spent half of the hour before train time wandering along Tremont and Washington Streets looking into shop windows, and the other half in the waiting room of the South Station.

Great and growing as was her curiosity, the girl asked no more questions. She was determined not to ask them. And the Captain, neither while in the city nor during the homeward journey, referred to the "hen" in which he and his friend from Chicago were mutually interested. It was not until nine o'clock that evening, when supper was over and Zoeth, having locked up the store, was with them in the sitting-room, that the hitherto secretive fowl came off the nest.

Then Shadrach, having given his partner a look and received one in return, cleared his throat and spoke.

"Mary-'Gusta," he said, "me and your Uncle Zoeth have got some news for you. I cal'late you've been wonderin' a little mite what that business of Mr. Keith's and mine was, ain't you?"

Mary-'Gusta smiled. "I have wondered—just a little," she observed, with mild sarcasm.

"Yes—yes, I ain't surprised. Well, the business is done and it's settled, and it's about you."

"About me? Why, Uncle Shad! How can it be about me?"

"'Cause it can and it is, that's why. Mary-'Gusta, me and Zoeth have been thinkin' about you a good deal lately and we've come to the conclusion that we ain't treated you just right."

"Haven't treated me right? *You?*"

"Yes, us. You're a good girl and a smart girl—the smartest and best girl there is in this town. A girl like that ought to do somethin' better'n than stay here in South Harniss and keep store. Keepin' store's all right for old hulks like Zoeth Hamilton and Shad Gould, but you ain't an old hulk; you're a young craft right off the ways and you ought to have a chance to cruise in the best water there is."

"Uncle Shad, what are you talking about? Cruise in the best water?"

"That's what I said. You ought to mix with the best folks and get a fine education and meet somebody besides drummers and—and Sol Higgins's son. Selling coffins may be a good job, I don't say 'tain't; somebody's got to do it and we'll all have to invest in that kind of —er—furniture sometime or 'nother. And Dan Higgins is a good enough boy, too. But he ain't your kind."

"My kind! Uncle Shad, what in the world have I got to do with Dan Higgins and coffins—and all the rest of it?"

"Nothin', nothin' at all. That's what I'm tryin' to tell you if you'll give me a chance. Mary-'Gusta, your Uncle Zoeth and I have decided that you must go to school up to Boston, at the Misses Cabot's school there. You'll board along with that Mrs. Wyeth, the one we met today. She's a good woman, I cal'late, though she is so everlastin' straight up and down. You'll board there and you'll go to school to those Cabot women. And——"

But Mary-'Gusta interrupted. The hen was off the nest now, there was no doubt of that, and of all unexpected and impossible hatchings hers was the most complete. The absurdity of the idea, to the girl's mind, overshadowed even the surprise of it.

"What?" she said. "Uncle Shad, what——? Do you mean that you and Uncle Zoeth have been in conspiracy to send me away to school? To send me away to Boston?"

Shadrach nodded.

"No conspiracy about it," he declared. "Me and Zoeth and Mr. Keith, we——"

"Mr. Keith? Yes, yes, I see. It was Mr. Keith who put the idea in your head. How perfectly silly!"

"Silly? Why is it silly?"

"Because it is. It's ridiculous."

"No, it ain't, it's common sense. Other girls go to city finishin' schools, don't they? That Irene Mullet's just gone, for one. Don't you think we figger to do as much for our girl as Becky Mullet can do for hers? Jumpin' fire! If you ain't worth a hogshead of girls like Irene Mullet then I miss my guess."

"Hush, Uncle Shad; what difference does that make?"

And now Zoeth put in a word. "Mary-'Gusta," he said, "you know what a good school like the one Shad's been speakin' of can do for a girl. I know you know it. Now, be right down honest; wouldn't you like to have a couple of years, say, at a school like that, if you could have 'em just as well as not? Didn't you say not more'n a fortni't ago that you was glad Irene Mullet was goin' to have such a chance to improve herself?"

Mary-'Gusta had said that very thing; she could not truthfully deny it.

"Of course I did," she answered. "And I am glad. But Irene's case and mine are different. Irene isn't needed at home. I am, and——"

Shadrach broke in. "Ah, ha! Ah, ha! Zoeth," he crowed, triumphantly. "Didn't I tell you she'd say that? I knew she'd say she wouldn't go 'cause she'd think she'd ought to stay here and look out for us. Well, Mary-'Gusta, you listen to me. Zoeth and I are your guardians, lawfully appointed. We're your bosses, young lady, for a spell yet. And you're goin' to do as we say."

"But——"

"There ain't any 'buts.' The 'buts' are all past and gone. Mr. Keith has arranged for you to board and room along with Mrs. Wyeth and I've arranged for your schoolin' at the Cabot place. Yes, and I've done more'n that: I paid for your first year's schoolin' this very afternoon. So there! *That's* ended."

It was not ended, of course. Mary-'Gusta went to her room that night declaring she would not leave her uncles to attend any finishing school. They went to theirs vowing that she should. The real end came the next day when Zoeth put the subject before her in a new light by saying:

"Look here, Mary-'Gusta; just listen to me a minute and think. Suppose the boot was on t'other foot: suppose you wanted us to do somethin' to please you, you'd expect us to do it, wouldn't you? Anyhow, you know mighty well we *would* do it. Now we want you to do this to please us. We've set our hearts on it."

Mary-'Gusta was silent for a minute or more. The partners watched her anxiously. Then she asked an unusual question, one concerning her own financial status.

"Can I afford it?" she asked. "Have I money enough of my own?"

Zoeth looked troubled. Shadrach, however, answered promptly and diplomatically.

"Haven't I told you," he said, "that Zoeth and me are your guardians? And didn't I say we'd gone into the thing careful and deliberate? And didn't I pay your first year's schoolin' yesterday? Don't that alone show what we think about the money. Be still, Zoeth; that's enough. Well, Mary-'Gusta?"

Mary-'Gusta considered a moment longer. Then she rose and, crossing the room, gave them each a kiss.

"I'll go," she said, simply. "I'll go because I think you mean it and that it will please you. For that reason and no other I'll go."

CHAPTER XI

THE Misses Cabot's school was to open on the fifteenth of September and, on the morning of the fourteenth, Mary-'Gusta bade her guardians good-by on the platform of the South Harniss railway station. Shadrach had intended going to Boston with her, but she had firmly insisted on going alone.

"I must get used to being away from you both," she said, "and you must get used to having me go. It will be best for all of us to say good-by here. It won't be for *very* long; I'll be home at Christmas, you know."

The three weeks prior to the fateful fourteenth had been crowded with activities. Twice the girl and Captain Shadrach had journeyed to Boston, where in company with Mrs. Wyeth, whose services had been volunteered in a crisp but kindly note, they visited shops and selected and purchased—that is, the feminine members of the party selected and the Captain paid for—a suit and waists and hats and other things which it appeared were necessary for the wardrobe of a young lady at finishing school. Shadrach would have bought lavishly, but Mrs. Wyeth's common sense guided the selections and Mary-'Gusta was very particular as to price. Shadrach, at the beginning, made a few suggestions concerning colors and styles, but the suggestions were disregarded. The Captain's taste in colors was not limited; he fancied almost any hue, provided it was bright enough. His ward would have looked like an animated crazy quilt if he had had his way.

He grumbled a little as they journeyed back to South Harniss.

"She may be all right, that Wyeth woman," he said, "but she's too everlastin' sober-sided to suit me. Take that hat you and she bought; why, 'twas as plain, and hadn't no more fuss and feathers than a minister's wife's bonnet. You ain't an old maid; no, nor a Boston first-family widow, neither. Now, the hat *I* liked—the yellow and blue one—had some get-up-and-git. If you wore that out on Tremont Street folks would turn around and look at you."

Mary-'Gusta laughed and squeezed his hand. "You silly Uncle Shad," she said, "don't you know that is exactly what I don't want them to do?"

Shadrach turned his gaze in her direction. She was at the end of the car seat next to the window and against the light of the setting sun her face and head were silhouetted in dainty profile. The Captain sighed.

"Well," he said, philosophically, "I don't know's we need to argue. I cal'late they'll look some as 'tis."

Her parting instructions to her uncles were many and diversified. Zoeth must be sure and change to his heavy flannels on the first of October. He must not forget rubbers when the ground was damp, and an umbrella when it rained. If he caught cold there was the medicine Doctor Harley had prescribed. He must not sit up after ten o'clock; he must not try to read the paper without first hunting for his spectacles. These were a few of his orders. Shadrach's list was even longer. It included going to church every other Sunday: keeping his Sunday shoes blacked: not forgetting to change his collar every morning: to get his hair cut at least once in six weeks: not to eat pie just before going to bed, "because you know if you do, you always have the nightmare and groan and moan and wake up everyone but yourself": not to say "Jumpin'" or "Creepin' Judas" any oftener than he could help: to be sure and not cut prices in the store just because a customer asked him to do so—and goodness knows how much more.

As for Isaiah Chase, his list was so lengthy and varied that the responsibility quite overwhelmed him.

"Gosh t'mighty!" exclaimed Isaiah, desperately. "I'll never be able to live up to all them sailin' orders and I know it. I've put some of 'em down on a piece of paper, but I ain't even got them straight, and as for the million or two others—whew! I'm to dust every day, and sweep every other day, and change the tablecloth, and see that the washin' goes when it ought to, and feed the horse the cat—no, no, feed the cat oats— Oh, consarn it! Feed the cat and the horse and the hens their reg'lar vittles at reg'lar times and—and—Oh, my soul! Yes, and let alone my own self and all that's laid onto me, I must keep an eye on Captain Shad and Zoeth and see that they do what's been laid onto *them*. I swan to man! I'm a hard-workin', painstakin' feller of my age, but I ain't as young as I used to be, and I'm human and not a walkin' steam-engyne. I'll do the best I can, but—but first thing you know I'll be drove into heavin' up my job. *Then* this craft'll be on its beam ends, I bet you! They'll appreciate me then, when it's too late."

The farewells at the railway station were brief. They were very hard to say and neither the partners nor Mary-'Gusta could trust themselves to talk more than was necessary. The train drew up beside the platform; then it moved on. A hand waved from the car window; Shadrach and Zoeth waved in return. The rear car disappeared around the curve by Solomon Higgins' cranberry shanty.

Mr. Hamilton sighed heavily.

"She's gone, Shadrach," he said. "Mary-'Gusta's gone."

Shadrach echoed the sigh.

"Yes, she's gone," he agreed. "I feel as if the best part of you and me had gone along with her. Well, t'other parts have got to go back to the store and wait on customers, I presume likely. Heave ahead and let's do it. Ah, hum! I cal'late we'd ought to be thankful we've got work to do, Zoeth. It'll help take up our minds. There are goin' to be lonesome days for you and me, shipmate."

There were lonely days for Mary-'Gusta also, those of that first month at Mrs. Wyeth's and at the Misses Cabot's school. For the first time in her life she realized what it meant to be homesick. But in the letters which she wrote to her uncles not a trace of the homesickness was permitted to show and little by little its keenest pangs wore away. She, too, was thankful for work, for the study which kept her from thinking of other things.

The Misses Cabot—their Christian names were Priscilla and Hortense—she found to be middle-aged maiden ladies, eminently prim and proper, and the educational establishment over which they presided a sort of Protestant nunnery ruled according to the precepts of the Congregational Church and the New England aristocracy. Miss Priscilla was tall and thin and her favorite author was Emerson; she quoted Emerson extensively and was certain that real literature died when he did. Miss Hortense was younger, plumper, and more romantic. She quoted Longfellow and occasionally Oliver Wendell

Holmes, although she admitted she considered the latter
rather too frivolous at times. Both sisters were learned,
dignified, and strict disciplinarians. Also, in the eyes
of both a male person younger than forty-five was
labeled "Danger—Keep Away." But one creature of the
masculine gender taught in their school; he was white-
haired Doctor Barnes, professor of the dead languages.
It was the prevailing opinion among the scholars that
Doctor Barnes, when at home, occupied an apartment
in the Greek Antiquity section of the Art Museum, where
he slept and ate surrounded by the statues and busts
of his contemporaries.

As for the scholars themselves, there were about forty
of them, girls—or young ladies: the Misses Cabot invariably referred to and addressed them as "young ladies"
—from Boston and New York and Philadelphia, even
from Chicago and as far south as Baltimore. Almost
all were the daughters of well-to-do parents, almost all
had their homes in cities. There were very few who,
like Mary-'Gusta, had lived all their lives in the country. Some were pretty, some were not; some were giddy
and giggly, some solemn and studious, some either according to mood; some were inclined to be snobbish,
others simple and "everyday." In short, the school
was like almost any school of its kind.

Mary-'Gusta entered this school and, doing so, ceased
to be Mary-'Gusta, becoming Miss Lathrop to her in-
structors and Mary to her intimates among the scholars. And at Mrs. Wyeth's she was Mary or Miss
Lathrop or Miss Mary, according to the age, length of
acquaintance, or station of the person addressing her.
But she always thought of herself as Mary-'Gusta and
her letters written to Uncle Shad or Uncle Zoeth were
so signed.

She found, after the hard work of beginning, that she could keep abreast of her class in studies without undue exertion. Also she found that, the snobs excepted, the girls at the Misses Cabot's school were inclined to be sociable and friendly. She made no bid for their friendship, being a self-respecting young person whose dislike of imitation was as strong as ever, but, perhaps because she did not bid or imitate but continued to be simply and sincerely herself, friends came to her. Most of these friends received monthly allowances far greater than hers, and most of them wore more expensive gowns and in greater variety, but she showed no envy nor offered apologies, and if she sometimes wished, being human, that her wardrobe was a trifle more extensive she kept that wish to herself.

Her liking for Mrs. Wyeth grew into a real affection. And the prim and practical matron grew more and more fond of her. The girl came to be considered, and almost to consider herself, one of the family. The "family" consisted of Mrs. Wyeth, Mary, Miss Pease, the other "paying guest," and Maggie, the maid, and Nora, the cook. Miss Pease was an elderly spinster without near relatives, possessed of an income and a love of travel which she gratified by occasional European trips. She and her closest friend, Mrs. Wyeth, disagreed on many subjects, but they united in the belief that Boston was a suburb of Paradise and that William Ellery Channing was the greatest of religious leaders. They attended the Arlington Street Unitarian Church, and Mary often accompanied them there for Sunday morning or afternoon service.

The conviction of the Misses Cabot that youthful manhood was dangerous and to be shunned like the plague Mary soon discovered was not shared by the majority of

the young ladies. If Miss Priscilla and Miss Hortense
had had their way Harvard University and the Institute
of Technology would have been moved forthwith to some
remote spot like the North Pole or San Francisco. There
were altogether too many "cousins" or "sons of old
family friends" calling at the school to deliver messages from parents or guardians or the said friends.
These messengers, young gentlemen with budding mus-
taches and full-blown raiment, were rigidly inspected and
their visits carefully chaperoned: but letters came and
were treasured and the cheerful inanity of their contents imparted, in strict secrecy, to bosom friends of
the recipients.

Mary received no such letters. No cousins or family friends called to deliver messages to her. No photographs of young fellows in lettered sweaters were
hidden among her belongings. Her friends in the school
thought this state of affairs very odd and they sometimes asked pointed questions.

Miss Barbara Howe, whose home was in Brookline
and whose father was the senior partner of an old and
well-known firm of downtown merchants, was the leading questioner. She liked Mary and the latter liked her.
Barbara was pretty and full of spirits and, although
she was the only child, and a rather spoiled one, in
a wealthy family, there was no snobbishness in her
make-up.

"But I can't see," she declared, "what you have been
doing all the time. Where have you been keeping yourself? Don't you know *anybody?*"

Mary smiled. "Oh, yes," she replied, "I know a good
many people."

"You know what I mean. Don't you know any of
the fellows at Harvard, or Tech, or Yale, or anywhere?

I know dozens. And you must know some. You know Sam Keith; you said you did."

Mary admitted that she knew Sam slightly.

"Isn't he fun! Sam and I are great chums. Doesn't he dance divinely!"

"I don't know. I never saw him dance."

"Then you've missed something. Do you know his friend, the one on the football team—Crawford Smith, his name is—do you know him?"

Mary nodded. "I—I've met him," she said.

"You *have?* Don't you think he is perfectly splendid?"

"I don't know. Is he?"

"Of course he is. Haven't you read about him in the papers? He made that long run for a touchdown in the Yale game. Oh, you should have seen it! I couldn't speak for two days after that game. He was just as cool and calm. All the Yale men were trying to get him and he dodged—I never saw anyone so cool and who kept his head so well."

"I thought the papers spoke most of the way he kept his feet."

"Then you did read about it! Of course you did! I'm just dying to know him. All the girls are crazy about him. Where did you meet him? Tell me!"

Mary smiled. On the occasion of her only meeting with Crawford Smith that young fellow had been anything but cool.

"I met him in my uncle's store at South Harniss," she said. "It was three years ago."

"And you haven't seen him since? He is a great friend of Sam's. And Sam's people have a summer home at the Cape. Perhaps you'll meet him there again."

"Perhaps."

"Goodness! One would think you didn't want to."

"Why, I don't know that I do, particularly. Why should I?"

"Why should you! Mary Lathrop, I do think you are the queerest girl. You don't talk like a girl at all. Sometimes I think you are as old as—as Prissy." "Prissy" was the disrespectful nickname by which the young ladies referred, behind her back, to Miss Priscilla Cabot.

Mary laughed. "Not quite, I hope," she said. "But I don't see why I should be so very anxious to meet Crawford Smith. And I'm sure he isn't anxious to meet me. If all the other girls are crazy about him, that ought to be enough, I should think."

This astonishing profession of indifference to the fascination of the football hero, indifference which Miss Barbara declared to be only make-believe, was made on a Saturday. The next day, as Mrs. Wyeth and Mary were on their way home from church, the former made an announcement.

"We are to have a guest, perhaps guests, at dinner this noon," she said. Sunday dinner at Mrs. Wyeth's was served, according to New England custom, at one o'clock.

"Samuel, Mr. John Keith's son, is to dine with us," continued Mrs. Wyeth. "He may bring a college friend with him. You have met Samuel, haven't you, Mary?"

Mary said that she had. She was a trifle embarrassed at the prospect of meeting Sam Keith in her new surroundings. At home, in South Harniss, they had met many times, but always at the store. He was pleasant and jolly and she liked him well enough, although she had refused his invitations to go on sailing parties and the like. She knew perfectly well that his mother and sister would not have approved of these invitations, for in the feminine Keith mind there was a great gulf fixed between the summer resident and the native. The latter was to be helped and improved but not encouraged socially beyond a certain point. Mary sought neither help nor improvement of that kind. Sam, it is true, had never condescended or patronized, but he had never called at her home nor had she been asked to visit his.

And now she was to meet him in a house where she was considered one of the family. His father had been influential in bringing her there. Did Sam know this and, if he did, what influence would the knowledge have upon his manner toward her? Would he be lofty and condescending or, on the other hand, would he pretend a familiar acquaintanceship which did not exist? Alone in her room she considered these questions and then put them from her mind. Whatever his manner might be, hers, she determined, should be what it had always been. And if any embarrassment was evident to others at this meeting it should not be on her part.

When she came downstairs, Mrs. Wyeth called to her to come into the parlor. As she entered the room two young men rose from the chairs beside the mahogany center table. One of these young men was Sam Keith; she had expected to see Sam, of course. But the other —the other was the very individual in whose daring deeds and glorified personality she had expressed a complete lack of interest only the day before, the young fellow whom she had last seen racing madly across the fields in the rear of Hamilton and Company's store with the larger portion of a sheet of sticky fly paper attached to his white flannels. Mr. Crawford Smith was taller and broader than on that memorable occasion but she recognized him instantly.

It was evident that he did not recognize her. Mrs.. Wyeth came to meet her.

"Mary," she said, "you know Samuel, I think. You and he have met before. Samuel, will you introduce your friend?"

Sam was staring at Mary with eyes which expressed a variety of emotions, intense surprise the most prominent. He was in a state which Barbara Howe would have described as "fussed," one most unusual for him. He had known of Mary's presence in the house; after the affair was settled John Keith told his family what he had done, facing with serene philosophy his wife's displeasure and prophecies of certain regrets. Sam had vivid and pleasing recollections of the pretty country girl in the South Harniss store. He had not told his college friend that they were to meet her that day, one reason being that he was not certain they would meet, and the other a secret misgiving that it might be well to wait and inspect and listen before boasting of previous acquaintanceship. Sam's mother had lectured him on the subject before he left home. "Don't be too familiar, Sam," was her warning. "You may be sorry if you do. The girl is well enough here in South Harniss, where she is accustomed to her surroundings, but in Boston she may be quite out of place and impossible. I have told your father so, but he won't listen, of course. Don't *you* be foolish, for my sake."

But here was no green country girl. The self-possessed young woman who stood before him looked no more out of place and impossible in Mrs. Wyeth's dignified and aristocratic parlor than she had in the store where he had last seen her. Her gown was simple and inexpensive but it was stylish and becoming. And her manner—well, her manner was distinctly more at ease than his at that moment. Mary had been but eight weeks among the Misses Cabot's young ladies, but she had used her eyes and her brain during that time; she was adaptable and had learned other things than those in the curriculum. Also, she was prepared for this meeting and had made up her mind to show no embarrassment.

So the usually *blasé* Samuel was the embarrassed party. He looked and stammered. Mrs. Wyeth was surprised and shocked.

"Samuel," she said sharply, "what is the matter with you? Why don't you speak and not stand there staring?"

Sam, with an effort, recovered some of his self-possession.

"Was I staring?" he said. "I beg your pardon, Cousin Emily. Er—How do you do, Miss Lathrop?"

Mrs. Wyeth sniffed.

"Mercy!" she exclaimed. "Is your acquaintance as formal as that? I thought you knew each other. The boys and girls of this generation are beyond me. 'Miss Lathrop,' indeed!"

Mary smiled. "Perhaps he didn't expect to see me here, Mrs. Wyeth," she said. "How do you do, Sam?"

She and Sam shook hands. Mrs. Wyeth asked another question.

"Didn't you know Mary was with me, Samuel?" she asked.

"Oh, yes, Cousin Emily, I knew. I knew she was here, of course. But—but I didn't—by George!" with a sudden outburst of his real feelings, "I hardly knew her, though. Really, I didn't."

Mary laughed. "Have I grown so much older in two months?" she asked.

"Oh, you haven't changed that way. I—I——" The young man, realizing that he was getting into deep water, seized an opportunity to scramble out. "Oh, I forgot!" he exclaimed. "Sorry, Crawford. Mary—Miss Lathrop, I want to present my friend, Crawford Smith. He's my roommate at college."

Mary and Crawford shook hands.

"I have met Mr. Smith, too, before," she said.

The young gentlemen, both of them, looked astonished.

"Have you?" cried Sam. "Oh, I say! I didn't know that. When was it?"

His friend, too, was plainly puzzled. "I hardly think so," he said. "I don't believe I should have forgotten it. I don't remember——"

"Don't you remember coming into my uncles' store at South Harniss with Miss Keith, Sam's sister? You bought some"—with a mischievous twinkle—"some marshmallows, among other things. I sold them to you."

"You? Great Scott! Are you—why that girl's name was—what was it?"

"It was the same as mine, Mary Augusta Lathrop. But in South Harniss they call me Mary-'Gusta."

"That was it! And you are Mary-'Gusta? Yes, of course you are! Well, I ought to be ashamed, I suppose, but I didn't recognize you. I *am* ashamed. I was awfully obliged to you that day. You helped me out of a scrape."

Sam, who had been listening with increasing curiosity, broke in.

"Say, what's all this?" he demanded. "When was this, Crawford? What scrape? You never told me."

"And you didn't tell me that Miss Lathrop was here. You didn't say a word about her."

"Eh? Didn't I? I must have forgotten to mention it. She—she *is* here, you know."

Mrs. Wyeth shook her head.

"Samuel, you're perfectly idiotic today," she declared. "Of course she is here; anyone with eyes can see she is. She is—ahem—visiting me and she is attending the Misses Cabot's school. There! Now, Mr. Smith understands, I hope. And dinner is ready. Don't any of you say another word until we are at the table. My father used to say that lukewarm soup was the worst sort of cold reception and I agree with him."

During dinner Sam was tremendously curious to discover how and where his friend and Mary had met and what the scrape might be to which Crawford had referred. But his curiosity was unsatisfied. Mr. Smith refused to tell and Mary only smiled and shook her head when questioned.

The young people furnished most of the conversation during the meal. The recent football season and its triumphant ending were discussed, of course, and the prospects of the hockey team came in for its share. Sam, it appeared, was out for a place on the hockey squad.

"You must see some of the games, Mary," he said. "I'll get tickets for you and Cousin Emily. You're crazy about sports, aren't you, Cousin Emily."

Mrs. Wyeth regarded him through her eyeglasses.

"I imagine," she observed, "that that remark is intended as a joke. I saw one football game and the spectacle of those boys trampling each other to death before my eyes, and of you, Samuel Keith, hopping up and down shrieking, 'Tear 'em up' and 'Smash 'em' was the nearest approach to insanity I ever experienced. Since that time I have regarded Doctor Eliot as President Emeritus of an asylum and *not* a university."

Sam was hugely delighted. "That's football," he declared. "I will admit that no one but lunatics like

Crawford here play football. Hockey, now, is different. *I* play hockey."

Crawford seemed surprised.

"Do you?" he asked, with eager interest. "No one has ever guessed it, not even the coach. You shouldn't keep it a secret from *him,* Sam."

Miss Pease, having been invited out that day, was not present at dinner. After the coffee was served the irrepressible Sam proposed a walk.

"You won't care to go, Cousin Emily," he said, "but I'm sure Mary will. It is a fine afternoon and she needs the air. Crawford isn't much of a walker; he can stay and keep Cousin Emily company. We won't be long."

Before Mary could decline this disinterested invitation Mrs. Wyeth saved her the trouble.

"Thank you, Samuel," she said, crisply. "Your kindness is appreciated, particularly by Mr. Smith and myself. I can see that he is delighted with the idea. But Mary and I are going to the afternoon service at the Arlington Street church. So you will have to excuse us."

This should have been a squelcher, but it was not. Sam announced that he and Crawford would go with them. "We were thinking of going to church, weren't we, Crawford? It is just what I suggested, you remember."

Mrs. Wyeth said "Humph," and that was all. She and Mary went to their rooms to get ready. Sam, surprised at the unexpected success of his sudden inspiration and immensely tickled, chuckled in triumph. But his joy was materially lessened when the quartette left the house.

"These sidewalks are too narrow for four," declared Mrs. Wyeth. "Samuel, you may walk with me. Mary, you and Mr. Smith must keep close at our heels and walk fast. I never permit myself or my guests to be late at church."

During the walk Crawford asked a number of questions. How long had his companion been in the city? How long did she intend staying? Did she plan returning to the school for another year? Where would she spend the Christmas vacation? Mary said she was going home, to South Harniss, for the holidays.

"It's a bully old place, Cape Cod," declared Crawford. "I never had a better time than I did on that visit at Sam's. Wish I were going there again some day."

"Why don't you?" asked Mary.

The young man shook his head. "Orders from home," he said. "Father insists on my coming home to him the moment the term closes. I made that visit to Sam's on my own responsibility and I got fits for doing it. Dad seems to have a prejudice against the East. He won't come here himself and he doesn't like to have me stay any longer than is absolutely necessary. When I wrote him I was at South Harniss he telegraphed me to come home in a hurry. He is Eastern born himself, lived somewhere this way when he was young, but he doesn't talk about it and has more prejudices against Eastern ways and Eastern people than if he'd lived all his life in Carson City. Won't even come on to see me play football. I doubt if he comes to Commencement next spring; and I graduate, too."

"I wonder he permitted you to go to Harvard," said Mary.

"He had to permit it. I've always been for Harvard ever since I thought about college. Dad was all for a Western university, but I sat back in the stirrups and pulled for Harvard and finally he gave in. He generally gives in if I buck hard enough. He's a bully old Dad and we're great pals, more like brothers than father and son. The only point where we disagree is his confounded sectional prejudice. He thinks the sun not only sets in the West but rises there."

The girl learned that he intended entering the Harvard Medical School in the fall.

"I had to fight for that, too," he said, with a laugh. "I've always wanted to be a doctor but Dad wouldn't give in for ever so long. He is interested in mining properties there at home and it was his idea that I should come in with him when I finished school. But I couldn't see it. I wanted to study medicine. Dad says there are almost as many starving doctors as there are down-at-the-heel lawyers; if I go in with him, he says, I shall have what is practically a sure thing and a soft snap for the rest of my days. That doesn't suit me. I want to work; I expect to. I want to paddle my own canoe. I may be the poorest M.D. that ever put up a sign, but I'm going to put that sign up just the same. And if I starve I shan't ask him or anyone else to feed me."

He laughed again as he said it, but there was a determined ring in his voice and a square set to his chin which Mary noticed and liked. He meant what he said, that was evident.

"I think a doctor's profession is one of the noblest and finest in the world," she said.

"Do you? Good for you! So do I. It doesn't bring in the dollars as fast as some others, but it does seem a man's job to me. The big specialists make a lot of money too, but that isn't exactly what I mean. Some of the best men I've met were just country doctors, working night and day in all sorts of weather and getting paid or not, just as it happened. That old Doctor

Harley down in your town is one of that kind, I think. I saw something of his work while I was there."

"Did you? I shouldn't have thought you had time for that, with all the picnics and sailing parties."

"I did, though. I met him at Sam's. Mrs. Keith had a cold or a cough or something. He and I got to talking and he asked me to come and see him. I went, you bet! Went out with him on some of his drives while he made his calls, you know. He told me a lot of things. He's a brick.

"It's queer," he went on, after a moment, "but I felt really at home down there in that little place. Seemed as if I had been there before and—and—by George, almost as if I belonged there. It was my first experience on and around salt water, but that seemed natural, too. And the people—I mean the people that belong there, not the summer crowd—I liked them immensely. Those two fine old cards that kept the store—Eh, I beg pardon; they are relatives of yours, aren't they? I forgot."

"They are my uncles," said Mary, simply. "I have lived with them almost all my life. They are the best men in the world."

"They seemed like it. I'd like to know them better. Hello! here's that confounded church. I've enjoyed this walk ever so much. Guess I've done all the talking, though. Hope I haven't bored you to death gassing about my affairs."

"No, you haven't. I enjoyed it."

"Did you really? Yes, I guess you did or you wouldn't say so. You don't act like a girl that pretends. By George! It's a relief to have someone to talk to, someone that understands and appreciates what a fellow is thinking about. Most girls want to talk football and dancing and all that. I like football immensely and dancing too, but there is something else in life. Even Sam—he's as good as they make but he doesn't care to listen to anything serious—that is, not long."

Mary considered. "I enjoyed listening," she said, "and I was glad to hear you liked South Harniss and my uncles."

On the way home, after the service, it was Sam Keith who escorted Mary, while Mrs. Wyeth walked with Mr. Smith. Sam's conversation was not burdened with seriousness. Hockey, dances, and good times were the subjects he dealt with. Was his companion fond of dancing? Would she accompany him to one of the club dances some time? They were great fun. Mrs. Wyeth could chaperon them, of course.

Mary said she was afraid she would be too busy to accept. As a matter of fact, knowing what she did of his mother's feelings, she would have accepted no invitations from Sam Keith even if nothing else prevented her doing so.

"My studies take a good deal of my time," she said.

Sam laughed. "You'll get over that," he declared. "I studied like blue blazes my freshman year, but after that—I should worry. Say, I'm mighty glad I came over here today. I'm coming again. I'll be a regular boarder."

The young men said good-by at the Wyeth door. Mrs. Wyeth did not ask them in, although the persistent Samuel threw out some pointed hints.

Crawford Smith and Mary shook hands.

"I've had an awfully good time," declared the former. Then, turning to Mrs. Wyeth, he asked: "May I call occasionally?"

Mrs. Wyeth's answer was, as usual, frank and unmistakable.

"Yes," she said. "I shall be very glad to see you—occasionally."

Crawford turned to Mary.

"May I?" he asked.

Mary scarcely knew how to reply. There was no real reason why he should not call; she liked him so far. His frankness and earnestness of purpose appealed to her. And yet she was not at all sure that it was wise to continue the acquaintance. In her mind this coming to Boston to school was a very serious matter. Her uncles had sent her there to study; they needed her at home, but that need they had sacrificed in order that she might study and improve. Nothing else, friendships or good times or anything, must interfere with the purpose with which she had accepted the sacrifice.

So she hesitated.

"May I?" repeated Crawford.

"Why, I don't know. I imagine I shall be very busy most of the time."

"That's all right. If you're busy you can send word for me to vamoose. That will be part of the bargain. Good-by."

Mrs. Wyeth's first remark, after entering, was concerning Sam's friend.

"I rather like that young person," she said. "Samuel idolizes him, of course, but Samuel would worship a hyena if it played football. But this Smith boy"—in Mrs. Wyeth's mind any male under thirty was a boy—"seems to have some common sense and a mind of his own. I don't approve of his name nor the howling wilderness he comes from, but he can't help those drawbacks, I suppose. However, if he is to call here we must know something about him. I shall make inquiries."

CHAPTER XII

THE school term ended on a Saturday morning in mid-December. Mary's trunk was packed and ready, and she and it reached the South Station long before train time. She was going home, home for the holidays, and if she had been going on a trip around the world she could not have been more delighted at the prospect. And her delight and anticipations were shared in South Harniss. Her uncles' letters for the past fortnight had contained little except joyful announcements of preparations for her coming.

We are counting the minutes [wrote Zoeth]. The first thing Shadrach does every morning is to scratch another day off the calendar. I never saw him so worked up and excited and I calculate I ain't much different myself. I try not to set my heart on things of this world more than I ought to, but it does seem as if I couldn't think of much else but our girl's coming back to us. I am not going to worry the way Shadrach does about your getting here safe and sound. The Lord's been mighty good to us and I am sure He will fetch you to our door all right. I am contented to trust you in His hands.

P. S. One or both of us will meet you at the depot.

Captain Shad's epistle was more worldly but not more coherent.

Be sure and take the train that comes right on through [he wrote]. Don't take the one that goes to Woods Hole.

Zoeth is so fidgety and nervous for fear you will make
a mistake that he keeps me on pins and needles. Isaiah
ain't much better. He swept out the setting-room twice
last week and if he don't roast the cat instead of the chicken
he is calculating to kill, it will be a mercy. I am the only
one aboard the ship that keeps his head and I tell them not
to worry. Be sure you take that through train. And look
out for them electric cars, if you come to the depot in one.
Better settle on the one you are going to take and then take
the one ahead of it so as to be sure and not be late. Your
train leaves the dock at quarter-past four. The Woods Hole
one is two minutes earlier. Look out and not take that.
Zoeth is afraid you will make a mistake, but I laugh at
him. Don't take the wrong train.

Mary laughed when she read these letters, but there
was a choke in the laugh. In spite of the perils of
travel by the electrics and the New Haven railroad, she
reached South Harniss safe, sound, and reasonably on
time. The first person she saw on the platform of the
station was Captain Shadrach. He had been pacing
that platform for at least forty minutes.

He spied her at the same time and came rushing to
greet her, both hands outstretched.

"And here you be!" he exclaimed with enthusiasm.

Mary laughed happily.

"Yes, Uncle Shad, here I am," she said. "Are you
glad to see me?"

Shadrach looked at her.

"*Jumpin'!*" was the only answer he made, but it was
fervent and sufficient.

They rode home together in the old buggy. As they
reached the corner by the store Mary expected the vehi-
cle to be brought to a halt at the curb, but it was not.
The Captain chirruped to the horse and drove straight on.

"Why, Uncle Shad!" exclaimed the girl. "Aren't you going to stop?"

"Eh? Stop? What for?"

"Why, to see Uncle Zoeth, of course. He's at the store, isn't he?"

Shadrach shook his head.

"No, he ain't," he said. "He's to home."

Mary was amazed and a trifle alarmed. One partner of Hamilton and Company was there in the buggy with her. By all the rules of precedent and South Harniss business the other should have been at the store. She knew that her uncles had employed no clerk or assistant since she left.

"But—but is Uncle Zoeth sick?" she asked.

"Sick? No, no, course he ain't sick. If he didn't have no better sense than to get sick the day you come home I'd—I'd—I don't know's I wouldn't drown him. *He* ain't sick—unless," he added, as an afterthought, "he's got Saint Vitus dance from hoppin' up and down to look out of the window, watchin' for us."

"But if he isn't sick, why isn't he at the store? Who is there?"

The Captain chuckled.

"Not a solitary soul," he declared. "That store's shut up tight and it's goin' to stay that way this whole blessed evenin'. Zoeth and me we talked it over. I didn't know but we'd better get Abel Snow's boy or that pesky Annabel or somebody to stay while we was havin' supper. You see, we was both sot on eatin' supper with you tonight, no matter store or not, and Isaiah, he was just as sot as we was. But all to once Zoeth had an idea. 'Shadrach,' he says, 'in Scriptur' times when people was real happy, same as we are now, they used to make a sacrifice to the Almighty to show how glad and grateful they was. Let's you and me make a sacrifice; let's sacrifice this evenin's trade—let's shut up the store on account of our girl's comin' home.' 'Good idea!' says I, so we did it."

Mary looked at him reproachfully.

"Oh, Uncle Shad," she said, "you shouldn't have done that. It was dear and sweet of you to think of it, but you shouldn't have done it. It didn't need any sacrifice to prove that you were glad to see me."

Shadrach winked over his shoulder.

"Don't let that sacrifice worry you any," he observed. "The sacrifice is mainly in Zoeth's eye. Fur's I'm concerned—well, Jabez Hedges told me yesterday that Rastus Young told him he cal'lated he'd have to be droppin' in at the store some of these nights to buy some rubber boots and new ileskins. We sold him the ones he's got four years ago and he ain't paid for 'em yet. No, no, Mary-'Gusta, don't you worry about that sacrifice. I can sacrifice Rastus Young's trade eight days in the week and make money by it. Course I didn't tell Zoeth that; have to humor these pious folks much as we can, you know."

Mary smiled, but she shook her head. "It's no use your talking to me in that way, Uncle Shad," she said. "I know you too well. And right in the Christmas season, too!"

Zoeth's welcome was as hearty, if not as exuberant, as Captain Shad's. He met her at the door and after the first hug and kiss held her off at arm's length and looked her over.

"My! my! my!" he exclaimed. "And this is our little Mary-'Gusta come back again! It don't seem as if it could be, somehow."

"But it is, Uncle Zoeth," declared Mary, laughing.

"And *isn't* it good to be here! Well, Isaiah," turning to Mr. Chase, who, aproned and shirtsleeved as usual, had been standing grinning in the background, "haven't you anything to say to me?"

Isaiah had something to say and he said it.

"Glad to see you," he announced. "Feelin' pretty smart? Got a new hat, ain't you? Supper's ready."

During the meal Mary was kept busy answering questions concerning school and her life at Mrs. Wyeth's. In her letters she had endeavored to tell every possible item of news which might be interesting to her uncles, but now these items were one by one recalled, reviewed, and discussed.

"'Twas kind of funny, that young Smith feller's turnin' up for dinner that time," observed Mr. Hamilton. "Cal'late you was some surprised to see him, wan't you?"

Mary smiled. "Why, yes," she said, "but I think he was more surprised to see me, Uncle Zoeth."

Captain Shad laughed heartily. "Shouldn't wonder," he admitted. "Didn't bring any fly paper along with him, did he? No? Well, that was an oversight. Maybe he thought fly time was past and gone. He seemed to be a real nice kind of young feller when he was down here that summer. He's older now; does he seem that way yet?"

"Why, yes, I think so. I only saw him for a little while."

Isaiah seemed to think it time for him to put in a question.

"Good lookin' as ever, I cal'late, ain't he?" he observed.

Mary was much amused. "Why, I suppose he is," she answered. "But why in the world are you interested in his good looks, Isaiah?"

Mr. Chase did his best to assume an expression of deep cunning. He winked at his employers.

"Oh, *I* ain't interested—not 'special," he declared, "but I didn't know but *some* folks might be. Ho, ho!"

He roared at his own pleasantry. Captain Shadrach, however, did not laugh.

"Some folks?" he repeated, tartly. "What are you talkin' about? What folks?"

"Oh, I ain't sayin' what folks. I'm just sayin' *some* folks. Ho, ho! You know what I mean, don't you, Mary-'Gusta?"

Before Mary could reply the Captain cut in again.

"No, she don't know what you mean, neither," he declared, with emphasis. "That's enough of that now, Isaiah. Don't be any bigger fool than you can help."

The self-satisfied grin faded from Isaiah's face and was succeeded by a look of surprised and righteous indignation.

"Wha—what's that?" he stammered. "What's that you're callin' me?"

"I ain't callin' you nothin'. I'm givin' you some free advice, that's all. Well, Mary-'Gusta, I cal'late, if you've had supper enough, you and me and Zoeth will go into the settin'-room, where we can all talk and I can smoke. I can always talk better under a full head of steam. Come on, Zoeth, Isaiah wants to be clearin' the table."

But Mr. Chase's thoughts were not concerned with table clearing just then. He stepped between Captain Shadrach and the door leading to the sitting-room.

"Cap'n Shad Gould," he sputtered, "you—you said somethin' about a fool. Who's a fool? That's what I want to know—who's a fool?"

The Captain grunted.

"Give it up," he observed. "I never was any hand

at riddles. Come, come, Isaiah! Get out of the channel and let us through."

"You hold on, Cap'n Shad! You answer me afore you leave this room. Who's a fool? I want to know who's a fool."

Captain Shad grinned.

"Well, go up to the post-office and ask some of the gang there," he suggested. "Tell 'em you'll give 'em three guesses. There, there!" he added, good-naturedly, pushing the irate Mr. Chase out of the "channel." "Don't block the fairway any longer. It's all right, Isaiah. You and me have been shipmates too long to fight now. You riled me up a little, that's all. Come on, folks."

Two hours later, after Mary had answered the last questions even Captain Shad could think of, had received answers to all her own, and had gone to her room for the night, Mr. Hamilton turned to his partner and observed mildly:

"Shadrach, what made you so dreadful peppery to Isaiah this evenin'? I declare, I thought you was goin' to take his head off."

The Captain grunted. "I will take it off some time," he declared, "if he don't keep the lower end of it shut when he'd ought to. You heard what he said, didn't you?"

"Yes, I heard. That about the Smith boy's good looks, you mean?"

"Sartin. And about Mary-'Gusta's noticin' how good-lookin' he was. Rubbish!"

"Yes—yes, I know, but Isaiah was only jokin'."

"Jokin'! Well, he may *look* like a comic almanac, but he needn't try to joke like one while that girl of ours is around. Puttin' notions about fellers and good looks and keepin' company into her head! You might expect such stuff from them fool drummers that come to the store, but an old leather-skinned image like Isaiah Chase ought to have more sense. We don't want such notions put in her head, do we?"

Zoeth rubbed his chin. He did not speak and his silence seemed to irritate his partner.

"Well, do we?" repeated the latter, sharply.

Zoeth sighed. "No, Shadrach," he admitted. "I guess likely we don't, but——"

"But what?"

"Well, we've got to realize that those kind of notions come—come sort of natural to young folks Mary-'Gusta's age."

"Rubbish! I don't believe that girl's got a single one of 'em in her mind."

"Maybe not, but they'll be there some day. Ah, well," he added, "we mustn't be selfish, you and me, Shadrach. It'll be dreadful hard to give her up to somebody else, but if that somebody is a good man, kind and straight and honest, why, I for one will try not to complain. But, Oh, Shadrach! Suppose he should turn out to be the other thing. Suppose *she* makes the mistake that I——"

His friend interrupted.

"Shh! shh!" he broke in, quickly. "Don't talk so, Zoeth. Come on to bed," he added, rising from his chair. "This very evenin' I was callin' Isaiah names for talkin' about 'fellers' and such, and here you and I have been sittin' talkin' nothin' else. If you hear me say 'fool' in my sleep tonight just understand I'm talkin' to myself, that's all. Come on aloft, Zoeth, and turn in."

The following morning Mary astonished her uncles by announcing that as soon as she had helped Isaiah with the breakfast dishes and the bed making she was going up to the store.

"What for?" demanded Captain Shad. "Course we'll be mighty glad to have your company, but Zoeth and me presumed likely you'd be for goin' round callin' on some of the other girls today."

"Well, I'm not. If they want to see me they can call on me here. I'm going up to the store with you and Uncle Zoeth. I want to help sell those Christmas goods of ours."

The partners looked at each other. Even Zoeth was moved to protest.

"Now, Mary-'Gusta," he said, "it ain't likely that your Uncle Shadrach and I are goin' to let you sell goods in that store. We won't hear of it, will we, Shadrach?"

"Not by a thunderin' sight!" declared Shadrach, vehemently. "The idea!"

"Why not? I've sold a good many there."

"I don't care if you have. You shan't sell any more. 'Twas all right when you was just a—a girl, a South Harnisser like the rest of us, but now that you're a Boston young lady, up to a fin—er—what-d'ye-call-it?— er—endin' school——"

"Finishin' school, Shadrach," corrected Mr. Hamilton.

"Well, whatever 'tis; I know 'twould be the end of *me* if I had to live up to the style of it. Anyhow, now that you're there, Mary-'Gusta, a young lady, same as I said, we ain't——"

But Mary interrupted. "Hush, Uncle Shad," she commanded. "Hush, this minute! You're talking nonsense. I *am* a South Harniss girl and I'm *not* a Boston young lady. My chief reasons for being so very happy at the thought of coming home here for my Christmas vacation were, first, that I should see you and Uncle Zoeth

and Isaiah and the house and the horse and the cat
and the hens, and, next, that I could help you with the
Christmas trade at the store. I know perfectly well
you need me. I'm certain you have been absolutely lost
without me. Now, really and truly, haven't you?"

"Not a mite," declared the Captain, stoutly, spoiling
the effect of the denial, however, by adding, although
his partner had not spoken: "Shut up, Zoeth! We ain't,
neither."

Mary laughed. "Uncle Shad," she said, "I don't believe you. At any rate, I'm going up there this minute to see for myself. Come along!"

She made no comment on what she saw at the store,
but for the remainder of the forenoon she was very
busy. In spite of the partners' protests, in fact paying
no more attention to those perturbed men of business
than if they were flies to be brushed aside when bother-
some, she went ahead, arranging, rearranging, dusting,
writing price tickets, lettering placards, doing all sorts
of things, and waiting on customers in the intervals. At
noon, when she and her Uncle Zoeth left for home and
dinner, she announced herself in a measure satisfied.
"Of course there is a great deal to do yet," she said, "but
the stock looks a little more as if it were meant to sell
and less as if it were heaped up ready to be carted off
and buried."

That afternoon the store of Hamilton and Company
was visited by a goodly number of South Harniss residents. That evening there were more. The news that
Mary-'Gusta Lathrop was at home and was "tendin'
store" for her uncles spread and was much discussed.
The majority of those who came did so not because
they contemplated purchasing extensively, but because
they wished to see what effect the fashionable finishing

school had had upon the girl. The general opinion
seemed to be that it "hadn't changed her a mite." This
result, however, was considered a desirable one by the
majority, but was by some criticized. Among the critics
was Mrs. Rebecca Mullet, whose daughter Irene also
was away at school undergoing the finishing process.

"Well!" declared Mrs. Mullet, with decision, as she
and her husband emerged from the store together.
"Well! If *that's* a sample of what the school she goes
to does for them that spend their money on it, I'm mighty
glad we didn't send our Rena there, ain't you, Christopher?"

Mr. Chris Mullet, who had received that very week a
bill for his daughter's "extras," uttered a fervent assent.

"You bet you!" he said. "It costs enough where
Rena is, without sendin' her to no more expensive
place."

This was not exactly the reply his wife had expected.

"Umph!" she grunted, impatiently. "I do wish you
could get along for two minutes without puttin' on poor
mouth. I suppose likely you tell everybody that you
can't afford a new overcoat account of Rena's goin' away
to school. You'd ought to be prouder of your daughter
than you are of an overcoat, I should think."

Mr. Mullet muttered something to the effect that he
was dum sure he was not proud of his present overcoat.
His wife ignored the complaint.

"And you'll be proud of Irene when she comes home,"
she declared. "She won't be like that Mary-'Gusta,
standin' up behind the counter and sellin' goods."

"Why, now, Becky, what's the matter with her doin'
that? She always used to sell goods, and behind that
very counter, too. And she certainly can *sell* 'em!" with
a reminiscent chuckle.

Mrs. Mullet glared at him. "Yes," she drawled, with sarcasm, "so she can—to some folks. Look at you, with all that Christmas junk under your arm! You didn't need to buy that stuff any more'n you needed to fly. What did you buy it for? Tell me that."

Chris shook his head. "Blessed if *I* know," he admitted. "I hadn't any idea of buyin' it, but she and me got to talkin', and she kept showin' the things to me, and I kept lookin' at 'em and——"

"Yes, and kept lookin' at her, too! Don't talk to *me!* There's no fool like an old fool—and an old man fool is the worst of all."

Her husband, usually meek and long-suffering under wifely discipline, evinced unwonted spirit.

"Well, I tell you this, Becky," he said. "Fur's I can see, Mary-'Gusta's all right. She's as pretty as a picture, to begin with; she's got money of her own to spend; and she's been away among folks that have got a lot more. All them things together are enough to spoil 'most any girl, but they haven't spoiled her. She's come home here not a mite stuck-up, not flirty nor silly nor top-lofty, but just as sensible and capable and common-folksy as ever she was, and that's sayin' somethin'. If our Rena turns out to be the girl Mary-'Gusta Lathrop is I *will* be proud of her, and don't you forget it!"

Which terminated conversation in the Mullet family for that evening.

But if the few, like Mrs. Mullet, were inclined to criticize, the many, like her husband, united in declaring Mary to be "all right." And her rearranging and displaying of the Christmas goods helped her and her uncles to dispose of them. In fact, for the three days before Christmas it became necessary to call in the services of Annabel as assistant saleslady. The store was crowded, particularly in the evenings, and Zoeth and Captain Shad experienced for the first time in months the sensation of being the heads of a prosperous business.

"Looks good to see so many young folks in here, don't it, Zoeth?" observed the Captain. "And not only girls, but fellers, too. Don't know when I've seen so many young fellers in here. Who's that young squirt Mary-'Gusta's waitin' on now? The one with the whittled-in back to his overcoat. Say, Solomon in all his glory wasn't arrayed like one of him! Must be some city feller, eh? Nobody I know."

Zoeth looked at his niece and her customer.

"Humph!" he said. "Guess you ain't rubbed your glasses lately, Shadrach. That's Dan Higgins."

Mr. Higgins it was, home for a few days' relaxation from the fatigues of coffin selling, and garbed as usual in city clothes the splendor of which, as Captain Shad said afterwards, "would have given a blind man eye-strain." Daniel's arms were filled with purchases and he and Mary were standing beside the table where the toys and games were displayed. Mary was gazing at the toys; Mr. Higgins was—not.

The partners regarded the pair for a moment. Shadrach frowned.

"Humph!" he grunted.

"Daniel's tryin' to find somethin' his little brother'll like," explained Zoeth.

"Yes," observed the Captain, dryly. "Well, he looks as if he'd found somethin' *he* liked pretty well. Here, Mary-'Gusta, I'll finish waitin' on Dan. You just see what Mrs. Nickerson wants, will you, please?"

Christmas Eve ended the rush of business for Hamilton and Company. The following week, the last of Mary's vacation, was certain to be dull enough. "Nothin' to do but change presents for folks," prophesied Captain Shad. "Give them somethin' they want and take back somethin' we don't want. That kind of trade is like shovelin' fog up hill, more exercise than profit."

Christmas was a happy day at the white house by the shore, a day of surprises. To begin with, there were the presents which were beside the plates at breakfast. Mary had brought gifts for all, Captain Shadrach, Zoeth, and Isaiah. There was nothing expensive, of course, but each had been chosen to fit the taste and liking of the recipient and there was no doubt that each choice was a success. Isaiah proudly displayed a jacknife which was a small toolchest, having four blades, a corkscrew, a screwdriver, a chisel, a button-hook and goodness knows what else besides.

"Look at that!" crowed Isaiah, exhibiting the knife, bristling like a porcupine, on his open palm. "Look at it! By time, there ain't nothin' I can't do with that knife! Every time I look at it I find somethin' new. Now, I wonder what that is," pointing to a particularly large and ferocious-looking implement which projected from the steel tangle. "I cal'late I've sized up about everything else, but I can't seem to make out what that's for. What do you cal'late 'tis, Cap'n Shad?"

Shadrach looked.

"Why, that's simple," he said, gravely. "That's a crust crowbar."

"A what?"

"A crust crowbar. For openin' one of them cast-iron pies same as you made for us last week. You drill a hole in the crust nigh the edge of the plate and then put that thing in and pry the upper deck loose. Good idea, Isaiah! I——"

"Aw, go to grass!" interrupted the indignant Mr.

Chase. "I notice you always eat enough of my pies, decks—yes, and hull and riggin', too."

Then there was *the* great surprise, that which the partners had prepared for their idolized niece. Mary found beside her plate a small, oblong package, wrapped in tissue paper and labeled, "To Mary-'Gusta, from Uncle Shadrach and Uncle Zoeth, with a Merry Christmas." Inside the paper was a pasteboard box, inside that a leather case, and inside *that* a handsome gold watch and chain. Then there was much excited exclaiming and delighted thanks on Mary's part, and explanations and broad grins on that of the givers.

"But you shouldn't have done it! Of course you shouldn't!" protested Mary. "It's perfectly lovely and I wanted a watch more than anything; but I *know* this must have cost a great deal."

"Never, neither," protested the Captain. "We got it wholesale. Edgar Emery's nephew is in the business up to Providence and he picked it out for us. Didn't begin to cost what we cal'lated 'twould, did it, Zoeth? When you buy things wholesale that way you can 'most always cal'late to get 'em lower than you cal'late to."

Mary smiled at this somewhat involved statement, but she shook her head.

"I'm sure it cost a great deal more than you should have spent," she said.

"But you like it, don't you?" queried Zoeth, hopefully.

"Like it! Oh, Uncle Zoeth, don't you *know* I like it! Who could help liking such a beautiful thing?"

"How's it show up alongside the watches the other girls have up to that Boston school?" asked Shadrach, with ill-concealed anxiety. "We wouldn't want our girl's watch to be any cheaper'n theirs, you know."

The answer was enthusiastic enough to satisfy even the Captain and Mr. Hamilton.

"I'm sure there isn't another girl in the school whose watch means to her what this will mean to me," declared Mary. "I shall keep it and love it all my life."

The partners heaved a sigh of relief. Whether or not the watch was fine enough for their Mary-'Gusta had been a source of worriment and much discussion. And then Isaiah, with his customary knack of saying the wrong thing, tossed a brickbat into the puddle of general satisfaction.

"That's so," he said; "that's so, Mary-'Gusta. You can keep it all your life, and when you get to be an old woman and married and have grandchildren then you can give it to them."

Captain Shadrach, who had taken up his napkin preparatory to tucking it under his chin, turned in his chair and glared at the unconscious steward.

"Well, by the jumpin' fire!" he exclaimed, with conviction. "The feller is sartinly possessed. He's lovesick, that's what's the matter with him. All he can talk about is somebody's gettin' married. Are *you* cal'latin' to get married, Isaiah?"

"Me? What kind of fool talk is that?"

"Who's the lucky woman?"

"There ain't no lucky woman. Don't talk so ridic'lous! All I said was that when Mary-'Gusta was old and married and had——"

"There you go again! Married and children! Say, did it ever run acrost your mind that you was a little mite previous?"

"I never said children. What I said was when she was old and had grandchildren."

"Grandchildren! Well, that's a dum sight *more* previous. Let's have breakfast, all hands, for the land sakes! Isaiah'll have us cruisin' along with the third and fourth generation in a few minutes. *I'm* satisfied with this one!"

That evening, at bedtime, as the partners separated in the upper hall to go to their respective rooms, Zoeth said:

"Shadrach, this has been a mighty nice Christmas for us all, ain't it?"

Captain Shad nodded emphatically. "You bet!" he declared. "Don't seem to me I ever remember a nicer one."

"Nor I, neither. I—I wonder——"

"Well, heave ahead. What are you waitin' for? What do you wonder?"

"I was just wonderin' if 'twas right for us to be so happy."

"Right?"

"Yes. Have we been—well, good enough this past year to deserve happiness like this?"

Shadrach grinned.

"I ain't puttin' in any testimony on my own hook," he said, dryly, "but I don't seem to remember your bein' desperately wicked, Zoeth. Course you *may* have got drunk and disorderly that time when Mary-'Gusta and I left you and went to Boston, but I kind of doubt it."

"Hush, hush, Shadrach! Don't joke about serious things. What I mean is have you and I walked the Lord's way as straight as we'd ought to? We've tried —that is, seems 's if we had—but I don't know. Anyhow, all this afternoon I've had a funny feelin' that you and me and Mary-'Gusta was—well was as if the tide had been comin' in for us all these years since she's been livin' with us, and as if now 'twould begin to go out again."

201

The Captain laughed. "And that's what you call a *funny* feelin'!" he exclaimed. "Zoeth, I've got a funny feelin', too, but I know what's the reason for it—the reason is turkey and plum puddin' and mince pie and the land knows what. When a couple of old hulks like you and me h'ist in a cargo of that kind it's no wonder we have feelin's. Good night, shipmate."

CHAPTER XIII

THE day after New Year's Mary went back to Boston and to school. The long winter term—the term which Madeline Talbott, whose father was a judge, called "the extreme penalty"—began. Boston's famous east winds, so welcome in summer and so raw and penetrating in winter, brought their usual allowance of snow and sleet, and the walks from Pinckney Street to the school and back were not always pleasant. Mrs. Wyeth had a slight attack of tonsillitis and Miss Pease a bronchial cold, but they united in declaring these afflictions due entirely to their own imprudence and not in the least to the climate, which, being like themselves, thoroughly Bostonian, was expected to maintain a proper degree of chill.

Mary, fortunately, escaped colds and illness. The walks in all sorts of weather did her good and her rosy cheeks and clear eyes were competent witnesses to her state of health. She was getting on well with her studies, and the Misses Cabot, not too easy to please, were apparently pleased with her. At home—for she had come to consider Mrs. Wyeth's comfortable house a home, although not of course to be compared with the real home at South Harniss—at Mrs. Wyeth's she was more of a favorite than ever, not only with the mistress of the house, but with Miss Pease, who was considered eccentric and whose liking was reported hard to win. The two ladies had many talks concerning the girl.

"She is remarkable," declared Miss Pease on one occasion. "Considering her lack of early advantages, I consider her ease of manner and self-possession remarkable. She is a prodigy."

Mrs. Wyeth sniffed. She enjoyed hearing Mary praised, but she objected to her friend's choice of words.

"For mercy sake, Letitia," she said, "don't call her that. The word 'prodigy' always reminds me of the Crummles infant, the one with the green parasol and the white—er—lingerie, in 'Nicholas Nickleby.'"

Miss Pease smiled with the superiority of the corrected who is about to correct.

"I don't see why that should bring the individual you mention to mind," she said. "If *I* remember correctly—and I was brought up on Dickens—she was a 'phenomenon,' not a prodigy. However, it makes no material difference what you and I call Mary Lathrop, the fact remains that she is an exceptionally well-behaved, good-mannered, polite——"

"Sweet, healthy girl," interrupted Mrs. Wyeth, finishing the sentence. "I know that as well as you do, Letitia Pease. And you know I know it. Now, what have you in your mind concerning Mary? I know there is something, because you have been hinting at it for more than a week. What is it?"

Miss Pease looked wise.

"Oh, I have a plan," she said. "I can't tell even you, Emily, just what it is as yet. You see, it isn't really a plan, but only an idea so far. She doesn't know it herself, of course."

"Hum! Is it a pleasant plan—or idea, whichever you call it? That is, will she think it pleasant when she learns what it is?"

"I certainly hope so."

"Look here, Letitia," with sudden suspicion, "you aren't planning some ridiculous sentimental nonsense for that child, are you? You're not trying to make a match for her, I hope?"

"Match? What are you talking about? If you mean am I trying to get her married to some *man*," with a scornful emphasis on the word, "I most certainly am not."

"Humph! Well, if she ever is married, I presume it will be to a man, or an imitation of one. All right, Letitia. I am glad your great idea isn't that, whatever it is."

"It is not. You know my opinion of marriage, Emily Wyeth. And, so far as matchmaking is concerned, I should say you were a more likely subject for suspicion. That young relative of yours, Sam Keith, appears to be coming here a great deal of late. He *may* come solely to see you, but I doubt it."

Mrs. Wyeth smiled grimly.

"Samuel has been rather prevalent recently," she admitted, "but don't let that trouble you, Letitia. I have had my eye on the young man. Samuel is as susceptible to pretty girls as children are to the measles. And his attacks remind me of the measles as much as anything, sudden outbreak, high fever and delirium, then a general cooling off and a rapid recovery. This seizure isn't alarming and there is absolutely no danger of contagion. Mary doesn't take him seriously at all."

"And how about that other young man?—Smith, I think his name is. He has called here twice since Christmas."

Mrs. Wyeth seemed to be losing patience.

"Well, what of it?" she demanded.

"Why, nothing that I know of, except, perhaps——"

"There is no perhaps at all. The Smith boy appears to be a very nice young fellow, and remarkably sensible for a young person in this hoity-toity age. From what I can learn, his people, although they do live out West— down in a mine or up on a branch or a ranch or something—are respectable. Why shouldn't he call to see Mary occasionally, and why shouldn't she see him? Goodness gracious! What sort of a world would this be if young people didn't see each other? Don't tell me that you never had any young male acquaintances when you were a girl, Letitia, because I shan't believe you."

Miss Pease straightened in her chair.

"It is not likely that I shall make any such preposterous statement," she snapped.

So the "young male acquaintance" called occasionally— not too often—Mrs. Wyeth saw to that; probably not so often as he would have liked; but he did call and the acquaintanceship developed into friendship. That it might develop into something more than friendship no one, except possibly the sentimental Miss Pease, seemed to suspect. Certainly Mary did not, and at this time it is doubtful if Crawford did, either. He liked Mary Lathrop. She was a remarkably pretty girl but, unlike other pretty girls he had known—and as good-looking college football stars are privileged beyond the common herd, he had known at least several—she did not flirt with him, nor look admiringly up into his eyes, nor pronounce his jokes "killingly funny," nor flatter him in any way. If the jokes *were* funny she laughed a healthy, genuine laugh, but if, as sometimes happened, they were rather feeble, she was quite likely to tell him so. She did not always agree with his views, having views of her own on most subjects, and if he asked her opinion the answer he received was always honest, if not precisely what he expected or hoped.

"By George! You're frank, at any rate," he observed,

rather ruefully, after asking her opinion as to a point of conduct and receiving it forthwith.

"Didn't you want me to be?" asked Mary. "You asked me what I thought you should have done and I told you."

"Yes, you did. You certainly told me."

"Well, didn't you want me to tell you?"

"I don't know that I wanted you to tell me just that."

"But you asked me what I thought, and that is exactly what I think. Don't *you* think it is what you should have done?"

Crawford hesitated; then he laughed. "Why yes, confound it, I do," he admitted. "But I hoped you would tell me that what I did do was right."

"Whether I thought so or not?"

"Why—well—er—yes. Honestly now, didn't you know I wanted you to say the other thing?"

It was Mary's turn to hesitate; then she, too, laughed.

"Why, yes, I suppose——" she began; and finished with, "Yes, I did."

"Then why didn't you say it? Most girls would."

"Perhaps that is why. I judge that most girls of your acquaintance say just about what you want them to. Don't you think it is good for you to be told the truth occasionally?"

It was good for him, of course, and, incidentally, it had the fascination of novelty. Here was a girl full of fun, ready to take a joke as well as give one, neither flattering nor expecting flattery, a country girl who had kept store, yet speaking of that phase of her life quite as freely as she did of the fashionable Misses Cabot's school, not at all ashamed to say she could not afford this or that, simple and unaffected but self-respecting and proud; a girl who was at all times herself and retained her poise and common sense even in the presence of a handsome young demigod who had made two touchdowns against Yale.

It was extremely good for Crawford Smith to know such a girl. She helped him to keep his feet on the ground and his head from swelling. Not that there was much danger of the latter happening, for the head was a pretty good one, but Mary Lathrop's common sense was a stimulating—and fascinating—reënforcement to his own. As he had said on the Sunday afternoon of their first meeting in Boston, it was a relief to have some-one to talk to who understood and appreciated a fellow's serious thoughts as well as the frivolous ones. His ap-proaching graduation from Harvard and the work which he would begin at the Medical School in the fall were very much in his mind just now. He told Mary his plans and she and he discussed them. She had plans of her own, principally concerning what she meant to do to make life easier for her uncles when her school days were over, and these also were discussed.

"But," he said, "that's really nonsense, after all, isn't it?"

"What?"

"Why, the idea of your keeping store again. You'll never do that."

"Indeed I shall! Why not?"

"Why, because——"

"Because what?"

"Because—well, because I don't think you will, that's all. Girls like you don't have to keep a country store, you know—at least, not for long."

The remark was intended to please; it might have pleased some girls, but it did not please this one. Mary's dignity was offended. Anything approaching a slur upon her beloved uncles, or their place of business, or South Harniss, or the Cape Cod people, she resented with all her might. Her eyes snapped.

"I do not *have* to keep store at any time," she said crisply, "in the country or elsewhere. I do it because I wish to and I shall continue to do it as long as I choose. If my friends do not understand that fact and appreciate my reasons, they are not my friends, that is all."

Crawford threw up both hands. "Whew!" he exclaimed. "Don't shoot; I'll come down! Great Scott! If you take a fellow's head off like that when he pays you a compliment what would you do if he dared to criticize?"

"Was that remark of yours intended as a compliment?"

"Not exactly; more as a statement of fact. I meant— I meant—Oh, come now, Mary! You know perfectly well what I meant. Own up."

Mary tried hard to be solemn and severe, but the twinkle in his eye was infectious and in spite of her effort her lips twitched.

"Own up, now," persisted Crawford. "You know what I meant. Now, don't you?"

"Well—well, I suppose I do. But I think the remark was a very silly one. That is the way Sam Keith talks."

"Eh? Oh, does he!"

"Yes. Or he would if I would let him. And he does it much better than you do."

"Well, I like that!"

"I don't. That is why I don't want you to do it. I expect you to be more sensible. And, besides, I won't have you or anyone making fun of my uncles' store."

"Making fun of it! I should say not! I have a vivid and most respectful memory of it, as you ought to know.

By the way, you told me your uncles had sent you their photographs. May I see them?"

Mary brought the photographs from her room. They had been taken by the photographer at Ostable in compliance with what amounted to an order on her part, and the results showed two elderly martyrs dressed in respectable but uncomfortable Sunday clothes and apparently awaiting execution. On the back of one mournful exhibit was written, "Mary Augusta from Uncle Shadrach," and on the other, "Uncle Zoeth to Mary Augusta, with much love."

"Now, don't laugh," commanded Mary, as she handed the photographs to Crawford. "I know they are funny, but if you laugh I'll never forgive you. The poor dears had them taken expressly to please me, and I am perfectly sure either would have preferred having a tooth out. They *are* the best men in the world and I am more certain of it every day."

Crawford did not laugh at the photographs. He was a young gentleman of considerable discretion and he did not smile, not even at Captain Shad's hands, the left with fingers separated and clutching a knee as if to keep it from shaking, the right laid woodenly upon a gorgeously bound parlor-table copy of "Lucille." Instead of laughing he praised the originals of the pictures, talked reminiscently of his own visit in South Harniss, and finally produced from his pocketbook a small photographic print, which he laid upon the table beside the others.

"I brought that to show you," he said. "You were asking about my father, you know, and I told you I hadn't a respectable photograph of him. That was true; I haven't. Dad has another eccentricity besides his dislike of the East and Eastern ways of living; he has a perfect horror of having his photograph taken. Don't ask me why, because I can't tell you. It isn't because he is ugly; he's a mighty good-looking man for his age, if I do say it. But he has a prejudice against photographs of himself and won't even permit me to take a snapshot if he can prevent it. Says people who are always having their pictures taken are vain, conceited idiots, and so on. However, I catch him unawares occasionally, and this is a snap I took last summer. He and I were on a fishing trip up in the mountains. We're great pals, Dad and I—more than most fathers and sons, I imagine."

Mary took the photograph and studied it with interest. Mr. Smith, senior, was a big man, broad-shouldered and heavy, with a full gray beard and mustache. He wore a broad-brimmed hat, which shaded his forehead somewhat, but his eyes and the shape of his nose were like his son's.

Mary looked at the photograph and Crawford looked at her.

"Well, what do you think of him?" asked the young man after an interval.

"Think?" repeated Mary absently, still staring at the photograph. "Why, I—I don't know what you mean."

"I mean what is your opinion of my respected dad? You must have one by this time. You generally have one on most subjects and you've been looking at that picture for at least five minutes."

"Have I? I beg your pardon; I didn't realize. The picture interested me. I have never seen your father, have I? No, of course I haven't. But it almost seems as if I had. Perhaps I have seen someone who looks like him."

"Shouldn't wonder. Myself, for instance."

"Of course. That was stupid of me, wasn't it? He

looks like an interesting man, one who has had experiences."

"He has. Dad doesn't talk about himself much, even to me, but he had some hard rubs before he reached the smooth places. Had to fight his way, I guess."

"He looks as if he had. But he got his way in the end, I should imagine. He doesn't look like one who gives up easily."

"He isn't. Pretty stubborn sometimes, Dad is, but a brick to me, just the same."

"Was your mother an Eastern woman?"

"No. She was a Westerner, from California. Dad was married twice. His first wife came from New England somewhere, I believe. I didn't know there had been another wife until I was nearly fifteen years old, and then I found it out entirely by accident. She was buried in another town, you see. I saw her name first on the gravestone and it made an impression on me because it was so odd and old-fashioned—'Patience, wife of Edwin Smith.' I only mention this to show you how little Dad talks about himself, but it was odd I should find it out that way, wasn't it? But there! I don't suppose you're interested in the Smith genealogy. I apologize. I never think of discussing my family affairs with anyone but you, not even Sam. But you—well, somehow I seem to tell you everything. I wonder why?"

"Perhaps because I ask too many questions."

"No, it isn't that. It is because you act as if you really cared to have me talk about my own affairs. I never met a girl before that did. Now, I want to ask you about that club business. There's going to be the deuce and all to pay in that if I'm not careful. Have you thought it over? What would you do if you were I?"

The matter in question was a somewhat delicate and complicated one, dealing with the admission or rejection of a certain fellow to one of the Harvard societies. There was a strong influence working to get him in and, on the other hand, there were some very good objections to his admission. Crawford, president of the club and one of its most influential members, was undecided what to do. He had explained the case to Mary upon the occasion of his most recent visit to the Pinckney Street house, and had asked her advice. She had taken time for consideration, of course—she was the old Mary-'Gusta still in that—and now the advice was ready.

"It seems to me," she said, "that I should try to settle it like this."

She explained her plan. Crawford listened, at first dubiously and then with steadily growing enthusiasm.

"By George!" he exclaimed, when she had finished. "That would do it, I honestly believe. How in the world did you ever think of that scheme? Say, you really are a wonder at managing. You could manage a big business and make it go, I'm sure. How do you do it? Where do you get your ideas?"

Mary laughed. His praise pleased her.

"I don't know," she answered. "I just think them out, I guess. I do like to manage things for people. Sometimes I do it more than I should, perhaps. Poor Isaiah Chase, at home in South Harniss, says I boss him to death. And my uncles say I manage them, too—but they seem to like it," she added.

"I don't wonder they do. I like it, myself. Will you help manage my affairs between now and Commencement? There'll be a whole lot to manage, between the club and the dance and all the rest of it. And then when you go to Commencement you can see for yourself how they work out."

"Go to Commencement? Am I going to Commencement?"

"Of course you are! You're going with me, I hope. I thought that was understood. It's a long way off yet, but for goodness' sake don't say you won't come. I've been counting on it."

Mary's pleasure showed in her face. All she said, however, was:

"Thank you very much. I shall be very glad to come."

But Commencement was, as Crawford said, still a good way off and in the meantime there were weeks of study. The weeks passed, some of them, and then came the Easter vacation. Mary spent the vacation in South Harniss, of course, and as there was no Christmas rush to make her feel that she was needed at the store, she rested and drove and visited and had a thoroughly happy and profitable holiday. The happiness and profit were shared by her uncles, it is unnecessary to state. When she questioned them concerning business and the outlook for the coming summer, they seemed optimistic and cheerful.

"But Isaiah says there are two new stores to be opened in the village this spring," said Mary. "Don't you think they may hurt your trade a little?"

Captain Shadrach dismissed the idea and his prospective competitors with a condescending wave of the hand. "Not a mite," he declared scornfully. "Not a mite, Mary-'Gusta. Hamilton and Company's a pretty able old craft. She may not show so much gilt paint and brass work as some of the new ones just off the ways, but her passengers know she's staunch and they'll stick by her. Why, Isaiah was sayin' that a feller was tellin' him only yesterday that it didn't make any difference how many new stores was started in this town, he'd never trade anywheres but with Hamilton and Company. That shows you, don't it?"

"Who was it said that, Uncle Shad?" asked Mary.

"Eh? Why, I don't know. Isaiah was tellin' me about it and we was interrupted. Who was it, Isaiah?"

"'Twas Rastus Young," replied Mr. Chase promptly.

Even the Captain was obliged to laugh, although he declared that Mr. Young's constancy was a proof that the firm's prospects were good.

"Rats'll always leave a sinkin' ship," he said, "and if Zoeth and me was goin' under Rat Young would be the first to quit."

Zoeth, when his niece questioned him, expressed confidence that the new competitors would not prove dangerous. "The Almighty has looked after us so far," he added, "unworthy as we be, and I guess he'll carry us the rest of the way, Put your trust in Him, Mary-'Gusta; I hope they teach you that up to school."

So Mary, who had been rather troubled at the news of Hamilton and Company's rivals in the field, dismissed her fears as groundless. Her uncles were old-fashioned and a little behind the times in business methods, but no doubt those methods were suited to South Harniss and there was no cause for worry concerning the firm's future. She made Isaiah promise to keep her posted as to developments and went back to Boston and her school-work.

CHAPTER XIV

THE spring term was an interesting one and there were other interests as well. Crawford called more frequently, the plans for Commencement requiring a great deal of discussion. Mary's fondness for managing was, or should have been, gratified, for the talent was in constant demand. Sam Keith, who, after meeting Mary at his cousin's house, had at first developed an amazing fondness for that relative's society, now came less often. He was in the second stage of the pretty-girl disease mentioned by his aunt; the fever and delirium had passed, and he was now cooling off. It cannot be said that the fever had been in the least encouraged. Mary was pleasant and agreeable when he called, but she would not treat him as a confidant or an intimate; she did not accept any of his invitations to dances or the theater, and she would not flirt even the least little bit. The last was the most unsatisfactory drawback, because the susceptible Samuel was fond of flirtations and usually managed to keep at least three going at the same time. Therefore, the cooling-off process was, in this case, a bit more rapid than usual. Sam's calls and dinners at his cousin Emily's residence had decreased from two or three times a week to an uncertain once a fortnight. Mary, of course, noticed this, but she felt no regret. Crawford, Sam's roommate, must have noticed it also, but if he felt regret he managed to conceal the feeling remarkably well.

Early in May Captain Shadrach came up to the city

to buy summer goods for the store. He positively refused to make his headquarters at Mrs. Wyeth's, although that lady sent an urgent invitation to him to do so. And, even when Mary added her own plea to that of her landlady, the Captain still refused.

Don't ask me, Mary-'Gusta [he wrote]. For the dear land sakes don't ask me to come to that place and stay. I'd do 'most anything for you, and I will do that if you are dead sot on it, but I do hope you ain't. I will come up there and see you of course and I'll even stay to supper if I get asked, but *don't* ask me to drop anchor and stay there night and day. I couldn't stand it. My backbone's sprung backwards now from settin' up so straight last time I was there.

So Mary had pity upon him and he took a room at the Quincy House where, as he said, he didn't have to keep his nose dead on the course every minute, but could "lay to and be comf'table" if he wanted to. He was invited to supper at the Wyeth house, however, and while there Mrs. Wyeth found an opportunity to take him aside and talk with him on a subject which he found interesting and a trifle disquieting.

"Now mind," said the lady, "I am by no means convinced that the affair is anything but a mere boy and girl friendship, or that it is ever likely to be more than that. But I did think I ought to tell you about it and that you should meet the young man. You have met him, you say?"

"Yes, ma'am," said Shadrach, "I've met him. 'Twan't much more'n that—he just came into our store down home, that's all. But I did meet him and I must say I thought he was a real likely young feller."

"I am glad you thought so. So do I. Has Mary written you of his calls here?"

"Oh, yes, ma'am, she's written. She ain't the kind of girl to keep anything back from us; at least, if she is, she's changed a heap since she came away to school. She's told us about his comin' here and about you and him and her goin' to that—what-d'ye-call-it—hookey game. She wrote all about that 'way last February."

"Yes, we did go to the hockey game. Samuel, my cousin John Keith's boy, played in it. Now, Captain Gould, I have a suggestion to make. It has been some years since you met Crawford Smith and I think, everything considered, you should meet him again and decide for yourself whether or not you still consider him a proper young person to call upon your niece. Suppose you dine with us again tomorrow evening and I invite young Smith also. Then——"

But the Captain interrupted. He had a plan of his own for the following evening and another meal at Mrs. Wyeth's was not a part of it.

"Er—er—excuse me, ma'am," he cut in hastily, "but I had a—a kind of notion that Mary-'Gusta and me might get our supper at a—a eatin'-house or somewhere tomorrow night and then maybe we'd take in—I mean go to a show—a theater, I should say. I didn't know but I'd ask this young Smith feller to go along. And—and——" remembering his politeness, "of course we'd be real glad if you'd come, too," he added.

But Mrs. Wyeth, although she thanked him and expressed herself as heartily in favor of the supper and theater party, refused to become a member of it. The Captain bore the shock of the refusal with, to say the least, manful resignation. He had a huge respect for Mrs. Wyeth, and he liked her because his beloved Mary-'Gusta liked her so well, but his liking was sea-

soned with awe and her no in this case was a great relief.

So the following evening at six Mary and her uncle
met Crawford at the Quincy House and the three dined
together, after which they saw the performance of "The
Music Master" at the Tremont Theater. Crawford
found the dinner quite as entertaining as the play. Captain Shadrach was in high good humor and his remarks
during the meal were characteristic. He persisted in
addressing the dignified waiter as "Steward" and in referring to the hotel kitchen as the "galley." He consulted his young guests before ordering and accepted
their selections gracefully if not always silently.

"All right, Mary-'Gusta," he observed. "All right,
just as you say. You're the skipper of this craft tonight, and me and Crawford here are just passengers.
If you say we've got to eat—what is it?—consummer
soup—why, I suppose likely we have. I'll take my
chances if Crawford will. Course, if I was alone here,
I'd probably stick to oyster stew and roast beef. I know
what they are. And it's some comfort to be sure of
what you're gettin', as the sick feller said when the doctor told him he had the smallpox instead of the measles.
You don't mind my callin' you 'Crawford,' do you?" he
added, turning to that young gentleman. "I'm old
enough to be your father, for one thing, and for another
a handle's all right on a jug or a sasspan, but don't seem
as if 'twas necessary to take hold of a friend's name by.
And I hope we're goin' to be friends, we three."

Crawford said he hoped so, too, and he said it with
emphasis.

"Good!" exclaimed the Captain with enthusiasm.
"And we'll cement the friendship—the book fellers are
always tellin' about cementin' friendships—with this sup-

per of ours, eh? If we only had some of Isaiah's last
batch of mincemeat we could sartinly do it with that;
it was the nighest thing to cement ever I saw put on a
table. I asked him if he filled his pies with a trowel
and you ought to have heard him sputter. You remember Isaiah, don't you, Crawford? Tall, spindlin' critter,
sails cook for Zoeth and me at the house down home.
He ain't pretty, but his heart's in the right place. That's
kind of strange, too," he added with a chuckle, "when
you consider how nigh his shoulder-blades are to the top
of his legs."

Between his stories and jokes he found time to ask
his male guest a few questions and these questions, although by no means offensively personal, were to the
point. He inquired concerning the young man's home
life, about his ambitions and plans for the future, about
his friends and intimates at college. Crawford, without
being in the least aware that he was being catechized,
told a good deal, and Captain Shadrach's appraising regard, which had learned to judge men afloat and ashore,
read more than was told. The appraisal was apparently
satisfactory for, after the young man had gone and the
Captain and Mary were saying good night in the Wyeth
parlor, Shadrach said:

"A nice boy, I should say. Yes, sir, a real nice young
feller, as young fellers go. I like him fust-rate."

"I'm glad, Uncle Shad," said Mary. "I like him,
too."

Shadrach regarded her with a little of the questioning scrutiny he had devoted to Crawford during dinner.

"You do, eh?" he mused. "How much?"

"How much?" repeated Mary, puzzled. "What do
you mean?"

"I mean how much do you like him? More'n you do your Uncle Zoeth and me, for instance?"

She looked up into his face. What she saw there brought the color to her own. He might have said more, but she put her finger-tips upon his lips.

"Nonsense!" she said hotly. "What wicked, silly nonsense, Uncle Shad! Don't you ever, ever say such a thing to me again. You *know* better."

Shadrach smiled and shook his head.

"All right, Mary-'Gusta," he said; "I won't say it again—not till you say it to me fust, at any rate. There, there, dearie! Don't blow me clean out of the water. I was only jokin', the same as Isaiah was tryin' to that night when you came home for your Christmas vacation."

"I don't like that kind of joking. I think it's silly."

"I guess maybe 'tis—for a spell, anyhow. We'll heave the jokes overboard. Yes, I like that Crawford Smith fust-rate. But the funniest thing about him is the way he reminds me of somebody else. Who that somebody is I can't make out nor remember. Maybe I'll think sometime or other, but anyhow I like him now for his own sake. I asked him to come down and see us sometime this summer. Wonder if he will."

Mary-'Gusta wondered, too, but she would have wondered more had she known what that coming summer was to mean to her. The morning after the theater party Captain Shadrach called to say good-by to Mrs. Wyeth. That lady asked some questions and listened with interest and approval to his report concerning Crawford Smith.

"I'm glad you were so favorably impressed with the boy," she said. "As I told you, I like him myself. And you approve of his friendship with your niece?"

The Captain rubbed his chin. "Why, yes, ma'am," he said. "I approve of that, all right, and I cal'late Zoeth would, too. Fact is, where Mary-'Gusta's concerned 'tain't nothin' *but* friendship, so fur, and I guess likely 'tain't on his part, either. If it ever should be more, then—well, then, if he turned out to be all that he'd ought to be I can't see where we old folks have much right to put our oar in, do you, ma'am?"

Perhaps Mrs. Wyeth was tired of the subject; perhaps she objected to being addressed as one of the old folks; at any rate, she made no answer, but asked a question instead.

"Captain Gould," she said, "what plans have you and Mr. Hamilton made for Mary this summer?"

"Plans, ma'am? Why, I don't know's we've made any. Of course, we're countin' on her comin' down to South Harniss when she gets through her school, and——"

"Just a moment, Captain. I have a friend who is very anxious to have you change that plan for one of hers. Come in, Letitia. Captain Gould, this is my friend, Miss Pease. Now, Letitia, tell the Captain your plan—the one you told me last night."

Miss Pease told of her plan and Captain Shad listened, at first with astonishment, then with a troubled expression and at last with a combination of both.

"There," said Miss Pease, in conclusion, "that is my plan. It means a great deal to me and I hope it may mean something to Mary."

"It will be a wonderful opportunity for her," declared Mrs. Wyeth emphatically.

"What do you think of it, Captain Gould?" asked Miss Pease.

Shadrach drew a long breath. "I—I don't know

hardly what to say, ma'am," he answered. "I can't hardly realize it yet, seems so. It sartinly would be a wonderful chance for her and it's somethin' me and Zoeth could never give her or think of givin'. But—but——"

"Of course," said Miss Pease, as he hesitated, "if she is needed very much at home—if you feel you cannot spare her——"

" 'Tain't that, ma'am," interrupted the Captain quickly. "Land knows Zoeth and me would miss her awful, but we wouldn't let that stand in the way—not of anything like this. But—but—well, to be right down honest, ma'am, I don't know's we'd feel like havin' somebody else do so much for her. Course we ain't well off, Zoeth and I ain't, but we ain't right down poor, either. We've been used to doin' for ourselves and——"

And then Miss Pease had an inspiration.

"Oh, dear me!" she broke in hastily. "I do hope you haven't made a mistake, Captain Gould. I hope you don't think I am offering this as a charity or purely as a favor to Mary. No, indeed! I am asking it as a favor to myself. I must have a companion, otherwise I cannot go. And Mary is just the companion I need. I am very fond of her and I think she likes me. I am not going to urge too much, Captain Gould, but I do hope you will consider the matter with Mr. Hamilton and let me hear from you soon. And I am hoping you will consent. I promise to take good care of your girl and bring her back safe and sound in September. And I shall not say one word of my great plan to her until you write me that I may."

So Captain Shadrach, the troubled expression still on his face, returned on the afternoon train to South Harniss to tell his friend and partner of Miss Pease's plan.

Mary, who accompanied him to the Boston station, wondered why he seemed so preoccupied and quiet. If she had known what his thoughts were she would have wondered no longer.

Miss Pease planned to travel through Europe during the summer months, and she had asked the Captain's permission to take Mary with her as her guest and friend and companion.

CHAPTER XV

I F time and space did not matter, and if even more important happenings in Mary-'Gusta's life were not as close at hand to claim attention, it would be interesting to describe at length those of that spring and the summer which followed it. Summarized in chronological order, they were these: First, the lengthy discussions between the partners concerning Miss Pease's plan, discussions which ended by Zoeth, as senior partner, writing Miss Pease:

Shadrach and I say yes. We ought to have said it afore but flesh is weak and we found it kind of hard to make up our minds to spare our girl all summer. But we know we ought to spare her and that it will be a splendid chance for her. So we say she shall go and we thank you more than we can say. She will need clothes and fixings to take with her and Shadrach and I wish to ask if you will be kind enough to help her pick out what she needs. Maybe Mrs. Wyeth will help too. It will be a great favor if you two will do this, Shadrach and I not being much good at such things. *We will send the money and will pay for all.*

Then came the breaking of the news to Mary herself. At first, after she could be made to believe the whole idea a perfectly serious one and realized that a trip to Europe—her dearest day-dream, even when a little girl, and the favorite play with the dolls in the attic at South Harniss—when she at last realized the opportunity that

225

was hers, even then she hesitated to accept it. There were her uncles—they needed her so much in the store—they would miss her so dreadfully. She could not go and leave them. The united efforts of Miss Pease and Mrs. Wyeth could not alter her determination to remain at home; only a joint declaration, amounting to a command and signed by both partners of Hamilton and Company, had that effect. She consented then, but with reluctance.

The steamer sailed from Boston—Miss Pease's civic loyalty forbade her traveling on a New York boat—on the thirtieth of June, the week after Commencement. Mary and Mrs. Wyeth attended the Commencement exercises and festivities as Crawford's guest. Edwin Smith, Crawford's father, did not come on from Carson City to see his son receive his parchment from his Alma Mater. He had planned to come—Crawford had begun to believe he might come—but at the last moment illness had prevented. It was nothing serious, he wrote; he would be well and hearty when the boy came West after graduating.

God bless you, son [the letter ended]. If you knew what it means for your old dad to stay away you'd forgive him for being in the doctor's care. Come home quick when it's over. There's a four-pound trout waiting for one of us up in the lake country somewhere. It's up to you or me to get him.

Crawford showed the letter to Mary. He was disappointed, but not so much so as the girl expected.

"I never really dared to count on his coming," he explained. "It has been this way so many times. Whenever Dad has planned to come East something happens to prevent. Now it has happened again; I was almost sure it would. It's a shame! I wanted you to meet him. And I wanted him to meet you, too," he added.

Mary also was a little disappointed. She had rather looked forward to meeting Mr. Smith. He was her friend's father, of course, and that of itself made him an interesting personality, but there was something more —a sort of mystery about him, inspired in her mind by the photograph which Crawford had shown her, which made her curious. The man in the photograph resembled Crawford, of course, but she had the feeling that he resembled someone else even more—someone she had known or whose picture she had seen. She was sorry she was not to meet him.

Commencement was a wonderful time. Mary was introduced to dozens of young fellows, attended spreads and sings and proms, danced a great deal, was asked to dance ever so much more, chatted and laughed and enjoyed herself as a healthy, happy, and pretty girl should enjoy a college commencement. And on the following Tuesday she and Miss Pease, looking down from the steamer's deck, waved their handkerchiefs to Mrs. Wyeth and Zoeth and Captain Shadrach and Crawford who, standing on the wharf, waved theirs in return as the big ship moved slowly out of the dock and turned her nose toward Minot's Light and the open sea. For the first time since Hamilton and Company put up a sign both partners had come to Boston together.

"Annabel's keepin' store," explained Shadrach, "and Isaiah's helpin'. It'll be the blind leadin' the blind, I cal'-late, but we don't care, do we, Zoeth? We made up our mind we'd see you off, Mary-'Gusta, if we had to swim to Provincetown and send up sky-rockets from Race P'int to let you know we was there. Don't forget

what I told you: If you should get as fur as Leghorn
be sure and hunt up that ship-chandler name of Peroti.
Ask him if he remembers Shad Gould that he knew in
'65. If he ain't dead I bet you he'll remember."

So Mary-'Gusta sailed away and for ten marvelous
weeks daydreams came true and attic make-believes
turned to realities. War had not yet come to sow its
seed of steel and fire and reap its harvest of blood and
death upon the fair valleys and hills of France, and the
travelers journeyed leisurely from village to cathedral
town and from the Seine to the Loire. They spent three
weeks in Switzerland and two in Italy, returning for the
final week to London where, under Miss Pease's expert
guidance, Mary visited the shops, the big ones on Regent
and Oxford Streets and the smaller, equally fascinating
—and more expensive—ones on Bond Street and Picca-
dilly, buying presents and remembrances for the folks
at home. And, at last, came the day when, leaning upon
the rail, she saw the misty headlands of Ireland sink beneath the horizon and realized that her wonderful holiday was over and that she was homeward bound.

The voyage was rather rough and stormy, as westerly
voyages are likely to be, but the ship was comfortable
and speedy and they made good time. Mary spent but
one day in Boston and, on the morning of the next,
started for South Harniss. She had one week before
school opened and that week was to be spent with her
uncles; no one else, she vowed, should have a minute
of it.

Great were the rejoicings in the white house by the
shore that day, and marvelous was the dinner Isaiah
served in honor of the occasion. Mary was obliged to
relate the story of her trip from start to finish, while
three rapt listeners nodded and exclaimed in sympathy

or broke in to ask questions. She had written faithfully, but, as Isaiah said, "writin' ain't tellin'." So Mary told and her uncles and Mr. Chase listened and questioned. It was twelve o'clock that night before anyone thought of going to bed, and next morning at the breakfast table the questioning began all over again.

"Mrs. Wyeth was down at the dock, I presume likely, to meet you when your ship made port?" queried Zoeth.

"Yes, she was there," replied Mary.

"Anybody else? How about that young Smith feller? Wa'n't he there, too?" asked Captain Shadrach with elaborate innocence.

Mary colored just a little. She knew it was foolish; there was no reason in the world why she should be embarrassed, but she could not help it.

"No, Uncle Shad," she answered. "He wasn't there. He has not returned from the West yet, but he will be in Boston next week when the Medical College opens."

"Been havin' a good time out West there, has he?" inquired the Captain, still with studied unconcern.

"Yes. At least he writes me that he has." She looked from one to the other of her trio of listeners and then added: "I have some of his letters here with me. If you'd like to hear them I'll read them aloud."

"No, no, you needn't do that," protested Shadrach hastily. But after another look at him Mary said, "I think I will," and departed in search of the letters.

Captain Shad, looking a trifle guilty, glanced at his partner.

"She needn't read 'em unless she wants to, need she, Zoeth?" he said. "I—I didn't mean for her to do that."

Mr. Hamilton's face expressed doubt and disapproval.

"Humph!" he said and that was all.

Mary returned bearing the packet of letters, some of which she proceeded to read. Crawford had spent the summer either at his home in Carson City or in camping with his father in the Sierras, where he had shot and fished and apparently enjoyed himself hugely. The letters were frank and straightforward, full of fun and exuberance, the sort of letters a robust, clean-minded young fellow ought to write and sometimes does. They were not sentimental; even Isaiah, with what Captain Shadrach termed his "lovesick imagination," would not have called them so.

The partners and Mr. Chase listened with interest to the reading of the letters and expressed their approval. Shadrach's applause was loudest of all, but he seemed to find difficulty in meeting his niece's eye. Just before bedtime, after Zoeth and Isaiah had gone upstairs and he was locking up for the night, Mary, whom he supposed had gone also, reëntered the dining-room and stood before him.

"Uncle Shad," she said severely, "come here a minute and sit down. I want to talk with you."

She led him to the big rocker. Then she took the little one beside it.

"Now, look me in the face," she commanded. "No," not out of the window—here. Um . . . yes. I don't wonder you turn red. I should think you might be ashamed."

"I—I—what's that?" stammered Shadrach, turning redder than ever. "What do you mean? Turnin' red! Who's turnin' red?"

"You are," said the young lady, firmly, "and you know it. Now, look me straight in the eye. Uncle Shad Gould, don't you think it would have been more honorable, if you wished to know whether Crawford

Smith and I corresponded, to have asked me instead of hinting? Don't you think it would?"

"Hintin'? Why—why, Mary-'Gusta, what—what——?"

His face was a study in expression. Mary bit her lip, but she managed to appear solemn.

"Yes, hinting," she said. "Instead of asking if Crawford and I had written each other you hinted. Well, now you know that we did write, and have heard his letters to me, have you any objection?"

"Objection? No, no, course not. Why—I—I think 'twas a fine thing. I—I like to get letters; a heap better than I do to write 'em," he added truthfully.

"Then why?"

"Well—well—I—I——"

"And aren't you ashamed?" repeated Mary.

"Why—why, yes, by the jumpin' fire, I am! There! I was ashamed when I done it."

"Then why did you do it?"

"Well—well, you see, Mary-'Gusta, I just wanted to know. Your Uncle Zoeth and me have been actin' as your pilots for a consider'ble spell. Course you're gettin' big enough now to cruise on your own hook—that is, in reason, you understand—but—but—well, we've got so used to takin' an observation every noontime, seein' how you're layin' your course, you know, that it's hard to lose the habit. Not that Zoeth was in on this," he added honestly. "He didn't do any of the hintin', as you call it. I imagine he'll preach my head off for doin' it, when he gets me alone."

"You deserve to have it preached off—or partly off, at any rate. Do you beg my pardon?"

"Sartin sure. I'd beg it on my bended knees if 'twa'n't for the rheumatiz."

"And you won't hint any more?"

"Nary a hint."

"That's right. If you want me to tell you anything, please ask. You must trust me, Uncle Shad. I shall always tell—when there is anything to tell."

"I know you will, Mary-'Gusta. I'm ashamed of my hintin'. God bless you, dearie. Now kiss me good night."

He kissed her and, holding her in his arms, looked fondly down into her eyes. And, as she returned his look, suddenly she blushed crimson and hid her face in his jacket. Then she broke away and with a good night ran from the room and up the stairs.

Shadrach looked after her, sighed, and, after finishing his locking up, went upstairs himself. There was a light in his partner's room and he entered to find Mr. Hamilton sitting at the little table with several sheets of paper covered with figures spread out before him. The Captain was so busy with his own thoughts that, for the moment, he did not notice the papers.

"Zoeth," he said, "our Mary-'Gusta's changed into a grown-up woman. Even this last summer has changed her. She don't look any older, and she's prettier than ever, but she thinks different, and I have a notion that, no matter how much we may want to, you and me ain't goin' to be able to keep her to ourselves as we—— Eh?" suddenly becoming aware of his friend's occupation. "Are you still fussin' over those things? Didn't I tell you not to worry any more, but to turn in and sleep?"

Zoeth shook his head. His usually placid, gentle face had lost some of its placidity. He looked worn and worried and the shadows thrown by the lamp deepened the lines in his forehead. He looked up over his spectacles.

"Shadrach," he said, "I can't help it. I try not to

" 'She mustn't know we're worried' "

worry and I try to heave my burdens onto the Almighty, same as we're commanded, but I can't seem to heave the whole of 'em there. If things don't pick up pretty soon, I don't know—I don't know—and I don't dare think," he added despairingly.

The sheet of paper he was holding rattled as his hand shook. Captain Shad scowled.

"If we didn't have our winter goods to buy," he muttered. "Our credit's good, that's one comfort."

"It is up to now, because the Boston folks don't know. But *we* know, or we're afraid we know, and that makes it worse. How can we go on buyin' from folks that has stood our friends ever since we went into business, knowin' as we do that——"

His partner interrupted.

"We don't know anything yet," he declared. "Keep a stiff upper lip, Zoeth. Nine chances to one we'll weather it all right. *What* a summer this has been! And when I think," he added savagely, "of how well we got along afore those new stores came it makes me nigh crazy. I'll go out with a card of matches some night and burn 'em down. Damn pirates! Callin' themselves good Cape Cod names—names that don't belong to 'em! Baker's Bazaar! Ugh! Rheinstein's Robbers' Roost would be nigher the truth. . . . Say, Zoeth, we mustn't hint a word to Mary-'Gusta about this. We've got cash enough on hand to pay her clearance charges up there at school, ain't we?"

"Yes, Shadrach, I've looked out for that. I don't know's I'd ought to. The money maybe had ought to go somewheres else, but—but right or wrong it's goin' for her and I hope the Lord'll forgive me. And what you say's true, she mustn't know we're worried. She's so conscientious she might be for givin' up her schoolin'

233

and comin' down here to help us. She'd be just as liable to do it as not."

"You're right, she would. Good thing she thinks she's got money of her own and that that money is payin' her schoolin' bills. She'd be frettin' all the time about the expense if 'twa'n't for that. You and I must pretend everything's lovely and the goose hangin' high when she's around. And we mustn't let Isaiah drop any hints."

"No. Isaiah has asked me two or three times lately if the new stores was hurtin' our trade. I shouldn't wonder if he had some suspicions down inside him."

"Umph! Well, that's all right, so long as they stay inside. If I see signs of one of those suspicions risin' above his Adam's apple I'll choke 'em down again. I'll put a flea in Isaiah's ear, and I'll put mucilage on its feet so's 'twill stick there."

So although Mary did notice that the two new shops in the village seemed to be prospering and that business at Hamilton and Company's was not rushing even for September, the answers to her questions were so reassuring that her uneasiness was driven away. Her Uncle Zoeth evaded direct reply and Captain Shadrach prevaricated whole-heartedly and cheerfully. Even Isaiah declared that "everything and all hands was doin' fine." But Mary made him promise that should it ever be otherwise than fine he would write her immediately. He gave the promise with some reluctance.

"I cal'late if Cap'n Shad caught me tellin' tales out of school he'd go to work and turn to and bust me over the head with a marlinespike," said Mr. Chase, with the air of one stating a fact.

Mary laughed. "Oh, no, he wouldn't," she declared. "I'll stand back of you, Isaiah. Now mind, you are to keep me posted on *just* how things are here."

CHAPTER XVI

MARY went back to Boston and to school, where old acquaintances were renewed and new ones made. The Misses Cabot welcomed her with fussy and dignified condescension. Barbara Howe hugged and kissed her and vowed she had not seen a girl all summer who was half so sweet.

"Why in the world someone doesn't run off with you and marry you this very minute I cannot see," declared the vivacious young lady. "If I were a man *I* should."

Mary, who was used to Miss Howe's outbursts, merely smiled.

"Oh, no, you wouldn't," she replied. "I should hope you would be more sensible. No one will run off with me; at least I wouldn't run off with them."

"Why not? Don't you think an elopement is perfectly splendid—so romantic and all that? Suppose you were head over heels in love with someone and his people were dead set against his marrying you, wouldn't you elope then?"

"I think I shouldn't. I think I should try to find out why they were so opposed to me. Perhaps there might be some good reason. If there were no good reason, then—why, then—well, I don't know. But I should hesitate a long while before I came between a person and his family. It must be dreadful to do that."

Barbara laughed. "Nonsense!" she cried. "It's done every day in the best families, my dear. And then the

235

reconciliation is all the sweeter. You just wait! Some of these days I expect to read: 'Elopement in South Harniss High Life. Beautiful Society Maiden Weds Famous Former Football—er—er—I want another F— Oh, yes, Famous Former Football Favorite.' Isn't that beautiful? Dear me, how you blush! Or is it sunburn? At any rate, it's very becoming."

The Famous Former Football Favorite called at Mrs. Wyeth's on the evening following that of Mary's return to Boston. He was as big and brown as ever and declared that he had had a wonderful vacation.

"And you're looking awfully well, too," he exclaimed, inspecting her from head to foot. "She is, isn't she, Mrs. Wyeth?"

Mrs. Wyeth admitted that she thought so. Crawford nodded emphatically.

"By George, you are!" he repeated.

There was no doubt of his sincerity. In fact, the admiration in his voice and look was so obvious and unconcealed that Mary, although she could not help being pleased, was a little embarrassed. The embarrassment wore away, however, when he began to tell of his summer in the Sierras and to ask for additional particulars concerning her European trip. He stayed longer than usual that evening and came again a few evenings later —to show them some photographs he had taken in the mountains, so he said. And the following Sunday he dropped in to accompany them to church. And—but why particularize? Perhaps it will be sufficient to say that during that fall and winter the boy and girl friendship progressed as such friendships are likely to do. Miss Pease, the romantic, nodded and looked wise and even Mrs. Wyeth no longer resented her friend's looks and insinuations with the same indignant certainty of denial.

"I don't know, Letitia," she admitted. "I don't know. I'm beginning to think he cares for her and may be really serious about it. Whether or not she cares for him is quite another thing and I am sure I shan't presume to guess. If she does she keeps it to herself, as she does so many other things. She knows how to mind her own business and that is a gift possessed by few, Letitia Pease."

Mary went home for the Christmas vacation and spent the holidays, as she had spent those of the previous year, in helping her uncles at the store. The Christmas trade, although not so brisk as she had seen it, was not so bad as to alarm her, and the partners were optimistic as ever. Isaiah, who had been talked to like a Dutch uncle by Captain Shad and was consequently in deadly fear of the latter's wrath, declared that as far as he could see everything was all right. So Mary left South Harniss and returned to school and the duties of the winter term with few misgivings concerning matters at home. Crawford met her at the train and came to the Pinckney Street house that evening to hear the news from the Cape. It was surprising, the interest in Cape Cod matters manifested of late by that young man.

On a day in early April, Mary, hurrying to Mrs. Wyeth's after school, found a letter awaiting her. She glanced at the postmark, which was South Harniss, and the handwriting, which was Isaiah's, and then laid it aside to be read later on at her leisure. After many postponements and with considerable reluctance she had accepted an invitation to dine with Barbara Howe at the latter's home in Brookline and this evening was the time appointed. It would be her first plunge into society—the home life of society, that is. The Howes were an old family, wealthy and well-connected, and

Mary could not help feeling somewhat nervous at the ordeal before her. She knew something of the number and variety of expensive gowns possessed by her young hostess and her own limited wardrobe seemed doubly limited and plain by comparison. But she summoned her unfailing common sense to her rescue and found consolation in the fact that Barbara and her people knew she was, comparatively speaking, a poor girl, and therefore could hardly have invited her with the expectation of seeing her arrayed in fine clothes. And if they had done so—here was a bit of the old Mary-'Gusta philosophy—their opinion was not worth consideration anyhow, and the sooner they and she reached mutual disgust and parting the better.

But although her best gown was not new nor expensive, and her jewels were conspicuous by their absence, the picture she made as she stood before the mirror giving the last touches to her hair was distinctly not an unpleasing one. Maggie, the maid, who entered the room to announce a caller, was extravagant in her praises.

"Ah, sure, Miss, you look fine," she declared. "You're that sweet one look at you would sugar a cup of tea. Ah, he'll be that proud of you and he ought to be, too. But he's a fine young man, and——"

"Who? What are you talking about, Maggie?" interrupted Mary. "Who will be proud of me and who is a fine young fellow?"

"Who? Why, Mr. Smith, of course; who else? He's down in the parlor waitin' for you now. I'll tell him you'll be down."

Before Mary could stop her she had left the room and was on her way downstairs. Mary followed a moment later. She had not expected a visit from Crawford, who had called already that week. She wondered why he had come.

She found him in the parlor. Mrs. Wyeth was out shopping with Miss Pease, and he and she were alone. He rose to meet her as she entered.

"Why, Crawford," she said, "what is the matter? Has anything happened? Why do you look so serious?"

He smiled ruefully. "I guess because I am rather serious," he answered. "I've had some news and I came to tell you about it." Then, noticing her gown, he added: "But you're going out, aren't you?"

"I am going out by and by. I am going to dine and spend the evening with Barbara Howe. But I am not going yet. Won't you sit down?"

"I will if you're sure you can spare the time. I hope you can, because—well, because I do want to talk to you. I've had bad news from home. My father is ill—and in the doctor's care."

"Oh, I'm so sorry. I hope it isn't serious."

"I don't know whether it is or not. It can't be desperately serious, because he wrote the letter himself. But at any rate it's serious enough for me. He wants me to give up my work here at the Harvard Medical and come West."

Mary gasped. "Give it up!" she repeated. "Give up your studies? Give up medicine? Surely he doesn't want you to do that!"

Crawford shook his head. "No, not quite that," he replied. "I wouldn't do that, even for him. But he writes that he is not well and is not likely to be better for a good while, if ever, and he would be very much happier if I were nearer at hand. He wants me to give up here at the Harvard Med. and take up my work again at Denver or Salt Lake City or somewhere out there. Even Chicago would seem much nearer, he says. It's a pitiful sort of letter. The old chap seems dreadfully down in the dumps. He wants me, that's plain enough, and he seems to think he needs me. Says if I were at Denver I could come home every little while, whereas here I can't. What ought I to do? I hate to say no, and I hate just as much to say yes."

Mary considered.

"I think you must decide for yourself," she said after a moment. "You have your career to consider, of course."

"Yes, I have. But, to be perfectly honest, I suppose my career would not be influenced greatly if I went. There are plenty of good medical colleges in the West. It is only that I am a Harvard man and I hoped to finish at the Harvard school, that is all. But I *could* go. What do you advise?"

Again Mary took time for consideration. Her face now was as grave as his. At last she said, without raising her eyes: "I think you ought to go."

He groaned. "I was afraid you would say that," he admitted. "And I suppose you are right."

"Yes, I think I am. If your father needs you and wants you, and if your career will not be influenced for harm, I—well, I think you should do as he wishes."

"And my own wishes shouldn't count, I suppose?"

"Why, no, not in this case; not much, at any rate. Do you think they should?"

"Perhaps not. But—but yours?"

"Mine?"

"Yes. Do *you* want me to go away?" He leaned forward in his chair and repeated earnestly: "Do you, Mary?"

She looked at him and her eyes fell before the look in his. Her heart began to beat quickly and she glanced apprehensively toward the partly opened door. He rose and closed it. Then he came close to her.

"Mary," he said, earnestly, "do you know why this appeal of Dad's has hit me so very hard? Why it is going to be so mighty difficult to say yes and leave here? It isn't because I hate to give up Harvard. I do hate that, of course, but I'd do it in a minute for Dad. It isn't that. It's because I can't—I just can't think of leaving you. You have come to be——"

She interrupted. "Please don't," she begged. "Please!"

He went on, unheeding:

"You have come to mean about all there is in life for me," he declared. "It isn't money or success or reputation I've been working and plugging for these last few months; it's just you. I didn't think so once—I used to think such things were just in books—but now I know. I love you, Mary."

Again she protested. "Oh, Crawford," she begged, "please!"

"No; you've got to hear me. It's true; I love you, and if you can care for me, I am going to marry you. Not now, of course; I've got my way to make first; but some day, if I live."

His teeth set in the determined fashion she had learned to know meant unswerving purpose. She looked up, saw the expression of his face, and for the instant forgot everything except her pride in him and her joy that she should have awakened such feelings. Then she remembered other things, things which she had spent many hours of many nights in debating and considering. As he bent toward her she evaded him and rose.

"Don't, Crawford! Please!" she said again. "You mustn't say such things to me. It isn't right that you should."

He looked puzzled. "Why not?" he asked. "At any rate, right or wrong, I must say them, Mary. I've been holding them in for months and now I've just got to say them. I love you and I want to marry you. May I?"

"Oh, no, Crawford! No! It is impossible."

"Impossible! Why? Is it—is it because you don't care for me? Don't you, Mary?"

She did not answer.

"Don't you?" he repeated. "Look at me! Can't you care, Mary?"

She was silent. But when he took a step toward her she raised her hands in protest.

"Please don't!" she pleaded. "No, you mustn't— we mustn't think—Oh, no, it is impossible!"

"It isn't impossible. If you love me as I do you it is the only possible thing in the world. Listen, dear——"

"Hush! I mustn't listen. Be sensible, Crawford! Think! We are both so young. You are only beginning your studies. It will be years before you can— before you should consider marrying."

"But we can wait. I am willing to wait if you will only promise to wait for me. I'll work—*how* I'll work! —and——"

"I know, but we both have others besides ourselves to consider. I have my uncles. They have done everything for me. And you have your father. Does he know—about me—about what you have just said to me?"

And now Crawford hesitated. Not long, but long

enough for Mary to know what the answer would be before it was spoken.

"He doesn't know," she said. "I thought not. Do you think he will approve?"

"I hope he will. There is every reason why he should and absolutely none why he shouldn't. Of course he'll approve; he's sensible."

"Yes, but he may have plans of his own for you, and your marrying an Eastern girl may not be one of them. You have often told me how prejudiced he is against the East and Eastern people. He may disapprove strongly."

Crawford squared his shoulders. There was no hesitation or doubt in his next speech.

"If he does it will make no difference," he declared. "I care a whole lot for Dad and I'd do anything on earth for him—anything but the one thing, that is: I won't give you up—provided you care for me—for him or for anyone else. That's final."

He certainly looked as if it were. But Mary only shook her head. In the new thoughts and new imaginings which had come to her during the past winter there had been a vague foreshadowing of a possible situation somewhat like this. She had her answer ready.

"Oh, no, it isn't," she said. "You are his son, his only child, Crawford. He cares so much for you. You have often told me that, and—and I know he must. And you and he have been so happy together. Do you think I would be the cause of breaking that relationship?"

He waved the question aside and asked one of his own.

"Do you love me, Mary?" he asked.

"You mustn't ask me, Crawford. Write your father. Tell him everything. Will you?"

"Yes, I will. I should have done it, anyway. If I go home, and I suppose I must, I shall tell him; it will be better than writing. But I want your answer before I go. Won't you give it to me?"

He looked very handsome and very manly, as he stood there pleading. But Mary had made up her mind.

"I can't, Crawford," she said. "Perhaps I don't know. I do know that it would not be right for me to say what you want me to say—now. Go home to your father; he needs you. Tell him everything and then—write me."

He looked at her, a long, long look. Then he nodded slowly.

"All right," he said; "I will. I will tell him that I mean to marry you. If he says yes—as he will, I'm sure—then I'll write you that. If he says no, I'll write you that. But in either case, Mary Lathrop, I shall marry you just the same. Your own no will be the only thing that can prevent it. And now may I come and see you tomorrow evening?"

"Not tomorrow, Crawford. When will you start for home?"

"Saturday, I think. May I come the day after tomorrow? Just to say good-by, you know."

Mary was troubled. She could not deny him and yet she was certain it would be better for them both if he did not come.

"Perhaps," she said doubtfully. "But only to say good-by. You must promise that."

There was a ring at the bell. Then Maggie, the maid, appeared to announce that the Howe motor car was waiting at the curb. A few moments later Mary was in her room adjusting her new hat before the mirror. Ordinarily, adjusting that hat would have been an absorbing and painstaking performance; just now it was done with scarcely a thought. How devoutly she wished that the Howe car and the Howe dinner were waiting for anyone in the wide world but her! She did not wish to meet strangers; she did not wish to go anywhere, above all she did not wish to eat. That evening, of all evenings in her life, she wished to be alone. However, accepted invitations are implied obligations and Mary, having adjusted the hat, gave her eyes a final dab with a handkerchief and cold water and hastened down to answer the call to social martyrdom.

It was not excruciating torture, that dinner in the Howe dining-room, even to a young lady who had just listened to a proposal of marriage and desired to think of nothing less important. Mr. Howe was big and jolly. Mrs. Howe was gray-haired and gracious and Barbara was—Barbara. Also, there was a friend of Mr. Howe's, an elderly gentleman named Green, who it seemed was one of a firm of wholesale grocers downtown, and who told funny stories and, by way of proving that they were funny, laughed heartiest of all at the ending of each. He sat next Mrs. Howe during dinner, but later, when they were all in the handsome drawing-room, he came over and seated himself upon the sofa next Mary and entered into conversation with her.

"You are not a born Bostonian, I understand, Miss Lathrop," he observed. "An importation, eh? Ho, ho! Yes. Well, how do you like us?"

Mary smiled. "Oh, I like Boston very much, Mr. Green," she answered. "I know it better than any other American city, perhaps that is why. It was the only city I had ever seen until quite recently. I am imported

—as you call it—from not so far away. My home is on Cape Cod."

Mr. Green regarded her with interest.

"So?" he said. "From Cape Cod, eh? That's rather peculiar. I have been very much interested in the Cape for the past day or so. Something has occurred in connection with my business which brought the Cape to mind. My attention has been—er—as you may say, gripped by the strong right arm of Massachusetts. Eh? Ho, ho!"

He chuckled at his own joke. Mary was rather bored, but she tried not to show it.

"What part of the Cape has interested you, Mr. Green?" she inquired for the sake of saying something.

"Eh? Oh—er—South Harniss. Little town down near the elbow. Do you know it?"

Mary was surprised, of course. The answer which was on the tip of her tongue was naturally, "Why, yes, I live there." But she did not make that answer, although she has often wondered, since, why. What she said was: "Yes, I know South Harniss."

"Do you, indeed?" went on Green. "Well, I don't, but I have known some people who live there for ever so long. My father knew them before me. They were customers of his and they have been buying of our firm for years. Two old chaps who keep what I believe they would call a 'general store.' Fine old fellows, both of them! Different as can be, and characters, but pure gold inside. I have had some bad news concerning them. They're in trouble and I'm mighty sorry."

Mary was bored no longer. She leaned forward and asked breathlessly:

"What are their names, Mr. Green?"

"Eh? Oh, the firm name is Hamilton and Company.

That is simple and sane enough, but the names of the
partners were cribbed from the book of Leviticus, I
should imagine—Zoeth and Shadrach! Ho, ho! Think
of it! Think of wishing a name like Shadrach upon a
helpless infant. The S. P. C. A. or C. C. or something
ought to be told of it. Ho, ho!"

He laughed aloud. Mary did not laugh.

"They—you said they were in trouble," she said
slowly. "What sort of trouble?"

"Eh? Oh, the usual kind. The kind of goblin, young
lady, which is likely to get us business men if we don't
watch out—financial trouble. The firm of Hamilton and
Company has not kept abreast of the times, that's all.
For years they did a good business and then some new
competitors with up-to-date ideas came to town and—
puff!—good-by to the old fogies. They are in a bad way,
I'm afraid, and will have to go under, unless—eh? But
there! you aren't particularly interested, I dare say. It
was your mention of Cape Cod which set me going."

"Oh, but I am interested; I am, really. They must go
under, you say? Fail, do you mean?"

"Yes, that is what I mean. I am very sorry. Our
firm would go on selling them goods almost indefinitely
for, as I have said, they are old customers and in a way
old friends. But they are absolutely honest and they
will not buy what they cannot pay for. We have some
pitiful letters from them—not whining, you know, but
straightforward and frank. They don't ask favors, but
tell us just where they stand and leave it to us to refuse
credit if we see fit. It is just one of the little tragedies
of life, Miss Lathrop, but I'm mighty sorry for those
two old friends of my father's and mine. And the worst
of it is that, from inquiries I have made, it would seem
that they have been sacrificing themselves by spending

their money lavishly and uselessly on someone else. They have a girl in the family, a sort of adopted niece, whatever that is, and, not content with bringing her up like a sensible, respectable country girl, they must dress her like a millionaire's daughter and send her off to some extravagantly expensive seminary where—— Why, what is the matter? Eh? Good heavens! What have I been saying? You don't know these people, do you?"

Mary turned a very white face toward his.

"They are my uncles," she said. "My home is at South Harniss. Please excuse me, Mr. Green."

She rose and walked away. A few minutes later, when Mr. Howe approached the sofa, he found his friend sitting thereon, staring at nothing in particular and fervently repeating under his breath, "The devil! The devil! The devil!"

Mary got away as soon as she could. Her looks attracted Barbara's attention and the young lady asked if she were not feeling well. Mary replied that she was not, and although it was not serious please might she be permitted to go home at once? She was sent home in the automobile and when she reached her own room her first act was to find and open Isaiah's letter which had arrived that afternoon. With trembling fingers she held it beneath the gas jet and this is what she read:

DEAR MARY AUGUSTA:

I had not ought to write you this and your Uncles would pretty nigh kill me if they knew I done so but I am going to just the same. Busines has gone to rack and ruin. Hamilton & Co. thanks to those and other darned stores, ain't making enough to keep boddy and soul together and they are making themselves sick over it. I don't know what will become of them to if something or someboddy does not think up some way to help them over the shoals. They do not tell

MARY-'GUSTA

anyone and least of all they wouldent want you to be told, but I think you ought to be. They have done a whole lot for you. Can't you think up some way to do something for them. For god Sakes write right off.

Yours truly,

ISAIAH CHASE.

CHAPTER XVII

PEOPLE grow older, even on the Cape, where hurry —except by the automobiles of summer residents—is not considered good form and where Father Time is supposed to sit down to rest. Judge Baxter, Ostable's leading attorney-at-law, had lived quietly and comfortably during the years which had passed since, as Marcellus Hall's lawyer, he read the astonishing letter to the partners of Hamilton and Company. He was over seventy now, and behind his back Ostable folks referred to him as "old Judge Baxter"; but although his spectacles were stronger than at that time, his mental faculties were not perceptibly weaker, and he walked with as firm, if not so rapid, a stride. So when, at eleven in the forenoon of the day following Mary's dinner at the Howes' home, the Judge heard someone enter the outer room of his offices near the Ostable courthouse, he rose from his chair in the inner room and, without waiting for his clerk to announce the visitor, opened the door himself.

The caller whose question the clerk was about to answer, or would probably have answered as soon as he finished staring in awestruck admiration, was a young lady. The Judge looked at her over his spectacles and then through them and decided that she was a stranger. He stepped forward.

"I am Judge Baxter," he said. "Did you wish to see me?"

She turned toward him. "Yes," she said simply. "I

should like to talk with you for a few moments, if you are not too busy."

The Judge hesitated momentarily. Only the week before a persistent and fluent young female had talked him into the purchase of a set of "Lives of the Great Jurists," the same to be paid for in thirty-five installments of two dollars each. Mrs. Baxter had pronounced the "Great Jurists" great humbugs, and her husband, although he pretended to find the "Lives" very interesting, was secretly inclined to agree with her. So he hesitated. The young woman, evidently noticing his hesitation, added:

"If you are engaged just now I shall wait. I came to see you on a matter of business, legal business."

Judge Baxter tried to look as if no thought of his visitor's having another purpose had entered his mind.

"Oh, yes, certainly! Of course!" he said hastily, and added: "Will you walk in?"

She walked in—to the private office, that is—and the Judge, following her, closed the door. His clerk stared wistfully at his own side of that door for a full minute, then sighed heavily and resumed his work, which was copying a list of household effects belonging to a late lamented who had willed them, separately and individually, to goodness knew how many cousins, first, second, and third.

In the private office the Judge asked his visitor to be seated. She took the chair he brought forward. Then she said:

"You don't remember me, I think, Judge Baxter. I am Mary Lathrop."

The Judge looked puzzled. The name sounded familiar, but he could not seem to identify its owner.

"Perhaps you would remember me if I told you my whole name," suggested the latter. "I am Mary Augusta

Lathrop. I think perhaps you used to call me Mary-'Gusta; most people did."

Then the Judge remembered. His astonishment was great.

"Mary-'Gusta Lathrop!" he repeated. "Mary-'Gusta! Are you——? Why, it scarcely seems possible! And yet, now that I look, I can see that it is. Bless my soul and body! How do you do? It must be almost—er—seven or eight years since I have seen you. South Harniss is only a few miles off, but I am getting—er—older and I don't drive as much as I used to. But there! I am very glad to see you now. And how are Captain Gould and Mr. Hamilton? There is no need to ask how you are. Your looks are the best answer to that."

Mary thanked him and said she was very well. Her uncles, too, were well, she added, or they were when she last heard.

"I am on my way home to them now," she added. "For the past two years I have been at school in Boston. I left there this morning and got off the train here because I wished very much to see you, Judge Baxter. Yesterday—last evening—I heard something—I was told something which, if it is true, is—is——"

She bit her lip. She was evidently fighting desperately not to lose self-control. The Judge was surprised and disturbed.

"Why, Mary!" he exclaimed. "I suppose I may call you Mary still; as an old friend I hope I may. What is the matter? What did you hear? What do you wish to see me about?"

She was calm enough now, but her earnestness was unmistakable.

"I heard something concerning myself and my uncles which surprised and shocked me dreadfully," she said.

"I can hardly believe it, but I must know whether it is true or not. I must know at once! You can tell me the truth, Judge Baxter, if you only will. That is why I came here this morning. Will you tell it to me? Will you promise that you will answer my questions, every one, with the exact truth and nothing else? And answer them all? Will you promise that?"

The Judge looked even more surprised and puzzled. He rubbed his chin and smiled doubtfully.

"Well, Mary," he said, "I think I can promise that if I answer your questions at all I shall answer them truthfully. But I scarcely like to promise to answer them without knowing what they are. A lawyer has a good many secrets intrusted to him and he is obliged to be careful."

"I know. But this is a secret in which I am interested. I am interested in it more than anyone else. I must know the truth about it! I *must!* If you won't tell me I shall find out somehow. *Will* you tell?"

Judge Baxter rubbed his chin again.

"Don't you think you had better ask your questions?" he suggested.

"Yes; yes, I do. I will. How much money did my stepfather, Captain Marcellus Hall, have when he died?"

The Judge's chin-rubbing ceased. His eyebrows drew together.

"Why do you want to know?" he asked, after a moment.

"Because I do. Because it is very important that I should. It is my right to know. Was he a rich man?"

"Um—er—no. I should not call him that. Hardly a rich man."

"Was he very poor?"

"Mary, I don't exactly see why——"

"I do. Oh, Judge Baxter, please don't think I am asking this for any selfish reasons. I am not, indeed I'm not! All my life, ever since I was old enough to think of such things at all, I have supposed—I have been led to believe that my stepfather left me plenty of money—money enough to pay my uncles for taking care of me, for my clothes and board, and now, during these last two years, for my studies in Boston. I never, never should have consented to go to that school if I hadn't supposed I was paying the expenses myself. I knew my uncles were not well-to-do; I knew they could not afford to—to do what they had already done for me, even before that. And now—last night—I was told that—that they were in great financial trouble, that they would probably be obliged to fail in business, and all because they had been spending their money on me, sacrificing themselves and their comfort and happiness in order that 'an adopted niece with extravagant ideas' might be educated above her station; that is the way the gentleman who told me the story put it. Of course he didn't know he was talking to the niece," she added, with a pathetic little smile; "but, Oh, Judge, can't you see now why I must know the truth—all of the truth?"

Her fingers clasped and unclasped in her lap. The Judge laid his own hand upon them.

"There, there, my dear," he said soothingly. "Tut, tut, tut! What's all this about your uncles failing in business? That isn't possible, is it? Tell me the whole thing, just as it was told to you."

So Mary told it, concluding by exhibiting Isaiah Chase's letter.

"It must be very bad, you see," she said. "Isaiah never would have written if it had not been. It is hard enough to think that while I was enjoying myself in

Europe and at school they were in such trouble and keeping it all to themselves. That is hard enough, when I know how they must have needed me. But if it should be true that it is their money—money they could not possibly spare—that I have been spending—wasting there in Boston, I—I—— Please tell me, Judge Baxter! Have I any money of my own? Please tell me."

The Judge rose and walked up and down the floor, his brows drawn together and his right hand slapping his leg at each turn. After seven or eight of these turns he sat down again and faced his caller.

"Mary," he said, "suppose this story about your uncles' financial and business troubles should be true, what will you do?"

Mary met his look bravely. Her eyes were moist, but there was no hesitation in her reply.

"I shall stay at home and help them in any way I can," she said. "There will be no more Boston and no more school for me. They need me there at home and I am going home—to stay."

"Whether it is your money or theirs which has paid for your education?"

"Certainly. Of course I never should have gone away at all if I had not supposed my own money were paying the expenses. Judge, you haven't answered my question—and yet I think—I am afraid that you have answered it. It was their money that paid, wasn't it?"

Judge Baxter was silent for a moment, as if in final deliberation. Then he nodded, solemnly.

"Yes, Mary," he said, "it was their money. In fact, it has been their money which has paid for most things in your life. Shadrach Gould and Zoeth Hamilton aren't, maybe, the best business men in the world, but they come pretty near to being the best *men,* in business or out of it, that I have met during seventy odd years on this planet. I think, perhaps, it will be well for you to know just how good they have been to you. Now, listen!"

He began at the beginning, at the day of Marcellus Hall's funeral, when he read the letter to Shadrach and Zoeth, the letter intrusting Mary-'Gusta to their care. He told of Marcellus's unfortunate investments, of the loss of the latter's fortune, and how, when the estate was settled, there were but a few hundreds where it was expected there might be a good many thousands.

"Don't make any mistake, Mary," he said earnestly. "Your uncles knew there was little or no money when they decided to take you. They took you simply for yourself, because they cared so much for you, not because they were to make a cent from the guardianship. Everything you have had for the past two years their money has paid for and you may be absolutely certain they never have grudged a penny of it. The last time I saw Captain Gould he was glorying in having the smartest and best girl in Ostable County. And Mr. Hamilton——"

She interrupted him. "Don't, please!" she said chokingly. "Please don't tell me any more just now. I—I want to think."

"There isn't any more to tell," he said gently. "I am going into the next room. I shall be back in a few minutes. Then, if you care to, we can talk a little more."

When he returned she had risen and was standing by the window looking out into the back yard. She was calm and even smiled a little as he entered, although the smile was a rather pitiful one. Of the two the Judge looked the more perturbed.

"Whew!" he exclaimed, after carefully closing the door behind him. "I've been doing a little thinking myself, young lady, since I left you here. I've been thinking that I had better take a trip to Canada or China or somewhere and start in a hurry, too. When your uncles find out that I told you this thing they have succeeded in keeping from you all this time—well, it will be high time for me to be somewhere else." He laughed and then added gravely: "But I still think I was right in telling you. Under the circumstances it seems to me that you should know."

"Of course I should. If you had not told me I should have found it out, now that my suspicions were aroused. Thank you, Judge Baxter. Now I must go."

"Go? Go where?"

"Home—to South Harniss."

"Nonsense! You're not going to South Harniss yet awhile. You're going to have dinner with my wife and me."

"Thank you. I can't. I must go at once. By the next train."

"There isn't any train until nearly four o'clock." Then, noticing her look of disappointment, he went on to say: "But that shan't make any difference. I'll send you over in my nephew's automobile. I'm not sufficiently up-to-date to own one of the cussed—excuse me!— things, but he does and I borrow it occasionally. I don't drive it; good heavens, no! But his man shall drive you over and I'll guarantee you beat the train. If you don't, it won't be because you go too slow. Now, of course, you'll stay to dinner."

But Mary shook her head. "You're very kind, Judge," she said, "and I thank you very much, but——"

"Well, but what?"

"But I—I can't. I—I—Oh, don't you see? I couldn't eat, or even try to—now. I want to get home—to them."

"And so you shall, my dear. And in double-quick time, too. Here, Jesse," opening the door to the outer office and addressing the clerk, "you step over and tell Samuel that I want to borrow his car and Jim for two hours. Tell him I want them now. And if his car is busy go to Cahoon's garage and hire one with a driver. Hurry!

"And now, Mary," turning to her, "can you tell me any more about your plans, provided you have had time to make any? If this story about your uncles' business troubles is true, what do you intend doing? Or don't you know?"

Mary replied that her plans were very indefinite, as yet.

"I have some ideas," she said; "some that I had thought I might use after I had finished school and come back to the store. They may not be worth much; they were schemes for building up the business there and adding some other sorts of business to it. The first thing I shall do is to see how bad the situation really is."

"I hope it isn't bad. Poor Zoeth certainly has had trouble enough in his life."

There was a significance in his tone which Mary plainly did not understand.

"What trouble do you mean?" she asked.

The Judge looked at her, coughed, and then said hastily: "Oh, nothing in particular; every one of us has troubles, I suppose. But, Mary, if—if you find that the story is true and—ahem—a little money might help to —er—tide the firm over—why, I—I think perhaps that it might be—ahem—arranged so that——"

He seemed to be having difficulty in finishing the sentence. Mary did not wait to hear the end.

"Thank you, Judge," she said quickly. "Thank you,

but I am hoping it may not be so bad as that. I am
going back there, you know, and—well, as Uncle Shadrach would say, we may save the ship yet. At any rate,
we won't call for help until the last minute."

Judge Baxter regarded her with admiration.

"Shadrach and Zoeth are rich in one respect," he declared; "they've got you. But it is a wicked shame
that you must give up your school and your opportunities
to——"

She held up her hand.

"Please don't!" she begged. "If you knew how glad
I am to be able to do something, if it is only to give up!"

The car and Jim were at the door a few minutes later
and Mary, having said good-by to the Judge and promised faithfully to keep him posted as to events at home,
climbed into the tonneau and was whizzed away. Jim,
the driver, after a few attempts at conversation, mainly
concerning the "unseasonableness" of the weather, finding responses few and absently given, relapsed into
silence. Silence was what Mary desired, silence and
speed, and Jim obliged with the latter.

Over the road by which, a dozen years before, she
had driven in the old buggy she now rode again. Then,
as now, she wondered what she should find at her journey's end. Here, however, the resemblance ceased, for
whereas then she looked forward, with a child's anticipations, to nothing more definite than new sights and
new and excitingly delightful adventures, now she saw
ahead—what? Great care and anxiety and trouble certainly, these at the best; and at the worst, failure and
disappointment and heartbreak. And behind her she was
leaving opportunity and the pleasant school life and
friends, leaving them forever.

She was leaving Crawford, too, leaving him without

a word of explanation. She had had no time to write even a note. Mrs. Wyeth, after protesting vainly against her guest's decision to leave for the Cape by the earliest train in the morning, had helped to pack a few essential belongings; the others she was to pack and send later on, when she received word to do so. The three, Mrs. Wyeth, Miss Pease, and Mary, had talked and argued and planned until almost daylight. Then followed an hour or two of uneasy sleep, a hurried breakfast, and the rush to the train. Mary had not written Crawford; the shock of what she had been told at the Howes' and her great anxiety to see Judge Baxter and learn if what she had heard was true had driven even her own love story from her mind. Now she remembered that she had given him permission to call, not this evening but the next, to say good-by before leaving for the West. He would be disappointed, poor fellow. Well, she must not think of that. She must not permit herself to think of anyone but her uncles or of anything except the great debt of love and gratitude she owed them and of the sacrifice they had made for her. She could repay a little of that sacrifice now; at least she could try. She would think of that and of nothing else.

And then she wondered what Crawford would think or say when he found she had gone.

CHAPTER XVIII

THE main street of South Harniss looked natural enough as the motor car buzzed along it. It was but a few months since Mary had been there, yet it seemed ever so much more. She felt so much older than on those Christmas holidays. When the store of Hamilton and Company came in sight she sank down on the back seat in order not to be seen. She knew her uncles were, in all probability, there at the store, and she wished to see Isaiah and talk with him before meeting them.

Isaiah was in the kitchen by the cookstove when she opened the door. He turned, saw her, and stood petrified. Mary entered and closed the door behind her. By that time Mr. Chase had recovered sufficiently from his ossification to speak.

"Eh—eh—by time!" he gasped. "I snum if it ain't you!"

Mary nodded. "Isaiah," she asked quickly, "are you alone? Are my uncles, both of them, at the store?"

But the cook and steward had not yet completely got over the effect of the surprise. He still stared at her.

"It *is* you, ain't it!" he stammered. "I—I—by time, I do believe you've come home, same as I asked you to."

"Of course I've come home. How in the world could I be here if I hadn't? *Don't* stare at me like that, with your mouth open like a—like a codfish. Tell me, are Uncle Shad and Uncle Zoeth at the store?"

"Eh—— Yes, I cal'late they be. Ain't neither of 'em come home to dinner yet. I'm expectin' one of 'em 'most

261

any minute. I'll run up and fetch 'em. Say! How in the nation did you get here this time of day?"

"I shall tell you by and by. No, I don't want you to get my uncles. I want to talk with you alone first. Now, Isaiah, sit down! Sit down in that chair. I want you to tell me just how bad things are. Tell me everything, all you know about it, and don't try to make the situation better than it is. And please *hurry!*"

Isaiah, bewildered but obedient, sat down. The command to hurry had the effect of making him so nervous that, although he talked enough to have described the most complicated situation, his ideas were badly snarled and Mary had to keep interrupting in order to untangle them. And, after all, what he had to tell was not very definite. Business was bad at the store; that was plain to everyone in town. "All hands" were trading at the new stores where prices were lower, stocks bigger and more up-to-date, and selling methods far, far in advance of those of Hamilton and Company.

"About the only customers that stick by us," declared Isaiah, "are folks like 'Rastus Young and the rest of the deadbeats. *They* wouldn't leave us for nothin'—and nothin's what they pay, too, drat 'em!"

The partners had not told him of their troubles, but telling was not necessary. He had seen and heard enough.

"They are right on the ragged edge of goin' on the rocks," vowed Isaiah. "Zoeth, he's that thin and peaked 'twould make a sick pullet look fleshy alongside of him. And Cap'n Shad goes around with his hands rammed down in his beckets——"

"In his what?"

"In his britches pockets, and he don't scurcely speak a word for hours at a stretch. And they're up all times

262

of the night, fussin' over account books and writin' letters and I don't know what all. It's plain enough what's comin'. Everybody in town is on to it. Why, I was up to the store t'other day settin' outside on the steps and Ab Bacheldor came along. He hates Cap'n Shad worse'n pizen, you know. 'Hello, Isaiah!' he says to me, he says. 'Is that you?' he says. 'Course it's me,' says I. 'Who'd you think 'twas?' 'I didn't know but it might be the sheriff,' he says. 'I understand he's settin' round nowadays just a-waitin'.' And Zoeth was right within hearin', too!"

"Oh!" exclaimed Mary indignantly.

"Yup, that's what he said," went on Isaiah. "But I got in one dig on my own hook. 'The sheriff don't wait much down to your house, Abner, does he?' says I. 'You bet he don't,' says he; 'he don't have to.' 'Well, he'd starve to death if he waited there long,' says I. Ho, ho! His wife's the stingiest woman about her cookin' that there is on the Cape. Why, one time she took a notion she'd keep boarders and Henry Ryder, that drives the fruit cart, he started to board there. But he only stayed two days. The fust day they had biled eggs and the next day they had soup made out of the shells. Course that probably ain't true—Henry's an awful liar—but all the same——"

"Never mind Henry Ryder, or Abner Bacheldor, either," interrupted Mary. "How did you happen to send for me, Isaiah?"

"Eh? Oh, that just came of itself, as you might say. I kept gettin' more and more tittered up and worried as I see how things was goin' and I kept wishin' you was here, if 'twas only to have somebody to talk it over with. But I didn't dast to write and when you was home Christmas I never dast to say nothin' because

Cap'n Shad had vowed he'd butcher me if I told tales to you about any home troubles. That's it, you see! All through this their main idea has been not to trouble you. 'She mustn't know anything or she'll worry,' says Zoeth, and Cap'n Shad he says, 'That's so.' They think an awful sight of you, Mary-'Gusta."

Mary did not trust herself to look up.

"I know," she said. "Go on, Isaiah."

"Well, I kept thinkin' and thinkin' and one day last week Ezra Hopkins, that's the butcher cart feller, he and me was talkin' and he says: 'Trade ain't very brisk up to the store, is it?' he says. 'Everybody says 'tain't.' 'Then if everybody knows so much what d'ye ask me for?' says I. 'Oh, don't get mad,' says he. 'But I tell you this, Isaiah,' he says, 'if Mary-'Gusta Lathrop hadn't gone away to that fool Boston school things would have been different with Hamilton and Company. She's a smart girl and a smart business woman. I believe she'd have saved the old fellers,' he says. 'She was up-to-date and she had the know-how,' says he. Well, I kept thinkin' what he said and—and—well, I wrote. For the land sakes don't tell Shad nor Zoeth that I wrote, but I'm glad I done it. I don't know's you can do anything, I don't know's anybody can, but I'm mighty glad you're here, Mary-'Gusta."

Mary sighed. "I'm glad I am here, too, Isaiah," she agreed, "although I, too, don't know that I can do anything. But," she added solemnly, "I am going to try very hard. Now we mustn't let Uncle Shad or Uncle Zoeth know that I have heard about their trouble. We must let them think I am at home for an extra holiday. Then I shall be able to look things over and perhaps plan a little. When I am ready to tell what I mean to do I can tell the rest. . . . Sshh! Here comes one of them now.

It's Uncle Zoeth. Look happy, Isaiah! *Happy*—not as if you were choking to death! Well, Uncle Zoeth, aren't you surprised to see me?"

Surprised he certainly was; at first, like Isaiah, he could scarcely believe she was really there. Then, naturally, he wished to know *why* she was there. She dodged the questions as best she could and Zoeth, innocent and truthful as always, accepted without a suspicion her vague explanation concerning an opportunity to run down and see them for a little while. Dinner was put on the table and then Isaiah hastened up to relieve Shadrach at the store in order that the partners and Mary might eat together.

The Captain arrived a few minutes later, red-faced, vociferous, and joyful.

"Well," he shouted, throwing his arms about her and kissing her with a smack which might have been heard in Abner Bacheldor's yard, "if *this* ain't a surprise! Zoeth said this mornin' he felt as if somethin' was goin' to happen, and then Isaiah upset the tea kittle all over both my feet and I said I felt as if it *had* happened. But it hadn't, had it! Well, if it ain't good to look at you, Mary-'Gusta! How'd you happen to come this time of year? Has the schoolhouse foundered?"

Mary repeated the excuse she had given Mr. Hamilton. It was sufficient. The partners were too happy at having her with them to be overcurious concerning her reasons for coming. Captain Shad talked and joked and laughed and Zoeth nodded and smiled in his quiet way. If Mary had not known their secret she would not have guessed it but, as it was, she noticed how pale and worn Mr. Hamilton looked and how the Captain had become prone to fits of unwonted silence from which he seemed to arouse himself with an effort and, after a glance at her, to talk and laugh louder than ever. Once she ventured to ask how business was and it would have been almost funny if it had not been so pathetic, the haste with which they both assured her that it was about the same.

After dinner she announced her intention of going up to the store. Her uncles exchanged looks and then Zoeth said:

"What makes you do that, Mary-'Gusta? Nice day like this I'd be out of door if I was you. We don't need you at the store, do we, Shadrach?"

"Not more'n a fish needs a bathin' suit," declared the Captain, with conviction. "You go see some of the girls and have a good time, Mary-'Gusta."

But Mary declined to go and see any of the girls. She could have a better time at the store than anywhere else, she said. She went to the store and spent the afternoon and evening there, watching and listening. There was not much to watch, not more than a dozen customers during the entire time, and those bought but little. The hardest part of the experience for her was to see how eager her uncles were to please each caller and how anxiously each watched the other's efforts and the result. To see Zoeth at the desk poring over the ledger, his lips moving and the pencil trembling in his fingers, was as bad as, but no worse than, to see Captain Shadrach, a frown on his face and his hands in his pockets, pace the floor from the back door to the front window, stop, look up the road, draw a long breath that was almost a groan, then turn and stride back again.

At six o'clock Mary, who had reasons of her own for wishing to be left alone in the store, suggested that she remain there while her uncles went home for supper.

Neither Mr. Hamilton nor the Captain would consent, so she was obliged to go to the house herself and send Isaiah up once more to act as shopkeeper. But at eleven that night, after unmistakable sounds from their rooms were furnishing proofs that both partners of Hamilton and Company were asleep, she tiptoed downstairs, put on her coat and hat, took the store keys from the nail where Zoeth always hung them, and went out. She did not return until almost three.

The next day she spent, for the most part, at the store. She wrote several letters and, in spite of her uncles' protests, waited upon several customers. That evening, as she sat behind the counter thinking, a boy whom Captain Shadrach identified as Zenas Atkins' young-one rushed breathlessly into the store to announce between gasps that "Mary-'Gusta Lathrop's wanted on the phone. It's long distance, too, and—and—you've got to scrabble 'cause they're holdin' the wire." Mary hurried out and to the telephone office. She had not answered Shadrach's question as to who she thought was calling. She did not know, of course, but she suspected, and for a cool-headed young business woman, a girl who had ruthlessly driven all thoughts except those of business from her mind, her heart beat surprisingly fast as she entered the closet which acted as a substitute for a telephone booth, and took down the receiver. Yet her tone was calm enough as she uttered the stereotyped "Hello."

The wire hummed and sang, fragments of distant conversation became audible and were lost, and then a voice, the voice which she was expecting but, in a way, dreading to hear, asked: "Hello! Is this Miss Lathrop?"

"Yes, Crawford."

"Mary, is that you?"

"Yes."

"I have just called at Mrs. Wyeth's and learned that you had gone. I am awfully disappointed. I leave for home tomorrow and I had counted on seeing you before I went. Why did you go without a word to me?"

"Didn't Mrs. Wyeth tell you?"

"She told me a good deal, but I want to know more. Is it true—that about your uncles?"

"I am afraid it is."

"Great Scott, that's too bad! I am mighty sorry to hear it. Look here, isn't there something I can do? Do they need——"

"Sshh! we mustn't talk about it over the phone. No, there is nothing you can do. I have some plans partially worked out; something may come of them. Please don't ask more particulars now."

"All right, I understand; I won't. But mayn't I come down and see you? I can start West the day after tomorrow just as well and that would give me time——"

"No, Crawford, no. You mustn't come."

"I've a good mind to, whether or no."

"If you do I shall not see you—then or at any other time. But you won't, will you?"

"No, Mary, I won't. It's mighty hard, though."

Perhaps it was quite as hard for her, but she did not reply.

"Will you write me—every day?" he went on. . . . "Why don't you answer?"

"I was thinking what would be best for me to do," she said; "best for us both, I mean. I shall write you one letter surely."

"*One!*"

"One surely. I want you to understand just what my coming here means and what effect it may have upon my future. You should know that. Afterward, whether I write you or not will depend."

"Depend! Of course you'll write me! Depend on what?"

"On what seems right to me after I have had time to think, and after you have seen your father. I must go, Crawford. Thank you for calling me. I am glad you did. Good-by."

"Wait! Mary, don't go! Let me say this——"

"Please, Crawford! I'd rather you wouldn't say any more. You understand why, I'm sure. I hope you will have a pleasant trip home and find your father's health much improved. Good-by."

She hung up the receiver and hastened back to the store. Shadrach and Zoeth looked at her questioningly. Finally the former said:

"Anything important, was it?"

"No, Uncle Shad, not very important."

'Oh!"

A short interval of silence, then—

"Mrs. Wyeth callin', I presume likely, eh?"

"No, Uncle Shad."

Shadrach asked no more questions, and Zoeth asked none. Neither of them again mentioned Mary's call to the phone, either to her or to each other. And she did not refer to it. She had promised her Uncle Shadrach, when he questioned her the year before concerning Crawford, to tell him "when there was anything to tell." But was there anything to tell now? With the task which she had set herself and the uncertainty before her she felt that there was not. Yet to keep silence troubled her. Until recently there had never been a secret between her uncles and herself; now there were secrets on both sides.

CHAPTER XIX

AT twelve o'clock on a night late in the following
week Captain Shadrach, snoring gloriously in his
bed, was awakened by his partner's entering the
room bearing a lighted lamp. The Captain blinked, raised
himself on his elbow, looked at his watch which was on
the chair by the bed's head, and then demanded in an
outraged whisper:

"What in the nation are you prowlin' around this
hour of the night for? You don't want to talk about
those divilish bills and credits and things, I hope. What's
the use? Talkin' don't help none! Jumpin' fire! I
went to bed so's to forget 'em and I was just beginnin'
to do it. Now you——"

Zoeth held up his hand. "Sshh! sshh!" he whispered.
"Hush, Shadrach! I didn't come to talk about those
things. Shadrach, there's—there's somethin' queer goin'
on. Get up!"

The Captain was out of bed in a moment.

"What's the matter?" he demanded, in a whisper.
"What's queer?"

"I—I don't exactly know. I heard somebody movin'
downstairs and——"

Shadrach grunted. "Isaiah!" he exclaimed. "Walkin'
in his sleep again, I'll bet a dollar!"

"No, no! It ain't Isaiah. Isaiah ain't walked in his
sleep since he was a child."

"Well, he's pretty nigh his second childhood now,
judgin' by the way he acts sometimes. It was Isaiah,

of course! Who else would be walkin' around downstairs this time of night?"

"That's what I thought, so I went and looked. Shadrach, it was Mary-'Gusta. Hush! Let me tell you! She had her things on, hat and all, and she took the lantern and lit it and went out."

"Went *out!*"

"Yes, and—and up the road. Now, where——?"

Shadrach's answer was to stride to the window, pull aside the shade and look out. Along the lane in the direction of the village a fiery spark was bobbing.

"There she goes now," he muttered. "She's pretty nigh to the corner already. What in the world can she be up to? Where is she bound—at twelve o'clock?"

Zoeth did not answer. His partner turned and looked at him.

"Humph!" he exclaimed. "Why don't you tell me the whole of it while you're about it? You're keepin' somethin' back. Out with it! Do *you* know where she's bound?"

Zoeth looked troubled—and guilty. "Why, no, Shadrach," he faltered, "I don't know, but—but I kind of suspect. You see, she—she did the same thing last night."

"She *did!* And you never said a word?"

"I didn't know what to say. I heard her go and I looked out of the window and saw her. She come back about three. I thought sure she'd speak of it this mornin', but she didn't and—and—— But tonight I watched again and—Shadrach, she's taken the store keys. Anyhow, they're gone from the nail."

The Captain wiped his forehead. "She's gone to the store, then," he muttered. "Jumpin'! That's a relief, anyhow. I was afraid—I didn't know—— Whew! I don't know *what* I didn't know! But what on earth has she gone to the store for? And last night too, you say?"

"Yes. Shadrach, I've been thinkin' and all I can think of is that—that——"

"Well—what?"

"That—that she suspicions how things are with us— somebody that does suspicion has dropped a hint and she has—has gone up to——"

"To do what? Chuck it overboard! Speak it out! To do what?"

"To look at the books or somethin'. She knows the combination of the safe, you recollect."

Captain Shadrach's eyes and mouth opened simultaneously. He made a dive for the hooks on the bedroom wall.

"Jumpin' fire of brimstone!" he roared. "Give me my clothes!"

A half-hour later an interested person—and, so far as that goes, at least every second person in South Harniss would have been interested had he or she been aware of what was going on—an interested and, of course, unscrupulous person peeping in under the shades of Hamilton and Company's window would have seen a curious sight. This person would have seen two elderly men sitting one upon a wooden chair and the other upon a wooden packing case and wearing guilty, not to say hang-dog, expressions, while a young woman standing in front of them delivered pointed and personal remarks.

Captain Shadrach and Zoeth, following their niece to the store, had peeped in and seen her sitting at the desk, the safe open, and account books and papers spread out before her. A board in the platform creaked beneath the Captain's weighty tread and Mary looked up and saw them. Before they could retreat or make up their minds what to do, she had run to the door, thrown it open, and ordered them to come in. Neither answered—they could not at the moment. The certainty that she knew what they had tried so hard to conceal kept them tongue-tied.

"Come in!" repeated Mary. "Come in! And shut the door!"

They came in. Also Captain Shadrach shut the door. Just why he obeyed orders so meekly he could not have told. His niece gave him little time to think.

"I did not exactly expect you," she said, "but, on the whole, I am glad you came. Now sit down, both of you, and listen to me. What do you mean by it?"

Zoeth sat, without a word. Shadrach, however, made a feeble attempt to bluster.

"What do *we* mean by it?" he repeated. "What do *you* mean, you mean! Perusin' up here in the middle of the night without a word to your Uncle Zoeth and me, and—and haulin' open that safe—and——"

Again Mary interrupted.

"Be still, Uncle Shad!" she commanded. "Sit down! Sit down on that box and listen to me! That's right. Now tell me! Why have you been telling me fibs for almost a year? Answer me! Why have you?"

Zoeth looked at Shadrach and the latter looked at him.

"Fibs?" stammered Mr. Hamilton. "Fibs? Why—why, Mary-'Gusta!"

"Yes, fibs. I might use a stronger word and not exaggerate very much. You have led me to think that business was good, that you were doing as well or better than when I was here with you. I asked you over and over again and you invariably gave me that answer.

And now I know that during all that time you have scarcely been able to make ends meet, that you have been worrying yourselves sick, that you——"

Captain Shad could stand it no longer.

"We ain't, neither!" he declared. "I never was better in my life. I ain't had a doctor for more'n a year. And then I only had him for the heaves—for the horse—a horse doctor, I mean. What are you talkin' about! Sick nothin'! If that swab of an Isaiah has——"

"Stop, Uncle Shad! I told you to listen. And you needn't try to change the subject or to pretend I don't know what I am talking about. I do know. And as for pretending—well, there has been pretending enough. What do you mean—you and Uncle Zoeth—by sending me off to school and to Europe and declaring up and down that you didn't need me here at home?"

"We didn't need you, Mary-'Gusta," vowed Zoeth eagerly. "We got along fust-rate without you. And we wanted you to go to school and to Europe. You see, it makes us feel proud to know our girl is gettin' a fine education and seein' the world. It ain't any more than she deserves, but it makes us feel awful pleased to know she's gettin' it."

"And as for the store," broke in the Captain, "I cal'late you've been pawin' over them books and they've kind of—kind of gone to your head. I don't wonder at it, this time of night! Hamilton and Company's all right. We may be a little mite behind in some of our bills, but —er—but. . . . *Don't* look at me like that, Mary-'Gusta! What do you do it for? Stop it, won't you?"

Mary shook her head.

"No, Uncle Shad," she said, "I shan't stop it. I know all about Hamilton and Company's condition; perhaps I know it better than you do. This is the fifth night that I have been working over those books and I should know, at least."

"The *fifth* night! Do you mean to say——"

"I mean that I knew you wouldn't tell me what I wanted to know; I had to see these books for myself and at night was the only time I could do it. But never mind that now," she added. "We'll talk of that later. Other things come first. Uncle Shad and Uncle Zoeth, I know not only about the affairs of Hamilton and Company, but about my own as well."

Zoeth leaned forward and stared at her. He seemed to catch the significance of the remark, for he looked frightened, whereas Shadrach was only puzzled.

"You—you know what, Mary-'Gusta?" faltered Zoeth. "You mean——?"

"I mean," went on Mary, "that I know where the money came from which has paid my school bills and for my clothes and my traveling things and all the rest. I know whose money has paid all my bills ever since I was seven years old."

Shadrach rose from his chair. He was as frightened as his partner now.

"What are you talkin' about, Mary-'Gusta Lathrop?" he shouted. "You know! You don't know nothin'! You stop sayin' such things! Why don't you stop her, Zoeth Hamilton?"

Zoeth was speechless. Mary went on as if there had been no interruption.

"I know," she said, "that I haven't a penny of my own and never did have and that you two have done it all. I know all about it—at last."

If these two men had been caught stealing they could not have looked more guilty. If, instead of being reminded that their niece had spent their money, they had been accused of misappropriating hers they could not have been more shaken or dumbfounded. Captain Shadrach stood before her, his face a fiery red and his mouth opening and shutting in vain attempts at articulation. Zoeth, his thin fingers extended in appeal, was the first to speak.

"Mary-'Gusta," he stammered, "don't talk so! *Please* don't!"

Mary smiled. "Oh, yes, I shall, Uncle Zoeth," she said. "I mean to do more than talk from now on, but I must talk a little first. I'm not going to try to tell you what it means to me to learn after all these years that I have been dependent on you for everything I have had, home and luxuries and education and opportunities. I realize now what sacrifices you must have made——"

"We ain't, neither!" roared the Captain, in frantic protest. "We ain't, I tell you. Somebody's been tellin' lies, ain't they, Zoeth? Why——"

"Hush, Uncle Shad! Someone *has* been telling me—er—fibs—I said that at the beginning; but they're not going to tell me any more. I know the truth, every bit of it, about Father's losing his money in stocks and— Uncle Shad, where are you going?"

Captain Shad was halfway to the door. He answered over his shoulder.

"I'm goin' home," he vowed, "and when I get there I'm goin' to choke that dummed tattle-tale of an Isaiah Chase! I'll talk to *you* after I've done it."

Mary ran after him and caught his arm.

"Come back, Uncle Shad!" she ordered. "Come back, sit down, and don't be foolish. I don't want you to talk to me! I am going to talk to you, and I'm not half through yet. Besides, it wasn't Isaiah who told me, it was Judge Baxter."

"Judge Baxter! Why, the everlastin' old——"

"Hush! He couldn't help telling me, I made him do it. Be still, both of you, and I'll tell you all about it."

She did tell them, beginning with her meeting with Mr. Green at the Howe dinner, then of her stop at Ostable and the interview with Baxter.

"So I have found it all out, you see," she said. "I'm not going to try to thank you—I couldn't, if I did try. But I am going to take my turn at the work and the worry. To begin with, of course, you understand that I am through with Boston and school, through forever."

There was an excited and voluble protest, of course, but she paid no heed whatever to commands or entreaties.

"I am through," she declared. "I shall stay here and help you. I am only a girl and I can't do much, perhaps, but I truly believe I can do something. I am a sort of silent partner now; you understand that, don't you?"

Shadrach looked doubtful and anxious.

"If I had my way," he declared, "you'd go straight back to that school and stay there long's we could rake or scrape enough together to keep you there. And I know Zoeth feels the same."

"I sartin do," agreed Zoeth.

Mary laughed softly. "But you haven't your way, you see," she said. "You have had it for ever so long and now I am going to have mine. Your new silent partner is going to begin to boss you."

For the first time since he entered the door of his store that night—or morning—Shadrach smiled. It wasn't a broad smile nor a very gay one, but it was a smile.

"Um—ya-as," he drawled. "I want to know, Mary-'Gusta! I am gettin' some along in years, but my memory ain't failed much. If I could remember any day or hour or minute since Zoeth and me h'isted you into the old buggy to drive you from Ostable here—if I could remember a minute of that time when you *hadn't* bossed us, I—well, I'd put it down in the log with a red ink circle around it. No, sir-ee! You've been *our* skipper from the start."

Even Zoeth smiled now and Mary laughed aloud.

"But you haven't objected; you haven't minded being— what shall I call it?—skipped—by me, have you?" she asked.

The Captain grinned. "Mind it!" he exclaimed. "Umph! The only time when we really minded it was these last two years when we ain't had it. We minded missin' it, that's what we minded."

"Well, you won't miss it any more. Now help me put these things back in the safe and we'll go home. Yes, home! Tomorrow morning—this morning, I mean— we'll talk and I'll tell you some of my plans. Oh, yes! I have plans and I am in hopes they may do great things for Hamilton and Company. But no more talk tonight. Remember, the skipper is back on board!"

So to the house they went and to bed, the Captain and Mr. Hamilton under protest.

CHAPTER XX

NEITHER Mary nor the Captain nor Mr. Hamilton slept much of the few hours until daylight, and Captain Shadrach, who was devoured with curiosity concerning the plans, would have asked particulars before breakfast, but Mary would not listen to questions. It was not until breakfast was over and they were back in the store that she consented to discuss the subject.

The safe was reopened and the books and papers spread out upon the desk. Mary took up one of the sheets of paper; it was covered with rows of figures in her handwriting.

"Now," she said, "it seems to me that the first thing is to find out exactly where we stand. When I say 'we,'" she added, with a nod of great importance, "I mean 'we,' because, as I told you last night, I am a silent partner in the business now."

"Don't seem to be so terrible much silence," observed Shadrach dryly.

"Hush! Another remark of that kind and I shall set you to sweeping out, Uncle Shad. Now, Uncle Zoeth, according to the books this is what we owe."

She read from the paper in her hand.

"That is the total, Uncle Zoeth, isn't it?" she asked. Zoeth groaned and admitted that he cal'lated it was nigh enough.

"Yes. But this," holding up another sheet of paper, "is what is owed us, and it is almost as much as the other."

It was Shadrach's turn to groan. "'Tis if we could get a-hold of it," he muttered. "The heft of the gang on that list ain't got a cent and the bulk of the rest of 'em wouldn't have if they paid what they owed."

Mary nodded determinedly.

"There are some that can pay," she said. "Jeremiah Clifford, for instance. According to the books he owes us over a hundred and ten dollars and part of the account is three years old. Mr. Clifford owns property. He can't be a poor man."

The Captain sniffed. "His wife owns the property," he said. "Every stick's in her name. Jerry Clifford's got enough, but he loves it too well to let go of it. Mean! Why, say! In the old days, when fishin' schooners used to run from South Harniss here, Jerry he was owner and skipper of a little hooker and Solon Black went one v'yage with him. There was another fo'mast hand besides Jerry and Solon aboard and Solon swears that all the hearty provision Jerry put on board for a four-day trip was two sticks of smoked herrin'. For two days, so Solon vows, they ate the herrin' and the other two they chewed the sticks. That may be stretchin' it a mite, but anyhow it goes to show that Jerry Clifford don't shed money same as a cat does its hair."

Zoeth put in a word.

"He says he'll pay pretty soon," he observed plaintively. "He's been sayin' it for over a year, though."

"Humph!" grunted Shadrach. "There's only a difference of one letter between 'sayin'' and 'payin',' but there ain't but two between 'trust' and 'bust.'"

Mary spoke. "Never mind," she said. "I shall see Mr. Clifford myself. And I shall see some of these others, too. Now about our own bills—those we owe. I have a list of the principal creditors. Mr. Green's firm is one of them; we owe them most of all, it seems. I think I shall go and see Mr. Green myself."

"For the land sakes, what for?" demanded Shadrach. "He knows how we're fixed, Zoeth wrote him."

"Yes, but I want to talk with him, nevertheless."

"But what for? You ain't goin' beggin' him to——"

"I'm not going begging at all. When I talked with him at the Howes' he, not knowing in the least who I was or that I was your niece, expressed sympathy for Hamilton and Company and wished there were some way of helping us out of our trouble—something he could do, you know. I'm not sure there isn't something he can do. At any rate, I am going to see him. I shall start for Boston Monday morning."

Zoeth ventured an observation.

"He'll be considerable surprised to see you, won't he?" he said.

Mary laughed. "I think he will," she replied. "Surprised and a little embarrassed. But I imagine his embarrassment will make him all the more anxious to be of service to me, and that's what I want from him—service."

Of course the partners asked hundreds more questions concerning the plans. Mary's answers were still disappointingly vague. Before she could tell just what she meant to do, she said she must be sure, and she was not sure yet. A great deal would depend upon her Boston trip. They must be patient until she returned from that.

So they were patient—that is to say, Zoeth was really so and Captain Shadrach was as patient as it was his nature to be. Mary was absent nearly a week. When she returned she had much to tell. She had visited Mr. Green at his office on Commercial Street. His surprise and embarrassment were all that she had prophesied. He offered profuse apologies for his blunder at the Howes'.

"Of course, if I had known of your relationship to Captain Gould and Mr. Hamilton," he began, "I should never—— Really, I am—I assure you I hadn't the slightest idea——"

He was floundering like a stranded fish. Mary helped him off the shoals by taking the remainder of his apologies for granted.

"Of course you hadn't," she said. "But I am very glad you told me, Mr. Green. It was high time I knew. Don't say another word about it, please. I have come to you to ask advice and, perhaps, help of a sort. May I have a little of your time?"

Mr. Green seized the opportunity thus offered. Indeed, she might have time, all the time she wanted. Anything in his power to do—and so on. Being a bachelor and something of an elderly beau who prided himself upon making a good impression with the sex, it had annoyed him greatly, the memory of his mistake. Also he had been distinctly taken with Mary and was anxious to reinstate himself in her opinion. So his willingness to atone was even eager.

"As it happens," he said, "I am not at all busy this afternoon. I can give you the rest of the day, if you wish. Now what can I do for you?"

Mary explained that she had come to speak with him concerning her uncles' business affairs, his house being Hamilton and Company's largest creditor. She told of her investigations, of the condition in which she had found the accounts, and of her determination to remain at South Harniss and work for the upbuilding of the concern.

"Of course I am not a business person like yourself, Mr. Green," she said. "I am only a girl. But I worked in my uncles' store and, in a way, managed it for two years or more before I came to Boston to school. Beside that I have talked during these last few days with some of South Harniss's most prominent people—permanent residents, not summer people. From what they and others tell me I am convinced that the sole reason why my uncles' business has fallen behind is because of a lack of keeping up to the times in the face of competition. Everyone likes Uncle Zoeth and Uncle Shadrach and wishes them well—they couldn't help that, you know."

She made this assertion with such evident pride and with such absolute confidence that Mr. Green, although inclined to smile, felt it might be poor judgment to do so. So he agreed that there was no doubt of Shadrach's and Zoeth's universal popularity.

"Yes," went on Mary, "they are dears, both of them, and they think everyone else is as honest as they are, which is a mistake, of course. So some people impose on them and don't pay their bills. I intend to stop that."

She evidently expected her listener to make some comment, so he said, "Oh, indeed!"

"Yes," continued Mary. "I intend to stop their trusting everyone under the sun and I shall try my hardest to collect from those they have already trusted. There is almost enough due to pay every bill we owe, and I believe two-thirds of that is collectible if one really goes after it."

"And you will go after it, I presume?"

"I most certainly shall. You are smiling, Mr. Green. I suppose it sounds like a joke, a girl like myself making such statements about things men are supposed to understand and women not to understand at all. It isn't a joke in this case, because I think I understand my uncles' business better than they do. I think I can collect what is owed us, pay what we owe, and make money there in South Harniss. But to do that I must have time and, by and by, credit, for we need goods. And that is what I came to talk to you about."

She had brought with her copies of the Hamilton and Company trial balance, also a list of the firm's debtors and creditors. These she put upon the desk before Mr. Green and ran a finger down the pages with explanatory remarks such as, "This is good, I know," "This can be collected but it may take a lawyer to get it," or, as in the case of 'Rastus Young's long-standing indebtedness, "This isn't worth anything and shouldn't be counted.

"You see," she said, in conclusion, "we aren't in such a *very* bad state; it isn't hopeless, anyway. Now here are the accounts we owe. Yours is the largest. Here are the others. All these bills are going to be paid, just as I said, but they can't be paid at all unless I have time. I have been thinking, thinking very hard, Mr. Green——"

Green nodded. "I can see that," he put in, good-naturedly.

"Yes. Well, this is what I want to ask you: Will you give us six months more to pay the whole of this bill in? I don't think we shall need so much time, but I want to be sure. And if at the end of two months we have paid half of it, will you give us credit for another small bill of goods for the summer season, so that we may be stocked and ready? The summer is our best season, you see," she added.

Mr. Green nodded. Her businesslike manner he found

amusing, although he by no means shared her confidence in the future.

"We shall be very glad to extend the time," he said. "You may remember I told you the other evening that so far as our house was concerned, we should probably be willing to sell your uncles indefinitely, for old times' sake."

His visitor frowned.

"We are not asking it for old times' sake," she said. "It is the new times I am interested in. And please understand this isn't sentiment but business. If you do not believe what I ask to be a safe business risk, that one your firm would be justified in accepting from anybody, then you mustn't do it."

Mr. Green hesitated. "Suppose I do not accept that risk," he said; "what then?"

"Then I shall go and see some other creditors, the principal ones, and make them similar propositions."

"And suppose they don't accept?"

"I think they will, most of them. If they don't— well, then there is another way. My uncles own their house and store. They have been thinking of selling their property to pay their debts. I should hate to have them sell, and I don't believe it is necessary. I have been talking with Judge Baxter over at Ostable—I stopped there on my way to Boston—and he suggested that they might mortgage and raise money that way. It could be done, couldn't it? Mortgages are a kind of business I don't know anything about. They sound horrid."

"Sometimes they are. Miss Lathrop, if I were you I shouldn't sell or mortgage yet. I am inclined to believe, judging by this balance sheet and what you say, that you have a chance to pull Hamilton and Company out of the fire, and I'm very sure you can do it if anyone can. Are you going to be in the city for a day or two? Good! Then will you let me consider this whole matter until—say—Thursday? By that time I shall have made up my mind and may have something to say which will be worth while. Can you come in Thursday afternoon at two? And will you? Very well. Oh, don't thank me! I haven't done anything yet. Perhaps I shall not be able to, but we shall hope for the best."

Mary went straight to Mrs. Wyeth's home on Pinckney Street and once more occupied her pleasant room on the third floor. In spite of her determination not to care she could not help feeling a little pang as she walked by the Misses Cabot's school and remembered that she would never again enjoy the privileges and advantages of that exclusive institution. She wondered how the girls, her classmates, had felt and spoken when they heard the news that she had left them and returned to Cape Cod and storekeeping. Some would sneer and laugh—she knew that—and some might be a little sorry. But they would all forget her, of course. Doubtless, most of them had forgotten her already.

But the fact that all had not forgotten was proved that very evening when, as she and Mrs. Wyeth and Miss Pease were sitting talking together in the parlor, Maggie, the maid, answering the ring of the doorbell, ushered in Miss Barbara Howe. Barbara was, as usual, arrayed like the lilies of the field, but her fine petals were decidedly crumpled by the hug which she gave Mary as soon as she laid eyes upon her.

"You bad girl!" she cried. "Why didn't you tell me you were in town? And why didn't you answer my letter—the one I wrote you at South Harniss? I didn't hear a word and only tonight, after dinner, I had the inspiration of phoning Mrs. Wyeth and trying to learn from her where you were and what you meant by dropping all your friends. Maggie answered the phone and said you were here and I threw on my things —yes, 'threw' is the word; nothing else describes the process—and came straight over. How *do* you do? And *what* are you doing?"

Mary said she was well and that she had been too busy to reply to Miss Howe's letter. But this did not satisfy. Barbara wanted to know why she had been busy and how, so Mary told of her determination to remain in South Harniss and become a business woman. Barbara was greatly excited and enthusiastic.

"Won't it be perfectly splendid!" she exclaimed. "I only wish I were going to do it instead of having to stay at that straight-up-and-down school and listen to Prissy's dissertations on Emerson. She told the Freshman class the other day that she had had the honor of meeting Mr. Emerson when very young—when *she* was young, she meant; she always tells every Freshman class that, you know—and one of the Freshies spoke up and asked if she ever met him afterwards when he was older. They said her face was a picture; I wish I might have seen it. But do tell me more about that wonderful store of yours. I am sure it will be a darling, because anything you have anything to do with is sure to be. Are you going to have a tea-room?"

Mary shook her head. "No," she said, laughing. "I think not. There's too much competition."

"Oh, but you ought to have one. Not of the ordinary kind, you know, but the—the other kind, the unusual kind. Why, I have a cousin—a second—no, third cousin, a relative of Daddy's, she is—who hadn't much money and whose health wasn't good and the doctor sent her

to live in the country. Live there all the time! Only
fancy! Oh, I forgot you were going to do the same
thing. Do forgive me! I'm so sorry! *What* a perfect
gump I am! Oh, dear me! There I go again! And I
know you abhor slang, Mrs. Wyeth."

"Tell me more about your cousin, Barbara," put in
Mary, before the shocked Mrs. Wyeth could reply.

"Oh, she went to the country and took an old house,
the funniest old thing you ever saw. And she put up
the quaintest little sign! And opened a tea-room and
gift shop. I don't know why they call them 'gift shops.'
They certainly don't give away anything. Far, far from
that, my dear! Daddy calls this one of Esther's 'The
Robbers' Roost' because he says she charges forty cents
for a gill of tea and two slices of toast cut in eight pieces.
But I tell him he doesn't pay for the tea and toast alone
—it is the atmosphere of the place. He says if he had
to pay for all his atmosphere at that rate he would be
asphyxiated in a few months. But he admires Esther
very much. She makes heaps and heaps of money."

"Then her tea-room and gift shop is a success?"

"A success! Oh, my dear! It's a scream of a success! Almost any day in summer there are at least a
dozen motor cars outside the door. Everybody goes
there; it's the proper thing to do. I know all this because it isn't very far from our summer home in Clayton
—in the mountains, you know."

"So she made a success," mused Mary. "Were there
other tea-rooms about?"

"Oh, dozens! But they're not original; hers is. They
haven't the—the something—you know what I mean,
Esther has the style, the knack, the—I can't say it, but
you know. And you would have it, too; I'm perfectly
sure you would."

Mary was evidently much interested.

"I wish I might meet your cousin," she said.

"Why, you can. She is here in Boston now, buying for the summer. I'll phone her and we three will lunch together tomorrow. Don't say you won't; you've just got to."

So Mary, rather reluctantly, consented to make one of the luncheon party. Afterward she was glad that she did, for Miss Esther Hemingway—this was the cousin's name—was an interesting person. She told Mary all about her tea-room and gift shop, how she started in business, the mistakes she made at first, and the lessons she had learned from experience. Because Barbara had asked her to do so she brought with her photographs of the establishment, its attractive and quaint exterior and its equally delightful interior.

"The whole secret," she said, "is in keeping everything in good taste and simple. Choose the right location, fit up your rooms in taste and cheerfully, serve the best you can find, and sell the unusual and the attractive things that other people do not have, or at least are not likely to have. Then charge adequate prices."

"Adequate being spelled A double D," observed Barbara significantly.

Mary parted from Miss Hemingway with a new idea in her head, an idea that sometime or other she meant to put into practice.

On Thursday afternoon she called upon Mr. Green. That gentleman, having had his opportunity to think, was ready with a proposition. Briefly it was this: He had personally seen the principal creditors of Hamilton and Company—they were all Boston business houses— and he and they had agreed to make the following offer: Hamilton and Company's credit upon debts already owed was to be extended six months. Mary was to go home, endeavor to collect what money she could, and with it buy for cash whatever goods were needed for the summer season. If that season was a success and the business promised well for the future, then arrangements could be made for future buying and for paying the old debt a little at a time.

"At any rate," concluded Mr. Green, "this postpones the mortgaging or selling for a time at least, and you always have it to fall back on if you can't make your new undertaking pay. I believe you can. I advise you to accept. Your other creditors feel the same way."

He did not add, as he might have done, that the opinion of those other creditors had been influenced almost entirely by his own and that in one or two instances he had been obliged practically to underwrite the payment of Hamilton and Company's indebtedness before gaining consent. He had talked with Mr. Howe, who in turn had called his daughter into consultation, and Barbara's enthusiastic praise of her friend had strengthened the favorable impression which the girl had already made upon both gentlemen. "Do you know, I believe she may win out," observed Mr. Howe.

"I am inclined to think she will," concurred Green.

"Of course she will!" declared Barbara hotly. "No one who ever knew her would be silly enough to think she wouldn't."

Hence Mr. Green's underwriting expedition and the proposition to Mary as the representative of Hamilton and Company.

Mary accepted, of course. She was very grateful and said so.

"I don't know how to thank you, Mr. Green. I can't

promise anything, but if trying hard will win, I can promise that," she said.

"That's all right, that's all right. I know you'll try, and I think you'll succeed. Now, why don't you go up and pick out some of those summer goods? You don't need them yet, and you needn't pay for them yet, but now is the time to select. Give my regards to your uncles when you see them and tell them I wish them luck. I may be motoring down the Cape this summer and if I do I shall drop in on you and them."

Mary had news to tell when she reached South Harniss. It was listened to with attention, if not entirely in silence. Captain Shadrach's ejaculations of "You don't say!" "I want to know!" and "Jumpin' fire, how you talk!" served as punctuation marks during the narration. When she had finished her story, she said:

"And now, Uncle Zoeth and Uncle Shad—now that you've heard the whole of it, and know what my plan is, what do you think of it?"

Both answers were characteristic. Zoeth drew a long breath.

"The Almighty sent you to us, Mary-'Gusta," he vowed. "There was a time a little spell ago when I begun to think He'd pretty nigh deserted us. I was almost discouraged and it shook my trust—it shook my trust. But now I can see He was just tryin' us out and in His good time He sent you to haul us off the shoals. He'll do it, too; I know it and I'll thank Him tonight on my knees."

Shadrach shook his head. "By fire!" he cried. "Mary-'Gusta, I always said you was a wonder. You've given us a chance to get clear of the breakers, anyhow, and that's somethin' we'd never have done ourselves. Now, if you can collect that money from Jeremiah Clifford

I'll—I'll—I swan to man I'll believe anything's possible, even Jonah's swallowin' the whale."

"Oh, Shadrach!" protested his partner. "If you wouldn't be so irreverent!"

"All right, I'll behave. But it's just as I say: if Mary-'Gusta can get Jerry Clifford to pay up I'll swallow Jonah and the whale, too. 'Twas Moses that hit the rock and the water gushed out, wa'n't it? Um—hm! Well, that was somethin' of a miracle, but strikin' Jerry Clifford for ten cents and gettin' it would be a bigger one. Why, that feller's got fists like—like one of those sensitive plants my mother used to have in the settin'-room window when I was a boy. You touch a leaf of one of those plants and 'twould shrivel up tight. Jerry's fists are that way—touch one of 'em with a nickel and 'twill shut up, but not until the nickel's inside. No, sir! Ho, ho!"

"If you knew all this, Uncle Shad," suggested Mary, "why in the world did you sell Mr. Clifford at all? If he wouldn't pay, why sell him?"

Mr. Hamilton answered.

"He always did pay," he said. "You see, he had to have groceries and clothes and such and whenever he needed more and thought he owed us so much we wouldn't put more on the bill he'd pay a little on account. That way we managed to keep up with him."

"Not exactly up with him," commented the Captain. "We was always a couple of laps astern, but we could keep him in sight. Now the new stores have come and he can get trusted there he don't buy from us—or pay, either. What's the use? That's what he thinks, I cal'-late."

Mary considered. "The mean old sinner!" she said. "I should judge, Uncle Shad, that what you told me once, when I was a little girl, about the Free Masons might apply to Mr. Clifford's pocketbook. You said that once in Masonry a man never got out. A dollar in Mr. Clifford's pocketbook never gets out, either, does it?"

Shadrach chuckled. "You bet it don't!" he agreed. "It's got a life sentence. And, so fur as that goes, they generally open a Mason lodge meetin' with prayer, but 'twould take more'n that to open Jerry's pocketbook, *I'll* bet you!"

"And, nevertheless," declared Mary, laughing, "I mean to make him pay our bill."

She did make the tight-fisted one pay up eventually, but months were to elapse before that desirable consummation was reached. In the meantime she set herself to collecting other amounts owed Hamilton and Company and to building up the trade at the store. The collecting was not so difficult as she had expected. The Captain and Mr. Hamilton had been reluctant to ask their friends and neighbors to be prompt in their payments, and largely through carelessness accounts had been permitted to drop behind. Mary personally saw the debtors and in most cases, by offering slight discounts or by accepting installments, she was able to obtain at least the greater part of the money due. In some cases she could obtain nothing and expected nothing, but these cases, among them that of 'Rastus Young, were rather to be considered in the light of good riddance even at the price. As Shadrach said, it was worth a few dollars not to have to listen to 'Rastus or Mrs. 'Rastus cry over their troubles whenever they wanted to hold up the firm for more plunder.

"Last time 'Rastus was in to buy anything," declared the Captain, "he shed so blamed many tears into my rubber boots that I got wet feet and sent the boots to the cobbler's to have 'em plugged. I cal'lated they leaked; I didn't realize 'twas Rat workin' me out of four dollars worth of groceries by water power."

The collections, then, those from Mr. Young and his ilk excepted, were satisfactory. Mary was enabled to buy and pay for a modest assortment of summer supplies, those she had selected while in Boston. The store she had thoroughly cleaned and renovated. The windows were kept filled with attractive displays of goods, and the prices of these goods, as set forth upon tickets, were attractive also. Business began to pick up, not a great deal at first, but a little, and as May brought the first of the early-bird summer cottagers to South Harniss, the silent partner of Hamilton and Company awaited the coming of what should be the firm's busiest season with hope and some confidence.

CHAPTER XXI

DURING all this time she had heard from Crawford at least once a week. He would have written oftener than that, had she permitted it. And in spite of her determination so bravely expressed in their interview over the telephone, she had written him more than the one letter she had promised. In that letter—her first—she told him the exact situation there at home; of her discovery that her uncles were in trouble, that the small, but to them precious, business they had conducted so long was in danger, and of her determination to give up school and remain at South Harniss where, she knew, she was needed. Then she went on to tell of her still greater discovery, that instead of being a young woman of independent means, she was and always had been dependent upon the bounty of her uncles.

You can imagine how I felt when I learned this [she wrote], when I thought of all the kindness I had accepted at their hands, accepted it almost as if it was my right, thinking as I did that my own money paid. And now to learn that all the time I had nothing and they had given of their own when they had so little, and given it so cheerfully, so gladly. And, Crawford, when I told them what I had done, they would not accept thanks, they would not let me even speak of the great debt I owed them. So far from that they acted as if they were the ones who owed and as if I had caught them in some disgraceful act. Why, if they could, they would have sent me back to Boston and to school, while they remained here to work and worry until the bankruptcy they expected came.

Do you wonder that I feel my first and whole duty is to them and that nothing, *nothing* must be permitted to interfere with it? I am going to stay here and try to help. Perhaps I shall succeed, and perhaps, which is just as probable, I may fail; but at any rate while my uncles live and need me I shall not leave them. They gave all they had to me when there was no real reason why they should give anything. The very least I can do is to be with them and work for them now when they are growing old.

I am sure you must understand this and that, therefore, you will forget——

She paused. "Forget" was a hard word to write. Fortunately she had written it at the top of a page, so she tore up that sheet and began the line again.

I am sure you will understand and that you will see my duty as I see it myself. It seems to me clear. Everyone has duties, I suppose, but you and I have ours very plainly shown us, I think. Yours is to your father and mine to my uncles.

Bringing that letter to an end was a difficult task. There were things which must be said and they were so very hard to say. At last, after many attempts:

I have not referred [she wrote] to what you said to me when we last met. It seems almost useless to refer to it, doesn't it? You see how I am placed here, and I have written you what I mean to do. And please understand I am doing it gladly, I am happy in having the opportunity to do it; but it does mean that for years my life and interest must be here with them. Even if I were sure of my own feelings —and perhaps I am not really sure—I certainly should not think of asking one I cared for to wait so long. You have your future to think of, Crawford, and you must think of it. And there is your father. Of course, I don't know, but I somehow feel certain that he will not wish you to marry me. Don't you think it better for us both to end it now? It seems so hopeless.

Which, she flattered herself, was brave and sensible and right. And, having reached this commendable conclusion and sealed and posted the letter, she came back to the house, went upstairs to her room, and, throwing herself upon the bed, cried bitterly for many minutes.

Yet, in a way, her tears were wasted. It takes two to make a bargain and although she might notify Crawford Smith that his case was hopeless, it by no means followed that that young gentleman would accept the notification as final. His reply to her letter was prompt and convincing. All the references to ending it were calmly brushed aside. There could be but two endings, one being their marriage—this, of course, the logical and proper ending—and the other Mary's notifying him that she did not love him. Anything else was nonsense and not worth consideration. Wait! He would wait fifty years if necessary, provided she would wait for him. He was about to take up his studies again, but now he would feel that he was working for her. His father, he was sorry to say, was not at all well. He was very nervous, weak and irritable.

I came home [he wrote] fully determined to tell him of you and my determination to marry you—always provided you will have me, you know—on the very night of my arrival. But when I saw how poor old Dad was feeling and after the doctor told me how very necessary it was that his nervous system be allowed a complete rest, I decided I must wait. So I shall wait; perhaps I shall not tell him for months; but just as soon as he is able to hear, I shall speak, and I am sure he will say, "Good luck and God bless you." But if he doesn't, it will make not the slightest difference. If you will have me, Mary dear, nothing on this earth is going to stop my having you. That's as settled and solid a fact as the Rocky Mountains.

He pleaded for a letter at least once a week.

You needn't put a word of love in it [he wrote]. I know how conscientious you are, and I know perfectly well that until your mind is made up you won't feel it right to encourage me in the least. But do please write, if only to tell me how you are getting on with Hamilton and Company. I only wish I were there to help you pull those fine old uncles of yours out of the hot water. I know you'll do it, though. And meanwhile I shall be digging away out here and thinking of you. Please write *often*.

So Mary, after considerable thought and indecision, did write, although Crawford's suggestion that her letters have no word of love in them was scrupulously followed. And so, while the summer came and went, the letters crossed and the news of the slow but certain building up of the business of Hamilton and Company was exchanged for that of Edwin Smith's steady regaining of health and strength.

And Hamilton and Company's business was reviving. Even the skeptics could see the signs. The revival began before the summer residents arrived in South Harniss, but after the latter began to come and the cottages to open, it was on in earnest. John Keith helped to give it its first big start. Mrs. Wyeth wrote him of Mary's leaving her school work to go to the rescue of

Shadrach and Zoeth, and the girl's pluck and uncomplaining acceptance of the task she considered set for her made Keith's eyes twinkle with admiration as he read the letter. The family came early to South Harniss and this year he came with them. One of his first acts after arrival was to stroll down to the village and enter Hamilton and Company's store. Mary and the partners were there, of course. He shook hands with them cordially.

"Well, Captain," he said, addressing Shadrach, "how is the new hand taking hold?"

Shadrach grinned. "Hand?" he repeated. "I don't know's we've got any new hand, Mr. Keith. Ain't, have we, Zoeth?"

Zoeth did not recognize the joke. "He means Mary-'Gusta, I cal'late, Shadrach," he said. "She's doin' splendid, Mr. Keith. I don't know how we ever got along without her."

"I do," put in his partner promptly; "we didn't, that's how. But, Mr. Keith, you hadn't ought to call Mary-'Gusta a 'hand.' Zoeth and me are the hands aboard this craft. She's skipper, and engineer, and purser, and —yes, and pilot, too. And don't she make us tumble up lively when she whistles! Whew! Don't talk!"

"She is the boss, then, is she?" observed Keith.

"Boss! I guess *so!* She's got *us* trained! Why, I've got so that I jump out of bed nights and run round the room in my sleep thinkin' she's just hollered to me there's a customer waitin'. Oh, she's a hard driver, Mary-'Gusta is. Never had a fust mate aboard drove harder'n she does. And it's havin' its effect on us, too. Look at Zoeth! He's agin' fast; he's a year older'n he was twelve months ago."

Keith laughed, Mary smiled, and Mr. Hamilton, judging by the behavior of the company that there was a joke somewhere on the premises, smiled too.

"You mustn't mind Uncle Shad, Mr. Keith," said Mary. "He talks a great deal."

"Talkin's all the exercise my face gets nowadays," declared the Captain instantly. "She keeps me so busy I don't get time to eat. What do you think of the store, Mr. Keith? Some improvement, ain't it?"

Keith, who had already noticed the trim appearance of the store and the neat and attractive way in which the goods were displayed, expressed his hearty approval.

"And how is business?" he asked.

"Tiptop!" declared Shadrach.

"It's improvin' consider'ble," said Zoeth.

"It is a little better, but it must be far better before I am satisfied," said Mary.

"How is the cottage trade?" asked Keith.

"Why, not so very good. There aren't many cottagers here yet."

When Keith reached home he called his wife into consultation.

"Gertrude," he asked, "where do we buy our household supplies, groceries and the like?"

"In Boston, most of them. The others—those I am obliged to buy here in South Harniss—at that new store, Baker's."

"I want you to buy them all of Hamilton and Company hereafter."

"*That* old-fogy place! Why?"

"Because the partners, Captain Gould and the other old chap, are having a hard struggle to keep going and I want to help them."

Mrs. Keith tossed her head. "Humph!" she sniffed. "I know why you are so interested. It is because of that upstart girl you think is so wonderful, the one who has been boarding with Clara Wyeth."

"You're right, that's just it. She has given up her studies and her opportunities there in Boston and has come down here to help her uncles. Clara writes me that she was popular there in the school, that the best people were her friends, and you know of her summer in Europe with Letitia Pease. Letitia isn't easy to please and she is enthusiastic about Mary Lathrop. No ordinary girl could give up all that sort of thing and come back to the village where everyone knows her and go to keeping store again, and do it so cheerfully and sensibly and without a word of complaint. She deserves all the help and support we and our friends can give her. I mean to see that she has it."

Mrs. Keith looked disgusted. "You're perfectly infatuated with that girl, John Keith," she said. "It is ridiculous. If I were like some women I should be jealous."

"If I were like some men you might be. Now, Gertrude, you'll buy in future from Hamilton and Company, won't you?"

"I suppose so. When your chin sets that way I know you're going to be stubborn and I may as well give in first as last. I'll patronize your precious Mary-'Gusta, but I *won't* associate with her. You needn't ask that."

"Don't you think we might wait until she asks it first?"

"Tut! tut! Really, John, you disgust me. I wonder you don't order Sam to marry her."

"From what Clara writes he might not have needed any orders if he had received the least encouragement from her. Sam might do worse; I imagine he probably will."

So, because John Keith's chin was set, the Keith custom shifted to Hamilton and Company. And because the Keiths were wealthy and influential, and because the head of the family saw that that influence was brought to bear upon his neighbors and acquaintances, their custom followed. Hamilton and Company put a delivery wagon—a secondhand one—out on the road, and hired a distinctly secondhand boy to drive it. And Mary and Shadrach and Zoeth and, in the evenings, the boy as well, were kept busy waiting on customers. The books showed, since the silent partner took hold, a real and tangible profit, and the collection and payment of old debts went steadily on.

The partners, Shadrach and Zoeth, were no longer silent and glum. The Captain whistled and sang and was in high spirits most of the time. At home he was his old self, chaffing Isaiah about the housekeeping, taking a mischievous delight in shocking his friend and partner by irreverent remarks concerning Jonah or some other Old Testament personage, and occasionally, although not often, throwing out a sly hint to Mary about the frequency of letters from the West. Mary had told her uncles of Crawford's leaving Boston and returning to Nevada because of his father's ill health. The only item of importance she had omitted to tell was that of the proposal of marriage. She could not speak of that even to them. They would ask what her answer was to be, and if she loved Crawford. How could she answer that—truthfully—without causing them to feel that they were blocking her way to happiness? They felt that quite keenly enough, as it was.

So when Captain Shad declared the illness of the South Harniss postmaster—confined to his bed with sciatica— to be due to his having "stooped to pick up one of them eighty-two page Wild West letters of yours, Mary-'Gusta, and 'twas so heavy he sprained his back liftin' it," Mary only laughed and ventured the opinion that the postmaster's sprained back, if he had one, was more likely due to a twist received in trying to read both sides of a postcard at once. Which explanation, being of the Captain's own brand of humor, pleased the latter immensely.

"Maybe you're right, Mary-'Gusta," he chuckled. "Maybe that's what 'twas. Seth [the postmaster] is pure rubber so far as other folks' mail is concerned; maybe he stretched the rubber too far this time and it snapped."

Zoeth did not joke much—joking was not in his line—but he showed his relief at the improvement in the firm's affairs in quieter but as unmistakable ways. When Mary was at the desk in the evenings after the store had closed, busy with the books, he would come and sit beside her, saying little but occasionally laying his hand gently on her shoulder or patting her arm and regarding her with a look so brimful of love and gratitude that it made her feel almost guilty and entirely unworthy.

"Don't, Uncle Zoeth," she protested, on one such occasion. "Don't look at me like that. I—I—— Really, you make me feel ashamed. I haven't done anything. I am not doing half enough."

He shook his head.

"You're doin' too much, I'm afraid, Mary-'Gusta," he said. "You're givin' up everything a girl like you had ought to have and that your Uncle Shadrach and I had meant you should have. You're givin' it up just for us and it ain't right. We ain't worthy of it."

"Hush, hush, Uncle Zoeth! Please! When I think what you have given up for me——"

" 'Twa'n't nothin', Mary-'Gusta. You came to your

Uncle Shadrach and to me just when we needed somethin' to keep our lives sweet. Mine especial was bitter and there was danger 'twould always be so. And then we brought you over from Ostable in the old buggy and—and the Almighty's sunshine came with you. You was His angel. Yes, sir! His angel, that's what you was, only we didn't know it then. I was pretty sore and bitter in those days, thought I never could forget. And yet—and yet, now I really am forgettin'—or, if I don't forget, I'm more reconciled. And you've done it for me, Mary-'Gusta."

Mary was puzzled. "Forget what?" she asked. "Do you mean the business troubles, Uncle Zoeth?"

Zoeth seemed to waken from a sort of dream. "Business troubles?" he repeated. "No, no; long, long afore that these troubles were, Mary-'Gusta. Don't let's talk about 'em. I can't talk about 'em even now—and I mustn't think. There are some troubles that—that——" He caught his breath and his tone changed. "I called you an angel just now, dearie," he went on. "Well, you was and you are. There are angels in this world—but there's devils, too—there's devils, too. There; the Lord forgive me! What am I talkin' about? We'll forget what's gone and be thankful for what's here. Give your old uncle a kiss, Mary-'Gusta."

He was happy in Mary's society and happy in the steady improvement of the business, but the girl and Captain Shadrach were a little worried concerning his general health. For years he had not been a very strong or active man, but now he looked paler and more frail than ever. He walked to and from the store and house several times a day, but he retired almost as soon as he entered the house at night and his appetite was not good.

"His nerves ain't back where they'd ought to be," declared Shadrach. "He was awful shook up when it looked as if Hamilton and Company was goin' to founder. He didn't keep blowin' off steam about it the way I did —my safety-valve's always open—but he kept it all inside his biler and it's put his engine out of gear. He'll get along all right so long's it's smooth sailin', but what I'm afraid of is a rock showin' up in the channel unexpected. The doctor told me that Zoeth mustn't worry any more and he mustn't work too hard. More'n all, he mustn't have any scares or shocks or anything like that."

"We must try to see that he doesn't have any," said Mary.

"Sartin sure we must, but you can't always see those things in time to head 'em off. Now take my own case. I had a shock this mornin'. 'Rastus Young paid me a dollar on account."

"*What?* 'Rastus Young *paid* you?"

"Well, I don't know's he paid it, exactly. He borrowed the dollar of one of those summer fellers over at Cahoon's boardin' house and he was tellin' Ab Bacheldor about it at the corner by the post-office. Ab, naturally, didn't believe any sane man would lend Rastus anything, so he wanted proof. 'Rastus hauled the dollar out of his pocket to show, and I who happened to be standin' behind 'em without their knowin' it reached out and grabbed it."

"You did? Why, Uncle Shad!"

"Yes. I told 'Rastus I'd credit his account with it, but I don't know's I hadn't ought to give it back to the summer feller. Anyhow, gettin' it was a shock, same as I said at the beginnin'. 'Rastus says he's goin' to sue me. I told him I'd have sued *him* long ago if I'd supposed he could *steal* a dollar, let alone borrow one."

CHAPTER XXII

IT was late in August when Mary received the letter from Crawford in which he told of his determination to wait no longer but to tell his father of his love for her. Edwin Smith was much better. By way of proof, his son inclosed a photograph which he had taken of his father sitting beneath a tree on the lawn of their home. The picture showed Mr. Smith without his beard, which had been shaved off during his illness. Either this or the illness itself had changed him a great deal. He looked thinner and, which was odd under the circumstances, younger. Mary, looking at this photograph, felt more than ever the impossible conviction that somewhere or other at some time in her life she must have met Mr. Edwin Smith.

So, in my next letter [wrote Crawford], I shall have news to tell. And I am sure it will be good news. "Ask your father first," you said. Of course you remember that, and I have remembered it every moment since. Now I am going to ask him. After that you will give me your answer, won't you? And it can't be anything but yes, because I won't let it be.

What Mary's feelings were when she received this letter, whether or not she slept as soundly that night and other nights immediately following, whether or not the sight of Isaiah returning from the post-office at mail times caused her breath to come a little quicker and her nerves to thrill—these are questions the answers to which must be guessed. Suffice it to say that she manifested no marked symptoms of impatience and anxiety during that week and when at last Isaiah handed her another letter postmarked Carson City the trembling of the hand which received it was so slight as to be unnoticed by Mr. Chase.

She put aside the letter until that night when she was alone in her room. Then she opened it and read what Crawford had written. His father had not only refused consent to his son's contemplated marriage but had manifested such extraordinary agitation and such savage and unreasonable obstinacy that Crawford was almost inclined to believe his parent's recent illness had affected his mind.

That is the only explanation I can think of [he wrote]. It seems as if he must be insane. And yet he seemed rational enough at the beginning of our first interview and during most of the second. Even when I had broken the news that there was a girl in whom I felt an especial interest he did not show any sign of the outbreak that came afterward. It wasn't until I began to tell how I first met you there at South Harniss, who you were, and about Captain Gould and Mr. Hamilton, that I noticed he was acting queerly. I was head over heels in my story, trying to make plain how desperate my case was and doing my best to make him appreciate how tremendously lucky his son was to have even a glimmer of a chance to get a girl like you for a wife, when I heard him make an odd noise in his throat. I looked up—I don't know where I had been looking before—certainly not at him—and there he was, leaning back in his chair, his face as white as his collar, and waving a hand at me. I thought he was choking, or was desperately ill or something, and I sprang toward him, but he waved me back.

"Stop! Wait!" he said, or stammered, or choked; it was more like a croak than a human voice. "Don't come here! Let me be! What are you trying to tell me? Who—who is this girl?" I asked him what was the matter—his manner and his look frightened me—but he wouldn't answer, kept ordering me to tell him again who you were. So I did tell him that you were the daughter of the Reverend Charles Lathrop and Augusta Lathrop, and of your mother's second marriage to Captain Marcellus Hall. "But he died when she was seven years old," I went on, "and since that time she has been living with her guardians, the two fine old fellows who adopted her, Captain Shadrach Gould and Zoeth Hamilton. They live at South Harniss on Cape Cod." I had gotten no further than this when he interrupted me. "She —she has been living with Zoeth Hamilton?" he cried. "With Zoeth Hamilton! Oh, my God! Did—did Zoeth Hamilton send you to me?" Yes, that is exactly what he said: "Did Zoeth Hamilton send you to me?" I stared at him. "Why, no, Dad," I said, as soon as I could say anything. "Of course he didn't. I have met Mr. Hamilton but once in my life. What *is* the matter? Sit down again. Don't you think I had better call the doctor?" I thought surely his brain was going. But no, he wouldn't answer or listen. Instead he looked at me with the wildest, craziest expression and said: "Did Zoeth Hamilton tell you?" "He told me nothing, Dad," I said, as gently as I could. "Of course he didn't. I am almost a stranger to him. Besides, what in the world was there to tell? I came to you because *I* had something to tell. I mean to marry Mary Lathrop, if she will have me——" I got no further than that. "No!" he fairly screamed. "No! No! No! Oh, my God, no!" And then the doctor came running in, we got Dad to bed, and it was all over for that day, except that I naturally was tremendously upset and conscience-stricken. I could see that the doctor thought I was to blame, that I had confessed something or other—something criminal, I imagine he surmised—to Dad and that it had knocked the poor old chap over. And I couldn't explain, because what I had told him was not for outsiders to hear.

Well, after a terribly anxious night and a worrisome forenoon the doctor told me that father was himself again and wanted to see me at once. "I've said all I can against it," said the doctor. "I don't know what sort of rumpus you two had yesterday, but it came dangerously near being the finish for him. And it must not be repeated; I'm making that as emphatic as I can." I assured him that so far as I was concerned there would not be a scene, and then went in to Dad's room. He looked white enough and sick enough but he was rational and his mind was keen and clear. He got me to tell the whole story about you all over again and he asked a lot of questions; in fact, he cross-examined me pretty thoroughly. When I had finished his tone was calm, but I noticed that his hand was shaking and he seemed to be holding himself in. "And so you think you want to marry this down-east country girl, do you?" he said. "I certainly do," said I. He laughed, a forced laugh—didn't sound like his at all—and he said: "Well, my boy, you'll get over it. It's a whole lot better to get over it now than to do so by and by when it's too late. It's a good thing I called you home when I did. You stay here and keep on with your studies and I'll keep on getting into shape again. By next summer, when we go on our fishing trip, you'll have forgotten all about your Down-Easter." Well, *that* was a staggerer, coming from him. It didn't sound like him at all, and again I had that feeling that his mind was going. You see, Mary, I never asked Dad for anything I didn't get—never. Now, I wasn't asking, I was just telling him what I had made up my mind to have, and he treated me this way. I answered him calmly and quietly, telling him I was serious and what you meant to me. He wouldn't listen at first; then when he did, he wouldn't agree. Pleaded with me—he was lonesome, I was his only son, he needed me, he couldn't share me with anyone else, and so on. There is no use going into all the details. We didn't get any nearer an agreement, we did get nearer and nearer to bad temper on my part and shouts and hysterics on his. So I left him, Mary. That was last night. I knew Dad was inclined to be stubborn, and I knew he had strong prejudices, but I never imagined he could behave like this to me. And I am sure he would not if he were himself. So I shall say no more to him on the subject for a day or two. Then, when he is better, as I am hoping he may be soon, he and I will have another talk. But understand, Mary dear, my mind was made up before I spoke to him at all. What he says or what he does will make no difference, so far as you and I are concerned. I know you are a believer in duty; well, so am I. I would stick by Dad through thick and thin. If I knew he was right in asking me to do or not to do a thing, even if I knew he had been wrong in asking other things, I would stick by him and try to do as he asked. But not this. I love Dad, God knows I do, but I love you, Mary, and as I have vowed to myself every day since I last saw you, I am going to marry you if you will only have me. As for Dad—well, we'll hope within a day or two I may have better news to write.

Mary read and reread the long letter. Then she leaned back in her chair and with the letter in her lap sat there —thinking. She had been right in her forebodings; it was as she had expected, had foreseen: Edwin Smith, man of affairs, wealthy, arbitrary, eccentric, accustomed to having his own way and his prejudices, however absurd, respected—a man with an only son for whom, doubtless, plans definite and ambitious had been made, could not be expected calmly to permit the upsetting of those plans by his boy's marriage to a poor "Down-Easter." So much she had foreseen from the first, and she had never shared Crawford's absolute confidence in his parent's acquiescence. She had been prepared, therefore, to read that Mr. Smith had refused his consent.

But to be prepared for a probability and to face a certainty are quite different. It was the certainty she was facing now. Unless Mr. Smith changed his mind, and the chances were ten to one against that, he and his son would quarrel. Crawford had inherited a portion of his father's stubbornness; he was determined, she knew. He loved her and he meant what he said—if she would have him he would marry her in spite of his father. It made her proud and happy to know that. But she, too, was resolute and had meant what she said. She would not be the cause of a separation between father and son. And, besides, marriage had become for her a matter of the distant future; for the present her task was set there at South Harniss.

What should she do? It was hard for Crawford, poor fellow. Yes, but it was hard for her, too. No one but she knew how hard. He would write her again telling her that his decision was unchanged, begging her to say she loved him, pleading with her to wait for him. And she would wait—Oh, how gladly, how joyfully she could wait—for him!—if she knew she was doing right in permitting him to wait for her. If she was sure that in permitting him to give up his father's love and his home and money and all that money could buy she was justified. There is a love which asks and a love which gives without asking return; the latter is the greater love and it was hers. She had written Crawford that perhaps she was not sure of her feeling toward him. That was not true. She was sure; but because she was fearful that his knowledge might be the means of entailing a great sacrifice on his part, she would not tell him.

What should she do? She considered, as the little Mary-'Gusta used to consider her small problems in that very room. And the result of her considerations was rather unsatisfactory. There was nothing she could do now, nothing but wait until she heard again from Crawford. Then she would write.

She brushed her eyes with her handkerchief and read the letter again. There were parts of it which she could not understand. She was almost inclined to adopt Crawford's suggestion that his father's mind might have been affected by his illness. Why had he received so passively the news that his son had fallen in love and yet become so violent when told the object of that love? He did not know her, Mary Lathrop; there could be no personal quality in his objection. And what could he have meant by asking if Zoeth Hamilton had sent Crawford to him? That was absolutely absurd. Zoeth, and Shadrach, too, had talked with Mary of Crawford's people in the West, but merely casually, as of complete strangers, which, of course, they were. It was all strange, but explainable if one considered that Mr. Smith was weak and ill and, perhaps, flighty. She must not think any more about it now—that is, she must try not to think. She must not give way, and above all she must not permit her uncles to suspect that she was troubled. She must try hard to put it from her mind until Crawford's next letter came.

But that letter did not come. The week passed, then another, but there was no word from Crawford. Mary's anxiety grew. Each day as Isaiah brought the mail she expected him to give her an envelope addressed in the familiar handwriting, but he did not. She was growing nervous—almost fearful. And then came a happening the shock of which drove everything else from her mind for the time and substituted for that fear another.

It was a Tuesday and one o'clock. Mary and Captain Shadrach, having had an early dinner, had returned to the store. Zoeth, upon their arrival, went down to the house for his own meal. Business, which had been very good indeed, was rather slack just then and Shadrach and Mary were talking together. Suddenly they heard the sound of rapid footsteps in the lane outside.

"Who's hoofin' it up to the main road at that rate?" demanded the Captain, lounging lazily toward the window. "Has the town pump got on fire or is somebody goin' for the doctor?"

He leaned forward to look. His laziness vanished.

"Eh! Jumpin' Judas!" he cried, springing to the door. "It's Isaiah, and runnin' as if the Old Boy was after him! Here! You! Isaiah! What's the matter?"

Isaiah pounded up the platform steps and staggered against the doorpost. His face flamed so red that, as Shadrach said afterward, it was "a wonder the perspiration didn't bile."

"I—I—I——" he stammered. "I—Oh, dear me! What shall I do? He—he—he's there on the floor and—and—Oh, my godfreys! I'm all out of wind! What *shall* I do?"

"Talk!" roared the Captain. "Talk! Use what wind you've got for that! What's happened? Sing out!"

"He's—he's all alone there!" panted Mr. Chase. "He won't speak, scurcely—only moans. I don't know's he ain't dead!"

"Who's dead? Who? Who? Who?" The irate Shadrach seized his steward by the collar and shook him, not too gently. "Who's dead?" he bellowed. "Somebody will be next door to dead right here in a minute if you don't speak up instead of snortin' like a puffin' pig. What's happened?"

Isaiah swallowed, gasped and waved a desperate hand. "Let go of me!" he protested. "Zoeth—he—he's down in a heap on the kitchen floor. He's had a—a stroke or somethin'."

"God A'mighty!" cried Shadrach, and bolted out of the door. Mary followed him and a moment later, Mr. Chase followed her. The store was left to take care of itself.

They found poor Zoeth not exactly in a heap on the floor of the kitchen, but partially propped against one of the kitchen chairs. He was not unconscious but could speak only with difficulty. They carried him to the bedroom and Isaiah was sent on another gallop after the doctor. When the latter came he gave his patient a thorough examination and emerged from the sickroom looking grave.

"You must get a nurse," he said. "This is likely to last a long while. It is a slight paralytic stroke, I should say, though what brought it on I haven't the least idea. Has Mr. Hamilton had any sudden shock or fright or anything of that sort?"

He had not, so far as anyone knew. Isaiah, being questioned, told of Zoeth's coming in for dinner and of his —Isaiah's—handing him the morning's mail.

"I fetched it myself down from the post-office," said Isaiah. "There was a couple of Hamilton and Company letters and the *Wellmouth Register* and one of them circulum advertisements about So-and-So's horse liniment, and, and—yes, seems to me there was a letter for Zoeth himself. He took 'em all and sot down in the kitchen to look 'em over. I went into the dinin'-room. Next thing I knew I heard him say, 'O God!' just like that."

"Avast heavin', Isaiah!" put in Captain Shadrach. "You're way off your course. Zoeth never said that. That's the way *I* talk, but he don't."

"He done it this time," persisted Isaiah. "I turned and looked through the doorway at him and he was standin' in the middle of the kitchen floor. Seems to me he had a piece of white paper in his hand—seem's if he did. And then, afore I could say a word, he kind of groaned and sunk down in—in a pile, as you might say, right on the floor. And I couldn't get him up, nor get him to speak to me, nor nothin'. Yet he must have come to enough to move after I left and to crawl acrost and lean against that chair."

The horse liniment circular and the *Wellmouth Register* were there on the kitchen table just where Mr. Hamilton had laid them. There, also, were the two letters addressed to Hamilton and Company. Of the letter which Isaiah seemed to remember as addressed to Zoeth personally, there was no sign.

"Are you sure there was such a letter, Isaiah?" asked Mary.

Mr. Chase was not sure; that is to say, he was not sure more than a minute at a time. The minute following he was inclined to think he might have been mistaken, perhaps it was yesterday or the day before or even last week that his employer received such a letter.

Captain Shadrach lost patience.

"Sure 'twan't last Thanksgivin'?" he demanded. "Are you sure about anything? Are you sure how old you are?"

"No, by godfreys, I ain't!" roared Isaiah in desperation. "I'm so upsot ever since I looked into that kitchen and see the poor soul down on the floor there that—that all I'm sure of is that I ain't sure of nothin'."

"Well, I don't know's I blame you much, Isaiah," grunted the Captain. "Anyway, it doesn't make much difference about that letter, so fur as I see, whether there was one or not. What did you want to know for, Mary?"

Mary hesitated. "Why," she answered, "I—perhaps it is foolish, but the doctor said something about a shock being responsible for this dreadful thing and I didn't know—I thought perhaps there might have been something in that letter which shocked or alarmed Uncle Zoeth. Of course it isn't probable that there was."

Shadrach shook his head.

"I guess not," he said. "I can't think of any letter he'd get of that kind. There's nobody to write it. He ain't got any relations nigher than third cousin, Zoeth ain't. Anyhow, we mustn't stop to guess riddles now. I'll hunt up the letter by and by, if there was one and I happen to think of it. Now I've got to hunt up a nurse."

The nurse was found, a Mrs. Deborah Atkins, of Ostable, and she arrived that night, bag and baggage, and took charge of the patient. Deborah was not ornamental, being elderly and, as Captain Shadrach said, built for tonnage more than speed; but she was sensible and capable. Also, her fee was not excessive, although that was by no means the principal reason for her selection.

"Never mind what it costs," said Mary. "Get the best you can. It's for Uncle Zoeth, remember."

Shadrach's voice shook a little as he answered.

"I ain't likely to forget," he said. "Zoeth and I've cruised together for a good many years and if one of us has to go under I'd rather 'twas me. I haven't got much money but what I've got is his, and after that so long as I can get trusted. But there," with an attempt at optimism, "don't you fret, Mary-'Gusta. Nobody's goin' under yet. We'll have Zoeth up on deck doin' the fishers' hornpipe in a couple of weeks."

But it was soon plain to everyone, the Captain included, that many times two weeks must elapse before Mr. Hamilton would be able to appear on deck again, to say nothing of dancing hornpipes. For days he lay in partial coma, rallying occasionally and speaking at rare intervals but evidently never fully aware of where he was and what had happened.

"He will recover, I think," said the doctor, "but it will be a slow job."

Mary did not again refer to the letter regarding which Isaiah's memory was so befogged. In fact, she forgot it entirely. So also did Captain Shad. For both the worry of Zoeth's illness and the care of the store were sufficient to drive trifles from their minds.

And for Mary there was another trouble, one which she must keep to herself. Three weeks had elapsed since Crawford's letter, that telling of his two fateful interviews with his father, and still no word had come from him. Mary could not understand his silence. In vain she called her philosophy to her rescue, striving to think that after all it was best if she never heard from him again, best that a love affair which could never end happily were ended at once, best that he should come to see the question as his father saw it—best for him, that is, for his future would then be one of ease and happiness. All this she thought—and then found herself wondering why he had not written, imagining all sorts of direful happenings and feeling herself responsible.

CHAPTER XXIII

ONE evening, about a week after Mr. Hamilton's sudden seizure, Mary was in her room alone. She had again reread Crawford's latest letter and was sitting there trying to imagine the scene as he had described it. She was trying to picture Edwin Smith, the man who—as his son had so often told her—indulged that son's every whim, was kindness and parental love personified, and yet had raved and stormed like a madman because the boy wished to marry her, Mary Lathrop.

She rose, opened the drawer of her bureau, and took out the photograph of Mr. Smith, the one which showed him without his beard, the one taken since his illness. Crawford had written that this photograph, too, had been taken on the sly.

"Dad's prejudice against photos is as keen as ever," he wrote. "He would slaughter me on the spot if he knew I had snapped him."

The face in the picture was not that of the savage, unrelenting parent of the old plays, who used to disinherit his sons and drive his daughters out into blinding snowstorms because they dared thwart his imperial will. Edwin Smith was distinctly a handsome man, gray-haired, of course, and strong-featured, but with a kind rather than a stern expression. As Mary had said when she first saw his likeness, he looked as if he might have had experiences. In this photograph he looked very grave, almost sad, but possibly that was because of his recent sickness.

She was looking at the picture when Isaiah's voice was heard outside the door.

"Hi, Mary-'Gusta," whispered Mr. Chase. "Ain't turned in yet, have you? Can I speak with you a minute?"

"Certainly, Isaiah," said Mary. "Come in!"

Isaiah entered. "'Twan't nothin' special," he said. "I was just goin' to tell you that Debby T. cal'lates Zoeth is a little mite easier tonight. She just said so and I thought you'd like to know."

By "Debby T." Isaiah meant Mrs. Atkins. Mary understood.

"Thank you, Isaiah," she said. "I am ever so glad to hear it. Thank you for telling me."

"That's all right, Mary-'Gusta. Hello! who's tintype's that?"

He had caught sight of the photograph upon the arm of Mary's chair. He picked it up and looked at it. She heard him gasp. Turning, she saw him staring at the photograph with an expression of absolute amazement— amazement and alarm.

"Why, Isaiah!" she cried. "What is the matter?"

Isaiah, not taking his eyes from the picture, extended it in one hand and pointed to it excitedly with the other.

"For godfreys mighty sakes!" he demanded. "Where did you get that?"

"Get what? The photograph?"

"Yes! Yes, yes! Where'd you get it? Where'd it come from?"

"It was sent to me. What of it? What *is* the matter?"

Isaiah answered neither question. He seemed to have heard only the first sentence.

"*Sent* to you!" he repeated. "Mary-'Gusta Lathrop,

319

have you been tryin' to find out—Look here! who sent you Ed Farmer's picture?"

Mary stared at him. "*Whose* picture?" she said. "What are you talking about, Isaiah?"

Isaiah thrust the photograph still closer to the end of her nose. Also he continued to point at it.

"Who sent you Ed Farmer's picture?" he repeated. "Where—where'd you get it? You tell me, now."

Mary looked him over from head to foot.

"I don't know whether to send for Uncle Shad or the doctor," she said, slowly. "If you don't stop hopping up and down and waving your arms as if they worked by strings I shall probably send for both. Isaiah Chase, behave yourself! What is the matter with you?"

Isaiah, during his years as sea cook, had learned to obey orders. Mary's tone had its effect upon him. He dropped one hand, but he still held the photograph in the other. And he stared at it as if it possessed some sort of horrible charm which frightened and fascinated at the same time. Mary had never seen him so excited.

"Ed Farmer!" he exclaimed. "Oh, I swan to man! I don't see how—— Say, it *is* him, ain't it, Mary-'Gusta? But of course 'tis! I can see 'tis with my own eyes. My godfreys mighty!"

Mary shook her head. "If I didn't know you were a blue ribboner, Isaiah," she said, "I should be suspicious. That photograph was sent me from the West. It is a picture of a gentleman named Edwin Smith, someone I have never seen and I'm perfectly sure you never have. Why in the world it should make you behave as if you needed a strait-jacket I can't see. Does Mr. Smith resemble someone you know?"

Isaiah's mouth fell open and remained so as he gazed first at the photograph and then at her.

"Ed—Edwin Smith," he repeated. "Edwin Smith! I—I don't know no Edwin Smith. Look here, now; honest, Mary-'Gusta, *ain't* that a picture of Ed Farmer?"

Mary laughed. "Of course it isn't," she said. "Who is Ed Farmer, pray?"

Isaiah did not answer. He was holding the photograph near the end of his own nose now and examining it with eager scrutiny, muttering comments as he did so.

"If it ain't him it's a better picture than if 'twas," was one of his amazing observations. "Don't seem as if two folks could look so much alike and not be. And yet—and yet I can see—I can see now—this feller's hair's pretty nigh white and Ed's was dark brown. But then if this feller was Ed he'd be—he'd be—let's see—he'd be all of thirty-five years older than he was thirty-five years ago and that would account——"

Mary burst out laughing.

"Do be still, Isaiah!" she broke in. "You are perfectly idiotic. That man's name is Smith, I tell you."

Mr. Chase heaved a sigh. "You're sartin 'tis?" he asked.

"Of course I am."

"Well, then I cal'late it must be. But if Ed Farmer had lived all these years and had had his tintype took he wouldn't get one to favor him more than that does, I bet you. My, it give me a start, comin' onto me so unexpected!"

"But who is Ed Farmer?" asked Mary. The name had meant nothing to her so far. And yet, even as she spoke she remembered. Her expression changed.

"Do you mean——" she cried, eagerly. "Why, Isaiah, do you mean the man in that old photograph I found in the garret ever and ever so long ago? The one you told me was a—a blackguard?"

Isaiah, still staring at Mr. Smith's likeness, answered emphatically.

"That's the one," he said. "That's the one I meant. My, this feller does look like him, or the way I cal'late he would look if he lived as long as this!"

"Is he dead, then?"

"I don't know. We don't any of us know around here. I ain't laid eyes on him since the day afore it happened. I remember just as well as if 'twas yesterday. He come out of the office onto the wharf where I was workin' and he says to me, 'Isaiah,' he says, knockin' on the head of a barrel with his hand—the right hand 'twas, the one that had the bent finger; he got it smashed under a hogshead of salt one time and it never came straight again—'Isaiah,' says he, 'it's a nice day, ain't it.' And I answered up prompt—I liked him fust-rate; everybody liked him them days—'Yes, sir,' I says, 'this is a good enough day to go see your best girl in.' I never meant nothin' by it, you understand, just a sayin' 'twas, but it seemed to give him a kind of start. He looked at me hard. 'Did anyone tell you where I was goin'?' says he, sharp. 'Why, no,' says I. 'Why should they?' He didn't answer, just kept on starin' at me. Then he laughed and walked away. I didn't know where he was goin' then, but I know now, darn him! And the next day he went—for good."

He stopped speaking. Mary waited a moment and then asked, quietly: "Went where, Isaiah? Where did he go?"

Isaiah, who was standing, the photograph still in his hand, started, turned and looked at her.

"What's that?" he asked.

"I say, where did this Mr. Farmer go?"

"Eh? Oh, I don't know. He went away, that's all.

Don't ask me any more questions. I've been talkin' too much, anyhow, I cal'late. Cap'n Shad would skin me alive if he knew I'd said as much as I have. Say, Mary-'Gusta, don't you say nothin' to either him or Zoeth, will you? You see—it's—it's a kind of little secret we have amongst us and—and nobody else is in on it. 'Twas this plaguey tintype got me to talkin'. No wonder neither! I never see such a look on two folks. I—there, there! Good night, Mary-'Gusta, good night."

He tossed the photograph on the bureau and hurried out of the room. Mary called after him, but he would neither stop nor answer.

After he had gone Mary took up the photograph, seated herself once more in the chair, and studied the picture for a long time. Then she rose and, lamp in hand, left the room, tiptoed along the hall past the door of Captain Shadrach's room, and up the narrow stairs to the attic, her old playground.

Her playthings were there still, arranged in her customary orderly fashion along the walls. Rose and Rosette and Minnehaha and the other dolls were seated in their chairs or the doll carriage or with their backs against Shadrach's old sea chest. She had never put them away out of sight. Somehow it seemed more like home to her, the knowledge that though she would never play with them again, they were there waiting for her in their old places. While she was away at school they had been covered from the dust by a cloth, but now the cloth had been taken away and she herself dusted them every other morning before going up to the store. As Shadrach said, no one but Mary-'Gusta would ever have thought of doing such a thing. She did, because she *was* Mary-'Gusta.

However, the dolls did not interest her now. She

tiptoed across the garret floor, taking great care to avoid the boards which creaked most, and lifted the lid of the old trunk which she had first opened on that Saturday afternoon nearly ten years before. She found the pocket on the under side of the lid, opened it and inserted her hand. Yes, the photograph of Hall and Company was still there, she could feel the edge of it with her fingers.

She took it out, and closed the pocket and then the trunk, and tiptoed down the stairs and to her room again. She closed the door, locked it—something she had never done in her life before—and placing the photograph she had taken from the trunk beside that sent her by Crawford, sat down to compare them.

And as she looked at the two photographs her wonder at Isaiah's odd behavior ceased. It was not strange that when he saw Mr. Edwin Smith's likeness he was astonished; it was not remarkable that he could scarcely be convinced the photograph was not that of the mysterious Ed Farmer. For here in the old, yellow photograph of the firm of "Hall and Company, Wholesale Fish Dealers," was Edgar S. Farmer, and here in the photograph sent her by Crawford was Edwin Smith. And save that Edgar S. Farmer was a young man and Edwin Smith a man in the middle sixties, they were almost identical in appearance. Each time she had seen Mr. Smith's photograph she had felt certain she must have met the original. Here was the reason—this man in the other photograph. The only difference was the difference of age. Edwin Smith had a nose like Edgar Farmer's, and a chin like his and eyes like his. And Isaiah had just said that Edgar Farmer had a crooked finger on his right hand caused by an accident with a hogshead of salt. Mary remembered well something Crawford had told her, that his father had a finger on the right hand which had been hurt in a mine years before he, Crawford, was born.

It could not be, of course—it could not be—and yet—— Oh, *what* did it mean?

CHAPTER XXIV

IN his own room at the end of the second-story hall, over the kitchen, Mr. Chase was sitting reading the local paper before retiring. It was a habit he had, one of which Captain Shadrach pretended to approve highly. "Best thing in the world, Isaiah," declared the Captain. "Sleep's what everybody needs and I can't think of any surer way of gettin' to sleep than readin' the South Harniss news in that paper."

Whether or not this unkind joke was deserved is not material; at all events Isaiah was reading the paper when he was very much startled by a knock at the door.

"Who—who is it?" he stammered.

"It is Mary," whispered a voice outside the door. "I want to speak with you, Isaiah. You're not in bed, are you?"

Isaiah reluctantly relinquished the paper. "No, no," he replied, "I ain't in bed. What's the matter? Zoeth ain't no worse, is he?"

"Let me in and I'll tell you."

"Come on in. You don't need no lettin'."

Mary entered. She was very grave and very earnest.

"What in the nation," began Isaiah, "are you prowlin' around this hour of the night for?"

"Hush! Isaiah, you must tell me everything now. There's no use to say you won't—you *must*. Who was Edgar Farmer and what wrong did he do my uncles?"

Isaiah said nothing; he did not attempt to answer. Instead he gaped at her with such an expression of guilty surprise, fright, and apprehension that at any other time she would have laughed. Just now, however, she was far from laughing.

"Come! come!" she said, impatiently. "I mean it. I want you to tell me all about this Edgar Farmer."

"Now—now, Mary-'Gusta, I told you——"

"You told me a very little. Now I want to know the rest. Everyone else in this family knows it and it is time I did. I'm not a child any more. Tell me the whole story, Isaiah."

"I shan't neither. Oh, by godfreys, this is what I get by sayin' more'n I ought to! And yet how could I help it when I see that tintype? It's just my luck! Nobody else but me would have had the dratted luck to have that picture stuck into their face and eyes unexpected. And 'twas just so when you found that other one years ago up attic. I had to be the one you sprung it on! I had to be! But I shan't tell you nothin'!"

"Yes, you will. You must tell me everything."

"Well, I shan't."

"Very well. Then I shall go straight to Uncle Shad."

"To who? To Cap'n Shad! Oh, my godfreys mighty! You go to him and see what he'll say! Just go! Why, he'd shut up tighter'n a clam at low water and he'd give you fits besides. Go to Cap'n Shad and ask about Ed Farmer! My soul! You try it! Aw, don't be foolish, Mary-'Gusta."

"I'm not going to be foolish, Isaiah. If I go to Uncle Shad I shall tell him that it was through you I learned there was such a person as the Farmer man and that there was a secret connected with him, that it was a disagreeable secret, that——"

"Hush! Land sakes alive! Mary-'Gusta, don't talk so! Why, if you told Cap'n Shad he'd—I don't know what he wouldn't do to me. If he knew I told you about Ed Farmer he'd—I swan to man I believe he'd pretty nigh kill me!"

"Well, you'll soon know what he will do, for unless you tell me the whole story, I shall certainly go to him."

"Aw, Mary-'Gusta——"

"I surely shall. And if he won't tell me I shall go to someone outside the family—to Judge Baxter, perhaps. He would tell me, I'm sure, if I asked. No, Isaiah, you tell me. And if you do tell me all freely and frankly, keeping nothing back, I'll say nothing to Uncle Shad or Uncle Zoeth. They shall never know who told."

Mr. Chase wrung his hands. Ever since he had been cook at the white house by the shore he had had this duty laid upon him, the duty of keeping his lips closed upon the name of Edgar Farmer and the story connected with that name. When Captain Shadrach first engaged him for his present situation the Captain had ordered him never to speak the name or mention the happenings of that time. And after little Mary Lathrop became a regular and most important member of the family, the command was repeated. "She mustn't ever know if we can help it, Isaiah," said Shadrach, solemnly. "You know Zoeth and how he feels. For his sake, if nothin' else, we mustn't any of us drop a hint so that she will know. She'll find out, I presume likely, when she gets older; there'll be some kind soul around town that'll tell her, consarn 'em; but *we* shan't tell her; and if *you* tell her, Isaiah Chase, I'll—I declare to man I'll heave you overboard!"

And now after all these years of ignorance during which the expected had not happened and no one of the village gossips had revealed the secret to her—now, here she was, demanding that he, Isaiah Chase, reveal it, and threatening to go straight to Captain Gould and tell who had put her upon the scent. No wonder the cook and steward wrung his hands in despair; the heaving overboard was imminent.

Mary, earnest and determined as she was to learn the truth, the truth which she was beginning to believe might mean so much to her, nevertheless could not help pitying him.

"Come, come, Isaiah," she said, "don't look so tragic. There isn't anything so dreadful about it. Have you promised—have you given your word not to tell? Because if you have I shan't ask you to break it. I shall go to Judge Baxter instead—or to Uncle Shad. But of course I shall be obliged to tell how I came to know— the little I do know."

Mr. Chase did not like the prospect of her going to the Captain, that was plain. For the first time his obstinacy seemed to waver.

"I—I don't know's I ever give my word," he admitted. "I never promised nothin', as I recollect. Cap'n Shad he give me orders——"

"Yes, yes, of course he did. Well, now I'm giving you orders. And I promise you, Isaiah, if it ever becomes necessary I'll stand between you and Uncle Shad. Now tell me."

Isaiah sat down upon the bed and wiped his forehead.

"Oh, Lordy!" he moaned. "I wisht my mouth had been sewed up afore ever I said a word about any of it. . . . But—but . . . Well," desperately, "what is it you want to know?"

"I want to know everything. Begin at the beginning and tell me who Mr. Farmer was."

Mr. Chase marked a pattern on the floor with his slippered foot. Then he began:

"He come from up Cape Ann way in the beginnin',"

he said. "The rest of the firm was Cape Codders, but he wan't. However, he'd been a-fishin' and he knew fish and after the firm was fust started and needed an extry bookkeeper he applied and got the job. There was three of 'em in Hall and Company at fust, all young men they was, too; your stepfather, Cap'n Marcellus Hall, he was the head one; and Mr. Zoeth, he was next and Cap'n Shad next. 'Twan't until three or four year afterwards that Ed Farmer was took in partner. He was so smart and done so well they give him a share and took him in.

"Everybody liked him, too. He was younger even than the rest, and fine lookin' and he had a—a kind of way with him that just made you like him. The way the business was handled was somethin' like this: Cap'n Marcellus, your stepfather, Mary-'Gusta, he and Cap'n Shad done the outside managin', bossin' the men—we had a lot of 'em on the wharf them days, too, and there was always schooners unloadin' and carts loadin' up and fellers headin' up barrels—Oh, Hall and Company's store and docks was the busiest place on the South Shore. You ask anybody that remembers and they'll tell you so.

"Well, Cap'n Marcellus and Cap'n Shad was sort of outside bosses, same as I said, and Zoeth he was sort of general business boss, 'tendin' to the buyin' supplies and payin' for 'em and gettin' money and the like of that, and Ed—Edgar Farmer, I mean—he was inside office boss, lookin' out for the books and the collections and the bank account and so on. Marcellus and Zoeth and Cap'n Shad was old chums and had been for years; they was as much to each other as brothers and always had been; but it wan't so very long afore they thought as much of Farmer as they did of themselves. He was that kind—you couldn't help takin' a notion to him.

"When I get to talkin' about Hall and Company I could

talk for a month of Sundays. Them was great days— yes, sir, great days for South Harniss and the fish business. Why I've seen, of a Saturday mornin' in the mackerel season, as many as forty men ashore right here in town with money in their pockets and their hats on onesided, lookin' for fun or trouble just as happened along. And Cap'n Marcellus and his partners was looked up to and respected; not much more'n boys they wan't, but they was big-bugs, I tell you, and they wore beaver hats to church on Sunday, every man jack of 'em. Fur's that goes, I wore one, too, and you might not think it, but 'twas becomin' to me if I do say it. Yes, sir-ee! 'Twas a kind of curl-up brim one, that hat was, and——"

"Never mind the hat now, Isaiah," interrupted Mary. "Tell me about Mr. Farmer."

Isaiah looked offended. "I am tellin' you, ain't I?" he demanded. "Ain't I tellin' you fast as I can?"

"Perhaps you are. We won't argue about it. Go on."

"Well—well, where was I? You've put me clear off my course."

"You were just going to tell me what Mr. Farmer did."

"What he did! What didn't he do, you'd better say! The blackguard! He smashed the firm flat, that's what he done! And he run off with Marcellus's sister."

"Marcellus's sister! My stepfather's sister! I didn't know he ever had a sister. Are you sure he had?"

"Am I sure! What kind of talk's that? Course I'm sure! She was younger than Marcellus and pretty—say, she *was* pretty! Yes, the outside of her figurehead was mighty hard to beat, everybody said so; but the inside was kind of—well, kind of rattly, as you might say. She'd laugh and talk and go on and Ed Farmer he'd hang over the desk there in the office and look at her. Just look—and look—and look. How many times I've seen 'em that way! It got so that folks begun to talk a little mite. Marcellus didn't, of course; he idolized that girl, worshiped her like a vain thing, so's to speak. And Cap'n Shad, course he wouldn't talk because he's always down on tattle-tales and liars, but I've always thought he was a little mite suspicious and troubled. As for poor Zoeth—well, it's always his kind that are the last to suspect. And Zoeth was as innocent then as he is now. And as good, too.

"And then one day it come out, come down on us like the mainmast goin' by the board. No, come to think of it, it didn't come all to once that way. Part of it did, but the rest didn't. The rest kind of leaked out along slow, gettin' a little mite worse every day. I can see it just as plain as if 'twas yesterday—Marcellus and Shadrach in the office goin' over the books and addin' up on pieces of paper, and it gettin' worse and worse all the time. And the whole town a-talkin'! And poor Zoeth lyin' in his bedroom there to home, out of his mind and ravin' distracted and beggin' and pleadin' with his partners not to chase 'em, to let 'em go free for her sake. And the doctor a-comin'! And——"

Mary began to feel that she, too, was in danger of raving distraction. Between her anxiety to hear the story and her forebodings and growing suspicions she was becoming more and more nervous as Isaiah rambled on.

"Wait! Wait, please, Isaiah!" she begged. "I don't understand. What had happened?"

Isaiah regarded her with surprise and impatience.

"Ain't I been tellin' you?" he snapped, testily. "Ain't I this minute told you? This Ed Farmer had cleared out and run off and he'd took with him every cent of Hall and Company's money that he could rake and scrape.

He'd been stealin' and speculatin' for years, it turned out. 'Twas him, the dum thief, him and his stealin's that made the firm fail. Wan't that enough to happen, I'd like to know? But that wan't all; no, sir, that wan't the worst of it."

He paused, evidently expecting his hearer to make some comment. She was leaning forward, her eyes fixed upon his face, but she did not speak. Mr. Chase, judging by her expression that he had created the sensation which, as story-teller, he considered his due, went on.

"No, sir-ee! that wan't the worst of it. You and me might have thought losin' all our money was the worst that could be, but Marcellus and Shadrach didn't think so. Marcellus was pretty nigh stove in himself—there was nothin' on earth he loved the way he loved that sister of his—but when he and Cap'n Shad thought of poor Zoeth they couldn't think of much else. Shadrach had liked her and Marcellus had loved her, but Zoeth had fairly bowed down and worshiped the ground she trod on. Anything she wanted, no matter what, she could have if 'twas in Zoeth's power to get it for her. He'd humored her and spiled her as if she was a child and all he asked for doin' it was that she'd pat him on the head once in a while, same as you would a dog. And now she'd gone—run off with that thief! Why——"

Mary interrupted again. "Wait! Wait, Isaiah," she cried. "I tell you I don't understand. You say—you say Captain Hall's sister had gone with Mr. Farmer?"

"Sartin! she run off with him and nobody's laid eyes on either of 'em since. That was why——"

"Stop! stop! What I don't understand is why Uncle Zoeth was so stricken by the news. Why had *he* humored and spoiled her? Was he in love with her?"

Isaiah stared at her in blank astonishment.

"In love with her!" he repeated. "Course he was! Why wouldn't he be? Wan't she his wife?"

There was no doubt about the sensation now. The color slowly faded from Mary's cheeks.

"His *wife?*" she repeated slowly.

"Sartin! They'd been married 'most five year. Didn't I tell you? She was a good deal younger'n he was, but——"

"Wait! What—what was her name?"

"Eh? Didn't I tell you that neither? That's funny. Her name was Patience—Patience Hall."

The last doubt was gone. Clear and distinct to Mary's mind came a sentence of Crawford's: "I saw her name first on the gravestone and it made an impression on me because it was so quaint and old-fashioned. 'Patience, wife of Edwin Smith.'"

She heard very little of Isaiah's story thereafter. Scattered sentences reached her ears. Isaiah was telling how, because of Zoeth's pleading and the latter's desire to avoid all the public scandal possible, no attempt was made to trace the fugitives.

"They went West somewheres," said Isaiah. "Anyhow 'twas supposed they did 'cause they was seen together on the Chicago train by an Orham man that knew Farmer. Anybody but Marcellus and your uncles, Mary-'Gusta, would have sot the sheriff on their track and hauled 'em back here and made that Farmer swab give up what he stole. I don't imagine he had such a terrible lot with him, I cal'late the heft of it had gone in stock speculatin', but he must have had somethin' and they could have got a-holt of that. But no, Zoeth he says, 'Don't follow 'em! For her sake and mine—don't make the shame more public than 'tis.' You see, Zoeth was the same then as he is now; you'd have thought *he* was to blame to hear him talk. He never said a word against her then nor since. A mighty good man, your Uncle Zoeth Hamilton is, Mary-'Gusta. Saint on earth, I call him."

He went on to tell how Marcellus and Shadrach had fought to keep the firm on its feet, how for a time it struggled on against the load of debt left it by their former partner, only to go down at last.

"Marcellus went down with it, as you might say," continued Isaiah. "Between losin' his sister and losin' his business he never was the same man afterwards, though he did make consider'ble money in other ways. Him and Cap'n Shadrach both went back to seafarin' again and after a spell I went with 'em. Poor Zoeth, when he got on his feet, which took a long spell, he started a little store that by and by, when Cap'n Shad joined in with him, was Hamilton and Company, same as now. And when Shadrach come I come too, as cook and steward, you understand. But from that day to this there's been two names never mentioned in this house, one's Patience Hall's and t'other's Ed Farmer's. You can see now why, when I thought that tintype was his, I was so took aback. You see, don't you, Mary-'Gusta? Why! Where you goin'?"

Mary had risen from her chair, taken up the lamp, and was on her way to the door.

"I'm going to my room," she said. "Good night, Isaiah."

"What are you goin' now for? I could tell you a lot more partic'lars if you wanted to hear 'em. Now I've told so much I might as well tell the rest. If I'm goin' to be hove overboard for tellin' I might as well make a big splash as a little one. If you got any questions to ask, heave ahead and ask 'em. Fire away, I don't care," he added, recklessly.

But Mary shook her head. She did not even turn to look at him.

"Perhaps I may ask them some other time," she said. "Not now. Thank you for telling me so much. Good night."

Alone in her own room once more she sat down to think. It was plain enough now. All the parts of the puzzle fitted together. Edwin Smith having been proved to be Edgar Farmer, everything was explainable. It had seemed queer to her, Mr. Smith's aversion to the East, his refusal to come East even to his son's graduation; but it was not at all queer that Edgar Farmer, the embezzler, should feel such an aversion, or refuse to visit a locality where, even after all these years, he might be recognized. It was not odd that he disliked to be photographed. And it certainly was not strange that he should have behaved as he did when his son announced the intention of marrying her, Mary Lathrop, stepdaughter of one of his former partners and victims and adopted niece and ward of the other two.

What a terrible surprise and shock Crawford's communication must have been to him! The dead past, the past he no doubt had believed buried forever, had risen from the tomb to confront him. His only son, the boy he idolized, who believed him to be a man of honor, whose love and respect meant more than the world to him—his only son asking to marry the ward of the man whom he had wronged beyond mortal forgiveness, asking to marry her and intimating that he would marry her whether or no. And the secret which he had guarded so jealously, had hidden from his son and the world with such infinite pains, suddenly threatening to be cried aloud in the streets for all, his boy included, to hear. Mary shuddered as she realized what the man must have felt.

It must have seemed to him like the direct hand of avenging Providence. No wonder he at first could not believe it to be merely accident, coincidence; no wonder that he asked if Zoeth Hamilton had sent Crawford to him, and had demanded to know what Zoeth Hamilton had told.

It was dreadful, it was pitiful. She found herself pitying Edwin Smith—or Edgar Farmer—even though she knew the retribution which had come upon him was deserved.

She pitied him—yes; but now she could spare little pity for others, she needed as much herself. For minute by minute, as she sat there thinking out this great problem just as the little Mary-'Gusta used to think out her small ones, her duty became clear and more clear to her mind. Edgar Farmer's secret must be kept. For Crawford's sake it must be. He need not—he must not—learn that the father he had honored and respected all his life was unworthy of that honor and respect. And her uncles— they must not know. The old skeleton must not be dug from its grave. Her Uncle Zoeth had told her only a little while before that he was learning to forget, or if not to forget at least to be more reconciled. She did not understand him then; now she did. To have him learn that Edgar Farmer was alive, that his son——Oh, no, he must not learn it! Ill as he was, and weak as he was likely to be always, the shock might kill him. And yet sooner or later he would learn unless the secret remained, as it had been for years, undisclosed.

And to keep it still a secret was, she saw clearly, her duty. She might rebel against it, she might feel that it was wicked and cruel, the spoiling of her life to save these others, but it was her duty nevertheless. Because she loved Crawford—and she was realizing now that she did love him dearly, that there could never be another love in the world for her—she must send him away, she must end the affair at once. If she did that she could save him from learning of his father's disgrace, could avert the otherwise inevitable quarrel between them, could make his career and his future secure. And her uncles would be happy, the skeleton would remain undisturbed.

Yes, she must do it. But it was so hard to do. Philosophy did not help in the least. She had tried to convince herself when she gave up her school work that it meant the end of her romance also. She had tried to tell Crawford so. But she had been weak, she had permitted herself to hope. She had realized that for the present, perhaps for years, she must work for and with the old men who had been father and mother both to her, but—he had said so—Crawford would wait for her, and some day —perhaps——

But now there was no perhaps—now she knew. She must receive no more letters from him. She must never see him again. The break must be absolute and final. And there was but one way to bring that about. He had said repeatedly that only her declaration that she did not love him would ever prevent his marrying her. Very well, then for his sake she must lie to him; she must tell him that very thing. She must write him that she had been considering the matter and had decided she could never love him enough to become his wife.

It was almost two o'clock when she reached this decision but she sat down at her desk to write then and there the letter containing it, the last letter she would ever write him. And when the morning light came streaming in at the windows she still sat there, the letter unwritten. She had made many beginnings, but not an end. She must try again; she was too tired, too nervous, too hopeless and heartbroken to make another attempt that morning, but before the day was over it should be done. She threw herself down upon the bed but she could not sleep. Why had she been selected to bear this burden? What had she done that God should delight to torture her in this way?

CHAPTER XXV

THAT difficult letter was never written. In the afternoon, business at the store being rather quiet and Mrs. Atkins, the nurse, desiring an hour's leave to do an errand in the village, Mary had taken her place in the sickroom. Zoeth was improving slowly, so the doctor said, but he took very little interest in what went on, speaking but seldom, asking few questions, and seeming to be but partially sensible of his surroundings. Best not to try to rouse him, the physician said. Little by little he would gain mentally as well as physically and, by and by, there was reason to hope, would be up and about again. Probably, however, he would never be so strong as he had been before his sudden seizure, the cause of which—if there had been a definite cause—was still unknown.

Just then he was asleep and Mary, sitting in the rocking-chair by the bed, was thinking, thinking, thinking. If she could only stop thinking for a little while! Uncle Zoeth, there on the bed, looked so calm and peaceful. If only she might have rest and peace again! If she might be allowed to forget!

The door opened gently and Mr. Chase appeared. He beckoned to her to come out. With a glance at the patient, she tiptoed from the room into the hall.

"What is it, Isaiah?" she asked.

Isaiah seemed to be excited about something.

"I've got a surprise for you, Mary-'Gusta," he whispered. "There's somebody downstairs to see you."

His manner was so important and mysterious that Mary was puzzled.

"Someone to see me?" she repeated. "Who is it?"

Mr. Chase winked.

"It's somebody you wan't expectin' to see, I bet you!" he declared. "I know *I* wan't. When I opened the door and see him standin' there I——"

"Saw him? Who? Who is it, Isaiah? Stop that ridiculous winking this instant. Who is it?"

"It's that young Crawford Smith feller from way out West, that's who 'tis. Ah, ha! I told you you'd be surprised."

She was surprised, there could be no doubt of that. For a moment she stood perfectly still. Had it not been that the hall was almost dark in the shadows of the late afternoon Isaiah would have noticed how pale she had become. But it was evident that he did not notice it, for he chuckled.

"I told you you'd be some surprised," he crowed. "Well, ain't you comin' on down to see him? Seems to me if I had a beau—excuse me, a gentleman friend— who come a-cruisin' all the way from t'other side of creation to see me I wouldn't keep him waitin' very long. Ho! ho!"

Mary did not answer at once. When she did she was surprised to find that she was able to speak so calmly.

"I shall be down in a moment," she said. "Isaiah, will you please go in and stay with Uncle Zoeth until I come?"

Isaiah looked chagrined and disappointed. Visitors from the far West were rare and especially rare was a young gentleman who Mr. Chase, with what Captain Shadrach termed his "lovesick imagination," surmised was Mary-'Gusta's beau. He wished to see more of him.

"Aw, say, Mary-'Gusta," he pleaded, "I'm awful busy. I don't see how I can set along of Zoeth—— Say, Mary-'Gusta!"

But Mary had gone. She was hurrying along the hall toward her own room. So Isaiah, remembering that the doctor had said Mr. Hamilton must not be left alone, grumblingly obeyed orders and went in to sit beside him.

In her own room Mary stood, white and shaken, striving to regain her composure. She must regain it, she must be cool and calm in order to go through the ordeal she knew was before her. His coming could mean but one thing: his father had still refused consent and he had come to tell her so and to beg her to wait for him in spite of it. If only he had written saying he was coming, if she had been forewarned, then she might have been more ready, more prepared. Now she must summon all her resolution and be firm and unwavering. Her purpose was as set and strong as ever, but ah, it would be so hard to tell him! To write the letter she had meant to write would have been easy compared to this. However, it must be done—and done now. She went down the stairs and entered the sitting-room.

He was sitting in the rocker by the window and when she came into the room he sprang to his feet and came toward her. His face, or so it seemed to her, showed some traces of the trouble and anxiety through which he had passed so recently. He was a little thinner and he looked less boyish. He held out his hands.

"Well, Mary," he cried, eagerly, "here I am. Aren't you glad to see me?"

He seized both her hands in his. She disengaged them gently. Her manner seemed odd to him and he regarded her in a puzzled way.

"*Aren't* you glad?" he repeated. "Why, Mary, what is the matter?"

She smiled sadly and shook her head. "Oh, Crawford," she said, "why did you come? Or, at least, why didn't you write me you were coming?"

He laughed. "I didn't write," he answered, "because I was afraid if I did you would write me not to come."

"I certainly should."

"Of course you would. So I took no chances but just came instead."

"But why did you come?"

"Why? To see you, of course."

"Oh, Crawford, please don't joke. You know I asked you not to come here. When we last spoke together, over the telephone, I told you that if you came here I should not see you. And yet you came."

His manner changed. He was serious enough now.

"I came," he said, "because—well, because I felt that I must. I had many things to tell you, Mary, and something to ask. And I could neither tell nor ask in a letter. Dad and I have quarreled—we've parted company."

She had expected to hear it, but it shocked and grieved her, nevertheless. She knew how he had loved his father.

"Sit down, Crawford," she said gently. "Sit down and tell me all about it."

He told her. There was little more to tell than he had written. His father had not become more reconciled to the idea of his marrying Mary. Instead his opposition was just as violent and, to his son's mind, as unreasonably absurd. Day after day Crawford waited, hoping that time would bring a change or that his own arguments might have an effect, but neither time nor argument softened Edwin Smith's obstinacy.

"He behaved like a madman at times," declared Crawford. "And at others he would almost beg me on his knees to give you up. I asked him why. I told him over and over again that he should be proud to have such a girl for his daughter-in-law. I said everything I could. I told him I would do anything for him—anything he asked—except give you up. That I would not do. And it was the only thing he seemed to wish me to do. Talked about bringing shame and disgrace on his head and mine —and all sorts of wild nonsense. When I asked what he meant by disgrace he could not tell me. Of course he couldn't."

That was true, of course he could not tell. Mary knew, and she realized once more the tortures which the man must have suffered, must be suffering at that moment.

"So at last we parted," said Crawford. "I left word —left a letter saying that, so far as I could see, it was best that I went away. We could not agree apparently, he and I, upon the one point which, as I saw it, was the most important decision of my life. And I had made that decision. I told him how much I hated to leave him; that I loved him as much as I ever did. 'But,' I said, 'I shall not give up my happiness and my future merely to gratify your unreasonable whim.' Then I came away and started East to you."

He paused, evidently expecting Mary to make some comment or ask a question, but she was silent. After a moment he went on.

"I haven't made any definite plans as yet," he said. "I have another year at the Medical School—or should have it. I am hoping that I may be able to go back to the Harvard Med. here in Boston and work my way through. Other chaps have done it and I'm sure I can.

And after that—well, after that I must take my chance at finding a location and a practice, like any other young M.D. But first of all, Mary, I want you to tell me that you will wait for me. It's a lot to ask; I know how much. But will you, Mary dear? That's what I've come here for—to get you to say that you will. After that I can face anything—yes, and win out, too."

Mary looked at him. His face was aglow with earnestness and his voice shook as he finished speaking. He rose and held out his hands.

"Will you, Mary?" he begged.

She looked at him no longer. She was afraid to do so—afraid of her own weakness. But no sign of that weakness showed itself in her tone as she answered.

"I'm sorry, Crawford," she said, gently. "I wish I could, but I can't."

"Can't! Can't wait for me?"

"I could wait for you, it isn't that. If it were merely a question of waiting—if that were all—how easy it would be! But it isn't. Crawford, you must go back to your father. You must go back to him and forget all about me. You must."

He stared at her for a moment. Then he laughed.

"Forget you!" he repeated. "Mary, are you——"

"Oh, please, Crawford! Don't make this any harder for both of us than it has to be. You must go back to your father and you must forget me. I can not marry you, I can't."

He came toward her.

"But, Mary," he cried, "I—I—— Of course I know you can't—now. I know how you feel about your duty to your uncles. I know they need you. I am not asking that you leave them. I ask only that you say you will wait until—until by and by, when——"

"Please, Crawford! No, I can't."

"Mary! You—— Oh, but you must say it! Don't tell me you don't love me!"

She was silent. He put his hands upon her shoulders. She could feel them tremble.

"Don't you love me, Mary?" he repeated. "Look up! Look at me! *Don't* you love me?"

She did not look up, but she shook her head.

"No, Crawford," she said. "I'm afraid not. Not enough."

She heard him catch his breath, and she longed—Oh, how she longed!—to throw her arms about him, tell him that it was all a lie, that she did love him. But she forced herself not to think of her own love, only of those whom she loved and what disgrace and shame and misery would come upon them if she yielded.

"Not enough?" she heard him repeat slowly. "You— you don't love me? Oh, Mary!"

She shook her head.

"I am sorry, Crawford," she said. "I can't tell you how sorry. Please—please don't think hardly of me, not too hardly. I wish—I wish it were different."

Neither spoke for a moment. Then he said:

"I'm afraid I don't understand. Is there someone else?"

"Oh, no, no! There isn't anyone."

"Then—— But you told me—— You have let me think——"

"Please! I told you I was not sure of my own feelings. I—I am sure now. I am so sorry you came. I should have written you. I had begun the letter."

Again silence. Then he laughed, a short, bitter laugh with anything but mirth in it.

"I am a fool," he said. "*What* a fool I have been!"

346

"Please, Crawford, don't speak so. . . . Oh, where are you going?"

"I? I don't know. What difference does it make where I go? Good-by."

"Stop, Crawford! Wait! It makes a difference to your father where you go. It makes a difference to me. I—I value your friendship very highly. I hoped I might keep that. I hoped you would let me be your friend, even though the other could not be. I hoped that."

The minute before she had asked him to forget her, but she did not remember that, nor did he. He was standing by the door, looking out. For a moment he stood there. Then he turned and held out his hand.

"Forgive me, Mary," he said. "I have behaved like a cad, I'm afraid. When a fellow has been building air castles and all at once they tumble down upon his head he—well, he is likely to forget other things. Forgive me."

She took his hand. She could keep back the tears no longer; her eyes filled.

"There is nothing for me to forgive," she said. "If you will forgive me, that is all I ask. And—and let me still be your friend."

"Of course. Bless you, Mary! I—I can't talk any more now. You'll—" with an attempt at a smile—"you'll have to give me a little time to get my bearings, as your Uncle Shad would say."

"And—and won't you go back to your father? I shall feel so much happier if you do."

He hesitated. Then he nodded.

"If you wish it—yes," he said. "I suppose it is the thing I ought to do. Dad will be happy, at any rate. Oh, Mary, *can't* you?"

"No, Crawford, no. Yes, your father will be happy.

And—and by and by you will be, too, I know. Are you going?"

"Yes, I think I had better. I don't feel like meeting anyone and your Uncle Shad will be here soon, I suppose. Your man here—Isaiah—told me of Mr. Hamilton's sickness. I'm sorry."

"Yes, poor Uncle Zoeth! He is gaining a little, however. Crawford, I won't ask you to stay. Perhaps it will be best for both of us if you do not. But won't you write me just once more? Just to tell me that you and your father are reconciled? I should like to know that. And do forgive me—Oh, do! I *had* to say it, Crawford!"

"I forgive you, Mary. Of course you had to say it. . . . But . . . Well, never mind. Yes, I'll write, of course. I hope . . . No, I can't say that, not now. I'd better go at once, I think, before I . . . Good-by."

He seized her hand, pressed it tightly, took his hat from the table and his bag from the floor and swung out of the door. In the doorway she stood looking after him. At the gate he turned, waved his hand, and hurried on. He did not look back again.

When at half-past six Captain Shadrach, having left Annabel and the boy in charge of the store, came home for supper, Isaiah had some news to tell him. It was surprising news.

"You don't say!" exclaimed the Captain. "Well, well, I want to know! All the way from out West, eh? Sho! Where is he now?"

Isaiah shook his head. "That's the funny part of it, he's gone," he said.

"Gone? Gone where?"

"*I* don't know. All I know is he come and said he

348

wanted to see Mary-'Gusta—I went up and told her and she come down to see him. I stayed up along of Zoeth until Debby T. came back from her shoppin' cruise. Then I come downstairs again and his hat and bag was gone. There wan't nobody here."

"Where was Mary-'Gusta? Where is she now?"

"Up in her room, I cal'late. I heard her movin' round there a spell ago."

Shadrach went up the stairs, along the hall, and knocked at Mary's door.

"Who is it?" asked a faint voice within.

"It's your Uncle Shad, Mary-'Gusta. Can I come in?"

"Yes."

He entered. There was no lamp and the room was dark.

"Where are you?" he demanded.

"Here, by the window, Uncle Shad."

She was sitting in the rocker by the window. He could not see her face, but as he bent and kissed her cheek he found it wet.

"Mercy on us! You've been cryin'!" he declared.

"Oh—Oh, no, I haven't! I——"

"Rubbish! Yes, you have, too. Settin' alone up here in the dark and cryin'! Mary-'Gusta Lathrop, come here!"

She had risen from the rocking-chair, but he seized her in his arms, sat down in the chair himself, and lifted her to his knee just as he used to do when she was the little Mary-'Gusta.

"Now there, dearie," he said. "You'll tell your Uncle Shad. What is it?"

"Oh, nothing, Uncle Shad, dear. I was—I'm feeling just a little silly this afternoon, I guess. You mustn't ask me."

"All right, I won't ask—I'll tell. That young feller from out West, the feller with the uncommon name—Brown—Jones—Oh, no, Smith, that was it—he came cruisin' around here and——"

"Uncle Shad, how did you know?"

"A little bird told me. A long-legged bird without much hair on top—a bald-headed eagle, I cal'late he must be. Hops round our kitchen daytimes and roosts in the attic nights."

"Isaiah! Of course he would tell."

"Of course he would—*bein'* Isaiah. Well, this Smith critter, he came and—and—well, I guess you'll have to tell me the rest."

"There isn't much to tell. He came and—and then he went away again."

"Went away—where?"

"Out to Carson City, I suppose."

"Ain't he comin' back any more?"

"No."

"Why? Don't you want him to come, Mary-'Gusta?"

"Oh, Uncle Shad, please don't. I don't feel as if I could answer. Don't ask me."

"There, there, dearie; don't you answer nothin'. You set still here and be my baby. I ain't had a chance to baby you for a long spell and it seems good."

Silence. Suddenly the Captain felt the head which nestled against his shoulder stir.

"Uncle Shadrach," said Mary-'Gusta, "what do you do when you want to forget?"

"Eh? Want to forget? Oh, I don't know! Cal'late I turn to and sail in and work a little harder, maybe. Why?"

"Oh, nothing. . . . But I am much obliged for the suggestion. Now I am going to work. I shall begin tomorrow morning. I wish it was tomorrow right now."

"Don't. Jumpin' fire! Don't wish time away; some of us ain't got too much to spare. But ain't you *been* workin', for mercy sakes? I should say you had."

Another interval of silence. Then Mary said:

"Uncle Shad, a good while ago, when you asked me about—about him, I promised you I would tell when there was anything to tell. I am going to keep my promise. He came today and asked me—asked me to marry him—not now, of course, but by and by."

Shadrach was not greatly surprised. Nevertheless it was a moment before he spoke. Mary felt his arms tighten about her and she realized a little of the struggle he was making. Yet his tone was brave and cheerful.

"Yes," he said. "Well, I—I kind of cal'lated that would come some day or other. It's all right, Mary-'Gusta. Zoeth and me have talked it over and all we want is to see you happy. If you said yes to him, Zoeth and I'll say 'God bless you' to both of you."

She reached for his hand and lifted it to her lips. "I know you would," she said. "All your lives you have been thinking of others and not of yourselves. But I didn't say yes, Uncle Shad. I am not going to be married now or by and by. I don't want to be. I am the silent partner of Hamilton and Company. I am a business woman and I am going to work—*really* work— from now on. No, you mustn't ask me any more questions. We'll try to forget it all. Kiss me, Uncle Shad, dear. That's it. Now you go down to supper. I shall stay here; I am not hungry tonight."

CHAPTER XXVI

CAPTAIN SHAD did ask more questions, of course. He asked no more that evening—he judged it wisest not to do so; but the next day, seizing an opportunity when he and his niece were alone, he endeavored to learn a little more concerning her reasons for dismissing Crawford. The Captain liked young Smith, he had believed Mary liked him very much, and, although he could not help feeling a guilty sense of relief because the danger that he and Zoeth might have to share her affections with someone else was, for the time at least, out of the way, he was puzzled and troubled by the abruptness of the dismissal. There was something, he felt sure, which he did not understand.

"Of course, Mary-'Gusta," he said, "I ain't askin' anything—that is, I don't mean to put my oar in about what you told me last night, but—well, you see, Zoeth and me was beginnin' to feel that 'twas pretty nigh a settled thing between you and that young man."

Mary was sitting at the desk—she and her uncle were at the store together—and she looked up from the ledger over which she had been bending and shook her head reproachfully. She looked tired and worn, so it seemed to Captain Shadrach, as if she had not slept well the night before, or perhaps for several nights.

"Uncle Shad," she said, "what did I tell you?"

"Eh? Why, you told me—— You know what you told me, Mary-'Gusta. What do you ask that for?"

"Because I think you have forgotten the most impor-

352

tant part of it. I told you we were going to forget it all. And we are. We are not going to speak of it again."

"But, Mary-'Gusta, why——"

"No, Uncle Shad."

"But do just tell me this much; if you don't I shan't rest in peace: you didn't send him away on account of Zoeth and me? It wan't just because you thought we needed you?"

"No, Uncle Shad."

"Then——"

"That's all. It's over with; it's done with forever. If you really care about me, Uncle Shad—and sometimes, you know, I almost suspect that you really do—you will never, *never* say another word about it. Now come here and tell me about this account of Heman Rodger's. Isn't it time we tried to get a payment from him?"

The Captain, although still uneasy and far from satisfied, asked no more questions of his niece. It was evident that nothing was to be gained in that way. He did, however, question Isaiah to learn if the latter had noticed anything unusual in Crawford's manner or if Crawford had said anything concerning his reason for coming on at that time, but Isaiah had noticed nothing.

"Umph!" grunted Shadrach, rather impatiently, for the mystery in the affair irritated him. "Of course, you didn't notice. *You* wouldn't notice if your head came off."

Mr. Chase drew himself up. "If *I* hove out such a statement as that," he observed, scornfully, "you'd call me a fool. 'If my head come off!' How could I notice anything if my head was off? You tell me that!"

His employer grinned. "I cal'late you could do it about as well as you can with it on, Isaiah," he said, and walked away, leaving the cook and steward incoherently anxious to retort but lacking ammunition.

So Shadrach was obliged to give up the riddle. Lovers' quarrels were by no means unusual, he knew that, and many young love affairs came to nothing. Mary had never told him that she cared for Crawford. But she had never said she did not care for him. And now she would say nothing except that it was "done with forever." The Captain shook his head and longed for Zoeth's counsel and advice. But Zoeth would not be able to counsel or advise for months.

And now Mary seemed bent upon proving the truth of her statement that she was henceforth to be solely a business woman. The summer being over—and it had been, everything considered, a successful one for Hamilton and Company—it became time to buy fall and winter goods, also goods for the holidays. Mary went to Boston on a buying expedition. When she returned and informed her uncle what and how much she had bought, he looked almost as if he had been listening to the reading of his death warrant.

"Jumpin' Judas!" he exclaimed. "You don't mean to tell me you bought all them things and—and got *trusted* for 'em?"

"Of course I did, Uncle Shad. It is the only way I could buy them; and, so far as that goes, everyone was glad to sell me. You see, our paying our bills up there in a shorter time than I asked for has made a very good impression. I could have bought ever and ever so much more if I had thought it best."

"Jumpin' fire! Well, I'm glad you didn't think it best. What in the nation we're goin' to do with all we have got *I* don't see."

"Do with it? Why, sell it, of course."

"Um—yes, I cal'lated that was the idea, probably; but who's goin' to buy it?"

"Oh, lots of people. You'll see. I am going to advertise this fall, advertise in the papers. Oh, we'll make Baker's Bazaar and the rest worry a little before we're through."

The Captain was inclined to fear that the most of the worrying would be done by Hamilton and Company, but he expressed no more misgivings. Besides, if anyone could sell all those goods, that one was his Mary-'Gusta, he was perfectly sure of that. He believed her quite capable of performing almost any miracle. Had she not pulled the firm off the rocks where he and his partner had almost wrecked it? Wasn't she the most wonderful young woman on earth? Old as he was, Captain Shad would probably have attempted to thrash any person who expressed a doubt of that.

And the goods were sold, all of them and more. The advertisements, temptingly worded, appeared in the county weeklies, and circulars were sent through the mails. Partly by enterprise and partly through influence —Mr. Keith helped here—Mary attained for Hamilton and Company the contract for supplying the furniture and draperies for the new hotel which a New York syndicate was building at Orham Neck. It was purely a commission deal, of course—everything was purchased in Boston —and Hamilton and Company's profit was a percentage, but even a small percentage on so large a sale made a respectable figure on a check and helped to pay more of the firm's debts. And those debts, the old ones, were now reduced to an almost negligible quantity.

The secondhand horse and wagon still continued to go upon their rounds, but the boy had been replaced by an active young fellow whose name was Crocker and who was capable of taking orders as well as delivering them. When Captain Shadrach was told—not consulted concerning but told—the wages this young man was to receive, he was, as he confided to Isaiah afterward, "dismasted, stove in, down by the head and sinkin' fast."

"Mary-'Gusta Lathrop!" he cried, in amazement. "Are you goin' stark loony? Payin' that Simmie Crocker fourteen dollars a *week* for drivin' team and swappin' our good sugar and flour for sewin'-circle lies over folks' back fences! I never heard such a thing in my life. Why, Baker's Bazaar don't pay the man on their team but ten a week. I know that 'cause he told me so himself. And Baker's Bazaar's got more trade than we have."

"Yes. And that is exactly why we need a better man than they have, so that *we* can get more trade. Simeon Crocker is an ambitious young chap. He isn't going to be contented with fourteen long."

"Oh, he ain't, eh? Well, *I* ain't contented with it now, I tell you that. Fourteen dollars a week for drivin' cart! Jumpin' fire! Why, the cart itself ain't worth more'n fifteen and for twenty-five I'd heave in the horse for good measure. But I'd never get the chance," he added, "unless I could make the trade in the dark."

Mary laughed and patted his shoulder.

"Never mind, Uncle Shad," she said, confidently, "Sim Crocker at fourteen a week is a good investment. He will get us a lot of new business now, and next summer—well, I have some plans of my own for next summer."

The Christmas business was very good indeed. Shadrach, Mary, Annabel, and Simeon were kept busy. Customers came, not only from South Harniss, but from West and East Harniss and even from Orham and Bayport. The newspaper advertisements were responsible for this in the beginning, but those who first came told others that the best stock of Christmas goods in Ostable County was to be found at the store of Hamilton and Company, in South Harniss, and so the indirect, word-of-mouth advertising, which is the best and most convincing kind, spread and brought results.

Christmas itself was a rather dreary day. Zoeth, although improving, was not yet strong enough to leave his room, and so the Christmas dinner lacked his presence at the table. Mary and Shadrach sat with him for an hour or so, but the doctor and nurse had cautioned them against exciting him, so, although the Captain joked continually, his jokes were rather fickle and in his mind was his partner's prophecy of two years before—that the tide which had, up to that time, been coming in for them, would soon begin to go out. Shadrach could not help feeling that it had been going out, for poor Zoeth at any rate. The doctor declared it was coming in again, but how slowly it came! And how far would it come? This was the first Christmas dinner he had eaten in years without seeing Mr. Hamilton's kindly, patient face at the other side of the table.

And Mary, although she tried to appear gay and light-hearted, laughing at her uncle's jokes and attempting a few of her own, was far from happy. Work, Captain Shad's recipe for producing forgetfulness, had helped, but it had not cured. And when, as on a holiday like this, or at night after she had gone to bed, there was no work to occupy her mind, she remembered only too well. Crawford had written her, as he promised, after his return home. He wrote that he and his father were reconciled and that he had resumed his studies. The letter was brave and cheerful, there was not a hint of whining or complaint in it. Mary was proud of him, proud of his courage and self-restraint. She could read between the lines and the loneliness and hopelessness were there, but he had done his best to conceal them for her sake. If he felt resentment toward her, he did not show it. Lonely and hopeless as she herself was, her heart went out to him, but she did not repent her decision. It was better, ever and ever so much better, as it was. He would forget and be happy by and by, and would never know his father's shameful story. And poor Uncle Zoeth would never know, either. As for her—well, she must work, work harder than ever. Thank God there were six working days in the week!

She did not answer that letter. After much deliberation she fought down the temptation and decided not to do so. What was the use? If one wished to forget, or wished someone else to forget, if it was a real wish and not merely pretending, the way to bring about that result was to do nothing to cause remembrance. Letters, even the letters of friends, the most platonic letters, were reminders. She had begged for Crawford's friendship—she could not bring herself to let him go without hearing that he forgave her and would think of her as a friend—but now she vowed she would not be so silly and childish as to torture him or herself unnecessarily. She would not do it. And so she did not write.

After Christmas came the long, dull winter. It was the most discouraging season the silent partner of Hamilton and Company had yet put in in her capacity as manager. There were no cottagers to help out with their custom, very few new customers, no fresh faces in the store, the same dreary, deadly round from morning till night. She tried her hardest and, with the able assistance of Sim Crocker who was proving himself a treasure, did succeed in making February's sales larger than January's and those of March larger than either. But she looked forward to April and the real spring with impatience. She had a plan for the spring.

It was in March that she experienced a great satisfaction and gave Shadrach the surprise and delight of his life by collecting the firm's bill against Mr. Jeremiah Clifford. Mr. Clifford, it will be remembered, had owed Hamilton and Company one hundred and ten dollars for a long time. There was every indication that he was perfectly satisfied with the arrangement and intended to owe it forever. Mary had written, had called upon him repeatedly, had even journeyed to Ostable and consulted her friend Judge Baxter. The Judge had promised to look into the matter and he did so, but his letter to her contained little that was hopeful.

There is money there [wrote the Judge]. The man Clifford appears to be in very comfortable circumstances, but he is a shrewd [there were indications here that the word "rascal" had been written and then erased] person and, so far as I can learn, there is not a single item of property, real or otherwise, that is in his own name. If there were, we might attach that property for your debt, but we cannot attach Mrs. Clifford's holdings. All I can advise is to discontinue selling him more goods and to worry him all you can about the old bill. He may grow tired of being dunned and pay, if not all, at least something on account.

When Mary read this portion of the letter to her Uncle Shadrach his scorn was outspoken.

"Get tired!" he scoffed. "Jerry Clifford get tired of bein' dunned! *Don't* talk so foolish! Why, he gets fat on that kind of thing; it's the main excitement he has, that and spendin' a cent twice a day for newspapers. Did you ever watch Jerry buy a paper? No? Well, you go up to Ellis's some day when the mornin' papers are put out for sale and watch him. He'll drive up to the door with that old hoopskirt of a horse of his—that's what the critter looks like, one of them old-fashioned hoop-skirts; there was nothin' to them but framework and a hollow inside, and that's all there is to that horse.—Well, Jerry he'll drive up and come in to the paper counter, his eyes shinin' and his nerves all keyed up and one hand shoved down into his britches pocket. He'll stand and look over the papers on the counter, readin' as much of every one as he can for nothin', and then by and by that hand'll come out of his pocket with a cent in it. Then the other hand'll reach over and get hold of the paper he's cal'latin' to buy, get a good clove hitch onto it, and then for a minute he'll stand there lookin' first at the cent and then at the paper and rubbin' the money between his finger and thumb—he's figgerin' to have a little of the copper smell left on his hand even if he has to let go of the coin, you see—and——"

Mary laughed.

"Uncle Shad," she exclaimed, "what ridiculous non-sense you do talk!"

"No nonsense about it. It's dead serious. It ain't any joke to Jerry, you can bet on that. Well, after a spell, he kind of gets his spunk up to make the plunge, as you might say, lays down the penny—Oh, he never throws it down; he wouldn't treat real money as disrespectful as that—grabs up the paper and makes a break for outdoors, never once lookin' back for fear he might change his mind. When he drives off in his buggy you can see that he's all het up and trembly, like one of them reckless Wall Street speculators you read about. He's spent a cent, but he's had a lovely nerve-wrackin' time doin' it. Oh, a feller has to satisfy his cravin' for excitement somehow, and Jerry satisfies his buyin' one-cent newspapers and seein' his creditors get mad. Do you suppose you can worry such a critter as that by talkin' to him about what he owes? Might as well try to worry a codfish by leanin' over the rail of the boat and hollerin' to it that it's drownin'."

Mary laughed again. "I'm afraid you may be right, Uncle Shad," she said, "but I shan't give up hope. My chance may come some day, if I wait and watch for it."

It came unexpectedly and in a rather odd manner. One raw, windy March afternoon she was very much surprised to see Sam Keith walk into the store. Sam, since his graduation from college, was, as he expressed it, "moaning on the bar" in Boston—that is to say, he was attending the Harvard Law School with the hope, on his parents' part, that he might ultimately become a lawyer.

"Why, Sam!" exclaimed Mary. "Is this you?"

Sam grinned cheerfully. "'Tis I," he declared. "I am here. That is to say, the handsome youth whose footfalls you hear approaching upon horseback is none other than our hero. Mary, you are, as usual, a sight to be thankful for. How do you do?"

Mary admitted that she was in good health and then demanded to know what he was doing down on the Cape at that time of the year. He sat down in a chair by the stove and propped his feet against the hearth before replying.

"Why! Haven't you guessed?" he asked, in mock amazement. "Dear me! I'm surprised. I should have thought the weather would have suggested my errand. Hear that zephyr; doesn't it suggest bathing suits and

outing flannels and mosquitoes and hammock flirtations?
Eh?"

The zephyr was a sixty-mile-an-hour March gale. Sam
replied to his own question.

"Answer," he said, "it does not. Right, my child; go
up head. But, honest Injun, I am down here on summer
business. That Mr. Raymond, Dad's friend, who was
visiting us this summer is crazy about the Cape. He has
decided to build a summer home here at South Harniss,
and the first requisite being land to build it on he has
asked Dad to buy the strip between our own property
and the North Inlet, always provided it can be bought.
Dad asked me to come down here and see about it, so
here I am."

Mary considered. "Oh, yes," she said, after a moment,
"I know the land you mean. Who owns it?"

"That's what I didn't know," said Sam. "But I do
know now. I asked the first person I met after I got off
the train and oddly enough he turned out to be the owner
himself. It was old Clifford—Isaiah, Elisha, Hosea—
Jeremiah, that's it. I knew it was one of the prophets."

"So Mr. Clifford owns that land. I didn't know that."

"Neither did I. He didn't tell me at first that he did
own it. Asked me what I wanted to know for."

"Did you tell him?" asked Mary.

For the first time since Mr. Keith's arrival that young
gentleman's easy assurance seemed a little shaken. He
appeared to feel rather foolish.

"Why, yes, to be honest, I did," he admitted. "I was
an idiot, I suppose, but everyone asks about everyone's
else business down here and I didn't think. He kept
talking and pumping and before I realized it I told him
about Raymond's being so anxious to get that property,
being dead set on it and all that, and about my being

commissioned to buy at any reasonable figure. A.
then, after a while, he astonished me by saying he owned
the land himself. Confound it! I suppose he'll jam the
price away up after what I told him."

"Oh, then you haven't bought?"

"Not yet. I was willing, but for some reason he
wouldn't sell at once—wouldn't even talk price. Wanted
to think it over, he said. I can't wait now, but I am
coming down again on Monday and we shall close the
deal then."

That evening Mary told Shadrach what Sam had
said. The Captain looked puzzled.

"I didn't know Jerry Clifford owned that land," he
said. "I don't believe he does."

"Of course he does, Uncle Shad. He wouldn't have
told Sam he did own it if he didn't. What in the world
would he gain by that?"

"Why, nothin', I presume likely. But he must have
bought it mighty recent. Last I heard Jimmie G. owned
that piece. 'Twas part of the property his father left
him. Next time I see Jimmie I'll ask him."

So, three days later, when Jimmie G.—his last name
was Peters—passed the store the Captain hailed him
and, inviting him in, went straight to the point.

"When did you sell Jerry Clifford that North Inlet
land of yours, Jim?" he asked.

Jimmie G. looked surprised. "How in time did you
know I had sold it?" he demanded. "It beats all how
things get around in this town. I never sold that land
until day afore yesterday evenin' and the deed didn't
pass till yesterday, and yet you know the whole business.
Not that I care; 'twas Jerry wanted it kept still. Who
told you?"

Captain Shad whistled. "I see," he said slowly. "I

e. Yes, yes. When Jerry told Sam he owned that
land he . . . Humph! It's just another case of the boy
lied, that's all. Tut, tut, tut! When you get ahead
of Jerry Clifford you've got to turn out early,
ain't you? I hope you got a good price for the land,
Jim."

"Well, I didn't; that is, not very big. What's up, anyway? What are you hintin' at, Cap'n Shad?"

Before the Captain could answer, Mary, who had been
listening to the conversation, broke in to ask a question.

"Mr. Peters," she cried eagerly, "would you mind
telling me this: Whose name is the new deed in, Mr.
Clifford's or his wife's?"

Jimmie G. laughed. "Why, that was kind of funny,
too," he said. "You know Jerry, Cap'n Shad; he never
has nothin' in his own name—it's all in his wife's. That's
a principle of his."

"I'd call it a lack of principle," grunted Shadrach.
"Never mind, Jim; go on."

"But he was in a terrible rush to close the sale, for
some reason or other," went on Peters, "and I forgot,
myself, and had the deed made in the name of Jeremiah
Clifford. He made a big row at first, but it seemed as
if he couldn't wait for me to have it changed, so he
handed over his check and——"

"Wait! Wait, please, Mr. Peters!" broke in Mary,
her eyes flashing with excitement. "Just tell me if I
understand you correctly. You sold that land to Mr.
Clifford and he owns it now *in his own name?*"

"Why, yes—sartin."

Mary waited to hear no more. She ran out of the
store and to the post-office. A few minutes later she
was talking with Judge Baxter over the telephone.

When she returned the Captain was curious to know where she had been, but she would not tell him.

"Wait," she said. "Wait, Uncle Shad; I think something is going to happen."

It happened on Monday morning. Mary was at the desk; Simeon was in the back room getting ready his early morning orders, and Captain Shad was standing by the window looking out. Suddenly Mary heard him utter an exclamation.

"What is the matter?" she asked.

"Oh, nothin'."

"You spoke as if you were in pain."

"No wonder. I'm lookin' at somethin' that gives me a pain. That wizened-up landshark of a Jerry Clifford is in sight, bound to the post-office, I cal'late. Goin' to put a one-cent stamp on a letter and let the feller that gets it pay the other cent, I suppose. He always asks the postmaster to lick the stamp, so's to save the wear and tear on his own tongue. That's a fact. . . . No," he added, a moment later, "he ain't goin' to the office; he's turnin' down the lane here. . . . Eh! Jumpin' fire of brimstone, I do believe—— *What* in the world?"

For Mr. Clifford's step was upon the platform of the store and in another moment the door opened and the tight-fisted one himself appeared. Shadrach said nothing; he could only stare in amazement. It had been more than two years since Jeremiah had crossed that threshold.

But he crossed it now. And, after a look about the place, ignoring the Captain completely, he walked over to the desk. He did not look happy. Mary, on the contrary, looked very much pleased.

"Good morning, Mr. Clifford," she said.

Jeremiah, who was a little thin man, looked up at her

from under his heavy gray eyebrows and above his spectacles. He did not acknowledge the salutation.

"Umph!" he grunted savagely. "You think you're smart, don't ye?"

Shadrach started forward.

"Why, you——" he began. Mary held up her hand.

"Don't interfere, Uncle Shad," she ordered. "This is Mr. Clifford's affair and mine. We understand each other perfectly." Then, turning to the frowning Jeremiah, she said: "Why, yes, thank you, Mr. Clifford, I do think I am rather clever—just now. Don't you think I am, yourself?"

Again the visitor ignored the question.

"What did you go and stick an attachment on that land of mine for?" he demanded.

"Surely you don't need to ask me that, Mr. Clifford. The amount is one hundred and ten dollars and sixty-three cents. I remember it and I should imagine you must; certainly it has been called to your attention often enough."

"Umph! Well, you can keep your darned old attachment."

"Very well; and you can keep your land—what is left, I mean. I think you will keep it for some time—after I tell Mr. Keith the facts. He will be here this afternoon, you know."

It was evident that Jeremiah was quite aware of the time of Sam Keith's arrival. His teeth—the few remaining—snapped together and, as Captain Shadrach said afterwards, he looked as if undecided whether to bite or put back his head and howl. Apparently he decided that howling was safer.

"I was cal'latin' to pay that bill of yours, anyhow," he said.

"Of course, and we were calculating that you would," said Mary sweetly. "Your calculations and ours are proving true, Mr. Clifford. That's nice, isn't it?"

From the direction of the back room, where Simeon was busy with his orders, came the sound of a smothered laugh. Shadrach, upon whom understanding of the situation was just beginning to dawn, slapped his knee. Mr. Clifford looked positively venomous.

"If I pay that bill—that—what was it?—that hundred and ten dollars you say I owe you—do I get that attachment off my land right away?" he demanded.

"If you pay the one hundred and ten dollars—and the sixty-three cents—I shall phone Judge Baxter the next minute," said Mary promptly.

Jeremiah hesitated no longer. He had considered the situation in all its phases before leaving home and the one hundred and ten dollars was but a small item compared to his expected profit on the sale of the North Inlet land. He reached into his pocket, produced a long, dingy leather pocketbook wound about with twine, unwound the twine, opened the pocketbook and produced a blank check.

"Give me a pen and ink," he snarled, "and I'll fill this in."

The Captain reached for the pen and ink bottle, but Mary interfered.

"Cash, if you please," she said sweetly.

Jeremiah looked at her steadily for what seemed a long time. Then she was surprised to see the corner of his lip twitch and notice a grim twinkle in his eye. Also there was a grudging note of admiration in his voice when he next spoke.

"Ain't takin' no chances, be you?" he said dryly.

"No. Don't you think we've taken enough already?"

Mr. Clifford did not answer. He replaced the blank check in his pocketbook and, from another compartment, extracted some bills rolled in a tight little cylinder and wound about with elastic.

"There you be," he said shortly. Then, turning to Shadrach, he added: "Don't I get nothin' off for payin' cash?"

From the back room came a vigorous "Haw, haw!" Even Mary laughed aloud. As for Captain Shad, he could only stare, struck speechless by his visitor's audacity. Mary, when she had finished laughing, answered for him.

"We shall deduct the interest we might have charged you, Mr. Clifford," she said. "Thank you. There is your change and there is the receipted bill. Now, I shall call up Judge Baxter."

When she returned from the post-office Jeremiah was still there. Shadrach, all smiles, was doing up parcels.

"What are those, Uncle Shad?" asked Mary. Mr. Clifford answered.

"Oh, I thought I might as well buy a little sugar and flour and such," he said. "Always come in handy, they do. Send 'em up when you get to it. Good-by."

His hand was on the door, but Mary called to him.

"Mr. Clifford," she called; "just a minute, please. Are you in any hurry for these things—the sugar and the rest of it?"

"No, don't know's I be, 'special'; why?"

"Oh, nothing, except that if you were in a hurry I should advise your paying for them. I told you, you remember, that we weren't taking chances."

For an instant Jeremiah stood there glowering. Then he did another astonishing thing. He took out the pocketbook once more and from it extracted a two-dollar bill.

"Take it out of that," he said, "and send me a receipted bill afterwards. I always cal'late to know what I've paid for. And say, you—what's your name—Mary-'Gusta, if you get tired of workin' for Shad Gould and Zoeth Hamilton, come round and see me. I've got—I mean my wife's got—two or three mortgages that's behind on the interest. I ain't been able to collect it for her yet, but—but, by time, I believe *you* could!"

He went out and the next moment Mary was almost smothered in her uncle's embrace.

"After this—after *this*," roared Shadrach, "I'll believe anything's possible if you've got a hand in it, Mary-'Gusta. If *you'd* been Jonah you'd have put the whale in your pocket and swum ashore."

CHAPTER XXVII

EARLY in April, when Mary announced that she was ready to put into operation her biggest and most ambitious plan, suggested the year before by Barbara Howe—the tea-room and gift-shop plan—the Captain did not offer strenuous opposition.

"I can't see much sense in it," he admitted. "I don't know's I know what it's all about. Nigh as I can make out you're figgerin' to open up some kind of a high-toned eatin' house. Is that it?"

"Why, no, Uncle Shad, not exactly," explained Mary.

"Then what is it—a drinkin' house? I presume likely that's it, bein' as you call it a 'tea-room.' Kind of a temperance saloon, eh? Can't a feller get coffee in it, if he wants to? I don't wake up nights much hankerin' for tea myself."

"Listen, Uncle Shad: A tea-room—at least a tea-room of the sort I intend to have—is a place where the summer people, the women and girls especially, will come and sit at little tables and drink tea and eat cakes and ice cream and look off at the ocean, if the weather is pleasant——"

"Yes, and at the fog, if 'tain't; and talk about their neighbor's clothes and run down the characters of their best friends. Yes, yes, I see; sort of a sewin' circle without the sewin'. All right, heave ahead and get your tea-room off the ways if you want to. If anybody can make the thing keep afloat you can, Mary-'Gusta."

So Mary, thus encouraged, went on to put her scheme

into effect. She had been planning the details for some time. About halfway down the lane leading to the house from the store was another small story-and-a-half dwelling of the old-fashioned Cape Cod type. It stood upon a little hill and commanded a wide view of ocean and beach and village. There were some weather-beaten trees and a tangle of shrubs about it. It had been untenanted for a good while and was in rather bad repair.

Mary arranged with the owner, a Bayport man, to lease this house and land at a small rental for three years. In the lease was included consent to the making of necessary alterations and repairs and the privilege of purchasing, at a price therein named, at the end of the three years, should the tenant wish to do so.

Then with the aid of soap and water, white paint and whitewash, attractive but inexpensive wall papers, and odds and ends of quaint old furniture, of which the parlor and best bedroom of the Gould-Hamilton home supplied the larger quantity, she proceeded to make over the interior of the little building. To every bit of nautical bric-a-brac, pictures of old sailing ships and sea curios she gave especial prominence. Then the lawn was mowed, the tangled shrubbery untangled and clipped and pruned; cheap but pretty lattices made to look like the shrouds of a ship, over which climbing roses were supposed—some day—to twine, were placed against the walls, and rustic tables set about under the trees and the grape arbor with ship lanterns hung above them. The driveway down to the lane was rolled and hardened, and a sign, painted by Joshua Bemis, the local "House, Boat and Sign Painter, Tinsmith and Glazier"—see Mr. Bemis's advertisement in the *Advocate*—was hung on a frame by the gateway.

Captain Shad's remarks when he first saw that sign

may be worth quoting. Mary had not consulted him concerning it; she deemed it best not to do so. When it was in place, however, she led him out to inspect. Shadrach adjusted his spectacles and read as follows:

THE FOR'ARD LOOKOUT
TEA AND GIFTS
DAINTY THINGS TO EAT
PRETTY THINGS TO BUY
ALL'S WELL!

There was the picture of a full-rigged ship, with every stitch set alow and aloft, sailing through a sea of thick green and white paint toward a kind of green wall with green feather dusters growing out of it.

Shadrach subjected this work of art to a long and searching stare. At last he spoke.

"Carryin' every rag she can h'ist," he observed; "nobody at the wheel, land dead ahead and breakers under the bows. Looks to me as if 'twas liable to be a short v'yage and a lively one. But the for'ard lookout says all's well and he ought to know; he's had more experience aboard gift-shop ships, I presume likely, than I have. What's those bristly things stickin' up along shore there—eel grass or tea grounds?"

For the first few weeks after the tea-room was really "off the ways" the optimistic declaration of the For'ard Lookout seemed scarcely warranted by the facts. Mary was inclined to think that all was by no means well. In fitting out the new venture she had been as economical as she dared, but she had been obliged to spend money and to take on a fresh assortment of debts. Then, too, she had engaged the services of a good cook and two waitresses, so there was a weekly expense bill to consider. And the number of motor cars which turned in at the new driveway was disappointingly small.

But the number grew larger. As people had talked about Hamilton and Company's assortment of Christmas goods, so now they began to talk about the "quaintness and delightful originality" of the For'ard Lookout. The tea was good; the cakes and ices were good; on pleasant days the view was remarkably fine, and the pretty things in the gift shop were temptingly displayed. So, as May passed and June came, and the cottages and hotels began to open, the business of the new tea-room and gift shop grew from fair to good and from that to very good indeed.

Mary divided her time between the store and the tea-room, doing her best to keep a supervising eye on each. She was in no mood to meet people and kept out of the way of strangers as much as possible; even of her former acquaintances who came to the For'ard Lookout she saw but few. If she had not been too busy she might have found it amusing, the contrasting studies in human nature afforded by these former acquaintances in their attitude toward her.

For instance, Mr. and Mrs. Christopher Mullet and daughter, Irene, the latter now through school and "finished" until her veneering actually glittered, sat drinking tea at a table on the lawn. Said Mrs. Mullet:

"And *this* is what it's come to; after all the airs and frills and the goin' to Europe and I don't know what all. Here she is keepin' an eatin' house. An eatin' house—just *think* of it! If that ain't a comedown! Wouldn't you think she'd be ashamed, 'Rena?"

Miss Mullet drooped a weary eyelid and sighed a hopeless sigh.

"Oh, Mother," she drawled, in deep disgust, *"can't*

you stop calling me by that outlandish name? I was christened Irene, I believe. *Please* remember it."

"All right, 'Re—all right, Irene; I won't forget again. Oh, there's Mary-'Gusta, now! Showin' herself out here with all these city folks, when she's nothin' but a hired help—a table girl, as you might say! *I* shan't notice her, anyway. I may buy her tea and stuff, but I— Who's that runnin' up to her and—and kissin' her— and—mercy on us! You'd think they was sisters, if you didn't know. Who is it? Looks kind of common, she does to me. Don't you think so, 'Rena—Irene, I mean?"

Irene sniffed.

"That," she said with cutting emphasis, "is Barbara Howe. Her people are building that big summer house at Osterville and her father is a millionaire, so they say. And her people wouldn't let her come to the school you sent me to because they thought it wasn't good enough for her. That's how common *she* is. I met her once, but she doesn't know me now, although she is perfectly crazy over that Mary Lathrop. I—Oh, there's Father drinking out of his saucer again! For heaven's sake, let's go home!"

And just then Barbara was enthusiastically hugging her former schoolmate and exclaiming:

"You did it! I knew you would if you would only try. I said it required a knack or a genius or something and that I was certain you had it. It's the dearest place of the kind I've ever seen, my dear, and if every single person I know who is in this vicinity doesn't come here at least once a week and spend lots and lots of money I'll never speak to them again. I'm going to turn myself into a walking phonograph, my dear, with just one record: 'If you love me visit the For'ard Lookout.' And of course everyone loves me—how can they help it? So—well, just wait and see what happens."

So far as spreading abroad the praises of the new tea-room was concerned, she was as good as her word. In August the patronage was so great and continuous that Mary found it necessary to hire three more waitresses and a salesgirl for the gift shop. She spent more of her own time there, leaving the care of the store to Shadrach, Simeon Crocker and a new clerk, who had been hired to help with the summer custom. When early September brought the beginning of the season's end the books of both the Lookout and of Hamilton and Company showed a substantial profit.

While all this was going on Zoeth was steadily gaining in health and strength. In July he was sitting in the sunshine upon the front porch. In August he was able to climb to the buggy seat and be driven up to the store, where day after day he sat in his armchair behind the counter, watching what was going on, listening to his partner's happy chatter—for Shadrach was in high spirits now—and occasionally saying a word or two himself. On pleasant Sundays he was driven to church and the Captain and Mary accompanied him. He was white and frail and thin, but the doctor assured them that, so far as he could see, there was no reason to expect anything but a complete recovery.

It did seem to Captain Shad, however, that his partner had something on his mind. He seemed often to be thinking deeply and at times to be troubled and disturbed. The Captain had never asked, never attempted by questioning to learn what the cause of the trouble—provided there was any—might be. He had been told often enough that the patient must not be excited, so he meant to take no risks, but Zoeth's long silences and the expression on his face as he sat there in the chair, evidently thinking deeply, puzzled and worried his friend and partner. He noticed the same expression at times when Mary was in the room. Zoeth's eyes would follow her as she moved about and in them was the look the Captain could not understand.

Shadrach had told his friend of Mary's sending young Smith away. Zoeth had asked concerning Crawford almost as soon as he was permitted to take part in a lengthy conversation. He appeared greatly interested, even eager.

"But, Shadrach," he said, "are you sure she sent him away because she didn't care for him? Are you sure that was the reason?"

"What other reason could there be?" demanded the Captain. "She as much as told me that was it, herself. I was some surprised, of course, for I'd rather cal'lated 'twas as good as settled between 'em, but it turned out that I didn't know what I was talkin' about. That *has* happened afore in my life, strange as it may seem," he added dryly.

Zoeth sighed. "I wish——" he said slowly, "I wish I knew——"

"What do you wish you knew?"

"Eh? Oh, nothin'. If—if I was only a little mite stronger I'd try to talk with Mary-'Gusta myself. I'd like—I'd like to have her tell me about it."

"Meanin' you don't believe me, eh? There, there, shipmate, it's all right. I was only jokin'. But I wouldn't ask Mary-'Gusta about that, if I was you. Course I know she cares as much or more for her Uncle Zoeth than for anybody on earth, and she'd tell him anything if he asked her; but I don't believe—— Well, I wouldn't ask, if I was you. You understand?"

"Yes, yes, Shadrach, I think I understand. You mean she felt bad to have to say—what she did say—to that young man and she wouldn't want to be reminded of it?"

"That's about it, Zoeth."

Silence for some minutes. Both partners were occupied with their thoughts. Then Zoeth said:

"Shadrach, I—I——"

He did not finish the sentence. The Captain ventured to remind him.

"Yes, Zoeth, what is it?" he asked.

"Nothin'. I—I can't tell you now. By and by, if the good Lord gives me strength again, I'll—— Never mind, now. Don't ask me, please."

So Shadrach did not ask, but he was puzzled and a little anxious. What was it his partner had to tell and found the telling so difficult?

CHAPTER XXVIII

IT was not until a day in mid-September that Captain Shadrach learned his partner's secret. He and Zoeth and Mary were at the store together. Business was still good, but the rush was over. The summer cottages were closing and most of the Cape hotels had already closed. The For'ard Lookout had taken down its sign at the end of the previous week. Its voyage for that year was over. It had been a prosperous one.

Mary was sorry that the busy season was at an end. She was very, very tired; she had allowed herself no rest, had taken no holidays, had done her best to think of nothing except matters connected with Hamilton and Company or the tea-room. These, fortunately, had given her enough to think of; other thoughts she resolutely crowded from her mind. Now there would be no tea-room to plan for, and, thanks to Sim Crocker and the competent way in which he had assumed care of the store, she no longer felt the absolute necessity of remaining there from daylight until late in the evening. Her Uncle Zoeth was almost well, also; she would no longer have his health as an additional burden upon her mind. She was in danger of being forced to think of herself, and that she knew she must not do. Thinking of herself would surely mean thinking of someone else and of what might have been. And what useless, hopeless thinking that would be! No, no! She must find something else to keep her thoughts occupied.

So she was planning the making over and enlarging

of the store front, putting in larger and better windows and strengthening the platform. She was discussing the plan with Shadrach and Zoeth when John Keith entered. The Keiths were leaving South Harniss rather early that year and the head of the family had dropped in to say good-by. Mr. Keith's liking for Mary was as strong as ever, and for her uncles he had, by this time, a very real regard, a feeling which was reciprocated by them.

Conversation began in the way the majority of conversations begin, with a discussion of the weather, its recent past, present, and probable future, shifted to the tea-room and its success and then to the visitor's recent trip to New York, from which city he had just returned. It was near the noon hour and there were few customers to interrupt. Those who did come were taken care of by Mr. Crocker.

"Anything new happenin' over there?" inquired Captain Shadrach, asking news of the metropolis exactly as he would have asked concerning the gossip of Harniss Center. "Meet anybody you knew, did you?"

Keith smiled. "Why, yes," he said. "I met the people I went to see. Mine was a business trip. I didn't meet anyone unexpectedly, if that's what you mean."

The Captain nodded. "Didn't get down on South Street, did you?" he asked. "No, I thought not. If you had you'd have met plenty. When I was goin' to sea I bet I never went cruisin' down South Street in my life that I didn't run afoul of somebody I wan't expectin' to. Greatest place for meetin' folks in the world, I cal'late South Street is. Lots of seafarin' men have told me so."

Keith's smile broadened as he was handed this nugget of wisdom. Then he said:

"You remind me, Captain, that I did meet someone, after all. In Boston, not in New York, and I met him only yesterday. It was someone you know, too, and Mary here used to know him quite well, I think—young Crawford Smith, Sam's Harvard friend. He visited us here in South Harniss one summer."

Shadrach was the only one of the trio of listeners who made any comment at all on this speech. Even he did not speak for a moment, glancing apprehensively at Mary before doing so. Mary said nothing, and Zoeth, leaning back in his chair, his face hidden from his partner's gaze by the end of the counter, did not speak.

"Sho!" exclaimed the Captain. "Sho! So you met him, did you! In Boston? That's funny. I had an idea he was out West somewheres."

"So did I. The last I heard concerning him he had given up his studies in the East here—he was studying medicine, as perhaps you know—and had gone back to his home in Nevada. His father, who was not at all well, asked him to do so. He had written Sam once or twice from out there. So I was surprised enough to see him in Boston. I met him in the South Station and we chatted for a few moments. He told me that his father was dead."

From behind the end of the counter where Zoeth sat came an odd sound, a sort of gasp. Shadrach leaned forward quickly.

"What's the matter, Zoeth?" he asked. Before Zoeth could answer Mary spoke:

"Dead!" she repeated. "Mr. Keith, I—did—did you say Crawford Smith's father was *dead?*"

Her tone was so strange that even Mr. Keith could not help noticing it. He looked at her, seemed about to ask a question, and then answered hers instead.

"Why, yes," he said; "he is dead. He had been in poor health for some time, so his son told me, and about two weeks ago he died. Crawford did not tell me any particulars, nor did he say what had brought him East. In fact, he didn't seem anxious to talk; acted as if he had something on his mind. Of course I said I was sorry and he thanked me and inquired regarding Mrs. Keith and Edna and Sam. Then I had to hurry for my train. . . . Oh, are you going, Mary? Well, then, I must say good-by until next summer; we leave tomorrow morning."

Mary explained, rather hurriedly, that she must speak with Simeon for a few minutes, said good-by, shook hands and hastened out. Keith looked after her.

"I hope I haven't made a blunder," he said, "in speaking of young Smith. She and he were quite—er—friendly at one time, weren't they. I understood so from some remarks of Sam's. Didn't put my foot in it by mentioning the boy's name, did I? I certainly hope not."

Zoeth did not speak. Shadrach hastened to reassure him.

"No, no!" he said. "There was one time when even me and Zoeth figgered there might be—er—well, we didn't know but what he and she was liable to be more'n just friends. But it's all off now, seems so. They don't even write each other, I guess. I cal'late maybe Mary-'Gusta got tired of him," he explained. "He was a real nice young feller, but he probably wan't quite good enough for her. Fur's that goes," he added, with the emphasis of absolute conviction, "*I* never laid eyes on one that was."

Keith looked relieved. "Well, I'm glad if I didn't make a mistake," he said. "She seemed so startled when

I said that the man was dead and her manner was so odd. Didn't you notice it yourself, Captain?"

Shadrach nodded.

"I noticed she seemed sort of sot all aback," he said, "but I don't know's that's so strange when you consider that she and Crawford used to be such friends. More'n probable she's heard him talk a good deal about his father."

"Well, perhaps so. No doubt that is it. I'm afraid she is working too hard and worrying too much over her various enterprises here. She is succeeding wonderfully, of course, but I don't like to see her losing those roses in her cheeks. They're much too precious to lose. Keep your eye on her, Captain, and don't let her wear herself out."

He soon said good-by. Captain Shadrach accompanied him to the door. Zoeth remained where he was, not rising even when he shook hands with his departing friend. But when the Captain turned back he saw his partner standing by the end of the counter and clutching it with one hand while he beckoned with the other. Shadrach gave him one look and then crossed the space between them in two strides.

"For the land sakes, Zoeth," he begged, "what's the matter?"

Zoeth waved him to silence. "Sshh! sshh!" he pleaded in a whisper. "Don't holler so; she'll hear you. Shadrach, I—I——"

"What *is* it?" broke in his friend. "What's the matter, Zoeth? Shall I fetch the doctor?"

"No, no. I'm—I'm all right, Shadrach. I've just had —had a kind of shock—a surprise, that's all. I ain't very strong yet and it—it kind of upset me. But, Shadrach, I want to talk to you. I want to tell you somethin' right away. I can't keep it to myself any longer. Can't we go home—to my room or somewheres—where we can talk? Please, Shadrach!"

"There, there, shipmate; take it easy. Go home? Course we can! Hey, Sim!" shouting to Mr. Crocker, who was in the back room. "You and Mary can take care of the store, can't you? Zoeth and me are goin' home for dinner."

Simeon replied that Mary was not there; she had gone out the back way, down to the house, he thought. "But you go ahead, Cap'n Shad," he added. "I can take care of the store all right."

At home, and in Mr. Hamilton's room, the Captain pulled forward the most comfortable chair, forced his partner to sit in it, closed and locked the door, sat down on the edge of the bed, and said:

"There! Now we're all taut and shipshape and nobody can get aboard to interrupt. Fire away, Zoeth. What is it you've got to tell?"

Zoeth, his hand trembling, reached into the inside pocket of his coat, took out an old-fashioned wallet and from it produced a much-crumpled envelope.

"Shadrach," he said, "I don't hardly know how to begin. It seems so strange to think that you and me, who've been so close to each other all these years, should have a secret between us, if only for a little while. It seems wicked. I guess 'tis wicked, and I'm the wicked one for keepin' it from you."

The Captain laughed.

"You couldn't be wicked if you was apprenticed to the Old Harry for ten years, Zoeth," he said. "You don't know how to be and the devil himself couldn't teach you. Now, don't waste time tellin' me I'm speaking lightly of sacred things," he added. "For one thing, the Old Scratch ain't sacred, as I know of, and for another I want to hear that secret. What is it?"

Zoeth shook his head. "I am wicked, all the same," he said, "but I guess I've been punished. There wan't any real reason why I shouldn't have told you afore, but somehow I couldn't make up my mind to speak of it. I just couldn't. But I'm goin' to tell you now, Shadrach."

He held up the crumpled envelope.

"You remember when I was took sick?" he said. "You remember I was struck down all of a heap in the kitchen? Yes; well, did you ever wonder what it was struck me down? I'll tell you. 'Twas a letter that came to me in the mail that morning. This was the letter. I managed to put it in my inside vest pocket that time when Isaiah run off after you and left me lyin' there. I didn't want him to see it. I didn't want anybody to— not then. Now I want you to read it, Shadrach. But before you do, let me warn you. You should ask the Almighty to give you strength. You're goin' to be surprised, Shadrach, surprised and shocked. Here it is; read it."

He handed the envelope to his partner. The latter took it, wonderingly, and looked at the inscription.

"Nobody's handwritin' that I know," he said.

"You knew it once well enough."

"I did? And it was mailed out in Carson City, Nevada. Why, that's where the Crawford Smith boy lives, ain't it? What on earth?"

He opened the envelope and from it took several sheets closely covered with finely written lines. He began to read and, as he read, his expression changed from curiosity to wonder, to amazement, to anger, to a mixture of the last three. The final sheet fell from his fingers to the floor. He looked up with a very white face.

"My God!" he said solemnly.

A half-hour later they were still talking. Shadrach had not entirely recovered from the surprise, but now he could think and speak more coherently, although the wonder of it all was overpowering.

"It seems as if the hand of the Lord was in it," he declared.

"It is," agreed Zoeth, with absolute conviction. "See how it worked out accordin' to His promise. The wicked flourished for a time, but God sent the punishment in due season, didn't He? Can't you see the poor feller's agonizin' in every line of that letter?"

"*Poor* feller! Good Lord above, Zoeth Hamilton, you ain't pityin' *him,* are you? You ain't sorry for him —*you?*"

Zoeth nodded. "I wan't at first," he said. "At first the whole thing, comin' on me out of a clear sky as you might say, knocked me flat. The doctor, when he came, said he thought I must have had a sudden shock. I did; that was it, that letter. But later on, when I was gettin' better and could think again, and when I was alone and had the chance and could read the letter again, I began to—to—well, not forgive him for what he done—I don't suppose I can ever do that."

"I should say not! Damn him!"

"Hush, Shadrach; he's dead."

"So he is. I forgot. Then he's damned, I guess, without any orders from me."

"He was damned here on earth, Shadrach. All his life—the last part of it, anyhow—must have been a torment. He must have idolized that boy of his. He says so in the letter, but it's plain on every line of the writin' without his sayin' it. And can't you just imagine him, as the boy grew up and they loved each other more and more, tremblin' and scared every minute for fear that somehow or other his son'll learn that the father he loves and respects is a—a thief—and—and worse? Seems to me I can imagine it. And then all at once the boy comes to him and says he wants to marry—Oh, my soul! Shadrach, think of it!—he wants to marry your girl and mine—Marcellus's stepdaughter. Why, it must have driven him nigh crazy. And then they quarrel, and the boy, the only bein' on earth he's livin' for, goes off and leaves him. And he knows he's comin' here—to us —and that some time or other he's sartin to learn everything. No wonder he wrote that letter. No won-der——"

The Captain interrupted.

"Writin' you, of all people!" he said. "Writin' you and beggin' you not to let Mary-'Gusta marry his son: and for what? To save the boy from somethin' bad? No! For all he knew, Mary-'Gusta might be what she is, the best and finest girl on earth. What he was beg-gin' for was himself—that his son shouldn't know what *he* was, that's all. No, Zoeth, I can't pity him much. He's dead, and that's a good thing, too. The wonder of it is that he's been alive all this time and we didn't know. And to think—but there; it's all wonderful."

Both were silent for a moment. Then Zoeth said:

"The one thing that's troubled me most in all this, Shadrach, is about Mary-'Gusta herself. How does she really feel towards Crawford? She sent him away, you told me that, but are you sure she did it because she didn't care enough for him to marry him? Are you sure there wan't any other reason?"

"She gave me to understand there wan't. What other reason could there be?"

"Well—well, Shadrach, it all depends, seems to me. You know Mary-'Gusta; the last person she thinks about on earth is herself. If she did think a sight of Crawford, if she thought *enough* of him, she wouldn't let him suffer on account of her, would she? She knew, probably, that he loved and respected his father and a father's good name must mean a lot to a son. Then, there is us—you and me, Shadrach. She wouldn't let us suffer, if she could help it. Do you see what I mean?"

"Humph!" mused the Captain, thinking aloud, "I cal'late I do, Zoeth. You mean if Mary-'Gusta had found out the facts about Ed Farmer, who he was and what he done, and if she knew Crawford Smith's dad *was* Ed Farmer and that Crawford didn't know it and we didn't know it—you mean that, *bein'* Mary-'Gusta, rather than bring sorrow and trouble on Crawford and on us, she'd sacrifice her own feelin's and—and would pretend she didn't care for him so as to get him to go away and save him and us. That's what you mean, I presume likely."

"That's it, Shadrach."

"Um—yes. Well, there's just one thing that makes that notion seem consider'ble more than unlikely. How in the world could she have found out that there ever was an Edgar Farmer——"

"Good many folks in South Harniss could have told her that if they'd had a mind to."

"Maybe so; but they couldn't have told her that Edwin Smith, of Carson City, Nevada, was ever Edgar Farmer. No, sir, they couldn't! Nobody knew it—but

Ed Farmer himself. How could our Mary-'Gusta know it?"

"I don't know, Shadrach, unless—she's awful smart, you know—somethin' might have put her on the track and she puzzled it out. I know that ain't likely; but, Shadrach, if she does care for Crawford and he cares for her, I—I want 'em to have each other. I do. They must."

Shadrach stared at him.

"Zoeth Hamilton," he exclaimed, "do you know what you're sayin'? You want our girl to marry the son of the man that—that——"

"I know what he did, Shadrach; you don't need to tell me. But he's dead, and his boy is a good boy—you liked him and so did I. And Shadrach, I've been thinkin' an awful lot about this since I got the letter and have been well enough to think. And I've made up my mind to just this: There has been sorrow and trouble enough brought on already by that wickedness. There shan't be any more. What wrecked all our lives thirty-five years ago shan't wreck these two, if I can help it. If Mary-'Gusta cares for him and he for her they must have each other and be happy. And you and I will be happy watchin' their happiness."

He paused and then added:

"So I wish, Shadrach, there was some way of findin' out for sure that she sent him away because she didn't care for him and not for any other reason."

Shadrach rose from his chair and laid his hand on his friend's shoulder. He cleared his throat once or twice before speaking and there was still a shake in his voice as he said:

"Zoeth, you're a better man than I ever hope to be. I declare you make me ashamed of myself."

Neither of them ate much dinner, although Isaiah had prepared a cranberry pie, made from the first fruit of the fall season, and was correspondingly disappointed when both of his employers left it untouched.

"Ain't a mite of use my slavin' myself to death cookin' fancy vittles for this crew," he grumbled. "I stood over that cookstove this mornin' until I got so everlastin' hot that every time the cold air blowed onto me I steamed. And yet I can't satisfy."

"Oh, yes, you can," observed Captain Shad, rising from the table. "You satisfied us too quick, that was the trouble. We was satisfied afore we got to the pie."

"Umph! I want to know! Well, Mary-'Gusta was satisfied afore that. She didn't eat hardly anything. Said she wan't hungry. I swan if it ain't discouragin'! What's the use of you folks havin' a cook? If you're goin' to have canary-bird appetites, why don't you feed on bird seed and be done with it? And I do believe I never made a better pie than that!"

"Where's Mary-'Gusta?" asked Zoeth.

"I don't know. She went up to her room. She may be there yet, or she may have come down and gone out again—I don't know. If she did come down I didn't see her."

Shadrach looked out of the window. It had been a dark, gloomy morning and now it was beginning to rain. The wind was whining through the tops of the silver-leafs and the moan of the breakers on the bar sounded with a clearness which denoted the approach of a northeaster.

"Dirty weather," observed the Captain. "And it'll be dirtier yet before night. You better stay here in snug harbor this afternoon, Zoeth. Simmie and the boy and Mary-'Gusta and I can tend store all right. Yes, yes, you stay right here and keep dry. Hope Mary-'Gusta took an umbrella when she went."

"I don't know as she has gone," said Isaiah. "She may be upstairs in her room yet. That's where she was."

Shadrach, after calling "Mary-'Gusta" several times at the foot of the stairs, went up to make sure. The door of Mary's room was closed but, as he received no answer to his knock, he opened it and entered. Mary was not there, although it was evident that she had been there very recently.

Apparently she had been writing a letter, for her writing case was spread out upon the table. Also the drawer in which she kept it had been left open, an unusual act of carelessness on her part, for, generally speaking, as her Uncle Shad said, "Nothin's ever out of place in Mary-'Gusta's room except some of the places, and that's the carpenter's fault, not hers."

The Captain stepped over to close the drawer. As he did so his attention was attracted by a photograph lying upon a pile of photographs in a box inside the drawer. He picked up the photograph and looked at it. It was that of Edwin Smith, taken when he seemed to be recovering from his illness, the one which showed him without a beard.

Shadrach's eyes opened wide as he looked at the photograph. He uttered an exclamation, stepped to the door of the upper hall and called, "Zoeth!" Then he returned to the table and took from the drawer the next photograph upon the pile in the box. It was the old, faded picture of the partners of Hall and Company.

Isaiah came stumbling up the stairs.

"Anythin' I can do for you, Cap'n Shad?" he asked. "Zoeth, he's gone out to shut up the barn door. Rain was liable to beat in, he said. I told him I'd do it, but—— Godfreys mighty!"

The Captain had paid no attention to him and he had entered the room and approached his employer from behind. Now over the latter's shoulder he saw the two photographs.

"Godfreys mighty!" cried the startled Isaiah.

Shadrach turned and looked at him.

"Well," he demanded, "what's the matter? What are you starin' like that for?"

"Them—them pictures," gasped Mr. Chase.

"Well, what about 'em? Where did Mary-'Gusta get 'em, do you know? Did—— Here! Where are you goin'?"

"I—I ain't goin' anywheres. I'm a-goin' downstairs. I got my dishwashin' to do. I—let go of me, Cap'n Shad! I got to go this minute, I tell you."

But the Captain did not let go of him. Instead, keeping a firm hold upon the collar of the frightened cook and steward, he twisted him around until he could look him straight in the eye. This was difficult, for Isaiah plainly did not wish to be looked at in that manner.

"Humph!" grunted Captain Shad, after a moment's inspection. "Humph! I cal'late I've got the right pig by the ear this time. Set down in that chair, Isaiah Chase; I want to talk to you."

CHAPTER XXIX

THE northeaster was developing. It was now raining hard and the wind was rising. The gusts swept across the top of the little hill and the window sashes of the For'ard Lookout rattled and the hinges of the ancient blinds squeaked. The yard, which had been so attractive, was shorn of its decorations. The tables had been carried inside; the lanterns taken down; the wonderful sign, pride of the talented Mr. Bemis, had been tenderly conveyed to the attic. Cook, waitresses and salesgirl had departed. The tea-room and gift shop had gone into winter quarters to hibernate until the following spring.

The rooms inside had been thoroughly swept and cleaned and most of the furniture and the best of the old prints covered with dust cloths. Some of the smaller articles, however, were still upon the shelves of the gift shop, Mary having ordered her assistants to leave them there, as she wished to look them over herself before putting them away. Some of her selections for stock had sold remarkably well and she had been obliged to reorder many times; others of which she had been quite confident when purchasing had not sold at all. Both good sellers and bad she meant to list as a guide to future choosing.

She was listing them now. Alone in the room which had once been the sacred best parlor of the little house, she was seated at the table, pencil in hand and memorandum books and paper before her. There was no particular reason why the listing should have been done that day; it might have been done any day until the weather became too cold to work in an unheated house. That morning she had had no idea of doing it that afternoon. She was doing it now because she felt that she must do something to occupy her mind, and because she wished to be alone. Up there at the For'ard Lookout she could combine the two—work and seclusion.

When Mr. Keith told, at the store that morning, the news of Edwin Smith's—or Edgar Farmer's—death she had been dreadfully shaken by it. It was so sudden, so unexpected—when she last heard the man was, so the doctors said, almost well. She had thought of him often enough during the past year; or, rather, she had thought of Crawford as being with him and of the father's joy in his son's return to him and the knowledge that his own disgraceful secret would not be revealed. And she had pictured Crawford as finding solace for his disappointed love in his father's society. That Edgar Farmer had been what Isaiah called him—a blackguard—she realized perfectly, but she was equally sure that, as Edwin Smith, he had been the kindest and most loving of fathers. And Crawford, although he had been willing to leave him because of her, loved him dearly.

And now he was dead, and Crawford was left alone. Somehow she felt responsible for the death. That it had been hastened by the terrible alarm and stress of the previous year was, of course, certain. She thought of Crawford alone and with this new sorrow, and this thought, and that of her responsibility, was almost more than she could bear.

She felt that she must write him, that he must know she had heard and was thinking of him. So, after leaving the store, she had hastened down to the house and up the back stairs to her room. There she had written a few lines, not more than a note, but the composing of that note had been a difficult task. There was so much she longed to say and so little she could say. When it was written she remembered that Crawford was in Boston and she did not know his address. She determined to send the letter to the Nevada home and trust to its being forwarded.

She took from the back of the drawer the box of photographs and looked them over. As she was doing so Isaiah called her to dinner. Then she heard her uncles come in and, because she felt that she could talk with no one just then, she avoided them by hastily going down the front stairs. She made a pretense of eating and left the house. Isaiah did not see her go. After stopping at the store long enough to tell Mr. Crocker she would be at the tea-room that afternoon, she climbed the hill, unlocked the door of the For'ard Lookout, entered and began her work.

The wind howled and whined and the rain beat against the windows. The blinds creaked, the sashes rattled, the gusts moaned in the chimney above the fireplace, and all the hundred and one groanings and wailings, the complaints of an old house in a storm, developed. All these sounds Mary heard absently, her mind upon her work. Then, little by little as they drew nearer, she became conscious of other sounds, footfalls; someone was coming up the walk.

She did not rise from her chair nor look up from her work when the outside door opened. Even when the footsteps sounded in the little hall behind her she did not turn.

"Yes, Uncle Shad," she said. "I am here, and I'm safe and I'm perfectly dry. Also I'm very, very busy.

Now, why did you come out in the rain to hunt me up? And I'm quite sure you haven't put on your rubbers."

And then the voice behind her said: "Mary."

She turned now—turned, looked, and rose to her feet. Her face went white, then flushed red, and then paled again.

"Oh!" she gasped.

Crawford Smith was standing there. His light overcoat—it was not a raincoat—dripped water; so did the hat in his hand. He stood there and looked—and dripped.

"Mary," he said again.

She caught her breath, almost with a sob.

"You!" she exclaimed. *"You!* Oh, how could you? *Why* did you come?"

He took a step toward her. "Because I felt that I must," he said. "I had to come. I came to see you once more. You must forgive me."

She did not speak. He continued:

"You must forgive me for coming," he said again. "There was a question I had to ask and only you could answer it. It isn't the question I asked before, although perhaps that—— But first I must tell you: Mary, my father is dead."

She nodded. She could scarcely trust herself to speak, but she tried.

"Yes, yes," she faltered. "I—I know."

"You know?" he repeated.

"Yes, Mr. Keith told us this morning. He said he met you in Boston."

"Yes, I had forgotten; so he did."

"That is how I knew. Oh, Crawford, I am so sorry for you. I have been writing you. But *why* did you come here again? It—it makes it so much harder for—for both of us."

He did not answer the question. "You knew my father was dead," he said again. "I wonder"—he was speaking slowly and his gaze was fixed upon her face—"I wonder how much more you know."

She started back. "How much——" she repeated. "How much more—— Oh, what do you mean?"

"I mean how much did you know about my father when you and I were together—when I came on here and asked you to marry me?"

She put a hand to her throat. "Oh!" she cried breathlessly. "*You* know! He told you!"

"Yes, Mary, he told me. Before he died he told me everything. And you knew it! I know now why you would not marry me—the son of a thief."

She looked at him in pained astonishment. The tears sprang to her eyes. "Oh, how can you!" she exclaimed. "How can you say that to me? How can you think it? As if that would make any difference! I learned your father's name and—and what he had done—by accident. It was only the night before you came. It would have made no difference to me. For myself I didn't care—but—— Oh, Crawford, how can you think it was because he was—that?"

His eyes were shining.

"I don't think it," he cried triumphantly. "I never have thought it, Mary. I believe—ever since I knew, I have dared to believe that you sent me away because you were trying to save me from disgrace. You had learned who and what my father had been and I did not know. And you feared that if you married me the secret might come out and I would be ashamed, my career would be spoiled, and all that. I have dared to believe this and that is why I came back to you—to ask if it was true. Can't you see? I *had* to come. *Is* it true, Mary?"

He came toward her. She would have run away if she could, but there was nowhere to run.

"Look at me, Mary," he commanded. "Look at me, and tell me this: It wasn't because you didn't love me that you sent me away? It wasn't really that, was it? Tell me the truth. Look at me now, and tell me."

She tried to look and she tried to speak, but her glance faltered and fell before his and the words would not come. She could feel the blood rushing to her cheeks. She put up her hands in mute protest, but the protest was unavailing. His arms were about her, his kisses were upon her lips, and he was telling her the things which are told in times like these. And she struggled no longer, but permitted herself to listen, to believe, to accept, and to be swept away by the wonderful current of love and destiny against which she had fought so long.

But the struggle was not entirely over. She made one more effort.

"Oh, Crawford!" she cried a little later. "Oh, Crawford, dear, this is all wrong. It can't be. It mustn't be. Don't you see it mustn't? We have forgotten Uncle Zoeth. He doesn't know whose son you are. If he should learn, it would bring back the old story and the old trouble. He isn't well. The shock might kill him."

But Crawford merely smiled.

"He does know, Mary," he said. "Father wrote him. I shall tell you the whole story just as Dad told it to me. Heaven knows it was not a pleasant one for a son to hear, but I am glad I heard it. The past was bad, but it *is* past. You and I have the future for our own and I mean to make it a clean one and a happy one for us both, God willing."

Shadrach came up the path to the tea-house, leading Isaiah by the arm. Mr. Chase moved reluctantly, as if led to execution or, at the very least, to immediate trial for his life.

"Now then," commanded Shadrach, "furl that umbrella and come along in here with me. I want you to make Mary-'Gusta understand that you've told me the whole business, about your tellin' her the Ed Farmer yarn and all. After that you can clear out, because I want to talk to her myself."

He opened the door and, still holding his captive by the arm, strode into the parlor. There he stood stock still, staring.

Crawford held out his hand and the Captain found himself shaking it warmly.

"Captain Gould," he said, "I know now what I did not know until two weeks ago, how greatly my father wronged you and your partners. I know the whole miserable story. But, in spite of it, I am here because I love Mary and I want to marry her. She has told me that she loves me. I don't know how you feel about it, but I hope——"

The Captain interrupted. "Wait a minute!" he ordered. "Heave to and come up into the wind a minute; let me get my bearin's. Young feller, if you're goin' to drop down out of the skies unexpected like this, you—— Tut! tut! tut! Whew!" He waited a moment, then he said:

"Mary-'Gusta, come here."

He held out his arms. She came to him and he held her close.

"Is it so?" he asked. "Do you care for this young feller enough for that? Do you, Mary-'Gusta?"

He put his finger beneath her chin and lifted her head

to look down into her face. The face was crimson.

"Do you, Mary-'Gusta?" he asked.

Mary looked up, wet-eyed but smiling.

"Yes, Uncle Shad," she said, "I think I do."

"And you want to cruise in his company all your life, eh?"

"Yes, Uncle Shad; but not unless you and Uncle Zoeth are willing."

He bent and kissed her.

"Bless your heart, dearie," he said, "it's all right. Zoeth and me were talkin' about this very thing a little while ago. And do you know what he said? He said: 'What wrecked all our lives thirty-five year ago shan't wreck these two, if I can help it. If Mary-'Gusta cares for him and he for her they shall have each other and be happy. And we'll be happy watchin' their happiness.' That's what he said. I don't know's I said 'Amen' exactly, but I thought it, anyhow. God bless you, Mary-'Gusta. Now you and Crawford go and see your Uncle Zoeth. He's down at the house. You just run along and tell him about it."

Mary turned to Mr. Chase.

"Well, Isaiah," she said, "haven't you anything to say to me?"

Isaiah looked at Crawford and then at her.

"I should say you'd better go somewheres, both of you, and get dry," he said. "His overcoat's soakin' wet and your waist ain't much better. I—I—don't know what sort of—of congratulations or—or whatever they be I ought to say, but—but I hope you'll be terrible happy, Mary-'Gusta."

"Thank you, Isaiah," laughed Mary.

"Yes, you're welcome. Now, just let me talk to Cap'n Shad a minute."

He swung about and faced the Captain and in his eye was triumph great and complete.

"Cap'n Shad Gould," crowed Isaiah, "a good many times in the last four or five year you've called me a fool for heavin' out hints that somethin' about like this was liable to happen. Well? *Well?* What have you got to say *now?* Who's the fool *now?* Hey? Who is?"

CHAPTER XXX

THE story of Mary-'Gusta Lathrop is almost told. Before Crawford left South Harniss, which was not until the end of another week, it had been decided that on a day in June of the following year she should cease to be Mary-'Gusta Lathrop. There was a great deal of discussion before this decision was reached, for many perplexing questions had to be answered.

First, there was the question of Crawford's future. His father had left a comfortable fortune and an interest in mining properties which would have rendered it quite unnecessary for the young man to keep on with his professional studies had he wished to discontinue them. But he did not so wish.

"As I think I told you that Sunday afternoon when we first met at Mrs. Wyeth's, Mary," he said, "I have always intended to be a doctor. Dad did not want me to be; he wanted me to come in with him, but I wouldn't do it. I love my work and I mean to stick to it and go on with it. If I were as rich as a dozen Rockefellers it wouldn't make any difference. But, as I see it, I am not rich. It is a grave question in my mind how much of that money out there belongs to me."

Mary nodded. "I think I understand what you mean," she said.

"Yes, I think there is no doubt that almost all of my father's money was made there in the West after"—he hesitated and then went on—"after the—the other died and after he married my mother. But nevertheless I shall always feel as if whatever there was belonged to your uncles, the surviving members of the old firm. If I could, I should give it to them."

Mary smiled. "Thank you for saying it, dear," she said, "and I know you mean it; but it would be no use to offer; they wouldn't take it."

"I know they wouldn't. So we must try and make it up to them in some other way. But suppose we leave that for a time and get back to my work. I'm going to keep on with it; I want to and you say that you want me to."

"I do, very much. I am sure you will be happier in that work than in any other, and besides—I suppose I am ever so unpractical, but I do feel it—I had rather you made your own way. Somehow the idea of our depending upon that money out there doesn't—doesn't—— Oh, I can't explain exactly, but I don't like the idea a bit."

"I know. I prefer to paddle my own canoe, if I can. But a young doctor's canoe is likely to move pretty slowly at first. And I intend taking a passenger, you know, and I want her to be comfortable."

Mary laughed, a contented little laugh. "She will be," she declared. "Did I tell you of the talk Uncle Shad and I had the other day? He saw me sitting by the dining-room window looking out at nothing in particular —and looking silly enough, too, I dare say—and he asked me what I was thinking. I said, 'Nothing much,' which wasn't true, and he said nothing must be good to think of, I looked so cheerful. I told him I was. Then I asked him—my conscience troubled me a little, you know—if he was sure that he and Uncle Zoeth were happy, because I shouldn't be unless they were."

"Well, that was characteristic. What did he say to that?"

"Oh, he laughed that big laugh of his and told me not to worry. '*I'm* feelin' pretty average satisfied with life just now, Mary-'Gusta,' he said, 'and as for Zoeth— well, he asked me this mornin' if I didn't cal'late 'twas wicked for him and me to be so contented with the things of this world, so I know *he's* all right. When Zoeth gets real happy he always begins to feel sinful.' I hope that a consciousness of sin isn't the only test of happiness," she added, "because I don't believe you feel wicked the least bit. At least you have never said you did."

Crawford laughed, and there followed one of those interruptions to conversation with which, although undoubtedly interesting to the participants, outsiders are not supposed to be concerned. When it was over Mary said:

"Of course I am not so foolish as to mean that you must not touch the money your father left. That would be ridiculous. But I mean I think we should not depend upon it; it should not change our plans or spoil your life work, or anything like that. It will make life easier for us, of course, and with its help we can make it easier for other people. I think that is what we should do with it."

"So do I, my dear. And our first duty, it seems to me, is toward your uncles. If they would consent, and I suppose there isn't the least chance that they would, I should like to sell out the store and the Lookout and the rest of it and take them with us, wherever we decide to go, and give them an easy, carefree time of it the rest of their lives."

Mary shook her head. "They wouldn't like it a bit,"

she said. "That precious old store is the joy of their lives. Without it they wouldn't know what to do; they would be as lost and lonesome and miserable as a pair of stray kittens. No, if we take care of them we must take care of Hamilton and Company, too. And we mustn't let them know we're doing it, either," she added with decision.

Crawford looked troubled. "I suppose you're right," he said; "but it is likely to be something of a puzzle, their problem. It will mean, of course, that you and I must go and leave them."

"Oh, no, we can't do that—not for some time, at any rate."

"It seems to me we must. We have decided, you and I, that I shall go back West, finish my preparatory work, then come here and marry you. After that—well, after that we have decided that I am to locate somewhere or other and begin to practice my profession. You'll go with me then, I presume?"

"Silly! Of course I will."

"I hoped so. But if we can't leave your uncles and they won't leave the store, what are we going to do? Put the store on a truck and take it with us?"

She looked up at him and smiled. "I have a plan," she said. "I haven't quite worked it out yet, but if it does work I think it's going to be a very nice plan indeed. No, I'm not going to tell you what it is yet, so you mustn't tease. You don't mind my planning for you and bossing you and all that sort of thing, do you? I hope you don't, because I can't help it. It's the way I'm made, I think."

"I don't mind. Boss away."

"Oh, I shall. I'm like that Scotch girl in the play Mrs. Wyeth took me to see in Boston—Bunty, her name was.

She made me think of myself more than once, although she was ever so much more clever. At the end of the play she said to her sweetheart, 'William, I must tell ye this: if I marry ye I'll aye be managin' ye.' She meant she couldn't help it. Neither can I. I'm afraid I'm a born manager."

Crawford stooped and kissed her.

"Do you remember William's answer?" he asked. "I do. It was: 'Bunty, I'll glory in my shame.' Manage all you like, my lady, I'll glory in it."

The plan did work out and it was this: Doctor Harley, who had practiced medicine for forty-one years in South Harniss, was thinking of retiring after two more years of active work. He was willing to sell out his practice at the end of that time. He liked Crawford, had taken a fancy to him on the occasion of his first visit to the town when he was a guest of the Keiths. Crawford, after Mary had suggested the idea to him, called upon the old doctor. Before the end of the week it was arranged that after Crawford's final season of college and hospital work he was to come to South Harniss, work with Doctor Harley as assistant for another year, and then buy out the practice and, as Captain Shad said, "put up his own shingle."

"I don't mean to stay here always," Crawford said, "but it will do me good to be here for a time. Harley's a tiptop old chap and a thoroughly competent general practitioner. He'll give me points that may be invaluable by and by. And a country practice is the best of training."

Mary nodded. "Yes," she said. "And at the end of this winter I shall have Simeon Crocker well broken in as manager of the store. And I can sell the tea-room, I think. My uncles don't care much for that, anyway.

They will be perfectly happy with the store to putter about in and with Simeon to take the hard work and care off their shoulders they can putter to their hearts' content."

"But suppose Simeon doesn't make it pay!" suggested Crawford. "That's at least a possibility. Everyone isn't a Napoleon—I should say a Queen Elizabeth—of finance and business like yourself, young lady."

Mary's confidence was not in the least shaken.

"It will pay," she said. "If the townspeople and the summer cottagers don't buy enough—well, you and I can help out. There is that money in the West, you know."

He nodded emphatically.

"Good!" he cried. "You're right. It will be a chance for us—just a little chance. And they will never know."

He went away at the end of the week, but he came back for Christmas and again at Easter and again in the latter part of May. And soon after that, on a day in early June, he stood, with Sam Keith at his elbow, in the parlor of the white house by the shore, while Edna Keith played "Here Comes the Bride" on the piano which had been hired for the occasion; and, with her hand in Zoeth's arm, and with Captain Shadrach and Barbara Howe just behind, Mary walked between the two lines of smiling, teary friends to meet him.

It was a lovely wedding; everyone said so, and as there probably never was a wedding which was not pronounced lovely by friends and relatives, we may be doubly certain of the loveliness of this. And there never was a more beautiful bride. All brides are beautiful, more or less, but this one was more. Isaiah, who had been favored with a peep at the rehearsal on the previous evening, was found later on by Shadrach in the kitchen in a state of ecstatic incoherence.

"I swan to godfreys!" cried Isaiah. "Ain't—ain't she an angel, though! Did you ever see anything prettier'n she is in them clothes and with that—that moskeeter net on her head? An angel—yes, sir-ee! one of them cherrybins out of the Bible, that's what she is. And to think it's our Mary-'Gusta! Say, Cap'n Shad, will checkered pants be all right to wear with my blue coat tomorrow? I burnt a hole in my lavender ones tryin' to press the wrinkles out of 'em. And I went down to the wharf in 'em last Sunday and they smell consider'ble of fish, besides."

The wedding company was small, but select. Judge Baxter and his wife were there and the Keiths—Mrs. Keith condescended to ornament the occasion; some of the "best people" had seen fit to make much of Mary Lathrop and Mrs. Keith never permitted herself to be very far behind the best people in anything—and Mrs. Wyeth was there, and Miss Pease, and Mr. Green who had received an invitation and had come from Boston, and Doctor Harley, and Simeon Crocker and his "steady company," one of the tea-room young ladies, and Annabel and—and—well, a dozen or fifteen more.

When the minister asked, "Who giveth this woman to this man?" Zoeth answered, bravely, "I do—that is, me and Shadrach." But no one laughed, because Zoeth himself was trying to smile and making rather wet weather of it. As for the Captain, his expression during the ceremony was a sort of fixed grin which he had assumed before entering the room and had evidently determined to wear to the finish, no matter what his emotions might be. But Miss Pease, always susceptible, had a delightful cry all to herself, and Isaiah, retiring to the hall, blew his nose with a vigor which, as Captain Shad said afterwards, "had the Pollack Rip foghorn soundin' like a deef and dumb sign."

Mary had managed everything, of course. Her uncles had tried to remonstrate with her, telling her there were plenty of others to arrange the flowers and attend to what the local newspaper would, in its account of the affair, be sure to call the "collation," and to make the hundred and one preparations necessary for even so small and simple a wedding as this. But she only laughed at their remonstrances.

"I wouldn't miss it for anything," she said. "I have always wanted to manage someone's wedding and I am certainly not going to let anyone else manage mine. I don't care a bit whether it is the proper thing or not. This isn't going to be a formal affair; I won't have it so. Uncle Shad, if you want to say 'Jumpin' fire' when Crawford drops the ring, as he is almost sure to do, you have my permission."

But Crawford did not drop the ring, and so the Captain's favorite exclamation was not uttered, being unnecessary. In fact there were no mishaps, everything went exactly as it should, reception and "collation" included, and, to quote from the South Harniss local once more, "A good time was had by all."

And when the bride and groom, dressed in their traveling costumes, came down the stairs to the carriage which was to take them to the station, Mary ran back, amid the shower of rice and confetti, to kiss Uncle Zoeth and Uncle Shad once more and whisper in their ears not to feel that she had really gone, because she hadn't but would be back in just a little while.

"And I have told Isaiah about your rubbers and oilskins when it rains," she added, in Shadrach's ear, "and he is not to forget Uncle Zoeth's medicine. Good-by. Good-by. Don't be lonesome. Promise that you won't."

But to promise is easy and to keep that promise is often hard, as Shadrach observed when he and Zoeth were alone in the sitting-room that evening. "I feel as if the whole vitals of this place had gone away on that afternoon train," the Captain admitted. "And yet I know it's awful foolish, 'cause she'll only be gone a couple of weeks."

"I'm glad that question about the name is settled," mused Zoeth. "That kind of troubled me, that did."

The partners had worried not a little over the question of whether Crawford's name was legally Smith or Farmer. If it were Farmer and he must be so called in South Harniss, they feared the revival of the old scandal and all its miserable gossip. But when they asked Crawford he reassured them.

"I consulted my lawyer about that," he said. "My father's middle name was Smith; that is why he took it, I suppose. Edwin Smith is not so very different from Edgar Smith Farmer, shorter, that's all. He and my mother were married under the name of Smith. Mother never knew he had had another name. I was born Smith and christened Smith and my lawyer tells me that Smith I am. If there had been any question I should have petitioned to have the name changed."

So that question was settled and Shadrach and Zoeth felt easier because of it.

"Zoeth," observed Shadrach, after replying to his friend's remark concerning the name, "do you know what I kind of felt as if we'd ought to have had here this afternoon?"

"No, Shadrach," replied Zoeth, "I don't. What was it?"

"Seemed to me we'd ought to had one of them music box chairs. I'd like to have put it under that Keith woman and seen her face when the Campbells started to come. Ho, ho!"

"What in the world made you think of that?" demanded his partner.

"Oh, I don't know. Thinkin' about Mary-'Gusta, I cal'late, set me to rememberin' how we fust met her and about Marcellus's funeral and all. That made me think of the chair, you see. I ain't thought of it afore for years."

Zoeth nodded. "Shadrach," he said, "that was a blessed day for you and me, the day when we brought that child home in our old buggy. The Lord put her there, Shadrach."

"Well, I guess likely he did, maybe, in a way of speakin'. Does seem so, that's a fact."

"Our lives was pretty sot and narrow afore she came. She's changed everything."

"That's so, Hello! What's that noise? I declare if it ain't Isaiah liftin' up his voice in song! In a hymn tune! What do you think of that?"

From the kitchen, above the rattle of dishes, Mr. Chase's nasal falsetto quavered shrilly:

"There shall be showers of blessin's——"

The Captain interrupted.

"Hi, you—what's your name—Jennie Lind—come in here," he hailed.

Mr. Chase appeared, his arms dripping soapsuds.

"What do you want, callin' me out of my name?" he demanded.

"Want to know what started you singin' about blessin's? Fust I thought 'twas the weathervane squeakin'. What tuned you up, eh?"

Isaiah looked rather foolish, but he grinned.

"I was thinkin' about Mary-'Gusta," he said.

"You was, eh? Well, she's been a blessin' to us, there's no doubt about that."

"Indeed she has," concurred Zoeth.

But Isaiah had the final word.

"Huh!" he declared, "she's more'n one blessin', she's a whole shower. That's what set me to singin' about 'em."

He departed for the kitchen once more, the falsetto rising triumphant:

"There shall be showers of blessin's,
    Send 'em upon us, oh Lord!"

Captain Shad looked after him. Then he turned to his friend and partner and said earnestly:

"Do you know, Isaiah's gettin' real kind of sensible in his old age."

(1)